OUR LADY OF THE PRAIRIE

OUR LADY
of the PRAIRIE

THISBE NISSEN

HOUGHTON MIFFLIN HARCOURT

BOSTON   NEW YORK

2018

Library of Congress Cataloging-in-Publication Data
Names: Nissen, Thisbe, 1972- author.
Title: Our lady of the prairie / Thisbe Nissen.
Description: Boston : Houghton Mifflin Harcourt, 2018.
Identifiers: LCCN 2017044908 (print) | LCCN 2017047823 (ebook)
| ISBN 9781328663054 (ebook) | ISBN 9781328662071 (hardback)
Subjects: | BISAC: FICTION / Contemporary Women. | FICTION / Literary. |
FICTION / Family Life. | GSAFD: Humorous fiction. | Love stories.
Classification: LCC PS3564.I79 (ebook) | LCC PS3564.I79 O95 2018 (print) |
DDC 813/.54--dc23
LC record available at https://lccn.loc.gov/2017044908

Book design by Victoria Hartman

Printed in the United States of America
DOC 10 9 8 7 6 5 4 3 2 1

All photographs are from the author's personal collection.

A portion of chapter 1, in altered form, previously appeared in *Story Quarterly*.

For Iowa, where a piece of my heart will always live,
and for Jay, who is my home

Do not be daunted by the enormity of the world's grief. Do justly now. Love mercy now. Walk humbly now. You are not obligated to complete the work but neither are you free to abandon it.

—*Pirkei Avot*

OUR LADY OF THE PRAIRIE

MY HUSBAND WAS DRESDEN

Our statistics are thrown off because we tend to remember
the unusual rather than the usual.

—William R. Corliss, *Tornados, Dark Days,*
Anomalous Precipitation, and Related Weather Phenomena:
A Catalog of Geophysical Anomalies

FROM THE MOMENT I saw Lucius Bocelli I wanted to go to bed
with him. If I'd known then what Michael would put me through
by way of penance—in twenty-six years of marriage you'd think if
he'd so badly needed to spank me he'd've found an opportunity—I
might have simply given in. Instead I spent three months in tortuous
longing before succumbing to all I felt for Lucius. But retrospect is
convenient, life less so. Even if I should have foreseen—or already
known of—my husband's peccadilloes, I still could not have gazed
into the future to know, say, the path that May's tornado would take
across Iowa, straight through our daughter's wedding. I met Lucius
in late January. I'd just arrived in Ohio for my semester's teaching
exchange; he was recently back from a year and a half in France, a
research sabbatical he'd extended with an additional six-month leave.
His work was on Nazi collaborationists of the Vichy regime, and

he'd be headed back to France that summer, but when we met it was only January. The Democrats hadn't even nominated someone to run against Dubya and bar him from a second term. Bernadette—the mother-in-law whose belligerent existence I'd suffered for more than half my life—was still alive and kicking me at every available opportunity, and Ginny wasn't yet married to Silas Yoder, or pregnant and off her psych meds and once again as miserable as she'd been before the electroshock. Orah and Obadiah Yoder were already dead—Silas and Eula's parents, hit head-on and killed by an SUV, in their own buggy in front of their own Prairie farm—and a year had done little to dissipate that pain. The birth of Eula's baby had diverted us, yes. My point is this: when I met Lucius my life was more stable than it had been in twenty-five years. I met him, and I wanted him—more clearly, and maybe less complicatedly, than I think I have ever wanted anything in this life.

There'd been a reading at the U of O—a progressive political commentator—with a gathering afterward at the dean's home, for the obligatory university-issue cheese-and-cracker platters and a Midwestern supermarket arrangement of crudités: concentric moats of gray-tinged cauliflower, parched baby carrots, and inedibly mushy grape tomatoes surrounding the ranch dip bowl. Guests represented the left of the U of O faculty, and there was a collective relief at being surrounded by other sane people at a time when the main—hell, the *only*—criteria for sanity were (a) abject terror at the state of the union, and (b) downright hatred of the president, who had about as much ability to run the country as one of our thickheaded, eighteen-year-old frat boys. And less humility, which is almost inconceivable. The wine flowed that night, and it was lousy, but it was on the U, so we drank with zeal. In Ohio, at the end of January, four-foot snowbanks turning the campus into a giant ice maze, you drink what's offered, and you're grateful.

I'd gotten a lift to the dean's house from Anthea Lingafelter, a Romanticist. As we entered, I saw, leaning in the arch of the foyer, a man I took instantly to be the actor Ed Harris. I'd like to imagine my next thought would have been, *What the hell is Ed Harris doing here?*, but Anthea had paused to make introductions and my hand was already extended as I heard her say, "Phillipa Maakestad—on loan to us—Theater." I was beaming a sort of I-thought-*Pollock*-was-brilliant smile when it seemed that, of this man whose hand I was shaking, Anthea was saying, "Lucius Bocelli, History." His expression mutated from pleased-to-meet-you to perplexity. I'd been holding his hand far longer than appropriate and dropped it abruptly, jerking away. A step behind my own actions, the soundtrack of my brain was out of sync with the picture. I shook hands with the others in the group, registering nothing. Then Anthea guided me away toward a den, slipping her parka onto a futon couch where coats were being piled.

"I thought he was Ed Harris!" I told her.

Anthea glanced back, her look inscrutable to me, and said, "Lucius?" When I made a face to say, *Yes, the Ed Harris look-alike, who else?*, she lifted her chin and let out a hoot—a hoot that only became clear much later when Lucius told me of the affair they'd had years before. Lucius, I will note, had nothing to do with Anthea's divorce.

I encountered him minutes later on line at the makeshift bar. He came up behind me. "The wine's no good," he said, "but it makes the socializing go down easier."

I was conscious of my own breath—I heard it like the rush of wind through a tunnel—and I'm not a woman often conscious of her own breath. "I'm so sorry." I lifted my hand toward the site of our introduction. "I thought you were Ed Harris." I shook my head in castigation for my absurdity. A smile spread across his face, crinkling his eyes, and I saw he was older than I'd realized. For no reason I can understand, it was this that hit my pelvis: realization of his age somehow turned my breathless giddiness into grave desire.

Lucius's eyes—pale, pale blue—were deeply set, corners striated with wrinkles, the skin there thin and tissuey as parchment. I had to physically restrain myself from lifting my hand to run a thumb across that delicacy. His face was so hard and sculpted it made that thin-thin skin at the corners of his eyes seem all the more fragile, their sadness devastatingly palpable. To see him smile felt like a triumph, and I may have known then that I would love this man with a ferocity, and an urgency, and a gravity I had never experienced before.

He dropped his chin, tucked it to his neck, and peered at me as if over reading glasses he wasn't actually wearing. "I suspect," he said, "you just can't tell one bald man from another."

"Come on," I said, "it's not like I mistook you for Danny DeVito."

His grin broke wide again—the shine of those sad, deep-set eyes. He conceded my point.

"Or Gandhi," I said.

"No," he said thoughtfully, mock-thoughtfully. "No, not Gandhi."

"Bruce Willis . . . Telly Savalas . . . Yul Brynner . . ."

"Now you're talking really bald—I have my scruff." He fluffed at his hair. "My *tufts*."

"Which," I pointed out, "is why I thought you were Ed Harris and got a bit tongue-tied."

Lucius looked suddenly disappointed. He'd glanced at my left hand: "You're married."

Without thinking, I shifted my hands on my hips to cover my knuckles, absurdly hiding the ring he'd already seen. "You?" I asked.

He tipped back his plastic glass, drained its dregs, stuck it in the underarm crook of his blazer, and held his hands out as though I'd asked to inspect his fingernails. Because of the cup, one arm was hitched up shorter than the other, his back bent as if in halfhearted Igor impersonation. His fingernails were clean, cut short, healthy pink, and he had small hands, downy with grayed hair I could tell had once been golden blond. They made me think of lifeguards on the California beaches of my childhood—muscled hands, thick-veined, wiry like the rest of him; he's sinewy and compact as a greyhound. He wore no ring. "Thrice was plenty," he said, then straightened and caught his cup as it fell.

I'd be lying to say I wasn't alarmed. *Three* marriages? But he was so forthcoming, and emotion overrode skepticism. I was already in love, and reconciled the question instantly. One failed marriage in this era barely warrants mention; at our age, two is hardly surprising. Three, though, calls for a story: a brief starter marriage, maybe, then a long-term one, ending in her death—cancer—and then an awful, grief-spurred, six-month catastrophe. That's what I imagined. "Kids?" I asked, and I'd like to think if he had more than, say, four—or any were still underage—I would have run, but I'd probably have found a way to reconcile that, too.

He was nodding. "Two, from my second marriage. Jesus, they're middle-aged," he said sheepishly. "Hannah and Tim. Both married. Kids of their own who aren't even kids anymore." He laid it out like he was coming clean.

"Grandkids—how old *are* you?" I'd assumed he was maybe Michael's age, sixtyish.

Lucius chuckled. "Put it this way: I'm Medicare-eligible."

"You are not."

His lips closed in a knowing line. "Oh, yes. Indeed I am. And yourself?"

"Fifty," I told him.

"And the rest?"

My eyes felt extraordinarily wide. I dropped my hands and faced him like a refugee. Like someone with nothing left to lose, which wasn't the case at all. "One daughter, Ginny. Twenty-five. Getting married in May." It was so easy to say. Just like that, I'd practically written Ginny a new life story—leapt over years of hospital corridors and caloric mandates, meth dens and court orders, razor blades and electroconvulsive shock—flew over it all and announced that I had a daughter about to be married. It wasn't a lie; it was entirely true—and it was glorious.

"Mazel tov," he said.

"You're a *Jew*?" I said.

"My mother was," he answered.

"Mine too," I said. "And my father."

"And you?" he asked.

"Me what?"

"You're a Jew? Unto yourself?"

"Not really."

"Me neither," he confessed.

"I never was, growing up, but in Iowa I sort of am, because no one else is. My parents weren't at all; my father's folks were — they were the ones who came over. A job at UC got my grandparents out of Germany early. Turned them into Golden State Jews."

"You're from California!" He looked delighted. "Where?"

"Bay Area, Berkeley."

Lucius smiled, tipped his empty cup to his chest. "L.A." He shook his head: "Two California Jews in the heartland . . ."

"My husband calls me a Murphyist." It was the wrong thing to say: giving voice to Michael made him real and present, and me terribly uncomfortable. To cover, to lose the word "husband" among others, I babbled: "An anything-that-can-go-wrong-will framework with a healthy Judaic fear of the *kinehora* thrown in: don't draw attention to the good or it will turn to shit. I'd call it a kind of nonsectarian superstitionism, if you will."

"I will," Lucius said. My memory goes a little funny from there. I'm pretty certain that's all we said, but I don't know how much time passed before I reawoke to our surroundings and realized we'd been staring at each other as the bar line split and re-merged around us, like a river past a boulder, there in the middle of Dean Sewell's living room.

Three months passed before Lucius and I succumbed to a fully consummate affair. Our relationship was not something I entered lightly; I understood the gravity with which it would bear upon my marriage. One does not simply step away after twenty-six unstrayingly married years. When Michael and I met, I was a young grad student, he my young professor. Such things were less taboo then, which is not to say that they happen now with any less regularity, just with a greater threat of lawsuit. I fell in love with my professor, and he with me, and when I finished my degree we married and I joined the department; they divided his teaching appointment in two, and I became his second half. We taught, and produced shows at the university theater. Michael practically grew up in the U's costume shop —Bernadette, his mother, ran it for decades—and he'd spent his childhood trolling the theater, raised, so to speak, in the wings. His ubiquitous lifelong presence made it only natural for him to assume an official role at the theater. Straight out of his own undergrad studies, they hired him as an assistant professor to do what he'd already been doing for years: run lights, sound, sets, etc., for the entire theater, and teach in a new major, theater design and technical production. My role in the department has always been more traditional, and more peripheral. I stage shows—they give me the musicals, of which I'm irrationally fond—which I've mostly enjoyed, and I teach acting, directing, history of theater, wherever they stick me. My own degree's in playwriting, but it's been a long time since I made specific use of it. I am the department's generic professor: I teach nearly everything we offer and, unqualified as I may be, I still usually know more than the average undergraduate. So it goes in American higher education. I think it was different once upon a time. My grandfather was a Berkeley professor, and—who knows?—maybe it was really all in the three-piece suits, the briefcase. Or in his stature as "Professor" or "Grandpa," but he certainly seemed more learned than the people I work with. He'd've been appalled by me. I can just hear his voice, that accent, thick: "What is it you have on, Phillipa? You're lecturing in your *pajamas*? These *hoodlums*—these are your *students*?"

Michael and I were married a year when Ginny was born and her difficult life—and ours—began. We raised her as best we could, and that had been my life for twenty-five years. Which is to say, Ginny's life had subsumed my own for a quarter-century. But she'd made it—

we'd all made it—through to an ease we'd never dreamed possible. In 2004, for the first time since 1979, I finally had a life again in which I was not my child's caretaker before all else. I was not unhappy with Michael. Certainly our marriage had, like so many, grown staid, but after all we'd gone through in Ginny's childhood, her adolescence and early adulthood, we were fine with staid. Everything was fine. Which is what Michael kept saying: "What happened? Everything was fine —*wasn't* everything fine?" Because it had been fine, and probably would have continued to be fine, if not for Lucius. That's not blame but acknowledgment: Lucius and I collided like a force of nature. We're no more to blame for the resulting combustion than air pressure fronts and atmospheric conditions are to blame for a tornado. Blame me, but blame me for inadequate shelter provisions, neglectful stormproofing, general lack of preparedness. Blame the tornado, if you must, though a tornado hurtles blindly. Or, fine: blame me! But blame me for my explanations and justifications and rationales, my refusal—here, again—to take responsibility or claim agency. Blame my acquiescence to forces I insist were beyond my control. What I won't back down from is this: Lucius and I met and we were a twister. We tried to keep ourselves apart, but some forces are too great. Some forces *are* beyond control.

OUR MUTUAL DESIRE was undeniable, but I was married. Period. So for three months I put myself through a battery of diversionary tactics, buffering my life with appointments and collegial lunches and outside projects, yet I moved from class to meeting to meal in a perpetual state of awareness that at any moment I might run into him and be entirely undone. So much of this life we spend holding ourselves together, when all we're really looking for is someone who might undo us completely.

Around me, Lucius was deferential, maintaining space between us as if legally bound to hover reverently on his own side of that ostensibly impenetrable Maginot Line. It was a dance: I moved, he moved, we moved together, our distance as constant and pressing as our attraction. It was excruciating. With every impulse in my being I felt compelled to touch this man. At times it was comical: we'd catch eyes across the room at some function, or over the whitened plain of a snowy quad, and like dumb little lab mice we'd bump against the Plexiglas maze wall and pass at a distance, rubbing our sore noses. Shaken by these proximal encounters, I barely remembered whether we were fighting to stay away from each other or trying with animal desperation to come together. This wasn't a show of resistance for appearance's sake, though that probably made us look all the more pathetic, like rescue workers doggedly pulling sandbags from one breached levee to fix another when anyone could have told us we were both already underwater.

Perhaps it's appropriate that we were ultimately done in by a torrential April rain. Classes hit a lull before the last push to semester's end, and on a nasty, wet Friday night, in a fit of seasonal pique, I took myself to a movie. It should have been no surprise that my instinct toward cushioned seating, passive entertainment, and heavily salted and buttered carbohydrates would be shared by other sentient Ohioans that evening, but this would not dawn on me until I was already downtown, Volvo in a lot, contraband convenience-store candy secreted in my handbag. Lucius had the same instinct that night, and was equally confounded to find the campus triplex sold out for both the seven and nine o'clock shows. We stood in the lobby gazing up at the SOLD OUT signs like travelers who've missed their train and can do nothing but stare at the departures board, hoping there's been some mistake.

Lucius saw me before I saw him. He did not approach, but I felt eyes on me in that Camplex lobby and turned to spot him, some fifteen feet away. He had his driver's license in hand, expectant as an undergraduate to be carded for his age, eager to prove himself. I loved him. I loved him already. I hunched my shoulders and constricted my chest muscles to protect the walloping heart inside. I hurt for loving him.

"Poor planning," he called to me, rooted where he stood.

"Speak for yourself." Was I trying to sass him, show my brassy bravado? I don't even know; no more came from my mouth. Lucius looked at me helplessly. Nothing mattered: it was over, our struggle futile. We lost hold and gravity got its way, and in that instant our pretending was born.

"Video rental?" Lucius asked, as if it were the next logical move. I shrugged my concession and went to him as though we'd come to the theater together and I'd only gone to use the ladies' room. Now, returning to him to find him ticketless, all shows sold out, what option was left us but to rent a film and go home to watch it? We exited the doors of the Camplex as though we'd entered through them together minutes before.

"My car's right here," Lucius said, and I suppose I made a significant choice right then, saying nothing of my own car in the ramp a block away. I simply got in. Mine was unfit for company anyway. Michael and Ginny mocked me for driving a dumpster: my big steel box of trash. I inherited it when my parents died, a late-eighties Volvo, in great shape, its first decade spent in California without snow or salt. My loyalty to it is, admittedly, sentimental, but I've never felt their ridicule to be quite fair. Yes, my car collects coffee cups and department mailings and gas receipts and plastic bottles and extra pairs of shoes and umbrellas and emergency Ziplocs of nuts in case I don't get a chance to eat before class. Would it be nice to drive a clean car? Sure. I'd also love it if my handbag didn't weigh ten pounds, with forgotten tape measures and Advil bottles and fortunes in loose change. But life is short, and I'm always late for something, grabbing my bag, racing out of the house. Time never slows enough for me to get on top of the accumulation. Once a year something happens to necessitate the dumping and sorting of my handbag, or a sack of potting soil opens in the back seat and I have to get everything out of the car to vacuum, but so help me I've never understood (a) how the hell other people manage to keep their cars clean and their handbags efficient, their offices tidy, etc. & etc., and (b) why it's so unfailingly hilarious that I can't. Big deal: my car's a mess! Still, that didn't mean I wanted Lucius to see it, at least not yet. And in that *not yet* was, I suppose, an admission that we had a future. And with *that* thought, we became a *we*.

Lucius held open the passenger door of his Honda, and I ducked out of the stinging drizzle and let him close me in. I leaned to unlock the driver's side, but there was no need. "I never bother," he said, climbing in. Then he shook his head. "That's not true. I *actively* don't bother. Sometimes I forget I haven't lived in L.A. for thirty years, and I lock it, and then I come back and unlock it because I think if it's locked someone's going to steal something out of spite, like, *I'll give you reason to lock it, buddy.* But who'd steal from an unlocked '87 Civic?"

We drove down Cuyahoga Street in silence. I flinched as the car swiped a low-hanging branch. Lucius reached to turn on the heat and defrost. "I like the video place in that mini-plaza," he said. "Tutty's? Tooty's? Something like that . . . Tuppy's?"

I shook my head. I hadn't seen a movie in more than three months. "Why does it smell like waffles?" The car had filled with a warm syrupy smell, like childhood breakfasts, overly sweet—not real maple syrup but Aunt Jemima, Mrs. Butterworth's, a taste we've grown so accustomed to that the real thing doesn't taste right anymore.

"I think the antifreeze is leaking. Or the AC coolant or something. Someone called *Car Talk* a few months ago about French toast in his heater. It's got to be the same thing."

We pulled into the parking area of a corner-lot office park whose unlikely entrance banner read: REBEL PLAZA. I thought maybe he'd chosen this place so we wouldn't run into anyone we knew; there was a Blockbuster much closer to the neighborhood where he lived and where I was subletting. Turned out he feels about Blockbuster the way I feel about McDonald's.

We pushed through the door of the family-owned video rental, on which the name *Alice's* was neatly scripted in lavender. *"Tuppy's?"* I asked.

Lucius waved his hands, abdicating from all activities involving coherent thought.

Students crammed the narrow aisles of the store I will now always think of as Tuppy's. We stood before a wall of swarming box covers; I could not focus on a single title.

"Prof Bocelli, hey." A dreadlocked young white man strode up wearing one of those thick hoodies that either smell like llama or always get worn by people who smell like llama.

Lucius greeted him, then said, "Do you know Professor Maakestad, on loan to us from Iowa, in Theater?" I shook hands with the student, who jostled my arm with buoyant enthusiasm. He did not offer his name or any other words, yet I had the sense that he thought nothing of seeing two professors at the video store together on a Friday night. It's likely he was too stoned to think at all—the pot aura around him nearly obscured the scent of llama—but what *was* there to think of two professors at the video store together on a Friday night? We'd run into each other, both squeezed from a sold-out movie. There was no reason to imagine our evening would involve anything beyond watching a film and consuming microwave popcorn. This thought made me both sick and emboldened at the same time. The idea of sitting alone in a room with Lucius and not touching him felt physically impossible, but a staunch defiance accompanied my own entitled outrage: how dare anyone assume anything about us! We'd stand firm on our moral high tundra and laugh at their base suspicions.

The student drifted away and Lucius and I were left to gaze at the wall of movies. Every title seemed either inauspiciously prophetic or indecorous or both: *In the Bedroom, The Last Seduction, My Life With-*

out Me, I Know What You Did Last Summer, Le Divorce, Crash, Titanic. In the end we opted for arguably the unsexiest movie in the store — *Mr. Death,* an Errol Morris documentary about a Holocaust-denying execution device designer — and left quite pleased with ourselves. Who rents *Mr. Death* to try and get someone into bed?

We made it as far as microwaving the popcorn. Lucius took out a ceramic bowl, but as he broke the bag's seal it released a bubble of fake-butter steam and his gumption seemed to fizzle. He looked up at me, face long, and ran a hand over his bald, scraggled head before he set down the bowl and leaned on the counter like he needed support to say what he was going to say. "I don't know what to do, Phillipa. I've steered clear. I don't want to be a homewrecker. An *anything* wrecker. Do you want to be here? Maybe you should leave?"

My head whirred, no thought staying long enough for recognition. Something propelled me, for I seemed to be moving toward him, though I didn't realize it until I saw him shrink back and hunch as if to protect his vital organs. I must have imagined him picking up the still-empty popcorn bowl in a last-ditch effort to put something between us, because he did not actually lift that pale blue ceramic bowl to him like a shield. It sat plump and benign on the counter and did not come between us. He put up no defense as I moved toward him, and when I got there nothing was between us but our sweaters and shirts and my bra, and we couldn't burrow past those fast enough. We needed to feel each other's flesh, pulse to pulse, heartbeat against heartbeat. His skin's softness defied everything I ever knew as soft. I felt that I could melt into his flesh, or as if, in touching him, I already had. We were inside each other's clothing, cocooned in wool and cotton and nylon/poly blend, entwined already by the time our lips met. They almost couldn't meet: my jaw was trembling, and his kept locking every time his body seized in a gasp. He kept gasping. We both kept gasping; we couldn't breathe right, or remember to breathe, or we were trying to breathe each other instead of air. His body convulsed against mine, breath coming out in spasms, and not just him, but us, quaking together. I don't know how long we stood in his kitchen, but it was a long time, gripping each other, grasping like it was the only thing we knew how to do. We didn't know how we'd move forward, though there was no question that we would. We had come together and could not now break apart. We hadn't knotted; we'd fused.

I feel compelled to note that I had not made love in some time. I cannot remember when Michael and I had last made love; there was no cause to remember one act amid various permutations of that act across a span of twenty-seven years. Why remember the once when you have no reason to think it will be the last? I can, however, very specifically recall the last time Michael and I had sex in a kitchen. It was not our kitchen but my mother-in-law's, at her old place on Carpathia, when we were moving her out of the house and into the first of a long string of nursing homes from which she's been un-ceremoniously, and justifiably, booted. Something had happened — I can't recall exactly. It had gotten late and we had just one car there, or we still had packing to do and it wasn't worth driving home only to drive back in the early morning. Something. So we stayed there, Michael and I, each on a living room sofa. The day had been miserable; Bernadette wasn't easy to deal with under the best circumstances. Yes, we were moving her from the house she'd lived in for forty-odd years, but everything took exponentially longer than it should have because she'd let us do nothing without supervision. She forbade us to pack so much as the contents of a dresser drawer if she wasn't in the room to oversee. Granted, we were getting rid of a lot, storing the rest in the attic there on Carpathia, in which she'd likely never again set foot. We planned to rent the house, not sell it. At the time, it had seemed that Ginny might live there someday — a small place, relatively near us, near the hospital. This was a couple of years before Gin's last round of shock and before the advent of Silas Yoder in her life, back when we still thought we'd be taking care of her the rest of our days, as we'd been doing more or less full-time for all her days on this planet preceding the blessed electroshock, and before she and Silas—acquaintances as kids, growing up—reencountered one another and fell in love.

Understandably, Bernadette felt protective during the sorting of her life's accumulations, watchful over the packing, but it was like she feared I'd try to make off with something, or as if there were certain things Michael and I were not to see. Very specific things had to go in very specific boxes with other very specific things. Some boxes we were not permitted to sort, only allowed to take to the attic. If one were inclined to imagine one's mother-in-law was, say, a Nazi in hiding, and not merely the retired lifelong costume mistress of the university theater, Bernadette did little to refute such fictions of the mind. Her paranoia certainly seemed to justify my suspicions that she was not who she claimed to be, but Michael forgave her everything: the woman had (ostensibly) lost her American soldier-husband in the war against Hitler. How could you blame such a person for harboring fears, however irrational? Well, you know what? If she'd told us *anything,* we wouldn't have to make up our own stories. My own father spent his entire life retelling *his* father's stories of family and friends lost in the war—you tell their stories, you keep them alive. Bernadette's family—what family? A great big void. She'd swept it clean, a holocaust of her ancestry. Bernadette hacked down her own family tree and used it for kindling.

The movers or storage company guys would be coming the next morning, and we hadn't realized that packing would take as long as it did. Bernadette went to bed early, grudgingly permitting us to box the contents of the kitchen cupboards. When we finished near midnight, well aware she'd be up and raring to go at four-thirty a.m., Michael and I stripped down to shirts and underwear, grabbed sheets and blankets from the Goodwill pile, threw them over the sofas, and tried in vain to get some sleep. Rankled, on edge, I felt infused with Bernadette's poison. I went to the kitchen and found, in a box of salvageable booze we'd unearthed, some brandy, circa 1952, which

I'm sure she'd bought for the tablespoon she needed in a Christmas pudding. In a cartoon-decorated Dixie cup probably left over from Ginny's childhood, I poured myself a brandy and stood in my underwear at the kitchen counter, willing the liquor to lull me.

Michael came in a minute later, assessed the situation, and smiled, slow and tired. I held the cup out to him and he accepted, sipped, and sidled in beside me against the counter in his boxers. I refilled the cup, and we stood in silence in Bernadette's kitchen passing the brandy between us. My legs were crossed, and Michael handed me the drink, then ran his hand down my thigh. He cleared his throat, let his hand rest just below my hip bone. We were side by side, looking out the kitchen door, through the dining room and into the living room where we should have been sleeping. "You looked rather fetching, standing here," my husband told me.

"But now you realize I'm just your same old lady."

He rubbed into the cleft of my thighs. "I realized: my old lady, she's fetching."

"You trying to seduce me?"

"Yes."

It felt like role-playing, something you'd learn in a Marriot conference room workshop: Keeping the Flame Alive—Sex and Long-Term Monogamy. But if his proposition was sad, my refusal would have been even sadder. I closed my eyes and drank down the brandy, then leaned into his hand and tried to open myself to it, talk myself into wanting. "You seduce all the girls this way?"

I felt Michael nodding. "Brandy in a Dixie cup, Mama sleeping up the stairs."

"So, once more for old times' sake before student renters trash the place?"

"Once more for the Gipper," he said.

"Do *not* bring the Republicans into this."

He quieted then, just rubbing. I focused on the warm flood of brandy and extended my hand, blindly reaching for the flap in his shorts. This was back when his underwear was still store-bought, before Eula had come to work for us and converted all his worn button-downs into boxers. I touched Michael's Fruit of the Looms, felt him hard beneath them, and slipped my hand inside the flap. The angle was awkward, so I turned him toward me and reached to pull his shorts down in back, but they caught in front, so I doubled back and remedied that, pushed them to his knees, and let him wriggle out. He pulled my underwear past my thighs, then held my arms and lifted me onto Bernadette's kitchen counter. When he pushed inside me, I had the reassuring thought that an orgasm might help me get to sleep, which seemed as good a reason as any to work for one. I could come with Michael; easier with a vibrator, but not undoable without. And if our sex wasn't passionate, it was reliable, and that gratified my sense of efficiency: the pleasing satisfaction in achieving a sought result. That sounds about as sexy as chem lab instructions, but also as effective, and that seemed enough. If not for Lucius, it would have continued to seem enough. Before him, what I had with Michael *was* enough. The *seemed like* only entered with Lucius. Lucius entered, and I made a choice that changed everything. And, at the risk of revealing myself as the hopelessly unrepentant lover of musical theater I am, I will quote the critically disastrous yet oddly compelling Andrew Lloyd Webber epic *Aspects of Love*—I directed it one summer for the StrawHat Guild in Vermont—to say this: *Love changes everything.*

I LEFT LUCIUS'S early the next morning and walked home to my sublet, where I sat on the bed, my hair vaguely knotted, lips chapped, the skin on my face rubbed raw from Lucius's beard, and called Michael to confess. Lucius, with dire reluctance, had dragged himself to a seven-thirty a.m. mandatory department meeting, making me swear on the cup of coffee he promised to bring me upon his return that I would not flee before he got back. "An hour," he told me. "One hour." I'd begun to dress when I heard the front door close behind him.

The phone rang once. I pictured Michael at our kitchen table, in his velour bathrobe, reading student papers or leafing through a Hy-Vee circular. The phone rang a second time and he answered. I could not bear to exchange a word before I told him. I could not bear the thought of him, later, replaying the conversation in his head and cursing me for those now-terrible moments of small talk and pleasantries, hearing the empty phrases again, as I inquired about Iowa weather, about Ginny, about anything other than what he would soon know I'd phoned to tell him. There are, I know, people who would call me selfish for telling my husband of my indiscretion at all — people utterly unfathomable to me, I'll add: to think anyone would prefer to live in ignorance than know the truth. To those people I say this: if my husband was Dresden and I was the firebomber, my explosives were already raining down. Would it have been cruel and unkind and self-serving to warn Dresden's citizens, to wake its inhabitants from their beds, yelling for them flee before the next wave of incendiaries? Before their city was ignited into a firestorm? Well, fine, then I'm selfish, and callous, and insensitive. Fine. I didn't do it for commendation as a savior; I did it to try and save something.

My husband picked up the phone and I said, "Michael, I have to say something and it's not something you're going to like to hear so I'm just going to say it because you have to know. Nothing is worth anything unless I say this. I've just come from Lucius Bocelli's house — the historian here I've mentioned to you — I've just come from his house where I spent the night with him. Sexually. I spent the night with him, in his bed, sexually. I slept with him. I left there and I came home — to this house, the sublet." I felt myself faltering. "I came here and I called you. I haven't taken off my shoes. I have not thought this through except to know I had to tell you."

There was silence on Michael's end of the line. Then he said, "Phillipa?"

"Of course it's *me!*"

He hung up.

Ginny has told me that in the throes of an episode—in the midst of her descent into that place in her mind I will never truly know—she visits a moment of such uncontestable clarity, such blatant truth, that she's compelled to abandon any previous notions of reality she may have held. All standing convictions as to the nature of existence are razed to the ground. The effect of my affair with Lucius on my marriage to Michael is possibly the closest I have come to understanding what she means. I had just toppled the logic of a partnership we'd lived more or less peaceably (Ginny notwithstanding) for nearly three decades. I *was* the firebomber. My husband *was* Dresden: unsuspecting, unprepared, and incinerated. And, yes, I speak from the relative safety of the plane, flying above the open target range below, but it's a nightmare from every angle, no matter where you're dreaming it from. And if you want a world to wake into, or land on, you'll have to build it yourself, because there's nothing left. *Love changes everything.*

I redialed our number. Michael waited nine rings. When he picked up, he said nothing.

"Michael?"

"What."

"Please say something."

"What? I can't . . . ." He took a breath. "I'm not sure what . . . what is . . . Is this happening?"

My relief was immeasurable. The helpless free fall of those nine long rings felt like something vital had been severed, but Michael's voice opened the line like a channel of possibility, and for an instant I felt the telephone connection literally, felt the fiber-optic canal hollow out from my ear to his. "It happened," I told him. The bed on which I sat—the bed of a professor of cultural criticism, on leave in

Berlin doing esoteric research on a subject I could never remember — the bed was soft and deflatable as a soufflé. As I waited for Michael to speak, I thought that this would not be a particularly good bed on which to conduct an affair, and I knew that no matter what Michael said or didn't say, this affair would be conducted.

THE AFFAIR: three weeks of Ohio May and then *who knows?* I felt like the college seniors all around me, throwing up their hands and partying until the end: *I'll deal with the aftermath in the aftermath!* The timing was, as such timing inevitably is, inauspicious, to say the least. Three weeks in the dawning Midwestern spring, and then I had to leave. It's not clear to me how much the people around us knew, but I may be deluding myself to think anyone was unaware. We took measures of propriety, didn't leave our cars parked all night on the street in front of each other's houses, didn't leave the house at which we slept and walk together to campus under the fluttery canopies of new-green leaves. We did not hold hands in public. But we were everywhere together: shared every meal, arrived and left together from every campus event we were professionally compelled to attend. It was as though we'd decided that since I was married, and nothing *could* be going on between us, then, for all outward purposes, nothing was. We'd clicked, we'd bonded, become fast and inseparable friends — we simply adored one another. I could even have imagined myself saying to Anthea Lingafelter, "Oh, I have such a *crush* on Lucius Bocelli," and she'd say, "No kidding!" or "Join the club" or "You're hardly the first, sweetheart," and he and I would go on, cutting things a little close for some people's comfort, pushing the line of our "friendship" further than credibility allowed while adamantly insisting our openness insured us against wrongdoing. *Well, we seemed to say, I'm sure I'd assume we were sleeping together, too — we look really suspicious, don't we?* Perhaps we only looked pathetic, but Lucius was so revered there: beloved, long-tenured, and single. They likely thought he deserved a little something. I was the outsider, the visitor who'd be on her way soon enough.

I had to leave a few days shy of the end of finals week to make it back for Ginny's wedding. Sometimes I wish the schedule hadn't been so unforgivingly tight and Michael and I had some time to contend with each other before the wedding. We tried to talk, but the phone felt impossible. Michael's birthday fell during that period. What does one say to one's cuckolded husband on his fifty-ninth birthday? Happy Midlife Crisis? Professors' worlds narrow at the end of the semester just like our students'; we, too, live on coffee and microwave pita pockets in our sprint to the finish line. With more time, Michael and I might have handled things better, but—and I say this at the risk of sounding like I believe in a power higher than Murphy—sometimes I think it's a blessing we had such little control over the unfolding events.

I left Ohio the afternoon of the third Thursday in May 2004. As I kissed Lucius goodbye in his mudroom against the upright washer/dryer, the dramatics swirling in me belonged far more appropriately to the hormone-riddled twenty-two-year-olds prancing around campus like spring-born gnomes. Like them, I had little sense of what awaited me beyond the college gates. I put my car on I-80 West and drove, unfortunately, straight into the sun. I left my prescription sunglasses, I realized too late, on Lucius's laundry room shelf, where he'd discover them, and then what? Call or email to say he had them? Find my address and mail them to me at home? Tuck them away until I returned? I had no idea; that's how new it was, how unarticulated our terms.

That evening, just past Gary, Indiana—facial muscles pinched, eyes strained from five hours of squinting—Chicago-area road construction narrowed the interstate to one lane and I spent three hours in traffic moving slower than an imperial cavalcade. In front of me, a glittery grape-colored Ford Aspire had a *Bush-Cheney '04* sticker and another that said *If You're Living Like There's No God You'd Better Be Right.* The license plate—primary colors, stick-figure drawings, a child's green handprints, KIDS FIRST—was from Indiana. The plate holder read: *Practice Safe Sex. Get Married and Be Faithful.* For three seething hours, crawling forward in spurts that never got me out of second gear, it was all I could do not to stick my head out the window and yell, *What about love? I was faithful for twenty-six years, then I fell in love—so what then? What would your goddamn god have me do then?* I knew the answer, I suppose. I didn't ask the question. Instead I put *La Cage aux Folles* on the stereo and sang along very, very loudly.

In the traffic ahead of the Aspire—*we aspire to build a decent car, really we do*—was the longest semi I've ever seen, hauling what I finally figured out was a church steeple in an enormous plastic bag, factory-pristine as a special-order game piece, ready to be ripped open, hoisted up, and deposited by crane atop a prefab church in some planned shopping mall community off the interstate, the steeple Lego-clicking into place. SUVs hulked over me like steroid-muscled henchmen, and I thought of the running joke circulating among the eco-crunchier of my students: they added the word "anal" to the macho-militaristic names of those gas-gorging, flab-assed RVs and SUVs to make Anal Trailblazers and Anal Pathfinders, Anal Excursions, Anal Rodeos, Anal Coachmen, Anal Odysseys. I once saw an Anal Prowler. But that day on I-80, when I spotted a brontosaurus-sized Anal Invader towing an army-green Anal Armada, I was near tears, about ready to abandon my car in the parking-lot-of-a-highway and march west on the median into the setting fireball sun. Orah and Obadiah Yoder were killed by an SUV—the driver never saw the Yoders' buggy as it crested the hill in front of their farm. They —Silas and Eula's parents—died in a catastrophe of horseflesh and blood and metal and fucking collard greens, and I blame every goddamn SUV owner for killing two of the best people I've known in this world. After the Yoders died I wanted never to drive again, to divorce myself from a society that allowed creation of the SUV. I wanted my own buggy. I wanted to move to Prairie, Iowa, and stake my own life against the world that had flown at Orah and Obadiah with the weight of all that American-made steel, obliterating those good, good people. The Amish, they forgive—they invite the murderer to the funeral, for chrissake!—and it's not that they're any less clobbered by loss than I am. They're sick with grief, but not with anger, not with the hateful bitterness I parade around. They have their heaven, and everything's better there, so they're not angry when a loved one crosses over. But me, I'm a selfish, angry, godless *Modern*, and I want the Yoders here, with me and Ginny and Silas and Eula and the grandchildren they'll never know. The Amish get past the Yoders' deaths in a way I never will—and I'm not sure I want to. I hate this America where there's no hope for a horse-drawn buggy to share the road. I'm so full of hate for it I don't know what to do with myself. Yet, law-abiding citizen that I am, I didn't abandon my vehicle on I-80 that day and wreak mayhem—this wasn't Woodstock, it was a fucking death march: the great death march that is life in America —I sat in my car, waiting out the traffic like everyone else. Good Phillipa, good American.

IT WAS TWO in the morning by the time I got home. Michael didn't rouse when I entered the bedroom; if he was awake, he didn't let on, just lay on his side of the bed as he had for all of our marriage. For longer than Ginny'd been a person on the earth, Michael had slept on his side of that bed, I on mine. To return home (albeit from an extended trip, in the course of which I'd broken my marriage vows) and *not* fall, exhausted, onto my side of the bed was something I had never done. I'd been going on adrenaline for three weeks by then. Adrenaline and—forgive me—sex. More sex than I'd been involved in for a long time. It is only luck that I did not kill anyone on I-80 that night. I should have been stopped at the toll plaza; in no way could I have appeared fit behind the wheel.

I got as far as the edge of the bed and couldn't go any farther. It felt wrong. I was degenerate with exhaustion. The dilemma of what to do if I *didn't* climb into the bed bloomed into such a paralytic cloud that I have no memory of sinking to the floor, but that's where I was when I next came to. The ensuing sequence I can only see as if it's part of a pretentious student-staged drama: each time the lights come up, the stage is set with a new tableau, a different arrangement of characters in space to mark the passage of time.

Lights rise on two figures. Him: asleep in bed. Her: sitting upright on the floor, asleep, head against the mattress. Lights down.

Lights up. Two figures. Him: slumped on the edge of the bed staring blankly out, his hand, flat and noncommittal, on the top of her head. Her: asleep, head on the metal bed frame, neck crooked at a distressing angle.

Two figures. Him: on the floor, legs crossed awkwardly, stiffly yogic. Her: head on his shoulder. He tilts toward it slightly, perhaps with affection.

Two figures. Him: lying ramrod-straight down the center of the bed, hands locked behind his neck. Her: fetal, on the floor, knees pressed to eye sockets.

Two figures. Him: on his belly, head sticking off the foot of the bed, face pressed to her hair as if a scent there might return them to another time. Her: seated, legs splayed like discarded crutches, arms fallen between them, empty palms open as if to catch a child's rolling ball.

Two figures.

MICHAEL WAS IN the shower when I woke the next morning on the floor, an unseasonal ache in my bones. I clutched the bedspread around me without knowing if I'd taken it or Michael had sacrificed it to me in the night. My sneakers lay on the carpet, laces tied. I pushed back into them, tightened my hair elastic, stood, and kept on.

There was so much to be done that day, but Ginny and Silas had left me and Michael free of demands until late afternoon when we were to transport Bernadette from the nursing home to the rehearsal dinner downtown, at the Sundry Heifer Café. Until then, we had the day to ourselves. Maybe they were being thoughtful, or maybe it would have only stressed Ginny more to have me involved. Perhaps she had an inkling of what sort of shape I might be in—maybe I was deluding myself in thinking I was deluding anyone as to the unhingedness of my life. Maybe they knew Michael and I would need time together after so long apart, though they could not have known why we needed that time or how we would use it. To tell Ginny what was going on between us would have been not only inappropriate, but impossible. We barely knew what was happening ourselves. What Michael and I did know was that we wouldn't have time to deal with anything for real until after the wedding. When we'd gotten Ginny and Silas on the honeymoon-bound plane to Paris, we could fall apart, not before, but we were unlikely to survive ten minutes of wedding propriety without some sort of processing beforehand. Love for Ginny aside, one of us would have cracked and blown. We just needed to get through the wedding, and in all honesty, I think the spanking was neither wholly ill conceived nor ill considered. It was born in Michael of valiant intention.

We spent the day before our daughter's wedding in negotiations tense enough to make the Geneva Convention seem like blowsy New Age conflict mediation. Michael claimed the seminal desire for the spanking had come to him during the night and grew that day as we railed in angry whispers and dramatic pantomime across the bedroom.

I'd led the U of O English and Theater Departments' trip to London over March break, so hadn't seen Michael since the end of January, when we loaded the Volvo in a snowstorm, Michael teasing that I already had enough in there to last the winter. Once it was packed, he tried to persuade me not to leave until the weather cleared, but classes began the next day and I hated to show up late. "You're no use to them dead on the highway," Michael said. I countered that death would be a good excuse to avoid add/drop week, and left in midstorm, snow-blind, *I'm Getting My Act Together and Taking It on the Road* playing loud enough to be heard in the other vehicles on the highway. With cars and semis piling up in the median like the aftermath of a demolition derby, it took me four hours to drive sixty miles before I pulled off, got a room at Motel 6, and watched HBO for the rest of the day while snow collected like windblown trash against the balcony door. I called Michael that night, lied, and told him I was in Ohio. I didn't want him proven right about driving in the storm. Still, I can't help but wonder if something began that day, with that small and seemingly negligible lie.

The day before the wedding, I don't know how long we negotiated until I got Michael to come out with the notion of the spanking. Hours, certainly. He'd agreed on the necessity of brokering a temporary truce—some way to slip a bookmark into our story so we could leave it upstairs on the bedside table (or secreted like a *Hustler* between the mattresses) and return to it when the weekend was over. But Michael could not get past *How could you?* and the clock was ticking. We needed to progress to *It's done, so what now?* And, I suppose, because he was the wronged, and I the wrong*er*, it came down to me finally, on my knees at the side of the unmade bed where my husband sat, my hands grasping his like a Dickensian beggar: *What do you need, Michael? What can I do to enable you to bear this?*

He shuddered and sank into himself, reminding me of Ginny as a child, clamped and encased in her own impossible fury, no answer an answer, the only remedy a time-travel pipe dream: *Go back and undo what's been done. Make it like it was before.* Then she'd throw a tantrum —a phrase that's always struck me, for its exact opposite is true. One does not take the initiative and *throw* a tantrum; the tantrum does the throwing. Ginny was victim, not victimizer, and I, her young mother, was frightened for and by her as she screamed on the floor of Toys "R" Us, or in the public pool dressing room, or at Samantha Slingerland's fifth birthday at the roller rink by the old highway, the O'Hare arrivals ramp, the Ground Round . . . Once a tantrum's begun, the only way out is to soothe. No matter how angry I was, how frustrated, how much I might have wanted to slap her, I had to be a drug. That's how I came to think of it: I had to become morphine and flood calm through her veins. In the midst of the shrieking and flailing, the gasps of a child spiraling in on herself, I had to become the eye of the storm and steer her down. This took a long time to learn.

But now, with Michael looking like he might get thrown by a tantrum of his own, I knew how to help him. I knelt at his feet, frightened of my husband as I had only ever been frightened of our daughter. He was scaring himself, and that scared me. He seemed afraid of his own thoughts, and I could only imagine that those thoughts were violent, that he wanted to do me harm and was deeply shaken by his own desires. On the bed above me he began to quake as if with fever. I tried to imagine what his mind had stuck on, what idea could cause him this degree of distress. *He wants to kill me,* I thought. Above me he cringed, as if in response. *He wants to rape me. My husband*—I was trying out possibilities, trying them on for fit—*father of my girl, this man I've slept beside for twenty-six years, has ideas of carving and mutilating me. Fantasies where he clubs my head in, smashes my body between his car and a brick wall, again and again and again . . . He wants to fuck me with pinking shears, crush my head in a vise, snap my neck the way cats kill bunnies in spring . . .* I was frightening myself. This wasn't *my* life, but it *was* the life of the woman who'd just spent three weeks in a near-perpetual state of orgasm. A practically menopausal woman wearing everyday panty liners to contend with a wetness she'd always thought was a lie breathed by phone sex operators revving up their johns. Now, this was my life.

"Michael, tell me what you want. You haven't *done* it. Thinking's not a crime—"

"Don't mock me, Phil."

"That's not—I wouldn't. Michael, *tell* me. We can't do anything otherwise. Say what you need to say. Tell me what you need." I held back; he did not respond well to psychologizing. I'd already decided I'd do whatever he asked. Ginny's wedding and all it represented was too important. That Ginny Maakestad and Silas Yoder found each other on this godforsaken earth might be some sort of proof we're not so forsaken as all that. But God or no God, forsaking, unforsaken, forsook, or forsooth, Michael and I were the only parents still alive to be part of this wedding, and we could not screw it up, not because of our own troubles, not for anything in the world. I'd told myself that whatever Michael thought would enable him to get through it, I'd do, and when he finally told me, it was not so bad as I'd imagined, not by a long shot.

He said: "I think if I could spank you . . ."

My head turtled toward him as I waited for more, but no more came. His eyes were shut like he couldn't bear to see my reaction, which was probably for the best, since I can't deny my disbelief: here we were at a dire moment in our lives, and Michael wanted to enact some kind of soft-porn domination fantasy? *This* was how we were to rise above our circumstance and behave like adults? *This* was his answer? But another part of me understood entirely. "You want to hurt me," I said. "I get it. I hurt you, you want to hurt me."

"I don't," he said. "I don't want to *hurt* you. I don't know why I want it. I'm ashamed to . . . but since I thought of it, I've imagined . . ." He broke off, and I appreciated how hard it was for him. I sympathized. I did. My feeling toward him wasn't precisely maternal, but it was certainly patronizing. As I slithered my way up to that condescending perch, though, something else happened, and the man on the bed became, for a brief moment, the man I'd married years before. He became what he'd first been to me: my teacher. Not my equal, but my superior. When I first knew Michael I was captivated by his knowledge, his stature. Just nine years my senior, he was a professor and I a lowly grad student—*his* lowly grad student. The authority in his voice has faded—or my ears are so accustomed I can no longer hear it. But my affair with Lucius had changed us, changed who we were and who we might be to one another, and for a moment in the bedroom that day he was the distant and unreachable — and infinitely desirable — man he'd once been. His jaw was so rigid it looked like he had an underbite, or was holding something in his mouth as he spoke, something caustic. His skin quivered, veins throbbing, teeth clenched. His words came in vicious points, each a stress of its own, as if he wanted me to know he'd carefully chosen each. "I want to hit you," he said. Then: "I want to whip you."

I was scared of the rage I'd seen in his muscles and bones, but in a moment the fear was gone and I felt what people apparently feel in times of horror or humiliation or pain. Part of my consciousness left my body and scuttled up on high to hover and observe. Part of me was still down there, sensate; I wasn't numb, but I was registering sensation without specific qualities. I *felt,* but didn't know *how* I felt, or *what* I felt. I experienced without processing. I sat above, recording it for later, when I could risk the scorn I might feel.

Ginny used to be unable to watch certain sporting events on TV — ice skating, ski jumping, gymnastics. The tension was too much, and she'd be tied in knots, her anxiety causing physical pain. Finally, she'd cover her eyes. But afterward she always asked for a narration of the events she'd hidden from. When we got a VCR, she had Michael tape the competitions, so once we'd told her how they turned out, she could then watch for herself and see the drama unfold. That's what I thought of as I removed myself from the situation in the bedroom. I thought I'd replay it later to experience it without the unbearable uncertainty of the outcome. And this is, I think, how a grown woman with no innate penchant for S&M submits herself to a spanking by her husband, who stands trembling before her in a brown velour bathrobe. I stepped outside myself. I said, "Okay."

Michael didn't reply, but stood slowly and went to my dresser like he'd already thought everything out. He opened the drawer where I kept ruined pantyhose I hadn't yet tossed.

I pushed myself onto the bed. I lay down. I turned over.

Michael moved like an automaton, physically forcing his every step. He came to the bedside and lifted my hands—one, then the other—to the headboard, holding squeamishly to my wrists as if I were diseased. He tied me to the headboard with knots he learned fifty years ago as a Cub Scout. Knots he demonstrated in 4-H county fair expos—oh, if the Scouts only knew how their lessons were being applied. Or maybe they know full well what their training's good for.

Bound to the headboard with my own Hanes-Her-Way "Barely There" Sandalfoot pantyhose, I lay facedown, waiting to be lashed by this zombie version of my husband. He retrieved his belt from the waist loops of khakis he'd slung over an armchair the night before, and approached, looking so whipped himself that I sympathized with him again. But sympathy turns so quickly to pity, and pity led me right to disdain, for Michael and the pathetic idea that his little S&M fantasy might clear the air between us. Back in Ohio with Lucius, I'd felt nothing but guilt with regard to Michael. Now, at home, with him hovering over me as if awaiting direction, I just wanted to get it over with so I could stop pretending to be bound to the bed and get on with my day. But then I'd gone again and lost sight of the larger picture, which wasn't about me and Michael and our marriage, but about Ginny and her marriage. We couldn't afford for this remedial measure to fail. In order to broker the peace we needed, I had to let the spanking serve its purpose. I could not float above, fly-on-the-wall-like. If it was to work, I had to be inside myself. Michael was not an idiot; he needed my submission, and so I needed to find a way to make myself feel demeaned, and to make him feel responsible for it.

As if he understood, Michael's voice grew authoritative. He said, "Take off your pants."

"Michael." There was too much reprimand in my voice, I knew. I flapped my elbows.

"Oh." He lay the belt on the bed, reached his arms under me, found and undid the button of my jeans. The way he held the fabric I thought he might yank and split my pants, rip them open the way he wanted to rip me open, but in a moment his fingers found the zipper pull and he dragged it haltingly down. Then he brought his hands gently up to my abdomen, palms flat against me, and slid them down into my underwear, pushing everything down in one clean motion until it all turned inside out at my ankles. Michael switched his position and pulled; I heard my clothes slump to the floor. My husband reclaimed his belt.

He stood a long while by the side of the bed, one hand in the crook between my thighs as if trying to warm it. Almost despondent, leather belt trailing from his hand, he seemed like a little boy who'd returned from walking the family dog with only a leash and empty collar. I felt a surge of tenderness, and would have reached for him with a palm of reassurance had I not (a) been tied to the headboard, and (b) thought my support just then was probably the last thing he needed. So much evidence of our trouble is right there: I didn't trust Michael to take care of his own needs.

I closed my eyes. I was so tired I thought I might actually sleep. My consciousness wavered. I fluttered to when I felt Michael sink to his knees, his hand coming to rest under one side of my ass, which he cupped with an excruciating tenderness. I was slipping away. I'm not sure I've ever been so profoundly exhausted in my life, a quivering exhaustion, spasmodic, my limbs and muscles like separate entities with twitching wills of their own. I fell asleep.

The first slap of the belt came from inside a dream, with a logic and a context of its own. I awoke with the second slap, which did not hurt so much as confuse me. I couldn't understand why it didn't hurt. It was, I thought, supposed to be painful, but maybe it wasn't painful because my body wasn't my body—it seemed to be the body of a horse, a big chestnut mare. The lash of leather was not a riding crop's switch, but more like a saddle girth or stirrup strap thwacking against me, thick and dull. When Michael let the belt fall to the floor and started in with the flat of his hand, I thought of a kind old horse groom laying down his currycomb to buffet the great beast with a few affectionate smacks to the flank. He brought his hand down with some force, then left it there, where it had struck, for a long moment. Then he began to rub the spot in circles as if to spread the pain around and prepare my flesh for the next onslaught. His skin against my skin was dry and warm. Above me, his breathing quickened, and he paused for a long time over the rubbing before he raised his hand again to strike. When he did, his hand retracted quickly, then came down again with a new quality of force, a speed and an astringency. I remember thinking of Fourth of July fireworks displays—those long minutes between singular blasts, as you wait, neck craned expectantly to the sky until the grand finale when everything comes together in an extended bombardment of relentless glory, bloom upon boom upon splash. The tiniest pause in dramatics and you think the show's over. And then it's not! It keeps coming, encore after encore after encore, until you think maybe you don't want another encore. Maybe you'd rather stand up, go home, feel the quiet . . . Only the encores won't stop, they just keep coming, slap after slap after slap, until you can't understand how he has the strength and energy to keep lifting his hand, to keep the blows coming. You start to question your own perception of time; has this really been going on as long as you *feel* it's been going on? Have you lost your hold on temporal relativity? Are you stuck in a glitch of time, a record caught in one groove? It's impossible to say, impossible to say anything, impossible that his hand is still rising and falling. Your flesh stings, prickly with electrostatic fuzz, and things start to go numb, like frostbite setting in. And still the smacking comes. You think maybe he'll beat you until your peripheral vision goes starry and blackness clouds in like carbon monoxide. You wonder if he'll simply pass out himself, from the exertion, although it almost seems rote now, mechanical, like he could go on forever, and this may truly never, ever end. The illogic's taking over, presenting itself through the scrim of your exhaustion as the sort of immutable truth you encounter in nightmares, a no-way-out, no-exit truth: all there is and will ever be is the rise and fall of this man's arm until the numbness has spread through your body and you're nothing. There's nothing left.

I didn't realize he'd stopped until I felt my wrist come free of the headboard from which I was apparently being untied. My hand dropped like dead weight and hit the night table, bouncing the clock and pencil jar, my knuckles cracking against wood. A tweaked and awkward pain shot up my arm like a blow to the funny bone. I still had bones! Michael was done, though the spanking seemed to continue, like a bell's toll still sounds in the eardrums long after the clapper has ceased to strike. When my bonds were loosed, Michael sank to the floor and laid his face against the side of my pummeled bottom. I winced, though I'm not sure I actually felt pain. A sob racked Michael's throat. If I'd had any sensation left in my hindquarters, I'd've felt his tears. I think he'd been crying all along.

The clock read ten past four when I rose from the bed that afternoon. I don't know how long we stayed there after my spanking, Michael crumpled in the spot on the floor where I'd spent much of the previous night. I stood and walked to the bathroom. Reaching behind the curtain to turn on the shower, I realized my shampoo would not be sitting in its place on the wall shelf; I hadn't been home in months. I turned to look in the medicine cabinet for something to wash my hair with—I wasn't about to go to the car for my toiletries, but if there was no conditioner—Michael never used it—my hair would be unmanageable. I wore a shirt, but that was all, and as I turned to the cabinet I caught sight of myself in the mirror over the sink. Rather, I caught sight of someone in the bathroom mirror and started at the recognition of my own ratted hair and shadowy face. I looked like a prisoner emerging from confinement. My top was loose, black cotton. My eyes went down to my hips, the dark nest of pubic hair. I thought, *How long has it been since I made love with my husband? Christmastime?*, but could locate no more precise memory than that. How long since I'd made love with Lucius? Less than twenty-four hours. In his mudroom. Against the washer/dryer—not to enact some sexy idea of fucking against the appliances, but because we could not be together without needing to merge, because anything less was unbearable. Looking in the bathroom mirror of my Iowa home at the reflection of my thighs, I was trying to see myself in the eyes of a man who wanted to make love to me. I tried to see myself through the eyes of a man who wanted to spank me. Then I turned my backside to the mirror and craned to take stock of my ass. The redness wasn't as shocking as the bruised imprints of his hand.

That sight propelled me into the shower like another blow. I stood under the water for what felt like a long time, though I don't know if it actually was. Then Michael came into the bathroom. He poked his head in at the edge of the shower curtain, and in a voice that was benign and sweet and just *normal,* he said, "Is there anything you need, Phil?" A rush of gratitude flooded through me. I looked at my husband and said, "I left my toiletries in the car," and he bowed away from the shower, disappeared, and then reappeared minutes later with my satiny, plastic-lined satchel. He laid it open on the toilet seat beside the shower for me to take what I needed, then slipped off his bathrobe and the houseclothes beneath it, let them fall to the floor, and stepped naked into the shower, where he held my wet body to his own.

MICHAEL OFFERED TO FETCH Bernadette at East Prairie Elder Living and come back for me once he'd dropped her at the Sundry Heifer, but it was ridiculous to do all that driving, too obvious an indication of *Something's the Matter with the Maakestads . . .* We had to get through the night and the whole next day; we might as well start with a twenty-minute car ride.

And so, not an hour after rising from our bondage bed, Michael and I were in the car on our way to the nursing home. What a strange, strange time. I don't know how to do it justice. My ass must have been numb; I don't recall pain. I remember a sense of displacement, the feeling that this person in Michael's passenger seat was not me. I was still in Ohio, with Lucius. Or maybe I'd crashed my car driving back to Iowa and this was purgatory, my coma-brain concocting the spanking to make sense of my body's numbness when, really, my legs had been severed from my torso when I sliced through the I-80 median somewhere in Indiana. This was limbo: a buzzing, static state, more radio wave than human, in which I would drift eternally through the life I'd be living if I weren't dead. If this was purgatory, though, it could be a hell of a lot worse than Iowa springtime: tulips, daffodils, blooming redbuds and dogwoods, students all getting the hell out of town, hauling their futon frames to the curb. The year before, Silas borrowed a trailer, hitched it to his Festiva, and drove around collecting futon frames. He painted them all white and used them to build us a garden fence. You could furnish whole houses just driving around River City before June 1. There was a glorious feeling in the air. Everything blossoming! Everything free for the taking! My daughter about to be married! Lucius and I in love! As little sleep and as much upheaval as I'd had in the past couple of days, it was hard to keep things straight. Driving through this lovely town in the thrumming spring, I had to remember who was beside me in the car, and where we were headed, and that I'd just been thrashed with a leather belt from the J. Crew catalog. Driving through River City, out into the farmland toward East Prairie, I felt a rush of goodwill toward Michael; I felt grateful. The yearning in my flickering womb was for Lucius, but the throb in my heart was for Michael, who may well have been right after all about the efficacy of a spanking to render us peaceable, coupled, and companionable. We slowed just inside East Prairie's downtown, such as it is, and Michael downshifted at the stoplight. As he idled, hand on the gearshift, I couldn't refrain from placing my hand on his, squeezing it there on the console between us. He looked to me as I touched him, confusion twitching in his eyes. Then the light turned green, he tensed to push the car into first, and my hand came away. He took a deep breath, sighing as he let up the clutch, and we rolled forward. I worried perhaps the spanking had done me more good than him.

Michael pulled into the East Prairie drive and, without words, left the car running and went in to get his mother. When they emerged, he carried her things in one hand and lent her his other arm for support, though this seemed largely symbolic. Yes, Bernadette took a number of medications and was nearly eighty, if not older, but she was as hale as a goddamn Clydesdale. In a pinkish summer suit with matching purse, she looked, as usual, oddly butch. Her hair was not old-lady-short-and-fluffed, but waved, parted on the side, styled à la Betty White, just over her ears, though the effect was less *Golden Girls* and more Robin Williams as Mrs. Doubtfire. Bernadette was a brick of a lady. It's amazing that someone with a bosom like hers could be so decidedly unfeminine, but there you have it. Michael's father must have been a tall and slender man; Michael inherited very little from Bernadette save her wavy hair, possibly her brute strength. How often I have wondered what the hypothetical Grandpa Maakestad looked like—I've gone so far as to search the U of I databases for information or images of a David Maakestad, but never come up with anything of note. There was a couple, now long deceased, husband and wife, both doctors—Dr. and Dr. Maakestad—up in northern Iowa, but as far as I can tell they had no children.

Michael got Bernadette and her bags in the car. I craned around, my face a frozen smile, but she settled in and buckled up before lifting her eyes to me, then nodded curtly. "Phillipa." No hello, just acknowledgment of my occupancy in the vehicle.

"Hi, Bernadette. Don't you look lovely." She brought the sarcasm out in me.

Michael shut Bernadette's door and climbed back into the driver's seat. "All set, Ma?"

She nodded and turned to the window, saying, "A little air might be nice," so Michael began to roll down her window from his control panel, but then she was saying, "You didn't tell me I'd need a ker-chief," so Michael reversed the window's direction, and rolled ours up too. He reached for the AC knob. "Just a touch," Bernadette cautioned, and he obliged. I have always found it painful to watch her emasculation of him, so I turned away, looked out my own window, dying to roll it down. *This* was purgatory: Bernadette in the back seat, eternally.

I moved through that evening in a bubble of amazing peace. As the night wore on and my physical numbness wore off, sitting down became uncomfortable, but even that seemed to contribute to my sense of well-being. I stood, claiming car fatigue—"I never want to sit down again!"—and friends nodded in sympathy. The event had all the cheer and falseness and censorious pressure of any family gathering, yet Michael and I struck a balance between internal and external pain that held us in a perfect, suspended equilibrium. We had something to conceal, together, from everyone else: a physical manifestation of our broken life. By some miraculous alchemy that Michael had enacted—I might go so far as to say calculated, engineered—he was upright and functional. He was bantering—a miracle unto itself. We made it through.

When we got home that night, Bernadette beat a hasty retreat to the basement guest room where she claimed to prefer staying when she visited, ostensibly so that her radio wouldn't disturb anyone. Bernadette decried all news sources as purveyors of propaganda, but kept one or another talk show piping into her ear twenty-four hours a day, as if she needed to know what was being said in order to disdain it. She'd sit in the basement in an old La-Z-Boy we picked up at an auction, her radio propped on the headrest, sewing project in her lap. When she was up above ground she often held the tiny transistor against her ear, as if she were intercepting top-secret exchanges. I suspect she chose the basement not for its privacy but so that she might let slip in casual conversation that at our house she was relegated to the cellar.

Upstairs in the living room Michael poured drinks. In our old life, we would come home from an outing, sip something on the couch, debrief through the evening, head up to bed. Now, the most natural thing in the world made me feel like an impostor in someone else's existence. *Twilight Zone*–ish: I looked like Phillipa, had all of Phillipa's memories, yet somehow we both knew I wasn't her. But what could we do? We kept playing along, pretending I was who I was and we were who we were, maybe waiting until we just couldn't do it anymore.

We stayed awake longer than we should have that night for lack of a governing plan. My exhaustion passed into delirium. I sat in one armchair, Michael the other, and I kept dozing off, waking up disoriented, too groggy even to panic over my confusion. Michael was tired too; it's not as if either of us had really slept the night before. Somewhere in my head I knew I could sleep in Ginny's old room, now the guest room—for those who didn't insist on the basement —but that would make a statement to Michael, and I didn't feel ready for declarations. We'd spent plenty of time apart in the course of our marriage, but I was hard-pressed to think of a night we spent in our River City home that we did not sleep together in our room, in our bed. Granted, we had spent nights with our backs to one another, tensed in postures of sleep but clenching our bodies in fury, fuming in self-righteous anger—but in the same bed. We had no precedent for sleeping separately in that house. I did not know how I could rise from the living room, climb the stairs, and turn right, instead of left, down the hall.

The thing that solved the problem—or doomed us, depending on your perspective—was toothpaste. Our bathroom was off our bedroom, and my toiletry bag was still in there from the afternoon's shower. In my haze of exhaustion I followed an illusive logic, by which I imagined I would go to our bathroom, brush my teeth, wash my face, and the next steps would reveal themselves. Perhaps Michael would stay downstairs, leaving the decision to me as to where

I'd lay my head. Perhaps he'd follow me upstairs and make his desires known. I very much wanted to do what *he* wanted. I know: I protest too much. I know my actions may appear to defy my intentions, but I swear: I wanted to make it easier for him, not to cause more pain.

Michael entered the bathroom as I was brushing my teeth. He took his toothbrush from the cup, dipped it under the running water, reached past me for the paste, then sat on the closed toilet to brush. The configuration was more than familiar. I'm a speedier brusher—Michael's thorough, methodical, and has fewer fillings—but I wash my face before bed and he doesn't, so we usually finished our ablutions in unison. As we stood at the sink—Michael replacing his brush in the cup, me patting my face dry—we ended up looking at ourselves, and each other, in the mirror. We stood and looked in the mirror as if waiting to see what these people might do next. They were a perfectly presentable couple—tired, yes, and showing it, but handsome in a nice-looking-older-people sort of way: he a good six inches taller than she, both of them with full heads of hair, gray dominating the brown, but not unattractively so, hers wavy to the shoulder, pulled back in a barrette, his a little shaggy, in need of a trim. The man wears a button-down—pale blue and white checks, open at the neck—and dark chinos, belted low, accommodating the slight belly a sixty-year-old man must accommodate. It's not unbecoming. His wife—his patronizing, neglectful, traitorous wife—is slender, but not without a bit of belly herself; may God bless the linen shift dresses of Eileen Fisher and the outlet malls that render such garments remotely affordable to mere mortals. This woman in the mirror spent a bit too much time in the sun as a girl and her freckles have turned to spots, but what can you do? There are crow's-feet and laugh lines, but the choices that begat them were made long ago and cannot be unmade. Standing there on the eve of their daughter's wedding, they watch as the man lifts an arm and places it lightly on his wife's hip, and begins to turn her away from the mirror toward their bedroom. She allows herself to be drawn, exhausted but willing. At the foot of the bed, the man turns his wife to him, takes hold of her dress and slip together, and lifts them over her head. Beneath she wears only underpants, and he takes hold of these at the waist and pulls them down. Lifting one leg and then the other, she acquiesces as he turns her slightly so he can see her from behind. He's hesitant, eyes squinted like he's ready to shut them quickly if he can't bear what he sees. There's a tiny gasp—his—an intake of air acknowledging what he's done, and as he places his palm tenderly over the hand marks— *his* hand marks—he is taking responsibility. He is sorry. It's a strange moment, as it's she who has so much to be sorry for, yet he's the one apologizing with every gesture. He lifts the quilt and sheet and helps his wife gently into bed, tucks her in, then rounds to his own side, sheds pants and belt in one sweep, undoes his shirt buttons, slips out of the shirt, and lays it on a chair. His watch, unbuckled, goes to the bedside table—how many times has she watched this ritual unfold? how many thousands of times?—and his boxer shorts slide from his waist. He steps free, leaves them, uncharacteristically, on the floor, and slides into the bed beside her, his wife.

In their bed, that night, they make love. Not passionately, but kindly, practically in their sleep, and, at the time, it does not feel wrong. At the time, it doesn't even feel confusing, for what is one more time in the context of countless times?

When I was in Ohio with Lucius I did not feel conflicted. I felt guilty, yes—guilty and bewildered by this strange turn of my life— but the pull toward Lucius was an undeniable force. In Ohio with Lucius I felt no pull toward Michael at all; my faraway husband felt like a vestigial limb that in time would fall away, dissolve. But then I returned to Iowa and, lo and behold, my living, breathing, feeling, autonomous husband received me not by confirming his obsoles- cence but by demonstrating he had more in him than I'd known. The spanking—which, in its conception and enactment, struck me as ri- diculous and sad and which I performed only out of duty—had be- gun to seem like a very deft move on Michael's part.

The spanking made me look at Michael differently, but I should qualify the character of this difference. I fear that Michael felt we'd transcended something, that from the rift in our marriage we were creating something new, opening another era. More than half asleep as we made love that night, I feared Michael thought we were repairing what was broken. I felt something new toward him, yes, but it wasn't about *us;* it was about what lay ahead for him, beyond me. I was seeing Michael in a fresh light, but I was no longer the lover taking him in with awe and inspiration. I was the friend, the sister, the mother, building him up after the fall: slapping his back, massaging his shoulders, the boxing coach in the corner of the ring, saying, *Get back in there, slugger!* But he didn't know I wasn't headed back into the ring behind him. I was sending him out there to take on others. I had someplace else to be, and as we made love that night, those were the terms in my mind, and I was aware they might not be the terms in his.

I blame my exhaustion and general state of confusion for what I did *not* think about that night: namely, Lucius. Not that he didn't cross my mind, but I didn't stop to think what my being with Michael might mean to him. In Ohio, Michael'd been nearly obliterated from my consciousness. Now, in Iowa, he crowded out everything else. Until I recrossed the threshold into my life with Michael, Lucius was the world — gorgeous, terrifying, a Technicolor world where I'd been too enraptured to think about home. Now, back in black and white with Auntie Em and Uncle Henry, there were cows to be milked and pigs to be slopped and no one cared to hear about my pretty dream. They drew me into the fold and baked me a black-and-white apple pie to say welcome home — because there's no place like it, right?

EARLY IN THE MORNING, Ginny and Silas arrived from Prairie, where they were living temporarily with Silas's sister, Eula, and her five-month-old baby, Oren. Born in December, shortly before I left for Ohio, Oren had been conceived the preceding March just after

Orah and Obadiah were killed. No one in this world save Eula knows who Oren's father is. After the Yoders' accident, Eula went to stay with Silas in River City, and when he went to work, she was left to herself, in town, for the first time in her life. Scarcely seventeen, she'd not yet taken the adult baptism into the church that follows an Amish teen's *rumspringa*, that time in Amish life when some degree of experimentation is expected. No one would be surprised if a regular American teenager who'd lost her parents, suddenly and violently, sought solace or escape in sexual activity—sex and death are so often conjoined. And maybe that was true for Eula, too, although in her case it seems more likely that she simply decided it was time to have a baby and set about the task. I've never known someone so profoundly accepting of the human life cycle. Perhaps I just don't know enough Amish, or perhaps my incapacity to grasp their understanding of God—or any notion of any god, for that matter—renders me a lost cause. I'm no Jew but for my need to question everything, and that's just neurotic, not divine. That Eula and I get along as well as we do is curious: me with my anxious nihilism, and Eula with her patient and tremendous love.

The morning of the wedding, Ginny and Silas dropped off Eula and Oren at our place. Bride and groom had lots to deal with, but before they dashed away we all stood in the kitchen for a few minutes, chatting while Eula took the baby upstairs to nurse. Into this scene entered Bernadette, reissuing the severe meteorological warnings she'd been hearing on her radio. Then the doorbell rang—exit Ginny stage left, reenter Ginny stage left moments later, the maid of honor on her arm. Enter Linda, wearing her usual size 50 carpenter pants and a hooded sweatshirt too warm for the season, lumbering in bearing enough Donutland donuts to feed an NA convention. Ginny gets everyone set up at the table for a wedding-day breakfast. They look like kids sitting down to an after-school snack. Bernadette scowls at her powdered pastry, though not necessarily in displeasure; a scowl is Bernadette's resting facial expression. Hard to imagine a child simply being born that way, disposition stamped into the structure of her face, and I might have guessed Bernadette's scowl had come to her later in life if not for one photograph—a photo half charred by her own hand, I'll note—that I have come to suspect is one of the sole artifacts of Bernadette's genuine identity.

After wedding-day donuts, Randall—whom I knew then only as Linda's NA sponsor—swung by for Linda in his poor Chevy Caravan, unaware that it was in the last hours of its automotive life, and the two of them headed off for an NA coffee klatch to prepare for the long day of non-narcotic-buffered socializing ahead. I don't know a ton about addiction—Ginny's problems, though drugs got involved, were never rooted there; drugs were just one of many means she tried to quell her demons. My sense, however, is that Randall and Linda had been drug addicts qua drug addicts. I remember wondering if all sponsor-sponsee relationships were as close as theirs, sobriety reliant on NA meetings, but also very heavily on each other. They seemed as addicted to togetherness as they may have once been to whatever it was they snorted or smoked or mainlined—I've never learned what they'd done, if they had the same habit, or just the same cure. I suppose it's true that you're always an addict; you just hope to find something benign, or less fatal, to be addicted to. *People don't change,* my father, a cynical clinical psychologist, used to say, *they just find different ways to be themselves.*

We all went our separate ways with plans to reconvene at the church at three, an hour before the ceremony. Ginny and Silas ran around doing last-minute God-knows-what, Bernadette retreated to her basement, and Eula got Oren down for a nap and was able to trim Michael's hair at the kitchen sink and spiff him up a bit. I went upstairs, ostensibly to lie down.

There was a phone in Ginny's old bedroom, a room where I never spent much time, amid the nostalgic curios that fill leftover bedrooms of adult children. Fresh paint, a new duvet cover, throw rugs, and toss pillows had rendered it suitable for the occasional guest, yet it remained studded with the artifacts of a time—and a person—past. These relics were mostly functional electronics we couldn't see fit to discard or replace: the plastic black-cat wall clock, its eyes and tail shifting back and forth to tick away the time; a thirteen-inch, antibiotic-pink television; the stylized 1980s big-button telephone, peeling Duran Duran sticker still half gummed to the receiver. I sat with that ridiculous phone on my lap, realizing I hadn't been alone since my return to Iowa, except for the five minutes I'd spent in the shower before Michael joined me. The grinning, watchful clock made me feel I still wasn't alone. I tried to get my head straight. I wanted to call Lucius, but what did I want to say? We hadn't spoken since I left Ohio—what, thirty-six hours before? It seemed impossible. I'd made love with two men in two days. I was young when I met Michael. I'd had a few boyfriends in college, a couple of lovers, one-night stands, but never in such proximity. Directly after the spanking, I'd felt such an imperative to tell Lucius everything, but the simplicity of that desire hadn't lasted. Ten hours later everything had changed again. I'd had sex with Michael, sex I somehow thought I could magically extract from time and sequester with all the other sex we'd had over the years, redistribute it from the night before into the past where it belonged. But now that logic only confused me. I sat under the cat's insipid, shifty gaze as time ticked on. It was ten-fifty-five; I had four hours to shower, dress, and get to the church. Was it enough time to call my lover and tell him that my husband had spanked me, and that we'd made love, but none of it mattered? I'd done what Michael needed, what the situation necessitated, and what our marriage and some respect for its longevity had seemed to call for. Who knew what would happen next? Even if I told Lucius everything, it would still be only a partial story, because the story continued. How do we ever simply tell anyone anything? How are we ever content to explain the way things *are*, when they're always inevitably changed by whatever comes next? I sat there flummoxed, clutching the phone beneath the grinning cat. By the time I took note of something other than the cat's ticking, it was after eleven. I had my dress to iron, nails to trim and paint, legs to shave. There wasn't time to call Lucius. Michael and I had done all we'd done in order to make it through Ginny's wedding together, and I couldn't risk a call embroiling me in my other existence. Squash it down a little longer, I told myself, stay here, in *this* life.

THAT GINNY HAD to contend with her period during the wedding seems like Murphy's idea of a joke. Having been too sick and too thin to bleed at all for so long, once Ginny finally did menstruate, it was terrible—and I know how bad the cramping can be, because I know how bad mine was before I had Ginny, and how bad my mother's was before she had me. Cramps used to wipe me out, like my entire reproductive system was trying to expel itself from the body cavity. I'd get clumsy from pain, sloppy, dropping things, misjudging distances, as if it took so much energy to contend with the pain there wasn't enough left to manage other bodily functions. Only monumental quantities of ibuprofen dulled it, and when you swallow that much Advil it dulls everything else, too. On Ginny's wedding day she was less the "recovered" Ginny I'd been coming to know, and more the way she'd been when she was just home from the final round of shock: slow, dragging, out of step. I had to keep reminding myself where we were in time.

I was impatient with her on her wedding day, I'm afraid. A church is not where I'd have preferred to see my daughter married. Granted, it was the least churchy of churches, a long-deconsecrated Catholic parish inhabited by a series of progressively less Jesus-y Christians, until it fell into the hands of scrap-bag, hippie Unitarian Universalists. The wooden sign outside—painted over many times with the names of many different churches—was always hard to read, and though the Virgin had long ceased to be the specific object of devotion inside, people still called it Our Lady of the Prairie, because nothing else ever stuck.

Frustrated with Ginny for her devotion to ecologically responsible tampons, I wished she'd conceded to old reliable Tampax — a
built-in applicator would have been much easier to manage in a wedding dress. But no. In the middle stall of the three in Our Lady of
the Prairie's ladies' room — with me and Linda standing on the toilet
seats of the stalls on either side, holding her dress out of harm's way
— Ginny struggled blindly inside the upsweep of taffeta to insert a
tampon without reducing her dress to something out of *Carrie*. Eula
had done a beautiful job on Ginny's dress, under the circumstances,
beset by setbacks one after another. There'd been a vole attack on the
tulle, then nail polish remover spilled accidentally across the hem.
Ultimately the choice to make it tea length made more sense than
starting over entirely.

So, yes, on Ginny's wedding day — my own marriage falling
apart, my ass mottled black and blue and purple, my body straining
east as though I might somehow reach Lucius by the power of my
want alone — yes, my patience faltered. Linda and I stood over Ginny
in the church bathroom stalls and held her dress like puppeteers as
Ginny painstakingly unwrapped the plastic shrink-wrap from around
that tiny white pellet.

I nearly dropped my side of the skirts when the tornado siren went
off, and a woman from the choir came crashing into the bathroom
to hustle us all down to the basement *immediately*. Nothing should
have been a surprise at that point. I should have thought: *Of course,
a tornado.* Only fitting that my daughter be married in a tempest. "Is
there *really* a tornado?" I asked, but the choir soloist just looked at me
as if in disbelief that I'd question the authority of an alarm system.
I couldn't stand her from moment one; I have so little patience with
the exudingly, performatively religious — Jews, Christians, the rest of
them alike — and she was so fervent and alarmist, white robes pro-
claiming her churchiness. She was a big help, though, getting Ginny
wet paper towels to clean her hands. And then she actually crawled
into the stall to hold up Ginny's dress from behind while she exited. I

looked down from my toilet perch as they emerged, the soloist holding Ginny's train above her own head, the pair of them stepping like a two-man sheep costume in Our Lady of the Prairie's Christmas pageant.

Outside the ladies' room we met a junior pastor–person who was waiting to lead us to a stairway at the end of the hall. Over the door, on the EXIT sign, a Magic Marker *S* had been snaked between the I and the T, so it read EXIST. It felt like we were following a trail of clues. The junior pastor was straight out of Tolkien or *The Wizard of Oz*, an appropriate guide into Our Lady's bomb shelter—the catacombs, he called it.

"There's not really a tornado, is there?" I asked.

He looked at me, his enormous black robe billowing as if it concealed a pair of flapping wings, and said ominously, "Funnels have been spotted." And I have learned enough in nearly three decades as an Iowan to know that when someone sees a funnel, you don't ask questions, you just get underground, even if you're led there by someone who looks like he might have donned his cloak one year for Mardi Gras, been mistaken for a church officiant, and been playing along ever since. He struck me as eccentrically out of place even for a Unitarian clergyman, and when he ushered us through the door marked by that symbol—the atomic bumblebee pinwheel, those three sinister triangles—I had the sensation of being led into a very hip, underground S&M club in some dark, foreboding eastern European city. Which made me think, too, of air raids, and wreckage. Of destruction. Of Michael, and Dresden. It's where my grandparents were from in Germany—before the firebombing. They got out before the war, but they lost people—friends, family—lost the site of all their memories.

On the landing, Linda stopped, peering down the dusty stairs, and said, "We're going to fuck the shit out of these dresses in there." When she heard how loud her declaration resounded in the echo chamber stairwell, she said, "Oh, fuck," then stripped down to her slip and passed it back up the stairs behind her. "Hang it on the banister or something," she called, then took Ginny by the shoulders, spun her around, skirts and train twisting her up like a stowed umbrella, and unfastened thirty-six pea-sized satin-covered buttons from their loopings as if they were so many snaps. Ginny came free. The soprano soloist valiantly held the train off the floor and swooped up the gown as it fell from Ginny's shoulders. She passed it up to hang on the rail beside Linda's. Their bouquets sat on a step like a pair of elaborately coifed and obedient lapdogs.

When we got to the bottom of the stairs, where a ramp extended the rest of the way into the underground bomb shelter, everyone cheered, and it almost felt like a surprise party, like they'd planned this all along. Ginny and Linda made it off the ramp and into the fray quickly, but the soloist and I got stuck merging into the crowd as people tried to settle on wooden benches along the walls. It was like a city bus at rush hour. A large part of the problem was that Bernadette had commandeered the church's standby wheelchair and was blocking traffic. She was likely as uncomfortable as I was to be in a church — if only Bernadette had admitted her distrust of organized religion, she and I might have had something over which to bond during our long, unpleasant relationship. She believed fraternal organizations to be the breeding grounds of fascism, and her suspicions extended to leagues (bowling, Little, Junior), lodges (Elk, Moose), clubs (Lions, book, country, golf, baseball-card-trading), and parties (Tupperware and political alike), as well as to VFWs, Jaycees, and Freemasons. When Michael joined the Boy Scouts, he did so without his mother's consent or knowledge; she'd forbidden it. Yet Bernadette refused to cop to her antagonism toward houses of worship, and left me isolated in the scorn I knew she held, too. That day in the church bomb shelter, she had amassed — on her lap, buffered by the arms of the wheelchair — an impressive collection of handbags. She'd either been designated the wedding's unofficial mobile bag-checker or was carrying out a strangely overt purse-snatching scheme — there's little I'd put past her. If I'd noticed Bernadette was without her usual lapful of needlework, I would have chalked it up to the occasion, though I'd've been unsurprised if she stitched straight through the wedding, a war widow ceaselessly at her piecework, ceremony notwithstanding.

Linda maneuvered herself and Ginny to the far end of the bunker where a child's playpen sat, blue-gray and ocher with mildew, so thickly draped in cobwebs it looked like a silver angora nest. The Fisher-Price kitchen set beside the playpen was like one Ginny had as a kid—it might've *been* hers, a Goodwill donation once she'd outgrown it. A slab of plastic sirloin lay thawing on the counter. Randall squatted on the floor beside a filthy Sit 'n Spin.

Silas cut a beeline to Ginny's side. Watching him shed his tuxedo jacket and ease it over Ginny's shoulders was, for me, more beautiful than any vows before a minister. In a matter of minutes, Ginny went from semitraditionally attired bride to pop queen circa 1984: white satin bustier, crinoline tutu, oversized topcoat with wilting pink boutonniere. She was glorious. *Who's that girl?* That's *my* girl.

Noticing Ginny kneading her cramped abdomen, Linda procured her some Advil, but Ginny had nothing to wash them down with until Randall came to the rescue. From his seat on the ancient Sit 'n Spin, he reached a stealthy hand into the front panel of his jacket, removed a sizable flask, and handed it to Ginny. She thoughtfully unscrewed the cap and took a whiff of its contents, then swigged. I assumed it was water, the flask merely an affectation. Randall liked messing with people. I can imagine him whipping it out at NA meetings just to turn heads, swallowing dramatically with a shimmy and sigh, as if feeling the burn slide down his throat.

Ginny swallowed hard, gave a shudder, shook herself, and cleared her throat loudly. Silas thumped her on the back. He has such an intuitive sense of Ginny's needs, uncannily perceptive, and I don't know if it's a product of his love for her or some genetically indicated, healing Amishness, but he cares for Ginny better than I ever did. I suppose he is caring for her post-brain-zapping, and I was contending with her before that miracle, but still, he's good for her in ways I never was. He's certainly a better partner to her than I've been to her father. When I feel strong, I have rationalizations for these things and am able to understand my life as something other than the collected ways in which I've failed the people I love. But in my weaker moments — well, we all know well enough what the weak moments are like.

Randall accepted the return of his flask, took a swig himself, and lifted it in a toast. He spoke in the voice of a bingo announcer, so loud and commanding it made people turn: "Keep off the junk!" He clinked an imaginary drinking partner, then stowed the flask and said, in that same thundering bass, "Sure you don't want me to marry you-all right now?" Silas looked mildly alarmed. I don't think Ginny was listening. She stood there smiling a sated-chipmunk smile, head swaying lazily as if some sultry song were being piped into her ears alone.

Meanwhile, Eula Yoder had, with typical foresight, brought a roll of heavy-duty trash bags down to the fallout shelter and was distributing them as makeshift seat covers, picnic blankets, and protective garb. The two little Bontrager flower girls opened the seams on one bag and sat cross-legged, facing each other, singing, *"Oh little playmate, come out and play with me . . . ,"* clapping and snapping and slapping their palms in choreographed ritual. Joan Silberstein had simply stuck her young Joshua into a trash bag feet-first and held him on her lap, his head and arms poking out the top like carrot greens too tall for the grocery sack. For herself, Eula fashioned a trash bag jumpsuit: a neck slit and arm holes in one made a smock, leg holes turned another into a pair of bloomers, the whole ensemble cinched at the waist with a Hefty belt. She'd become a walking garment bag for the bridesmaid's dress she still wore. And, over it all, Oren slept in a quilted baby sling Eula wore as proudly as a pageant sash. I hoped she wouldn't try nursing him under a Hefty privacy poncho — that seemed inadvisable.

The crowd in the fallout shelter clustered most densely by a kerosene lantern someone'd managed to light, and they strained like seedlings there toward a banana-yellow shower radio from which the emergency weather broadcast emanated weakly amid bursts of static. I made my way over, for Michael was among them, and it wasn't until I arrived at his side that I realized I had no reason, outside habit, to gravitate toward him. He stood beside the hired flutist, who seemed unaware that he was the father of the bride. "Is it the whole state?" she asked, and Michael said, "Sounds like something touched down over in Story City, and now they're worried about the ones coming up from south-central—Appanoose, Wapello, Keokuk counties—up between Ottumwa and Oskaloosa. There was a hit at Indian Hill Community College. Sounds like it's headed for us, through Joetown, Prairie, Frytown, up through River City, then northwest— Morse, Mount Vernon, Mechanicsville . . ." He grew self-conscious then, realizing his response was out of proportion to the question, but what I heard in this exchange between Michael and the flutist lifted my mood immeasurably. I imagined Michael talking this way to other young women, telling them the sad story of the disintegration of his marriage, provoking reactions of sympathy and desire. Though he was certainly in great tumult, I looked at my husband there in that basement and thought: *Michael's going to be fine.* Once a professor who marries his grad student, always a professor capable of marrying a grad student.

The flutist was very polite. "Did they say until when?"

Michael checked his watch. "Four-forty-five."

"What time is it now?"

Michael checked his watch again, as though it might have changed. "Four-fifteen." He seemed grateful for the weather reports—maybe for the tornado itself, something outside us to focus on, to track and watch and fear.

The flutist—who, we learned, also played jazz clarinet in a Music Department quintet—said, "It's just that I'm supposed to play another gig after this. Up at the riverboats in Dubuque."

"Oh," said my husband.

I spoke then. "I don't know a riverboat's where you want to be in a tornado," and both the flutist and Michael turned, surprised; they hadn't known I was there, or realized I was me.

Nearby, the Bontrager girls on their trash bag flying carpet abandoned the clapping game for a song, each seeming to think she knew the words better than the other. They chirped and twittered, coming together on one repeated line, their voices so high and slight they sounded like they were imitating little girls singing: "*. . . part of your world. La la la la la, part of your world . . .*"

The flutist, beside Michael, opened her mouth as if to speak, but instead began to sing along. She *did* know the words, and the Bontrager girls heard and followed her lead, three voices echoing sweetly through the basement chamber. The girls jumped to their feet, bouncing with excitement, the littler one crying "Ariel!," the name bursting from her as if in a flash of religious ecstasy. The flutist paused, held up a finger—*wait*—and went to look for something on a bench. From a black case she removed the pieces of her flute and returned, assembling it. She played a few warm-up notes, and the chamber quieted, and I thought of a story I heard often as a child. It came to my grandparents from one of our "European cousins," who were not actual cousins but Jews who'd survived the war and landed in Berkeley, to be taken in by my grandparents' community there. In the story, a concert is being given in a large city—Paris, maybe, or London—a city with a metro system. When an air raid begins, the audience exits the concert hall and crowds into an underground station for protection. A few of the performing musicians, who could no more leave behind their instruments than they would their children, carry violins and oboes and piccolos into the shelter, where they play for the people while bombs fall overhead. The story always sounded to me like a scene from a movie, as if it couldn't have really happened. Like the band playing on while the *Titanic* sank—they didn't, *really*, did they? But in Our Lady's bomb shelter that day, the flutist began, without fanfare, to play the Little Mermaid's song. The Bontrager girls fairly shook with excitement, trying to figure out where to join in. I once sat on the thesis committee for a women's studies major's ardent exposé of sexism in animated movie musicals, and was earnestly instructed in the antifeminist offense of *The Little Mermaid*. Still, I can't help my affection for Ariel's song—far more appropriate than the soprano-soloed, flute-accompanied "Let Hope and Sorrow Now Unite," whoever idea *that* was.

It dawned on me then that Reverend Hrkstra, the officiating minister, was not among us. I inquired, but no one, including our soprano savior from the bathroom, recalled seeing him before the sirens. I sought out the junior pastor. "Nope," he said, "the Reverend hadn't arrived yet when we came down here." Alarm overtook his face. "Oh, I hope he wasn't on the road. He was driving from a wedding in What Cheer . . . that's the path of the storm! Oh my!" He looked like he wanted to run, to check on his boss—friend, lover, whatever his relation to that other man of the cloth—but there was nothing to be done. Such a terrible feeling of impotence, that. I stood with him awhile, listening as storm reports and severe warnings repeated until it seemed we were surrounded, checkmated by twisters. After a time I excused myself to look for Eula, whom I found behind the cobwebbed playpen in a circle on the floor with the flutist and the Bontrager girls. Eula had joined in their song, and she, too, appeared to know all the words.

The weather radio issued several loud burps of static, then lost reception, buzzing until someone thought to turn the volume down. Thunder exploded with such violence it seemed to come from the very earth around us. There were gasps, a hush, the muffled cries of a child. And then the flutist resumed her song. Across the basement, Silas was talking with Angus—a Yoder cousin, I think, less strictly Amish and more Mennonite-ish—who'd gone up to look out the porthole in the emergency exit door at ground level. "Can't see a foot outside," he reported. "I was afraid to get too close to the glass, case it blew. Felt like I was in a submarine!" He thrilled at the image, but then dark shame took over his face: sinful to fantasize oneself into a submarine. "You know," he qualified, "what with the water against the window."

The radio didn't get a signal for another fifteen minutes, but once it did, Michael, our unofficial correspondent, announced the National Weather Service's clearance to emerge. I was one of the last up to ground level, since I was in the depths of the shelter with Eula and the Bontrager girls, and the poor flutist, who grew increasingly agitated about her gig in Dubuque, which was also apparently some sort of audition. For a good five minutes before we actually got out of the building, she had cell reception and got word that Dubuque hadn't been under so much as a tornado *watch*. Everything was on for the show. When we emerged, blinking in the daylight, our flutist was nearly apoplectic. She turned to me pleadingly.

"Go, go," I said, "go, and good luck. Who knows when we'll get on with things here. You go. Drive carefully." You'd think I'd granted the girl a stay of execution. She took off for her car, which appeared undamaged. A beaver dam of debris blocked the exit, but without much hesitation she drove straight through a decimated flower bed. I wonder if she made it to the gig.

The rest of us remained to bear witness to the destruction. The iris bed, marked by the fleeing flutist's tire tracks, was now a patch of crushed green stems and torn petals, purples and yellows quivering in the wind. Petals were everywhere—flecks of color against the asphalt, oddly beautiful, like when scarlet larkspur and hillside monkeyflower came up from the char after a California wildfire, or the way they say fireweed emerged in Europe's bomb-blackened fields after the war. On one side of the lot, crushed beneath a willow that had earlier offered a parking spot of plentiful shade, lay what remained of Randall's poor old Chevy Caravan, flower petals wet-slapped and fluttering against its broken windows and mangled sliding door.

People inspected their cars for damage, grabbing each other—*My God! Look at that!*—pointing like it was a competition. They talked on cell phones. The junior pastor was speaking in great animated bursts, seemingly to no one, as he paced the rectory pathway, impatient as a stock trader. He spotted me and strode fast in my direction, and I could see then that he wore a cell phone headset. "Reverend Hrkstra's fine," he called, and I dramatized a posture of great relief at the news. With a predatory intensity one doesn't usually associate with a man of the church, the junior pastor came at me. "The Reverend was on 22, coming east from What Cheer." He was as excited as a gossiping middle schooler. "They warned him—the folks at the other wedding—warned him against leaving. He promised he'd keep the radio on and pull over if it got dangerous. He was about to Keswick when he heard it was coming up near 149 from Sigourney toward Webster, and then he saw signs for 149, and then they said anyone driving 22 between Thornburg and Riverside, pull over and get in a ditch. So he did! He saw it pass! The sky turned purple, then green, then purple again, and black. He said he never saw anything like it in his life—and Reverend Hrkstra's no young man. It was God, he said, touching down in his—"

"But he's okay?" I asked.

"Oh, yes," he cried. "Oh, yes!"

"Well, that's a relief."

"Oh, yes."

"And does he think he'll be able to get here?"

"*Oh, no!* No no no no *no*. The roads are im*pass*able. *Im*passable. Oh, no, certainly not."

"Of course," I said. "Of course, I'm sorry."

"He's been in a ditch! In a tornado!"

"I'm sorry, I wasn't thinking."

He inhaled, as if preparing to sing a difficult high note, but then his breath fizzled and he deflated, eyes closed. His chin dropped to his chest. For a moment I suspected narcolepsy.

I reached out to touch him, but stopped. "I'll let the bride and groom know."

Without lifting his head, the junior pastor nodded sleepily.

Humans do not cease to confound me.

I spotted Ginny, Silas, Randall, and Linda by the scrap heap of Randall's van and brought to them what the junior pastor had told me. All eyes went expectantly to Randall, who rose from his crouch with a look like *For real?* "I *am* what-do-you-call-it?" he said.

"Ordained," Linda told him.

"Right," Randall said. "Online. Church of the Fellowship of Something. Legal as a priest, swear to God." He held up three fingers. "By the power vested in me by cyberspace—"

"You got ordained by an online church?" I asked.

"Yeah. Of the Brotherhood of the Fellowship of the Something."

I just said, "Why?"

"Married some folks at NA last weekend, but I'm good all month. I'm no priest, but—"

"Thank God," I said.

Randall laughed and looked to Ginny and Silas. "You do got everybody here and all."

Silas and Ginny faced each other. I don't know if they spoke, but I imagine her eyes asking him if he could abide, how his folks would have felt, if they'd been here. And I imagine Silas saying: *This is how it is. Everything happens for a reason. This is where we are and what we're faced with.* I imagine him saying: *I love you, Ginny Maakestad. I pledged my life to you long ago. Let's let Randall make it official. Really, who better to marry us?*

Randall piped in, "I still got the words here"—he gestured to the wreck—"if I can get to them. From Corinna and David's, the whole what-you-say thing." A crowbar appeared, and Randall set to prying open the van's back doors.

"Where's Daddy?" Ginny asked me. "How do we tell everyone?"

At that moment Randall burst the jammed doors apart, propped them open with fallen tree limbs, reached in, and procured a gigantic bullhorn. He switched it on. "Ladies and gentlemen," he boomed, "thanks for being so cool during that little tornado there. Now come on gather here and we'll have ourselves a wedding!"

I found Michael still in the basement, futzing with the radio, tracking the storm. "They're going to do their vows, Michael. Randall's e-ordained!" It was absurd enough to be glorious.

Michael looked at me with unwavering blankness.

"Michael—"

He opened his mouth and warbled a few notes: "*One-nine-six-five at Orinciqua . . .*"

It was my old Camp Orinciqua song. I don't think I said anything, just stared.

"You *must* remember," he said.

"Of course I *remember.*"

Michael seemed lost in time. He looked to the radio like it was a periscope, a link to the outside. He must have felt so peripheral—to my life, to Ginny's, to his own as he'd known it. He probably couldn't imagine we'd notice his absence. "What a stoic you've become," he said.

I bristled. "This is for Ginny! Why did we go through all of that? This isn't me being unfeeling. I'm holding it together. For today, for Ginny—Jesus!"

"I meant about tornadoes," Michael said. "You were so frightened that first time."

I felt humbled and cowed, but of course that's not how I sounded. "I wasn't *frightened,* I'd never been through one. You grew up with them. There aren't tornadoes in California."

Michael smiled, like he'd forgotten we weren't at home, in our own basement, looking at reel-to-reels, reminiscing, indulging in nostalgia's guilty gluttony. "Right, Phil, you're right, you weren't scared at all." He nearly grinned, his voice warm and lifelike again, and for a moment we were what we had once been: Michael, the wise professor, and Phillipa, the ambitious young grad student. All of which was silly even then—*professor!*—he was thirty-two years old. As for wisdom, the man's lived his entire life in the same Iowa university town. I grew up in Berkeley, a family of Jewish intellectuals, a teenager there, so near to San Francisco, in the late sixties. But we balanced out somehow: his expertise, extraordinary technical proficiency, the professorship at such a young age, the confidence of a smart, good-looking man, sure of his trade and of himself. I was younger, yes, but more worldly, a city girl, a *Jew*—the exoticism of it in Iowa in the 1970s! Through Midwestern eyes, I was practically a hippie. When we married the university hired me, a spousal appointment; that's the way it was done. It carried an onus, of course, kept me a little behind and below him. Which seemed appropriate then, good for the balance—it kept us even. And by the time the equilibrium might have begun to erode, Ginny arrived, and kept us busy, and worried, and ever occupied. Michael and I were good for each other through Ginny's troubles—which is to say, approximately the first twenty-three years of her life. Over those years, Michael and I had both spent semesters away—he did a year in London, I had several summers at the StrawHat Guild in Vermont—but neither of us ever had an affair. I'm certain Michael has been honest about that. It's impossible to say whether I'd have fallen in love with Lucius if I'd met him at another point in my life, but, likewise, I can't help but wonder if there were men I would have loved, had circumstances been different. There was a man in the company one summer in Vermont—they brought him in to play Tevye, a giant wallop of a man. We'd become fast friends, inseparable, but he was married, and I was married, and neither of us quite had room for outside possibilities. Maybe it's a testament to a time in my relationship with Michael when I couldn't imagine giving up the life we made together. By the time I met Lucius, I was willing. Whether I was willing and then along came Lucius, or along came Lucius and thus I was willing, I can't know. Is Lucius a better man than Michael? Probably not. Any better for me? Who knows?

Ginny would probably say that things had gotten too calm for her drama-queen mother, so I'd had to go and summon a tornado. But tornadoes aren't parties; you don't *throw* a tornado. Tornadoes, like tantrums, do the throwing themselves.

The first tornado I lived through hit in July of my first year in Iowa, 1976. Though my degree program at the U was an MFA in playwriting, I was taking Michael's sound design course that summer — to learn sound design, yes, and because it was taught by the attractive young professor. We became friends — a cup of coffee here, a beer there — and had made plans to visit opening evening at the Prairie County Fair. This was before Doppler, before satellites and advance-warning systems, back when word of an approaching tornado came because someone spotted a twister coming across a field and called it in to the local radio station.

Poor, starving graduate student that I was, I didn't have a telephone. Michael was to pick me up, early evening, in his truck. The storm hit midafternoon, and the fair didn't open that night — it took some clearing and rehab before it opened at all — but Michael arrived as promised and found me in the basement. The house where I lived was subdivided into apartments; I was the only resident home for the storm. I'd brought my cat, Maude, with me to the basement, along with an electric radio, which obviously did me no good whatsoever. The power was out, and I had no way of knowing if and when the tornado had passed. I had some vague notion of a tornado's calm center eye whose peaceful aura might give the illusion that the storm was over, while in reality the eye could suck you up and spit you out like a centrifuge. I could hear the way they'd talk about me, idiot grad student from California: *Girl had enough sense to get to the basement, not enough to stay there.* I'd poke my head out the cellar door, Maudie under my arm, fur blowing like Toto's, and we'd be whisked into the funnel, which had been hovering conveniently over the storm door of my student rental just waiting for a silly girl like me to mistake the eye for the end. So I stayed put on the basement floor of that old house on North Dodge and sang Maudie the entire libretto of *Pirates of Penzance* to pass the time. When Michael showed up I had moved on to camp songs. Imagine him approaching my house, suddenly catching wind of a tune, a lone voice rising from underground. *"One-nine-six-five at Orinciqua, no other year the same. Sunshine and joy all summer through . . ."* You can imagine the ensuing mockery I endured, but it served its purpose: a vehicle for the flirtation we were clearly going to engage in, appropriate or otherwise. I suppose you could say Michael and I began and ended in a tornado, but maybe beginnings and endings always feel like a whirlwind: love snatches you up where you live and plunks you down somewhere in Oz.

Michael and I climbed from Our Lady's bomb shelter, up the ramp and the stairs, toward the light of the vestibule, and out to the slapped, strewn, disheveled churchyard. The shattered trunk of the willow had been transformed into an altar while I was underground, and Randall, the master of ceremonies, stood there shuffling a stack of crumpled papers like he was cramming for a final. Stuck in the splintered willow trunk was the memorial bouquet for Orah and Obadiah. Someone had fetched it from the chancel. Someone had also retrieved the dresses; Ginny and Linda were no longer in their skivvies, as my grandfather used to say. Eula had removed her Hefty bag garb and knelt on it now, rebraiding the Bontrager girls' pigtails. Bernadette sat, magisterial in her wheelchair—had she been carried *in it* up the stairs? Among the bags and purses, she looked smugly satisfied by the weather's corroboration of her morning forecast.

Silas stood, handsome and collected, Ginny beside him. As Michael and I emerged from the bomb shelter, she looked both ways, fast, as if someone was going to catch her, and then, with great gumption, hiked up her bridal skirts and dashed toward us across the church lot, running like it was the last sprint of her childhood, and *goddamn* she'd make it a good one. She was a streak of white, a flash of lightning, luminous in that strangely bleary, still afternoon. The light was like an eclipse—depths blurred, outlines stark—the air perfectly clear. Everything seemed unreal and startlingly real at the same time, as though what we'd known as light had been redefined, and now we saw this—*ah! this!*—and knew it was what we'd meant by light all along.

When she reached us—breathing hard, flushed, the veins and muscles in her thin arms pulsed out and corded with the effort of gripping her skirts to free her legs for the run—all the energy and attention of the crowd was beamed where we stood. At the makeshift altar there was a shuffling, then a calm, and then the clear, baby-soprano voices of the Bontrager girls rang out alongside Eula's powerful alto, deep and alarmingly sexy.

Ginny dropped her skirts, stepped between her father and me, and took our arms in hers, and we walked down that aisle like it was the goddamn yellow brick road, making our way to Ginny's best friend in the world, waiting there at the altar, Randall at her side and ready to deliver vows cribbed from weddingsRus.com, to invoke the power vested in him by the Church of the Fellowship of Who the Hell Even Cares—by the Church of the Fellowship of Everything That Is Good and Right and Truly Deserved in This World—to pronounce Silas Yoder and Virginia Maakestad husband and wife.

2

THE STORIES

They aren't just entertainment.
Don't be fooled.
They are all we have, you see,
all we have to fight off
illness and death.

You don't have anything
if you don't have the stories.

—Leslie Marmon Silko, *Ceremony*

T HAT GINNY AND SILAS were married outside the church—near, but not in it—made a symbolic sense we couldn't have engineered any better. And the Mennonite Festival Barn reception took place without electricity, the way Silas was raised, which felt like a beautiful, if unintentional, gesture of respect for Orah and Obadiah. There was lantern-lit dancing to improvised jigs: a friend of Silas's happened to have a lap steel guitar in his truck, and he was joined by Randall on harmonica and the maid of honor on a borrowed fiddle. Who knew Linda fiddled? Not I. She changed out of her dress into a T-shirt and gym shorts, tucked that instrument under her neck, and played like she was raised in an Appalachian shack by bluegrass virtuosos. You learn a lot about people when the power goes out.

I was leaning against a barn post, looking out at the dancers, when I felt a hand on my shoulder. Ginny had gone to a Montessori preschool where to get an adult's attention the kids placed a hand on the grown-up, registering their presence and desire to speak. The teacher'd be standing there sometimes with eight, ten kids laying on hands. Ginny never lost the habit. I felt her hand on my shoulder at the reception and reached to cover it with my own. "It's perfect, Gin."

"It is," she said, and we stood there marveling. She seemed better than she had that morning, more in control of herself, sharper, less Advil'd. We've been through so many drug cocktails in Ginny's time —pharmaceutical combinations that worked for a while, and we'd all hold our breath, waiting for the nosedive, the fail—but since the electroshock, or at least since the shock of the shock wore off, she'd been mostly steady. There were dips still, yes, lapses into disquietude, disequilibrium, but for the most part she'd really been okay. I had to swallow tears.

When Ginny spoke again, her voice was earnestly solemn. "Thank you, Ma."

"You guys did it all, Gin. I hardly—"

"No," she said, "thank you for getting me to this day, not giving up on me. For making me live long enough to find Silas, keeping me in the world." She reined back tears; mine spilled. "You're the squeakiest wheel there is. I know how lucky I am to've had you squeaking on my behalf all these years. You've been squeaking for me since the day I was—" and there Ginny broke down, too. Through tears, I said, or tried to say, "And we all know it's the squeaky wheel that gets—" but Ginny broke in before I could finish. "The electroshock!" she cried, and then we were both crying, and laughing, and I'll say this: to be able to laugh about the horror that is electroconvulsive shock therapy is a pretty good indication of how far we'd come.

When Ginny composed herself, she began again, as if she'd sworn she was going to say these things to me before her wedding day was through: "I would not still be here if not for you, Ma. I know that. Daddy knows that. And you know that. I fought you every fucking step, and you kept fighting—for me. You *made* me make it—against my own will mostly! For so long I didn't think I'd ever be okay, and I'm so grateful to be here . . ."

I couldn't speak, I was crying so hard. I squeezed her hand and we stood there, wet-faced, watching the wedding dancers gallop and twirl. Linda fiddled like a West Virginian Jascha Heifetz, and Randall slapped a tambourine against his knee. On the sidelines, sweet, sweet Silas squatted by Bernadette's wheelchair, trying to persuade her to dance. She batted his attentions away flirtatiously; she looked as happy as I had ever seen that woman look in twenty-five years.

I glanced around for Michael, finally spotting him against a post just like mine across the barn. He was propped with his feet out in front, a champagne flute in one hand. Ginny had spent months collecting Goodwill glassware for the reception; I held one from the ALPHA PHI WINTER FORMAL, FEBRUARY 26, 1983. Michael appeared relaxed, handsome. Sometimes a few glasses of prosecco can round the edges just enough. Ginny once had a doctor who thought Zoloft should go into the drinking water, like fluoride. Maybe then every day would feel like you'd had a few glasses of bubbly at your daughter's wedding. I might be unable to complain.

It was close to ten when Michael and I began to say our goodbyes. I found Ginny and Silas with Linda, Randall, and a few other friends sprawled among some hay bales. They looked sleepy and content, like overgrown children at a slumber party. Ginny saw me and pushed herself up, then teetered, but was caught by hands from all sides and set upright on her bare feet. She put a hand out to Silas and pulled him up, and together they scuffed through the hay. Ginny — tiny Ginny, half a foot shorter than me — wrapped her arms around my waist and hugged me tight. I held her close. When we parted, Silas was standing by, attentive and patient, and Ginny and I drew him in. They smelled sweaty and grassy and loamy and wonderful.

"We can't stay much longer either," Ginny said once we let go. "Our flight's early. I don't know why we didn't plan for a day of recovery. We never even thought of it."

"You'll recover on the plane," I assured them. "It's going to be great!" I'd pictured them in Paris, strolling in the Tuileries, hand in hand, although, as in a dream, the characters kept shifting: Ginny and Silas were themselves, then they were me and Lucius, then me and Michael. Eras ran together—the past, the soon-to-be present, the dreamed-of future. Sometimes it's hard to know which life you're living, which you've already lived, and which is someone else's. Dividing lines are so porous. Unable to express any of this, I said, simply, "France . . ."

Silas, though tired, looked buoyant with anticipation. Twenty-two years old: today, married; tomorrow, his first airplane ride.

"It's going to be wonderful," I said again, and they nodded, beaming. I drew them to me again—so mortifyingly similar to the way my grandparents used to envelop me in their arms and refuse to let me go. I used to think it was an affectation of old Jews—Jews of a certain age who'd lost so much and held histrionically tight to whatever they loved—but I understand now that it's more universal than that, a fundamentally irresistible desire, a need to hold as close as humanly possible those who are dear to you. When we're forced to pull away, the loss feels crushing, but also strangely buoying. Love is so bizarrely nourished by the desolate emptiness of separation, so perversely fortified by longing.

Rather than ferry Bernadette back to East Prairie, we brought her home with us again. I was trying to hold on to the joy of the barn and Silas and Ginny, but Bernadette was a buzz kill. Michael parked and she let him help her from the back seat as if she were docile and helpless; she cultivated the myth of her own infirmity the way some people build tax shelters.

The tornado had done little damage in our university neighborhood. If not for the digital blinking 12:00 on the microwave, we might have been unaware of the afternoon's power outage. Michael made his way through the house resetting clocks, Bernadette went down to her basement, and I picked up the phone to hear the day's voicemail:

one message from East Prairie Elder Living informing us that their utilities building had taken a direct hit in the storm. Damages were extensive; evacuations had been necessary. It might be weeks before the community was fully functional and safe for residents to return. They were "so relieved" Bernadette had been with us, said the administrator diplomatically on behalf of the East Prairie "family"—all of whom were undoubtedly thanking every star in the damn sky that Bernadette Maakestad was not, just then, their burden to bear. East Prairie hoped we were all safe, that the wedding hadn't been impeded by the weather, and they suggested we come by the next day to collect whatever Bernadette might need from her room.

Michael passed by and I called to him. He looked exhausted, like he'd aged since my return. I held out the phone and shook my head, amazed. "East Prairie." I pressed Replay and put the receiver to Michael's ear. He took it without touching my hand, and I left the room.

In the kitchen I put the kettle on for a cup of tea, and when the exterior water burned off and stopped hissing I heard Michael's voice and leaned back into the dining room to see what he needed, but he wasn't talking to me. He was on the phone, and I knew by his tone—devoted, and crushable—that it was Ginny. Michael's love for her is defenseless ardor. "We need to allot . . . what?" he was saying. "Six hours? We don't know how the roads'll be . . . The flight's four-thirty-five? Two hours for international? So eight-thirty. I'll come after breakfast. Okay, Gin. No—you're welcome. Of course." He hung up, already shaking his head. "I'm assuming you probably don't want to drive them to O'Hare tomorrow?"

"What? Why?"

"Storm damage at the airport here. Everything's grounded until at least the day after tomorrow, but if they can get to Chicago, they can still catch the connection to Paris. But if I'm driving them, you'll have to take my mother to East Prairie for her things."

I slept in Ginny's room that night, in my dress. When I woke in the morning Michael'd already left. I changed my clothes, went downstairs, made coffee, and chugged it down when I heard Bernadette ascending from her dungeon. When she was settled in the Volvo's passenger seat, I tuned the radio to the infernal, chattering-white-noise station she loves, drove at exactly the speed limit, refrained from flipping off the barn on Route 26 with the two-story *W* for Bush painted on it, and nodded "Mmm-hmm" in an attempt at polite acknowledgment as Bernadette read road signs and advertisements aloud: "Get your MBA in just eight weeks," "Stumps grinded 358-1926," "Life Is Fragile—Handle with Prayer," "Cherry Juice, Tue 1–3," "Pray for Bob." She read without apparent expectation of response; I doubt she could hear much in a moving car anyway. Bernadette had hearing problems, among various other ailments—arthritis, high blood pressure—for which she took a number of medications. I never fully knew the details of her health; *decent* people, apparently, did not talk of such things. Bernadette was ever intent on informing me of the way in which *decent* people conducted their lives. For how could I possibly know what decent people did? Like so many of the churchly Americans Bernadette distrusted, she, too, was superficially decent and fundamentally dishonest. She claimed, for instance, to be Midwestern, but anyone who ever heard her speak could tell her accent was decidedly foreign to the heartland, if it was from this land at all. In the years I knew Bernadette she had, at various times, referred obliquely to her past in Iowa, Ohio, and Idaho, all of which sounded the same to her. Any attempt I made to press for clarification was met with annoyance and scorn, as if I'd rudely corrected her grammar. *Lay, lie, Iowa, Idaho, who cares?* I don't know which Michael would corroborate, since he had never in his life simply demanded to know where in hell his mother was really from. Ohio—or Idaho, or Iowa —she said, and he accepted it, conflicting evidence be damned. The woman sounded more foreign than my immigrant bubbie and zadie. Twenty-six years married to Bernadette's son, a number of those in which we all worked for the same university department, and here's what I knew: Her "ancestors" were "from Europe." Michael's father,

her late husband, was supposedly killed toward the end of the Second World War when Michael was a few months old. The young widow was so deeply traumatized she never spoke of him again. And I have tried to empathize, tried to imagine a man she loved so completely and so singularly that, when he died, the only way she could keep on was to willfully eradicate all memory of him. I've also imagined it could have been hatred, not love, that kept Bernadette from the memory of her husband. Or something more complicated and gray than love or hate. Or maybe the whole damn thing's a lie, and the less she talked about it, the less she risked getting caught. Michael must have learned very early that one did not curry favor with Bernadette by asking questions, and his need for favor trumped his curiosity. He'd grown, in turn, to be ferociously defensive of his mother's privacy. He had never seen a photograph of his own father; Bernadette burned them, Michael told me, upon news of his death.

"How odd," I had commented.

"It's not *odd*," Michael snapped. "She was mad with grief. She had an infant to care for. What good would photos do her? She had to move on."

This was an explanation my husband had likely spent his entire childhood constructing, an explanation that enabled *him* to get on with *his* life, and it was not a story I felt I had a right to demolish. There are, of course, things one lets slide in a marriage. My inquiries into Michael's family history were met by such an absolute black hole that at some point I stopped trying, not for lack of interest, but out of frustration and fruitlessness. We had other things to deal with. We drifted into a kind of complacency, an acceptance of The Way Things Are. I was, up until that day, guilty of never having simply asked my mother-in-law outright to explain the origin of her accent. It had always sounded French to me. When Ginny was a child, she shortened "Grandma Maakestad" to "Grandma Ma," which sounded like "Grandmama," which sounds French, especially in Bernadette's voice. This was all my own projection. French is the only foreign language I know. My forebears were German and Russian Jewish immigrants who spoke nothing but English in the home, embraced their own acculturation with the zeal of converts, and raised American-born children, my own parents: progressive Californians, "foodies" before the term was coined, unrepentant and unapologetic Francophiles.

As Bernadette and I drove toward East Prairie the morning after the tornado, with the town and my marriage to her son in shambles, I felt a little like a looter. I said, "Maybe while we're there today, you can find your family album, the one you mentioned? For the wedding gift I'm having made for Ginny and Silas?"

Bernadette only sniffed ostentatiously.

Months earlier, before I left for my semester in Ohio, I saw something at a crafts show in Cedar Rapids: an artist's rendering of a couple's personalized family trees, coming together and growing entwined. I liked the thought of giving them something that contained a kind of homage to Orah and Obadiah. And my idea had practical applications as well: if Ginny and Silas decided to have children, they'd need to know what sorts of screenings their genetic union might necessitate. I was determined to get the information out of Bernadette somehow. I'd contacted the artist, and had been trying to track down and compile the requisite ancestry to fill in the tree's branches. Bernadette had hemmed and hawed at my queries and led me down a series of false paths to dead ends. Michael stood firmly against bringing up anything related to his dead father; it was against his express wishes that I'd asked Bernadette if she had any family photographs. If I couldn't get names, the tree artist said she could do something with photo-collage, so I'd inquired, half expecting Bernadette would claim that, like the Yoders, her family was Amish, and that's why she had no photos. Instead she surprised me by referring to an album "packed away somewhere." So she hadn't burned *everyone's* pictures. She did keep photos of us — Michael, Ginny, and me — in frames in her room at East Prairie, though she probably tolerated my face in those shots with her beloved son and granddaughter the way she tolerated my actual presence: grudgingly, and with unconcealed displeasure. I always imagined that, if Michael and I split up, she'd relish X-ACTOing me out or sticking something over my face —an Easter Seal, a Chiquita banana sticker. *That's not my daughter-in-law, that's just PLU #4011.*

Tornado damage out by East Prairie was far worse than in River City. The funnel had skipped across the state, intermittently making land and blowing apart whatever it touched. The landscape looked like a targeted-missile strike zone: one house standing as though painters had just brushed on the last coat of trim, the next a pile of splinters, oven door wrapped around a tree branch forty feet off, bathroom toilet a throne in the rubble, a wicker basket of potpourri perched on the tank, fragrant and untouched.

As we neared the nursing home, Bernadette grew agitated. I tried reassuring her, but her anxiety confounded me: she worried who would be in the room as she packed, and where she would store things at our house. "What am I permitted to take?" she asked, as if I were Gestapo.

"Just whatever you'll need to be away a little while. Clothes, toiletries, your sewing things." Bernadette sewed the way people chain-smoke, like it was the only thing preventing her from jumping out a window. I should show a little more respect and gratitude: she taught Ginny to sew, and there have been times when the push and pull of thread through fabric may well have kept my daughter from a defenestration of her own. When Bernadette was still at the U, she was ever at work on some costume, something for a show or an outside commission—that war widow doing piecework late at night in her kitchen for a few extra pennies a day. In retirement, she was always sewing something "for charity," though what she made and for what sort of charity was never clear. I imagined her secreting away her embroidered creations, ironed and folded and tucked in a trunk under lock and key like an illicit trousseau for some imaginary, dreamed elopement. She probably took them out to stroke and finger when no one was around.

At my mention of her sewing things, Bernadette snorted with impatience, waving off her dolt of a daughter-in-law who clearly didn't understand the intricacies of the situation—of which she had no intention of enlightening me. I didn't learn until much later about the changes in her medications, the new one for blood pressure interacting badly with the arthritis pills she'd taken for years. Switching arthritis meds had caused her symptoms to flare, the pain and swelling inhibiting her ability to sew. I'd've had sympathy if I'd known, but the woman never shared a single thing. I suppose I was never all that receptive an ear. Should I have noticed her hands were not busy? Mea culpa. I was distracted with loving a man five hundred miles away. Mea maxima culpa.

Utilities were still down in East Prairie. The skinny cop directing traffic at the sole stoplight looked more like an Eagle Scout than a law enforcement official. Stores on Main Street were closed—though that may have been a Sunday thing, not the tornado—but generators were powering the nursing home into a kind of slow-motion mayhem. I pulled into the circular drive and stopped the car. Winds had divested the main building of its kitchen and most of the dining room roof, the tables now *en plein air,* detritus of the evening meal lying in half-eaten waste. As Bernadette checked her face in the visor mirror, I watched a little girl in a pink jogging suit move unsupervised among the tables, gathering goodies in the upturned belly of her sweatshirt. The snapping clasp of Bernadette's purse I took as my cue to get out of the car, but as I popped my seat belt, I felt her bristle. "You stay here." She sounded strangely afraid.

"Bernadette, that's silly. I'm glad to help. There'll be things to carry."

In response, she flung off her seat belt, heaved open the door, levered herself out, and slammed it shut while I sat having flashbacks of dropping Ginny at court-mandated shrink sessions. I got out and followed at a safe distance up the walk. Tornado debris had been cleared and piled up like shoveled snow. We checked in at a makeshift reception desk and were led inside by a dark-skinned African orderly with a bouncy stride and mellifluous accent.

Everything was in perfect order in Bernadette's wing, but our guide informed us that the utilities building had been virtually de- molished: no air filtration or climate control. He held open the door to Bernadette's room. "If I may be of assistance . . . ?" he offered.

"You can go," Bernadette snapped.

The man bowed away. "I shall be here, in the hall, should you re- quire my aid."

Bernadette panned the room, pointed to an indestructible rubber plant capable of going years without attention or water, and told me to take it to the car.

"Bernadette, the staff will care for your plants just like always, they've said—"

"Phillipa." She regarded me piteously. "You know you can't trust these people."

So I bent down, scooped up the ugly plant, and went out without another word. The orderly stood in the hall text-messaging on a cell phone the size of a Zippo. He looked up as I emerged; the phone whooshed into his pocket. His hands reached for the plant.

"It's okay. I think I'm banished." I shrugged. The orderly nod- ded, his patience luminous, and bowed back against the wall. No East Prairie employee was innocent to the wiles of Mrs. Maakestad. She took everything as a personal slight—the size of her dinner portion, the wattage of a closet bulb, the thoroughness of cleaning services, the scent of the laundry's detergent—and railed against whomever she decided to blame for the gross injustices she was forced to en- dure.

Back out on the debris-strewn lawn, the unchaperoned girl in pink had settled herself cross-legged on the underside of a table flipped by the wind, its legs stuck in the air like a dead animal. She was dividing her loot into piles, the way Ginny used to sort her Halloween candy, and looked plumply contented with her bounty of saltine cracker packs, stale dinner rolls, and salad dressing pouches. She had an impressive assortment of tea bags. "Nice haul," I called over my rubber plant. The girl's head snapped up. I fought the instinct to set down the pot amid her treasures and make for the car, gun off, leave my mother-in-law to fend for herself.

Walking the hallway back to Bernadette's room I smelled smoke, and I remember thinking the orderly might be sneaking an unsanctioned cigarette in the post-tornado disorder, and hoping he wouldn't get sniffed out by someone in authority. Was he in the U.S. legally? I didn't know, and Bush's Department of Homeland Security would probably make his life miserable regardless. My Nazi mother-in-law is welcome in this glorious country where the government creates any excuse it needs to purge "undesirables." But this guy, he's from Africa, you say? Africa's close to the Middle East, right? He's probably a terrorist. Lock him up, kick him out, keep America safe. Homeland Security: the SS of a new age.

But the orderly wasn't in the hall having a smoke. As I approached, I heard his voice coming from inside Bernadette's room. I sped up, confused and alarmed. The scene into which I stepped came together in pieces. First: the orderly, face wide with incredulity, seized upon me as I entered, begging me to believe him. "Ma'am," he cried, "your mother has started a fire!"

My first, primal instinct was to correct him—*That is not my mother!*—but I'd've had to outshout Bernadette, who was trying to wrench herself away from the orderly. He had her firmly by the upper arm, and she decried his abuse, demanding release. "I am getting rid of trash—old trash! Is that a crime? It's a crime to dispose of trash?"

The orderly and I gaped: Bernadette seemed insane. Then something changed in the orderly's face and he turned to me with new-found horror, asking, "She has the Alzheimer?"

"No, no, no!" Bernadette and I cried in unison, like a demented protest rally. The orderly's body caved in relief. He let go of her arm, but she kept arguing: "How is it a crime —?"

The source of the smoke was a plastic trash basket in the corner, which I lifted to the window's light, then found two pens to use as tongs to retrieve the smoldering thing inside. Behind me, Bernadette huffed and stamped like a rankled horse. Feeling like a child playing detective, I closed my pincers. The item they held was an old photograph. Professionally mounted on dense, embossed card stock, from a time when even insignificant things were finished beautifully. Three distinct burns blackened two of the corners and the bottom center where Bernadette must have held her match before the orderly caught a whiff from the hall and wrestled himself between her and the photo she was bent on incinerating. That was the first time I saw the picture of the three little girls, and though seventy or eighty years had probably passed since the portrait was made, I'd wager anything that the snub-nosed kid on the right, peering scornfully into the camera—her sadness and fear nearly palpable—was Bernadette Maakestad.

"Bernadette?" I turned to her. The orderly stood by, ready to take her down if she tried anything funny. "Bernadette," I said again, "who is this?"

She'd busied herself with something in a closet. "Who's who?"

"These girls in the photo." I sounded like a *Law & Order* cop, or a Jew-hunting Nazi—*or*, perhaps more accurately, a Nazi-hunting Jew.

"How should I know?" Bernadette shrugged, blithely unconcerned. "No one *I* recognize."

It's a good thing there was a witness; I really might have throttled her. "Then why," I seethed, "were you trying to burn it?"

When she finally faced me, her features were hard, her stare as scornful as the little girl's, but without her pitiable sadness. "Why keep a picture of people I don't know?"

I was past propriety. "You've got to be kidding."

She gazed at me, blank and blameless, and gave another exaggerated shrug to show her marvel at my gall. "*You're* the one who asked me to look for photographs."

"These girls are members of your *family*?" I tried once more: "Who are they?"

She threw her hands in the air. "I haven't the foggiest idea, Phillipa." She pronounced my name like a disease. "I've told you, it's not mine." If the photo had ever been connected to her life, she divested herself of it entirely now, excised it, scalpeled it out like a frontal lobe.

Bernadette packed her own going-away bag. The orderly fled, and I stood outside like a hallway monitor, my backside still too sore to sit for long. While I waited, fuming, I studied the half-charred photograph, the three little girls dolled up in white cotton smocks, christening gowns, maybe. Bernadette's is the fussiest, more layered and encumbering than her sisters'—and there's no way they're anything but sisters. Posed for some kind of angelic, churchy something: three little Aryans. In my anger it all made sense: her dissembling about her past, her disdain for me. I decided right then: Bernadette Maakestad was a Nazi. Her accent wasn't French but German. She'd been in hiding since the war. And wasn't it just like Murphy to make sure her American-born son went and married a dirty Jew? Bernadette probably lived in fear of being ushered to the gallows at Nuremberg. I stood in the hall relishing news-flash visions of sensational headlines —IOWA JEWESS UNMASKS NAZI MOTHER-IN-LAW—until a movement at the end of the corridor startled me and I shoved the photograph into my bag as if I'd stolen it.

Coming down the hall was Bernadette's neighbor, Vivvy Rehak, here to collect her own belongings, in the care of her meathead frat-boy grandson. We said hello, and she invited me in to visit. The kid, reeking of stale beer, plopped onto a recliner and promptly fell asleep, so I helped Vivvy pack her things. When she asked me about the wedding, I found I liked the story: my daughter was married in a tornado. Now the newlyweds were off to see Europe by rail. They started in Paris, which may just be where they found the cheapest airfare, but is also where Michael and I took our honeymoon. We went because I was twenty-four and still fully in thrall to my Francophilic upbringing—a romance I admit is not quite over—and because it seemed to be the place where one was supposed to honeymoon, but once we'd seen the Eiffel Tower and Notre-Dame and strolled the Left Bank, Michael was bored, so we crossed the channel and spent the week in the London theater. We saw two shows a day if we could. Back then, there was no place Michael and I would rather be than in a dark theater, side by side. It's been so long since that was the case I have difficulty conjuring the feeling now, but once upon a time—before it was a job and a contractual obligation, semester after semester after semester—the theater was my favorite place in the world.

Sometimes I fear my life looks like a series of decisions that have only led me away from my vocation. I went to school, fell in love, got married, was offered a job, took it gratefully. We had a child, and she had troubles, and so job security, insurance, and flexible schedules became all the more important. Time passed, and there you have it:

a life. I once passionately loved the theater; my rib cage grew fluttery just thinking of the next show, the immersion, the possibilities, a darkened cavern we could turn into anything. I hadn't felt like that for years. Until Lucius.

Bernadette took another two hours to pack; I should have expected as much after the ordeal of moving her out of Carpathia. Even if she hadn't shunned help, the East Prairie staff wouldn't exactly have fallen over themselves to offer assistance. Her first week there, Bernadette so inundated the front desk with requisitions and demands that an amendment was made to the nursing home charter limiting residents to two service calls a day. At number three they started charging a buck a call. Which might have discouraged Bernadette — the woman was thrifty, if nothing else — except that she simply walked down to complain in person and avoided the call charge. That's when her room assignment precipitously changed, and she was relocated to an alcove as far from the front desk as they could put her, about which she complained incessantly.

Bernadette permitted me to carry everything to the car like a porter. She held her own pocketbook, and something wrapped in a Sam's Club bag, its corners poking through. I reached for it and she nearly hissed, clutching the parcel. "I'll show you at home. Then maybe you'll stop haranguing me with this family tree nonsense," and I realized then what it was she held.

My voice glutinous with sarcasm, I said, "Oh, Bernadette, your family album!" but she didn't acknowledge my tone. I wonder if she was simply unable to register such modulations. Unless they were grossly exaggerated, I don't imagine I'd be able to detect nuanced cadences or inflections that alter or subvert a word's meaning in a language not my native tongue.

As we pulled into the driveway at home, Bernadette seemed anxious to get inside and suggested we leave the unloading to Michael, who hadn't yet returned. The ensuing scene I now present, burdened with limited commentary so as to preserve the drama in its naked bizarreness. Bernadette and I sit on the living room sofa so closely you might think we liked one another.

The velveteen album cover, once burgundy, is worn to a blotched, dusty rose, dull as weathered canvas; the only soft velvet is a bit of fuzz at the edges of the tin title, *Album,* tacked on in cheap, ornate Victorian script. The book nearly crumbles at the touch. Bernadette perches primly on the center sofa cushion, the decomposing album propped on her lavender wash-and-wear knees. Taking a deep breath, she lifts the cover; it clings to the spine by a fraying strip of tape. She lays it open, but suddenly slams it shut again and leaps to her feet, coughing with forced intensity. She sputters the start of ten different sentences before settling on "Excuse me" and resuming her seat. With a phlegmy *ahem*—that grandiose signifier of frog-in-throat— she clasps the album to begin anew, the first page clamped to the cover with her thumb.

"Wait." I point. "You're skipping a page there."

She gives no reaction at first, then seems to make a decision and lifts her thumb. The book falls open. Her gaze remains fixed ahead; there's something on the first page she does not want to see. I present that page here. (I scanned it later.) Mea maxima culpa. I'm a terrible person.

I read the words nearest me — "Compliments of Hazel" — then lean over Bernadette to see the dedication: "Ida M. . . . Wombold? Hormbold? Bernadette, how do you pronounce . . . ?"

Bernadette will not even glance down, only mutters some variation of whatever I've just said. Before I can ask who Hazel and Ida are, she's turning the page with a huff of annoyance. There is but one version of this guided family tour Bernadette's willing to give.

BERNADETTE: There's my mother.

ME: She was very beautiful.

BERNADETTE: Yes.

ME: What was her name?

BERNADETTE: Ida.

ME: So this book belonged to your mother?

BERNADETTE: Yes. My mother.

ME: And what was her maiden name?

BERNADETTE: Hormbold. Ida Hormbold.

ME: *Hormbold?* That's how you pronounce . . . ?

BERNADETTE: (No answer.)

ME: Ida M. Hormbold. And the *M* . . . ?

BERNADETTE: Her middle initial.

ME: Right. Which stood for . . . ?

BERNADETTE: Mary.

ME: Ida Mary Hormbold.

BERNADETTE: My mother. (She turns the page.) Here. As a young girl.

ME: She certainly was very pretty.

BERNADETTE: Yes.

ME: You're sure that's her?

BERNADETTE: (Flipping the page quickly.) Perhaps it's me as a girl.

ME: *There's* the same Ida!

BERNADETTE: Yes.

ME: And, with her, that's . . . ?

BERNADETTE: My father.

ME: He looks so much like your mother. They could be brother and sister.

BERNADETTE: (Silence.)

ME: Your father's name was . . . ?

BERNADETTE: Harmon.

ME: And your maiden name, Bernadette . . . I'm forgetting . . . It's . . . ?

BERNADETTE: Harmon.

ME: No, no, your maiden name — your last name before you married.

BERNADETTE: *Harmon.*

ME: Your father's name was Harmon Harmon?

BERNADETTE: Don't be ridiculous. My father's name was John. (She turns the page.) My mother . . . (She makes to turn again.)

ME: (Trying to make her turn back to "Ida and John.") Wait — that's not the same person.

BERNADETTE: (Keeping the book clamped open as it is.) Well, it must be Hazel. Always was hard to tell them apart.

ME: Hazel? Hazel who gave the book to Ida?

BERNADETTE: Twins.

ME: Your mother was a twin? I didn't realize there were twins in the family.

BERNADETTE: Only two.

ME: I see.

BERNADETTE: Here I am. With my brother, John. He was killed in the war.

ME: I didn't know you lost both your brother and your husband in the war.

BERNADETTE: (Flipping the page.) May they rest . . .

BERNADETTE: So handsome.

ME: Your father?

BERNADETTE: My brother.

ME: John? And that was your father's name as well? And Michael's father was Dave?

BERNADETTE: (Moving on.) Such a beautiful towheaded child!

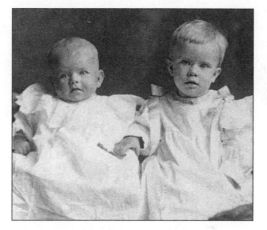

ME: John?

BERNADETTE: (Opens hands. *Yes, John. Are you a moron?*)

ME: Then who's that with him?

BERNADETTE: Me.

ME: But you were older than John in the last . . .

BERNADETTE: (Flipping the page.) Well, I suppose that's someone else, then. Here's John with his puppy.

ME: What was the puppy's name?

BERNADETTE: (Making a noise like a child's imitation of a steam engine.)

ME: Are you saying *choo-choo*? Like a train? Or *shoe-shoe*? (Pointing at my foot.) Or *shoo-shoo*? As in *scat*? *scram*? (Whisking out my hands.) Are you saying *chou*? Like *Chou-chou*? What is that, like, *little cabbage*?

BERNADETTE: Yes, sure, probably . . . (Turns the page.) Me and John.

BERNADETTE: (Turns the page.)

ME: Whose family is that?

BERNADETTE: Cousins ... (Flipping quickly through a series of pages. All young men are "cousins killed in the war." Babies "all look alike—who could tell them apart?" until, finally ...) Me and John.

ME: That is *not* the same boy who had the puppy back—

BERNADETTE: I know my own brother, Phillipa. Rest his soul. (Turns the page.)

ME: I suppose that's also you and John, then?
BERNADETTE: Oh, Phillipa, don't be ridiculous. That's Ida and Hazel.
ME: I thought you said they were twins.
BERNADETTE: They could have been, couldn't they?

And with that, Bernadette slapped shut her album, wrestled it into the Sam's Club bag, and stood. We'd been in the house ten minutes, max. I started to ask if I might copy down the relevant information, but didn't get far. "I'll write it up *for* you, dear." Her tone made it clear that to insist would be to refuse her "generosity." Press further and the "offer" would be rescinded, the subject placed off-limits evermore. Album clutched to her bosom, Bernadette got as far as the basement door and turned. "A stop at the market on the way home might have been nice."

My propriety was gone. "Bernadette, why exactly do you have a foreign accent?"

Her reply issued forth with such calm disinterest you'd think this question got posed to her every day. "Well, from my father. You know he came over from France."

You know? How would I know anything? But I wondered if Ginny knew of this supposed French ancestry . . . Were she and Silas honeymooning in Grandma Ma's homeland? Or was Bernadette copping to France because France was on our minds? If Ginny and Silas went on honeymoon to Australia, would Bernadette have claimed she descended from wallaby wranglers?

She continued, then, unprompted: "Since my mother was deaf, it's my father's voice we imitated, you know, learning to speak."

"Your mother was deaf?"

"Of course." Her face was a cipher of absolute boredom. "Runs in the family," she said. "I'm lucky to have my ears at all. My mother —stone deaf before she was thirty, rest her soul."

When Michael returned that evening—five hundred miles the worse for wear, smelling of burnt coffee and restroom air freshener

—he was reserved and cold. I knew how things probably looked to his eyes: I'd done what he asked to get through the wedding—submitted to spanking and sex, to gentleness and intimacy—and now that it was over, I'd absented myself, left him, again.

Perfunctorily, he asked, "How was East Prairie?" Then he poured a scotch and sank into a chair as far from the couch where I sat as he could get.

I craved, indecorously, to tell him how his mother—his *French* mother—had nearly burned down the nursing home, but just said, "We got it done." He wasn't really listening. When the silence got oppressive, I said, "Then, back here, she showed me her family album."

Tired, exasperated, and in no mood, Michael said, "Family album?"

I nodded. "Old photos. Her and her brother. Her mother and aunt as children. Her mother and father . . ." I tried to express my skepticism without sounding like that's what I was doing. Michael's face was disconcertingly unreadable. When he nodded absently and began glancing through the mail, was he attempting to conceal the fact that I'd just told him more than he'd ever known of his mother's family? How could he possibly have been uninterested? I kept thinking about the dedication, the elaborate fountain pen flourishes: *December 25th*. A Christmas present from Hazel to Ida, 1899. I'd always had the impression that Bernadette was young—maybe twenty—in 1945 when she had Michael, which would put her own birth around '25. The handwriting on that dedication page was not a child's penmanship, and whether Hazel and Ida were twins or not, even if they'd been teenagers in 1899, that would still have Ida giving birth to Bernadette when she was past forty. Which was possible, I suppose, though I think it's more likely that Bernadette's mother wasn't yet born in 1899, or was only a baby. Maybe Hazel and Ida weren't twins, and the gift was made to an infant Ida . . . ? But in the photos Hazel isn't much older than Ida—a bit young to have mastered the art of calligraphy, no? Nothing added up. I thought about the clothes in those photographs, wondering what Lucius might know of historical fashion. The flouncy bow tie on Bernadette's "brother" "John"? Was it the 1930s or '40s? It all felt wrong. I wanted — and with, I'll admit, an unseemly drive — to get another look at the album. Perhaps this is how strange obsessions are born: the semiconscious avoidance of problematic circumstances in one's own life leads to a sudden overwhelming compulsion to work puzzles whose solution is (a) unlikely and (b) decidedly unimperative.

Across the room, Michael had fallen asleep in his chair. He didn't snore, just breathed deeply, head lolling on his chest. I went over, placed a hand on his arm. "Michael." He woke smoothly — not the startling type, my husband — and gave a soft *hmm,* as if to express agreement. I started to say, *Come to bed,* but *come* implied *with me,* so I said, "Michael, before you get a crick in your neck . . ." He collected himself obediently and rose from the chair, then went upstairs, closing our bedroom door behind him. After the instant sting, I felt relieved.

Under Ginny's old duvet I huddled to the telephone receiver the way Ginny might have as a teenager, if there'd been anyone to whom she confided over the phone, late at night, the way teenagers should. There was Linda, later, but Linda's no big talker. Their friendship began in the hospital, and continued in support groups until they went their separate therapeutic ways, Ginny to shock, and then Silas, Linda to NA and to Randall's sponsorship. Now they did normal things together, like have coffee, or go for a walk, see a movie. But Ginny didn't do those things as a teenager; she was too busy starving, or snorting, or fucking random methheads. That she's free of horrific consequences — brain damage, organ damage, incurable STDs — is just stupid, dumb, blind luck. And grateful as I am, I do mourn the adolescence she missed out on, the way I imagine soldiers' mothers mourn their children's missing limbs. It's a pain I keep to myself.

As I listened to the phone ring in Lucius's house, I could almost smell his bed all the way in Ohio, almost smell Lucius himself — pine, wintergreen, coriander, Barbasol, a twinge of tiger balm, something like cloves—nothing more than his own scents mixed with the scents of his ablutions, but it made wings flutter against my pelvic floor. I had never known such intensity of want. I did not just desire to be with him, I wanted him wedged inside me—crammed, glutted in me as deeply as anything has ever penetrated. How does one say any of this without sounding vulgar or downright pornographic? How could Lucius say what he'd say to me, what he'd say when he was so far inside there was no closer we could be? He'd beg, *Open your womb to me,* and it was as if I could. We turned each other inside out.

"Hi." His voice came from somewhere distant and dreamed, his *hi* a long, drawn-out word.

"Hi," I said, and like children with paper cups against either side of a door, we strained to feel our connection. We breathed together.

"Come to me," he said.

My breath came out ragged, a choke of admission that I was not already there.

"What do we do, Phillipa?" His question had no answer. "What am I doing without you?"

"Let's drive tomorrow," I said. "Meet halfway. Gary, or Chicago. For as long as we can. I need to feel you. I have so much I have to say —so much to tell you. To ask."

"Just get up and drive to each other?" he asked.

"Yes, get up and drive. Get a motel. Steal a few hours. It doesn't have to be seedy."

"Oh, but I want to do terribly seedy things to you." He sighed.

"*You* can be as seedy as you like. On clean sheets."

"You're serious," he said. "Really?"

"Yes. Please, let's. My body doesn't know what to do without your body anymore."

"Can it drive? When can it leave? How soon can I have it?"

"If I get out by seven," I said, "I could be there, depending where, by say twelve-thirty, my time."

"If we meet on your side of the line, then I get an extra hour with you."

I laughed into the sheets, into Ginny's old duvet. "My side, then."

"Gary. Let's aim for Gary."

We stayed on the line another twenty minutes just listening to each other breathe.

MY ALARM WENT OFF at six-thirty. It was not enough sleep and it didn't matter. I felt like a teenage boy, perpetually exhausted by my own exuberant growth, but still up for sex, always up for sex, ever ralliable for sex, even from the depths of slumber.

Bernadette was already in the kitchen, drinking her weak coffee, crunching her pale toast.

"Morning, Bernadette, how'd you sleep?" I did try to be nice. I did.

"Oh, not well. But I never do." She slurped through crumbed lips.

"More coffee?" I readied to dump the rest of her pot. "Or can I make some for myself?"

"Oh." She thought I thought myself too good for her Maxwell House swill.

"Sorry?" I asked. "Was that a yes or a no?"

"Oh, I'm all done here," she said.

And down the drain it went.

"You're up early," she accused me.

I ground coffee beans in reply, then said, "Headed to an auction. Don't want to miss anything!" Oh, the falsehood! The chipperness! As an alibi, I thought an auction would hold up nicely. But in our old life, Michael always joined me for an auction, and the idea that we'd never go auctioning together again wrenched something unexpected in me. I turned on the faucet just as my windpipe seized, and I sucked a gasp of air, the sound muffled by water pounding into the decanter. This life was already over. These banal, domestic morning rituals in the company of a woman I'd so disliked for so very long —it would all be gone, and I felt fear. I know: I chose it. But it's like choosing to ride the roller coaster: you buy your ticket, wait in line, strap yourself in, feel the slow climb . . . Still, when the bottom drops out, that's real fear.

I cleared her dishes, but Bernadette did not leave the table. I busied myself collecting things that might serve as a pile of dirty laundry; the washer and dryer were in the basement.

Michael came downstairs as the coffee was finishing its brew. "Morning, Ma."

"Good morning, Michael." Bernadette's *Michael* always sounded forced, like she had to fight her own tongue not to call him *Michel*.

Before coffee, even Michael had trouble with Bernadette. He searched for a question to occupy her and buy himself some time. "So," he said, "how was East Prairie?"

As Bernadette launched in, I asked, "Anything for laundry?" and backed toward the stairs. They shook their heads, and I slithered down to the basement where I could not help but notice, on the old recliner by the washing machine, a certain Sam's Club shopping bag. I could hear her voice upstairs, but couldn't tell what she was saying, which is a shame, for I'd've liked to hear her version of the previous day's events. Still, I was more interested in the album. I opened it carefully to the dedication page, but then, upstairs, Bernadette's voice dropped off, and I grabbed the bag to slide the album back in. That's when I noticed, stuck to the inside, a small white price tag. I heard Michael speak and Bernadette begin to respond, and I squinted to read the worn print on the sticker. It said 35702, and, below that, $15.00. I recognized it: this was River City Consignments' tagging system. 35702 was the consignor's number, and they always used recycled sacks from other stores. I stuck the book in the sack, the sack on the chair, and my load of not-dirty laundry in the washer, and there is, to this day, very little anyone could say to convince me that

Bernadette didn't purchase the Hom-Wom-Wormbold family album and the ancestry contained therein at River City Consignments for fifteen dollars, plus tax. *Chou-chou* the puppy my ass.

THERE'S THE DRIVE to describe. Interstate 80, the same stretch Michael'd driven the day before. Five hours with my sore rear on a seat cushion I wished were a little cushier. I listened to *Pippin,* to *Hair* and *Godspell,* before I gave up and drove in silence. Farmland, road signs green as Astroturf, the Mississippi flat and wide, a thick brown ribbon dangling from the hat brim of a homely girl, America. Car dealerships lined the strip as far west as Joliet. The traffic around Chicago is traffic that never clears: funneled traffic, stalled and stopped traffic, *Slow down, my daddy works here* traffic. Through the exit, toll booth, town of shopping centers like a maze of nightmares. I was headed only one place: to the hotel, to Lucius, there, leaning against the hatchback of his burgundy two-door Honda in the midday sun of the Best Western parking lot, Gary, Indiana, May 2004. In rust-colored corduroys gone thin and coppery in the thighs, and a striped button-down — always a button-down from a seemingly infinite supply, as if he were once a suit-wearing banker. This one was white, rolled at the cuffs, with a thin red stripe and a thinner, intermittent green-blue. It was worn through at the elbows, but he wouldn't retire the shirt until the sleeves ripped open and hung flapping like wings. He had no Eula to turn his used shirts into boxer shorts, as she did with Michael's. Lucius's discards landed in the rag bin under his mud-room sink; he used them to wipe down his cross-country skis. Lucius is fit — small and lean-muscled. His skin, pale and freckled with age and exposure, is always warm and feels powder-dusted against mine. He wears glasses only for reading, little half-lenses perched at the tip of his nose. What hair he has left is gray and white, wisped at the fringes of his skull, a baby's scattered peachy fuzz over the dome of his head. I love the hair on his forearms, exposed below the rolled shirt cuffs, light — it makes me think of wheat fields. He was blond in his youth, the photographs attest. His skin is spotted with age, forearms like lichen-covered tree roots. He's strong, a man at home shoveling snow. I have never seen him shovel snow, but I imagine him scooping great heaps of fresh powder, curb to front door, clearing the way so I can come to him.

I linger, now, in describing Lucius, but that day nothing moved fast enough. I spotted him, parked my car, and then I can't track specifics. We got inside as quickly as we could, careering like blind-hurtling drunks, down the hall, through the antiseptic air to plunge key card in slot. Did we speak? I don't know, we just moved until we'd gotten rid of the clothes between us, clothes that conspired with toll plazas and speed limits and directions and lane changes until we tore them aside and made it to each other, flesh to flesh, skin on skin. Deep inside one another, we could finally breathe. Fifty mostly decorous years I'd been alive, and then came this desire.

Not until after we made love could we pull our heads away and actually look at each other. "Hi," we said. And then he was asking, "How was your drive?" and I was saying, "You made good time, no?" and then we were laughing, holding each other, our laughter reverberating in one another's ribs. And then we were making love again. Somehow we were not too old for this—miraculously, we weren't yet too old. Defying age and time, our desire stronger than the laws of decay. It was like we'd gotten a free pass: he was not yet in need of Viagra, I was not yet menopausal. My body'd hit an amazing stage of perpetual and barely contained arousal. We coasted on the magic carpet of our luck.

Afternoon sun tried to worm in under the heavy, industrial drapes, but it wasn't strong enough, got stopped at the borders. We had business with the darkness, and such a tiny, stolen snip of time. "I have so many things I have to tell you," I said, and he said, "Tell me." He held me in his arms and said, "Tell me everything," and I did, and when I got to the hardest parts to tell—the spanking, and the sex with Michael after the rehearsal dinner—Lucius held me closer, as if we were watching a movie and these were the brutal scenes, he held me to say: *We are in this together.* He stroked my hair, kissed my head, as though I'd done some brave thing.

"How?" I asked. "How do you understand this?"

"I've been married and divorced three times, Phil. I understand." If I should have taken caution at this, it's probably obvious that I did not. I knew, by then, the circumstances of Lucius's three marriages: each entered earnestly, each failed for its own specific reasons. Each lasted about ten years; he was a serial monogamist who believed in marriage. I did not feel cautious, I felt understood. When the sun passed to the other side of the building, the air in our room felt newly still and empty. We lay beneath the sheet, the length of our bodies pressed together, face-to-face, my knee bent up between his thighs, his legs clutching mine. His hand gently circled the still-tender, purpled skin of my backside, and he said, "Just for the record: if I really wanted to spank you, I wouldn't wait twenty-five years to ask."

When the clock glowed 5:00 p.m., Lucius reluctantly said, "We should eat." I hid the clock with a pillow instead. When I forced myself to check again, it was 5:15, and I conceded that I would love a glass of wine.

"No chance," Lucius said sternly. "Coffee. You have five hours of driving ahead."

It was all so radically untenable. In a few short weeks, Lucius would leave for two more months of research in France, and I was committed, without a wiggle of leeway, to teaching a six-week intensive course back at Iowa that I'd put off the summer before. It began the following day, would meet twice a week, Tuesday/Thursday, for three-hour blocks: Musical Theater History and Script Analysis I—about as exciting as the course title suggests. In the fall, I had to direct a mainstage production of *The Mystery of Edwin Drood,* and teach, the next spring, an advanced directing course without which four of our majors—all advisees of mine—would be unable to graduate. Neither Lucius nor I was ready—nor could we afford—to retire. If we were younger, we might have put ourselves on the job market, hoping to wangle appointments in reasonable proximity to one another. I'd never been on the job market; I married into my job, practically married into tenure. At my age, my rather undistinguished career mostly behind me, how could I account to a search committee for the twenty-five years in which I did my job, no more and no less, and raised a not-easy-to-raise daughter? Maybe if we were younger, five hours in a car to an exit-route motel would have seemed a reasonable way to conduct a relationship.

By six that evening we were sitting in a chain diner, overlooking a parking lot full of fat American cars with *W* bumper stickers, in a booth surrounded by other booths full of fat American families. A few tables over sat a bevy of Mennonites—not fat—their hats and snoods sticking out the top of the booth. We ordered breakfast for dinner, but the coffee looked so bad I ordered a Coke and sat half listening to conversational strands of other diners, people so afraid of life without a Candyland heaven at the end, they'd vote for a man who'd no sooner fight for their rights than he fought for the country he claims to love. They'd vote for him because he reminded them of their own recovered-alcoholic fathers every time he said "God bless." Here's something I'd like to ask: what ever happened to "may"? *May* God bless—*if* he so chooses, *if* he is pleased. We goddamn Americans shorten everything. No time to lose! Conserve a word: don't ask, just demand. *God: bless us.* How about asking for once, America? How about some manners? How about a goddamn "please"?

"How about we join the Peace Corps," I said, "you and me? If Bush wins again."

"If Bush wins," Lucius said, "I'm sure he'll abolish the Peace Corps. *Peace* . . . makes us sound weak." He fluttered his fingers like a rain of fairy dust.

"Wasn't Hitler all about peace at the outset? Or is that just in *The Producers*? Peace through nationalism, peace through Aryan supremacy?"

Lucius sounded like he'd already devoted a good deal of thought to the subject when he said, "Dubya's no Hitler. He's not lacking charisma, but it's not the right charisma, not enough steeliness behind it. Too shambly, too house dog–ish. Like there's not quite the . . . If Bush and Cheney were one person, I think we'd be in real, no-jokes trouble. Someone comes along with the the charisma and the vicious intellect combined — or someone who convinces the disenfranchised white American masses that he's going to buck the system for them — and this *will* be 1929 Germany, no question. And it'll be too late to get anywhere. We'll be fighting for survival right here." He patted the table, warbling, *"From California to the New York Island . . ."*

"Woody Guthrie must never have visited Gary," I said. "Who would fight for Gary?"

"What about France?" Lucius asked. When I didn't respond, he said, "I've had contact with another: a man, and his sister. He's in his eighties. Was a soldier then — French, but fought alongside the Nazis, *for* them. She's younger — was twelve, maybe thirteen during the occupation. Lost it completely after the war. Institutionalized by sixteen."

"Jesus." The Lord's name rippled in vain through the restaurant. I said it again, louder.

Lucius smiled, shook his head slightly, not in annoyance like Michael, but appreciatively.

"I think my mother-in-law's a Nazi," I said.

"Whose isn't?" Lucius said. "So everyone thinks the guy's dead twenty years. Then, 1965, he suddenly shows up in France. His folks have *both* committed suicide, couldn't face what they'd done. But he finds his sister in the asylum, gets her out, spends his life taking care of her."

"How do you find these people?"

"This found me," he said. "I gave a talk. A woman — French — approached me afterward. She'd been contacted by a brother she hadn't seen in sixty years. She'd married an American soldier at the end of the war, got out, never knew what happened to the rest of her family. Then came the Internet, and it turns out the brother's still there, with the other sister, in the town where they grew up, living in the family's old tailor shop on rue des Brebis."

Our eggs arrived. We bent ourselves out of the waitress's way. "More Coke?" she asked. I shook my head, and she tucked our bill daintily under the jam. "You-all have a good day."

I leaned over my steaming plate. "And this guy's willing to talk to you?"

He nodded. "We've been corresponding." Confusion must have crossed my face, for Lucius smiled coyly. "Even former collaborationists can sign up for Yahoo accounts."

"You're emailing with a Nazi?"

"*Collaborationist.* In a complicated time." He unfurled his silverware from the napkin.

"Indeed."

"Will you come?" he asked. "To France? Join me? When your class is done?"

My composure melted. Something flipped in my diaphragm, fizzed, then flipped again.

"It's stopgap." Lucius inventoried his own emotions as he spoke. "But it's something."

I nodded helplessly, tears welling. It felt like a proposal, and all I knew was *yes.* For a few seconds the future seemed okay. Then I remembered what I had to go home to, and groaned.

"What?" Lucius looked at me with alarm.

"I dread my own house, going back to Michael *and* his mother." I took a bite.

"How long will she be there?"

"Unclear," I said, chewing. I swallowed. "I keep wondering: What if she weren't there? Would *I* move to the basement? Ginny's room? Until what? Am I leaving him?"

Lucius was slow to reply. "I don't know how to answer that question, Phil. Are you leaving your husband? I don't think it's my question to answer." He looked at his plate.

"I know," I said. Those two words now seemed to imply their opposite, a silent "don't" stuck between them. What did I want, anyway? For my lover of less than a month to say *Yes, leave your husband, marry me, become my fourth wife*? When you fall in love, do you promptly move out of your home and leave your husband of twenty-six years? I had no prior experience.

"How long are Ginny and Silas gone for?" Lucius asked. "Could you go to Eula's?"

I honestly hadn't thought of it. "I'll call Eula on my way home and ask," I said, but Lucius looked puzzled and I didn't know why. "What?" Now I was confused.

"The Amish get phones nowadays?" He waggled a piece of toast in the air.

"It's Silas's. His cell. While they're away. Eula's not exactly traditional, anyway." For no reason, I got suddenly shy, but Lucius reached to lift my face, my chin in his hand. I felt fifteen and melty. We were still like that when the waitress came to clear our plates, and we were a maudlin sight that evening in the parking lot: two old fogies, faces pressed together in the shopping-strip dusk, in tears. When we let go and Lucius opened his car, I saw the books—his books that I'd asked him for—on the passenger seat. "For me?" I reached in.

"This is really how you want to think of me while I'm away?" Lucius grimaced. "The guy obsessed with French Nazis?"

"Collaborationists," I corrected. "It was a complicated time." From the seat I collected a stack of his books. There's actual heft to the evidence of this man's life, his work here in this world. I make no apology for my admiration, nor for my envy. It must be very satisfying to know you've made something—other than a child, which any dumb fuck can do. *Friends of the Führer: Collaborators in the Vichy Regime. Give Me Your Watch and I'll Tell You the Time: The French Under Nazi Occupation. We Were All Comrades: The Legion of French Volunteers* in the Anti-Bolshevik Crusade. This But Begins the Woe: From Cooperation to Collaboration. The Carrot and the Stick: How Hitler Controlled the Masses. Blood Will Have Blood: The Occupiers and the Occupied, France 1940–1944. A Past That Does Not Pass: Repression in French Memory of the Vichy Era. An oeuvre of titles and subtitles, overarching ideas and pointed explorations. Lucius Bocelli, PhD, is a man who long ago found his calling in the world, and I am moth-drawn to the flame of such purpose.

It was nearly seven-thirty before we were in our separate cars, ready to steer our noses in opposite directions down that black swath of road. I-80, the bulging empire waistline of our thick-waisted nation. When Lucius started his car, I looked up at the rumble, forced a smile to show him I was okay, and waved him off, a gesture to say, *I'll go in a second.* He waved back, nodding sad and slow, and backed out of his parking spot. I let myself bawl as he pulled away, just sat there in my car and sobbed, the stack of his books on my passenger seat, his name printed thousands of times over, but such a desperate and pathetic substitute for him, for his being, his body. When my phone rang, I answered without speaking. He said: "You're not moving." I looked up. His Honda sat at the parking lot exit, blinkers flashing.

"Oh, can't you let a woman sob in peace?!"

"A man born in 1939 can't leave a lady crying under any circumstance."

I laughed through my tears.

"Okay, good. That's a start. You can laugh and drive, but no crying and driving."

"Which is why I'm getting it out now. So would you just get out of here already, please?"

"I love you," he said.

"Oh, stop that!" I wailed. "You'll start me all over. I love *you.* Now get out of here!"

We hung up. He switched off his flashers and pulled onto the I-80 East ramp. I sobbed as I watched him go, digging in my purse for a Kleenex. My *bag*—my enormous satchel—a Coach I'd wanted and Michael bought me years ago, then teased me about forever after because of course I'd asked for the Mary Poppins bag, a kitchen sink lost somewhere at the bottom. The joke was born tired. Maybe it was time to get myself a new damn handbag.

Finally I found a tissue. And, also—in a side pocket I slip things into and then forget about—I found the photograph of the three little girls that Bernadette had tried to burn. It smelled of char, and so would everything I put in that pocket forever after. I sat in my car in the hazy dusk, the strip-mall sodium vapor lights buzzing on as I tried to stop crying. Staring bleary-eyed at the photo—the "Harmon" girls, the three young daughters of "Ida and John" as presented, *Compliments of Hazel,* in the "family album"—I wondered if anything in Bernadette's life *didn't* warrant scare quotes. Such a bizarre woman, the deceits—her accent, for God's sake! I could hear her voice in my head, her own name the way *she* spoke it—*Behr-na-det*—lips spreading, tongue pressing back, the sounds catching as she ground out those hard, phlegmy *r*'s. Her concession to French and deaf ancestry made sense, if it wasn't just one more evasion. French, not German. Or Alsatian, maybe, the French spoken along the Rhine, on either side of the Franco-German border. *Behr-na-det Ahr-maw.* I said it aloud to myself, consonants scraping my throat. *Behr-na-det Ahr-maw,* a name like a cat hacking hairballs. Futile tears for Lucius were still wet on my face, and a fresh wave of rage at Bernadette swept over me, a flood of anger on behalf of those discarded little girls. She disowned them—her sisters, herself—stripped their names and identities, took a match to their images, left them smoldering in a nursing home trash basket.

The one in the middle is so lovely I want to hold her safe, whisper, *Sweet Mignon.* Was that something Lucius said? To me? An endearment—Mignon, short for something, maybe, like Marianne, or Mallorie—or a nickname. Mignon: humble, those hooded eyes beaming steadily ahead, willing herself to lift them, though to look

up is only to confirm what she already knows: that death is there, just
ahead, hanging like a carrot, or a noose. She's six years old at most,
the wisped hair at her temples still downy as a newborn's, and already
death is right there on her small face. She'll be a suicide, Mignon Armond. She'll die young.

She probably won't even be the first. I can imagine brothers, too
—unpictured here, the brothers Armond. Small boys from a tiny
French village just over the German border, swept up as young men
and forced to fight in a German uniform. Or gone willingly—Lucius
says plenty did—to die in borrowed Nazi duds. And if they don't
die in the war, they'll take their own lives once it's over, after liberation, when it's clear what they've done and who they've been. Or
one brother dies fighting, the other shoots himself in the woods with
his Nazi-issue rifle, unable to bear the responsibility for his own acts.
They won't find his body, devoured by animals, his gun pilfered by
another lost and wandering soul.

Or maybe, like Lucius's collaborationist, he's simply assumed
dead, but isn't, and the only person who knows it is his sister—his
twin sister. The middle sister, the beautiful one, far left in the photo,
the one who looks, truly, like Ginny. What's the French form of
Virginia? *Virginie?* Virginie knows that if a bullet entered her twin
brother's brain she'd've felt it, and she's sure: he is not dead. But such
knowledge can drive a person mad, and it does. Oh, Virginie, you'll
step into that madness so trustingly, and it will claim you, lock you
in another world inside your own lovely, mad head. Poor girl. She'd
have been so beautiful, too.

And then there's little Bernadette. You never trusted a thing, did
you? Little Berna, little Dettie, little Bena, little girl . . . How old are
you, there, in your frouffy white gown, lopsided ribbons in your thin
blond curls? Two? Three? Suspicion marked you from the start, your
brow creased in worry even then. The youngest, and the smallest—
small the way a runt is small: piggy, and grabby, and always wronged,
right from the start. Not enough blood down the cord or milk at the

teat, not enough attention, never enough time. You were set against the world before you entered it, Bernadette, set to face it down and show you wouldn't stand for being shafted. I want to pity you, her, this angry girl in her frothy white dress beside her sisters, dead and mad. I try to pity her the life she'll have to lead, but my resentment's an obstacle to sympathy. What an unsympathetic person you became, Bernadette. Maybe hardening yourself was the only way through, steeling yourself against the world the only way to live. Were you brave, Bernadette, in your own way? Maybe all you really ever had going for you was that bullheaded, iron-gutted instinct for survival. You hated this life from the very start, little Bena, and you were the one who'd have to see it out, belligerently alive and wretchedly sane.

I WASN'T ON the road an hour before even *Hello, Dolly!* couldn't keep me awake, and I had to stop at a rest area to nap. When I woke and opened my eyes to a stream of Mennonites flooding from a mini-van like circus clowns, I thought I was dreaming. The line for the la-dies' room was like a *Little House on the Prairie* casting call.

It was one a.m. when I got home to River City. The door to our bedroom was closed, so I spent another night in Ginny's room. My first class of the summer session was scheduled for three that after-noon, and I'd prepared nothing. They were undergrads; we'd play name games.

When I went downstairs at around ten in the morning, Berna-dette wasn't in sight, but Michael was ensconced on the living room sofa, a legal pad on his lap, the phone book splayed open at his side, telephone crooked between his cheek and shoulder. He seemed to be on hold. I lifted a hand in tentative greeting as I passed, and he raised his head stiffly, acknowledging my presence, but nothing more. He looked angry.

As I reheated coffee and made cereal, I overheard a few things and gleaned that Michael was on the phone with someone at a nursing home or care facility, but not East Prairie. He seemed to be inquiring about vacancies. I took my coffee and stood in the doorway to wait for him to finish. He made a note—or just doodled—and looked distantly off, squinting in demonstrable calculation. When he hung up, he sat a minute, flipping through the phone book, as if to show he had important things to do. Finally he looked up and spoke, his tone accusing: "I cannot understand how you could possibly not tell me about the fire."

"What?"

"We've been asked to remove my mother from East Prairie."

"You're kidding," I said.

"Do I look like I'm kidding?"

I don't think I replied; my face was screwed up in a bewilderment that spoke for itself.

"They feel," Michael said, and then spoke as if quoting someone, *"she poses a danger to the other residents* and they'd like for us to *find alternate accommodations* for her. Stat."

I made a sound of disgust. We'd been through this before.

"They're hoping to reopen late next week, and they'd like her gone before then, to *minimize the disruption to the other residents.*"

I wasn't speaking, just trying to process it all, and this clearly annoyed Michael, though there's little I could have done that *wouldn't* have annoyed Michael.

"She's been accused of many things," he began, "but attempted arson's something new. They say if we get her out fast they won't press charges."

"Attempted arson?" I repeated. *"That's* what they said?"

Michael widened his eyes and spread his hands to say, *I only know what they told me.*

"I didn't tell you," I began. "I wanted to, but I thought it would sound petty, like tattling. She tried to burn an old photo in a wastebasket. It wouldn't light. There was no fire. She struck maybe three matches. It made no sense, but I have for a long time attempted to refrain—at your request—" My tone was growing self-righteous and I made an effort to temper it. "I didn't tell you because I thought you'd find it catty. The incident was so insignificant."

Michael was trying to figure out whether to believe me or not. "She was trying to *burn an old photo?*" He didn't understand. "From the album? The family album thing?"

"Maybe?" I shrugged. "The girls in the photo weren't elsewhere in the album . . . Of the same era, maybe, but the actual children—" And then I realized I could show it to him. I grabbed my bag, fished in the side pocket, pulled out the three little girls in their charry frame, and handed it to Michael. My fingers came away sooty, and I wiped them on my jeans. Then, instinctively, lifted my hand to my nose and inhaled the scent of burn.

I'm still not sure how to interpret Michael's reaction to the photograph. Whatever he thought, he said nothing aloud, though he looked at the photo for a long time, his face registering shifting emotions. I don't imagine he could possibly look at the little girl on the right and not think: *That is my mother.* That little girl *is* Bernadette Maakestad, or whatever her name really was—all of us Maakestads may well be going by a name born of someone's imagination. I suppose it's no stranger than Jews' names getting Americanized or de-Jewified at Ellis Island, or hippies denouncing patriarchy and discarding their fathers' names at Woodstock, their own offspring becoming Melissa Starlight or Leif Morningdew. Still, those people can trace back and learn that Topliss was Teplitzky, and Ms. Starlight might've been Ms. Strauss; there's a lineage, a story. I married into a family name that could have been plucked from a phone book for all I know. Of the lives of my own parents and grandparents I have an attic full of documentation—photographs, marriage licenses, death certificates, other crap I should sort through: mortgage loan approvals from 1942, illegible mimeographed report cards, staple-bound synagogue community cookbooks. I have the artifacts of their lives. And I have the stories they told, *more* evocative than the ephemera. Michael has nothing. Nothing. He has this name, Maakestad, and he has Bernadette's perfunctory, begrudging, highly suspect origin story. That's it, in toto. Until this photograph. But he didn't have time for ancestral speculation, not with so much else to deal with. Maybe he told himself he'd think about it someday, once his mother was gone. Whatever Michael might have liked to know about those little girls, he just couldn't go there, not then. He handed back the photo and resumed his present concerns, though he seemed not so angry as before. "Well," he said, "Operation Find Mother a Home begins yet again." Then his tone turned dark. "There's a seventy-six-person waiting list at Riverview." The only river in view at Riverview Senior Residence is a sewage drain behind the meat-packing plant.

I said, "Everyone in River City got old all of a sudden?" There was no waiting list at Riverview; word about Bernadette, Nursing Home Terror, must have simply gotten out.

Michael pursed his lips, shrugged, and turned back to the Yellow Pages.

"Does she know?" I asked.

He shook his head, a little ashamed at his reluctance to break the news. "I'll tell her."

"When will you go to—"

Michael cut in: "They don't even want her on the premises."

That was pretty absurd, as if Bernadette were actually dangerous. I wanted to offer something—help, something. "I teach this afternoon, but I can go with you tomorrow."

Michael was ready to decline whatever I had to give. "You don't have to."

"Please, Michael, it'll go a lot faster with two. It's fine. I'm glad to help."

Michael glumly nodded his acquiescence.

I excused myself on the pretense of class prep and went upstairs to search online for cheap flights to Paris. I listened in on Michael and Bernadette's conversation. Within minutes they were both angry, with raised voices that neither seemed to care if I heard. Bernadette was very displeased by the news of her East Prairie expulsion and was, despite Michael's defense of me, convinced that I'd ratted her out for the photo-burning, that I'd exaggerated, "like you know she does," Bernadette said, "makes a mountain of a molehill." Her eviction was, she felt, my fault. She also blamed the orderly — "that African," she called him, which wouldn't have been a racial epithet, as the man *was* African, except that Bernadette called all blacks Africans, with the implication that she'd put up no protest if someone shipped them back to that far-off continent from whence she figured they'd all come. God, I loathed her.

Bernadette said something, and Michael growled back, short-tempered and frazzled, "Do you really think Phillipa wants you here any more than you want to be here?"

Bernadette shot back: "Here?"

"You've just about exhausted your options in this town, Ma."

"Well, stick me in that Riverview cesspool and be done with it."

"You'd be lucky to get a room at Riverview." He informed her of the wait list. "Unless you want Motel 6 or have a better idea, you're staying here for now whether you like it or not."

There was some further protest, but she came to accept the situation as she understood it: beyond her control, forced on her by Michael, acting as my agent. What surprised me was how little she argued about our clearing out her East Prairie room without her. Then I realized she'd already disposed of anything we might have discovered. And then the thought of spending a day with Michael — déjà vu all over again, packing his mother's things — without any prospect of revelation or insight grew very depressing, more depressing even than the class I had to teach that day. Lucius was leaving for France so soon, and I wanted to ditch everything — job, family, all of it — and join him. I was a fifty-year-old delinquent teenager.

In the end I did not go with Michael to East Prairie; I stayed home with Bernadette. When Michael returned, I helped him load everything into the garage, and only then did we learn, via much huff-ing, that Bernadette had anticipated having her things with her in the basement, and she grew miffed when Michael refused to accommodate her. He remained hopeful about finding her another place to live.

Though I could not hear the argument that ensued, just their raised voices emanating from the basement, I imagine it was during this heated exchange that Michael let slip in anger that he and I were having problems—or told her outright that I'd had an affair. Whatever he said, Bernadette's attitude and demeanor toward me changed dramatically. For twenty-seven years she had treated me with distrust, disdain, and forced, false solicitude, but the evening that Michael moved her things out of East Prairie and into our garage, I went from being an annoyance in Bernadette's life to being a pest so loathsome she'd have exterminated me without a second thought. The next morning when I entered the kitchen, where she sat in her housecoat slurping weak coffee and crunching dry toast, I greeted her as usual and she looked at me, set down her toast as if suddenly nauseated, pushed back her chair, and stalked from the room.

It soon became clear that Bernadette intended to shun me such as to make Amish ostracism look downright benevolent, and I lasted another day and a half before I called Eula and begged to come stay with her and Oren in Prairie. I told her the situation with Bernadette had become untenable and, prudent or not, I also told her that Michael and I were having problems and needed time apart—never mind that we'd just had months apart. I did not tell Eula about Lucius, and whatever she may have thought or suspected, she asked nothing, simply welcomed me into her home. She was eighteen years old and the most gracious, mature, generous human being I think I have ever encountered.

Michael neither registered surprise nor argued when I told him I was going to stay with Eula to help with the baby while Ginny and Silas were away. It was an easy bluff, a ready excuse if anyone asked. Once I was out of sight, Bernadette could pretend I'd never existed.

Ginny would still be Michael's daughter, Bernadette's granddaughter, but with a hazy origin story—left on the doorstep, perhaps, the mother run off, never to be known, never to be named.

The following day, Michael took his mother to the beauty parlor, then out to lunch and a movie matinee, to give me time to extricate myself from the house. I will admit that I also took the opportunity, while doing laundry, to glance around the basement. Deep in a bag, back on a shelf, I found Bernadette's ALBUM. In a different bag, in an unmarked envelope, I unearthed another piece of the bizarro puzzle: two photographs that, unlike the album, I believe to be genuine artifacts of the woman's life. And, God help me, before I left for Prairie I took all these things upstairs and scanned them. No proof ties them to Bernadette, and I doubt I'll ever learn who the subject is, but I contend that these are two photographs of the same man, young and old.

You may question the eyebrow, the nose, but I say: look at the hairline, jawline, ears. He may have fought in a war, been injured, scarred, changed. Who knows what life he led? I do not think he is

Michael's father—he bears far too great a resemblance to Bernadette. But the Armond girl he most resembles is the beautiful one. He looks like Virginie; Ginny is who he looks like.

In addition to the photos, I have the paper they were wrapped in, a piece of old ledger bearing a list of names. Since its discovery, seventeen other renditions of the same list have surfaced among Bernadette's things, but this is the first one I found, and the one I think of as the original.

I did the research: most of these names match the names of World War II U.S. military personnel. Aside from the parenthetical nicknames, their format follows a dog tag's: first, middle initial, last. Some of these men are still alive, some not. I haven't attempted contact. What would I say? *Hi, I found your name in the possession of a woman I knew as Bernadette Maakestad, though her maiden name may have been something like Armond, but that's hard to be sure of as well. I could tell you what I know of her, but I doubt any of it is true.* It all sounded like an email scam: *Goodmorning my dear Sir, Utmost importantly I write you to of News you have Son 60 years old with Nazi, lady. Please Kindness as to wire $10,000 USD OK! And so no body learn of past insurrection private matter of family. Beesseched you by Phillippa Maakestad, MFA, your daughter inLaw marries to half Nazi son yours.*

3

W HAT

[A] good quiltmaker's mind was free of all preconceived notions of how a quilt should be created, even from an influence as close as one's mother.

—Alvia Wardlaw, "The Quilts of Gee's Bend"

THE YODER FARMHOUSE sits atop a lolling hill on Iowa Route 1, three miles east of Prairie. Approaching by car, the way the road's configured, you can't see the house until you're past it. The driveway's blind, and now there's a shiny DOT sign at the site of the accident that says as much. No morbid roadside shrine to Orah and Obadiah Yoder—though there's no one in the county who doesn't know what happened here—just HIDDEN DRIVEWAY, and also the yellow sign with the black buggy on it. They're reminders: this is where.

Surrounded by miles of cultivated corn and soy, the Yoder parcel is just three acres, the house, the barn, a few outbuildings. Commercial ag bought up the land but, as is common around here, had no interest in the house. Orah and Obadiah had worked out a rent-to-own arrangement when they first got to Prairie from their previous community, wherever that was, and the fifteen-year agreement was paid in full shortly before they died, so the house and its acreage be-

long to Eula and Silas outright. The Yoders always kept a huge garden
—cooked, canned, and ate what they grew. The remaining land some
might call overgrown, but I prefer "prairie restoration"—a graceful
return to native grasses and wildflowers, a tiny pocket amid the reg-
imented rows of genetically superior corn brought to us by Monsanto, the Mengele Institution of American Agriculture.

Like many an Iowa farmhouse, the Yoders' has rooms aplenty,
added on year by year as some Amish family grew, and outgrew, their
living quarters. I chose a small room upstairs with a couple of windows for some modicum of cross-ventilation and began a new life.
An illusion, I know; I'd just grabbed a few books and teaching things,
some summer clothes from our River City house where a quarter-
century of life's accumulation remained, but it was nice to flee to a
place where very little is required, and where listening to crickets is a
fine way to pass an evening.

In Prairie, Eula was mistress. Twice a week I went into River City
to teach my joke of a class—the students and I were just clocking the
time—otherwise, I helped Eula in the garden and the kitchen, with
the baking and with Oren, and did what I could to free up her hands
for stitchery. Inept with a needle and thread myself, I served as Eula's ironer—and have the burn scars to prove it—to earn my keep.
Also, I chauffeured. We took Oren's car seat from Silas's Festiva and
installed it in the Volvo, and I drove Eula and her cookies and quilts
to Bluntmore's Auction on Wednesday evenings and to the Friday-
afternoon River City Farmers' Market—the same market where for
years I'd bought her mother's heirloom tomatoes and rhubarb pies,
tasting Orah's recipes as they matured, watching her children grow,
and chatting with her in a way I now know was not looked upon fa-
vorably by her Amish neighbors.

It was at Bluntmore's, one Wednesday evening back in the early
spring of 2002, that Orah mentioned Eula's interest in taking a job
outside Prairie. I'd gone to the auction feeling those late-March, early-
April muddy Iowa doldrums and wanting to get out of the house.

Orah and Obadiah sat behind a table laden with plastic-wrapped pies and potato breads and baggies of snickerdoodles and molasses crisps. Behind them hung a quilt of Orah's; others lay appealingly folded on an upturned crate beside the table. I hadn't seen the Yoders since market season ended the previous fall with the last of the gourds and pumpkins, and when I'd paid for my apple butter, a loaf of dill bread, and the crosshatched peanut butter cookies Michael loves, I stood awhile by the table catching up with Orah. Most Amish women do not pass time with a customer—a *Modern*—trading updates on gardens and children, but Orah was no ordinary Amish, traditional as she may have appeared beside her children. Silas and Eula are in many ways like the first-generation American-born students I teach, acculturated in manners entirely their own.

Eula'd just turned sixteen in 2002 and was ready for her *rumspringa*. Though the transplanted Yoders had their issues with the Prairie Amish community, they'd been deeply saddened by Silas's defection a few years before. In his own Amish way, I think Silas brought his parents as much anguish as Ginny brought us. The Yoders had decided that when Eula came of age they'd handle things differently, so when they asked her what steps she'd like to take toward worldly knowledge, and she said, "I'd like to work a job. Not in Prairie. In River City," it seemed a reasonable request as far as *rumspringas* went, and Orah took up the task of securing employment for her daughter. She might put her domestic skills to use, Orah suggested: cleaning, baking, sewing, some carpentry even. I had always liked this family a great deal, and I welcomed the chance to know them better—in a way I hope wasn't merely fetishistic or opportunistic. Also, I'd lost my weekly household helper back in December when she'd graduated from the university, and had an eye out for someone to replace her, so it all felt fortuitous.

Ginny had spent the better part of that year at a Quad Cities care facility undergoing the electroshock therapy that ultimately enabled her to live her life instead of skittering toward its end like a guttered pinball. Eula began her *rumspringa* job with us around the time Ginny came home. On Saturday mornings, Silas would leave his River City rental apartment, drive to Prairie to fetch Eula from their parents' house, bring her to us, and then collect her again in the early evening to get her back to the farm. Since he'd left the Church, declining the adult baptism, Silas lived on his own in a shabby studio in town and worked construction with a bunch of other lapsed Amish and Mennonites. At first, the chauffeuring seemed a lot to ask of him — all that county highway travel just so his sister could iron my placemats — but it soon became clear that Silas would've gladly driven Eula, daily, to Timbuktu and back if it meant a chance to see Ginny Maakestad.

Of course they'd met before, had seen each other almost weekly at markets and auctions since they were kids. Once, when Ginny was a teenager, doing drugs, and disappearing for days at a time, she went to the farmers' market hoping to find me and ask for money, but I had a rehearsal and didn't make it to the market that afternoon, and it was Orah who spotted Ginny huddled behind the public restrooms. To be driven home in a buggy no doubt had an effect on my daughter, but it was Silas, age twelve or thirteen at the time, who I imagine was most affected by the experience. Scary as Ginny may have looked — skinny, doped up, wild-eyed — she was still lovely, even in her seediness, and maybe all the more intriguing to a boy like Silas.

Seven, eight years later, when Silas was tasked with ferrying his sister to and from her job with us, yes, he did have ulterior motives. But so, too, did Eula. A job for its own sake wasn't all she wanted; Eula had her eyes on a sewing machine, not a treadle one like Orah's, but a motorized Singer. Ultimately, she'd have it converted to run off an air compressor or a car battery, as the Amish do, but when Silas took her to the Mennonite Consignment Store so she could spend her first month's pay on the deposit and sign a payment plan, it was to our house in River City that they brought the machine. We set it up in the little sunroom downstairs, and thereafter Eula spent part of her Saturday working for me and part of it on her quilts.

By then Silas was no longer just dropping Eula off in the morning and picking her up at the end of the day. Each week he returned earlier and earlier to fetch her, until he arrived not at five p.m. but noontime, and he'd spend the afternoon helping us with projects around the house while Eula quilted. Eventually he quit the pretense of dropping her off, and just parked the car and spent the day replacing rotted porch boards, weeding the garden, or driving Ginny in his little orange Festiva for lunch at the Slidy Diner. It's an amazing thing watching two people discover that it's to each other that their individual lives finally make sense. And if one of those people should happen to be the daughter you thought might not live to see fifteen, let alone twenty-five, your feelings of salvation and gratitude and sheer beatific glory might be impossible to overstate.

Two years later the Yoders were dead, Eula had a baby, Ginny and Silas were married, and I'd left Michael and gone to live in Prairie, among, but not of, the Amish. When I was not chauffeuring Eula, watching Oren, or helping with house and garden and baking work or with Eula's quilts, I passed the time on the front porch or in my hot little second-floor room, not prepping for my fall show but reading the collected works of Lucius Bocelli. I began with *A Past That Does Not Pass: Repression in French Memory of the Vichy Era,* his discussion of the inadequacy of a standard historical approach to address "the history of memory." His scholarly interests centered on the conflicts between collective, "dominant" memories and individual, dissenting ones—between the history a society might prefer to perpetuate of itself, and any contradictory, less persuasive, less flattering histories. "Vichy syndrome" is how the experts describe the apparently widespread failure of French memory to account for Nazi collaboration.

What I understood of Lucius's work worried me for reasons that had nothing to do with Lucius or Vichy. I was worried about memory: although Michael and I hadn't ruined Silas and Ginny's wedding in real time, we *would* ruin it retroactively, once the truth was out. For what *is* an event but the stories we tell of it? History is determined by dominant, persuasive memories, their telling and retelling. No one at the wedding knew what was going on with me and Michael at that time; the popular version of the wedding story might be rosy—until they found out we'd split up soon thereafter, that I'd been having an affair. Then the event could no longer exist in any light except that cast upon it by concurrent happenings, retrospectively revealed. However the wedding may have seemed as it happened, once Ginny knew the truth, she would never be able to believe the story as she'd experienced it, only the one shadowed by my sins.

She and Silas sent Eula one postcard from France, a vintage reproduction: *Grande Semaine Maritime Française du 9 au 16 Juillet 1906*. The illustration is of the port at Le Havre as seen from a hill, ships and sailboats dotting the distant water. In the foreground, a woman in a white plumed hat and boa holds a pair of binoculars in one gloved hand, while the other hand waves a white hankie in *adieu* to a departing steamer. On the flip side it says: *Bonjour!* ♥, *G&S*. If they sent anything to the house in River City, I never heard about it.

They were due home at the end of the first week of June. Michael was to fetch them from the airport—Cedar Rapids, not Chicago, barring tornadic interference. He and I spoke on the phone the day before, and I asked how he thought we should tell them about us.

"How? We just tell them." He'd grown belligerent alone in that house with his mother.

"Yes, but, together? Separately? You'll see them first—or I could come to the airport—"

"You want to have them get off the plane—"

"Michael—"

"—jet-lagged and exhausted, and truck them off to a booth at Perkins so they can learn our marriage is over, over a nice slice of pie and a cup of decaf?"

I laughed. I couldn't help it.

"Don't," he warned, but I didn't know what exactly he was cautioning against.

"You sound like me," I said.

"Wonder of wonders."

"Could you *not* say anything right off? I'll be at Eula's. When you drop them we can—"

"Great," Michael said. "Welcome home! Bam!"

"It's not ideal," I began, "but—"

"Tell them you couldn't last another day in a house with my mother—it's not a lie."

"It's hardly the whole truth."

Michael was silent then. Resigned, he said, "Do what you like, Phil. I'll bring them to Eula's. You want to greet us with iced tea and misery, great." He paused. "Great," he said again.

The day they returned was unseasonably hot. Ginny'd wanted to be back for Jazz Fest in River City that coming weekend—live music downtown, vendors, crafts, sidewalk sales, tastings, reunions. I pictured her, with Silas, running into former teachers and classmates. They'd all known her as such a basket case, but now, when they asked how she'd been, Ginny could say, "I'm well. This is my husband, Silas. We just got back from our honeymoon." It's not actually something Ginny would say; it's what I would say if I were Ginny, and I must remind myself once again—no matter how much better off I think Ginny would be if she'd just do what *I* would do if I were her—that she is *not* me. She's really nothing like me. You might think twenty-five years would be long enough for this to sink in, but I could probably tattoo it on my arm—GINNY IS NOT YOU—stare right at it, and still not understand why she won't just do as I do.

Michael picked them up at the airport; Eula, Oren, and I awaited their arrival on the front porch. That time of day, the porch was cooler than the house, but still we were sweltering. Eula rocked in the porch swing, working a bit of embroidery onto the quilt top she was doing for Ginny and Silas—all white, shades of white, different textures and prints, bits left over from Ginny's wedding dress, Orah's aprons, old sheets, flour and feed sacks, all embroidered white on white. She inherited her mother's gift, her technical skill and craft, but it wasn't until Eula bought that sewing machine and started quilting Saturday afternoons at our house that she began to improvise and experiment, to move beyond the traditional Amish geometrics. The quilts she and Orah stitched by hand are beautiful, of course, but compared to what Eula does now, they're so staid. What Orah might have thought of Eula's quilts I can't say, for Eula's quilts, as they are now, would not exist if Orah were still alive.

That hot June day, as we waited on the porch for the honeymooners to return, I was reading—or pretending to—in a chair so old its wooden seat was cushiony with rot. I kept looking over at the baby, penned by couch cushions into a makeshift playpen, as he ran his hands over the quilt beneath him, fingertips feeling the changes in texture, patch to patch. Eula made Oren's quilt from scraps of things that belonged to members of the family, those he knew and those he'd never know. There were bits of Obadiah's coveralls, strips of Orah's old dresses, wedges of a shirt I remembered on Silas years ago. I don't know if Eula sneaked in something of Oren's father's, if she *had* anything. Occasionally I'd spot a bit of material I hadn't noticed before, point, and ask, "Eula, what's that, there? The tan, with the flecks?" Inevitably, it was something from Orah's scrap bag or a bit of an old tablecloth. What did I imagine? That one day I'd ask and Eula would say, *Oh, that? That's the shirt Oren's father wore the night Oren was conceived. I tore it off him in a fit of passion and then hid it away in my sewing box.*

I once saw a poster in the Gas Stop convenience store advertising a concert at the Prairie Park pavilion: a Christian folk duo from Montana—probably evangelicals out to save the Amish—two handsome young men gazing out from a Xeroxed wheat field. The timing's off—Eula got pregnant just a month or two after her parents were killed—still, I have pictured her and the hippie songsters staging their own tiny Woodstock in Prairie, Iowa. The minstrels are invited to park their van on the Yoders' land, and Eula slips out of her room and into the night to join them. In my imagination, her parents are asleep upstairs—an impossibility, for they were dead before Oren was conceived, but it's my imagination, goddammit, so there, if nowhere else, Eula *can* slip out and leave Orah and Obadiah asleep in the house while she joins the boys at their campfire. When the three climb into the back of the van, it's at Eula's bold suggestion: "It's getting chilly, isn't it, outside here? May we go in? Into your van?" She's like something sent from God, this one—that's their capital G, not mine—this lovely, ample, deep-voiced girl, a mane of thick, dark, freshly brushed hair curtaining her beautiful face. Awed, these two earnest, Christ-loving boys and Eula sit cross-legged beneath billowing Indian tapestries staple-gunned to the van's ceiling. They smoke a joint—I don't even know if it's Eula's first. The scene isn't tawdry but lovely, all three trying to suppress giddy grins. Eula initiates, reaches out toward the face of one young man and the hand of the other at the same time. She draws the face to hers, kissing this one's mouth while placing the other's hand beneath her heavy breast. In this way I do feel partly responsible: the only place I can imagine her having access to any of these ideas is in some book or video from our shelves in River City. Perhaps it's perversely appropriate: I'm "Grandma Phil," as close to a grandparent as Oren will ever come, with Orah and Obadiah gone and his father's identity a mystery.

Michael's car pulled up the farm drive, and Michael got out. He saw us on the porch, fixed his eyes on mine, and shook his head emphatically. It took me a second: he was indicating that we were absolutely *not* going to tell Ginny and Silas anything just then. The car's rear doors opened simultaneously and I went slack, suddenly inhumanly exhausted. I'd learned this with Ginny: if you go limp, like an abused animal, you can avoid the most brutal injury. I felt my *self* contract, hiding under layers of meat and organ, muscle, flesh. I shrank to a speck, peering out from inside, my eyes like periscopes into the world. Both rear doors opened, but only Silas emerged, and the blood rushed in my veins again. My first thought: she twisted an ankle at the Eiffel Tower. She's broken a leg! Sprained a knee! Michael's alarm was unnecessary—she was *fine*.

Silas rounded the car and squatted by Ginny's open door; I couldn't see their exchange. Michael went to pop the trunk and retrieve their bags. Then Ginny emerged, levering herself from the back seat like she weighed three hundred pounds. Another wave of relief. *She's carsick!* I thought. *Or airsick! Heatsick! But everything's fine.* And then I saw her face, the ferocious set of her jaw, the anger pulsing in her eyes, and I knew nothing was fine at all.

Michael and Silas bore backpacks and shopping bags toward the house. Ginny slung her duffel over her small frame and grabbed up a poster tube—it made her look like some military flag-bearer. A great sigh blew from her lower lip and fluttered the bangs against her forehead as she humped her burdens through the heat. Michael came up the steps. Silas waited for Ginny to catch up, then followed her onto the porch.

"The travelers return!" Michael's bravado was so false, Eula physically shrank from it.

I stood as Ginny leaned in—contorted by her oversized bag, holding the poster tube out of the way—to kiss me. Her lips brushed my cheek, and I had a flash of vain, desperate hope that perhaps her air was just a laconic European affectation she'd picked up, a French suavity. I half expected that, like the French, she'd bend and kiss my other cheek, but she didn't, just hoisted the bag higher on her shoulder and said, "Hi, Ma. We're beat. I've got to go to bed." She gave Eula and Oren the same wafty, absent kisses and went in through the screen door.

Silas stepped forward to greet me, but his burdens precluded an embrace. "Hello, Phillipa." He's still awkward calling me by my first name. "It was a long trip," he said.

"The flight?" I was suddenly afraid the whole honeymoon had been one long trial.

"Yes." He looked confused. "The airplane. People, all so close together."

"Was Ginny claustrophobic?" But Ginny likes confinement; it's infinity that's trouble.

"No, no, just a lot of people," Silas assured, "in one place, for a long time. All the viewpoints and opinions . . . No, we had a wonderful time. I think Ginny wished we could stay."

I forced a laugh. "Look, at this point, if Bush gets reelected, or slithers his way into office again somehow, I might seriously consider a move to France myself."

Silas looked like he'd bitten something foul. His eyes were glassy. He was exhausted.

I mustered some motherliness and said, "Silas, sweetheart, get yourself to bed before you keel over. Tell us later. You go now and lie down."

Silas nodded wearily, not a spark of resistance, and went into the house.

Michael set down the bags he was carrying and looked like he might slide down the wall beside them onto the porch floor. But Eula, with Oren in one arm, reached for a folding chair with the other and deftly shook it open beneath Michael. He sank into it obediently.

"What's going on?" I sat too, eyes shut against whatever Michael was about to say.

"Dada!" Oren squawked, intent and purposeful. "Dadadadadadadada!" Loaded syllables for this child, perhaps already figuring out how to taunt his mother. Someday he would want to know who his dada was. I had no idea what Eula planned to say. For now, she only hushed him.

In his folding chair, Michael sighed heavily. "I think she's off her meds."

My throat filled. I wanted to scream—at Michael. In that moment, it felt like his fault. "Off her meds?" My voice was a croak, a whisper.

"She says she's been tapering down, but I don't know exactly what that means."

I was caught in shock, seemingly only able to repeat what was said. "Tapering down?"

"Tapering down. Lowering her dosage gradually. Or so she says."

"I know what it means. You think she's lying?"

Michael looked at me piteously. "Wouldn't be the first time."

It felt like a time warp, like the good years had disappeared and we were back in the horror, doomed to it forever. "Why would she be tapering down?" It sounded like something repugnant. Why would she be *eating rat poison? plucking out her own fingernails?*

Michael sighed again, so tragically I wanted to hit him. "To try to get pregnant," he said.

"Oh, Jesus." It was my fault: I'd thought about it, entertained a daydream of Ginny well and stable enough to have a baby. A little Orah or Obadiah. Or Sky, I'd thought, for a girl or a boy — in *Guys and Dolls,* Sky Masterson's real name is Obediah — but I might be the only one who'd appreciate that. Like an idiot, I'd been naming imaginary grandchildren, not thinking about Ginny's meds. I'd worried about her ability to conceive, given God-knows-what she did to herself in those years of starving and doping and attempting to die. Stupid. I'd been stupid and starry-eyed. Of course she'd have to come off her meds to host a fetus. I didn't even know what she was on anymore. I liked imagining that the shock therapy had blasted all the trouble out. I knew she still took drugs, but I realized I had cast these as some kind of buffer medications, boosters, training wheels just in case she got wobbly, but no longer vital to her sanity or survival. I'd been telling myself a lie; Ginny had never been riding that big-girl two-wheeler all by herself.

Michael was saying something in the worn-out voice I knew so well, the voice of defeat he'd been using since my return from Ohio.

"I just spent forty-five minutes listening to her rant about a woman on the plane wearing a *W* cap." Michael ran a hand through his hair. Still thick, it would serve him well with the willowy, ambitious grad students who would love him.

As far as Michael'd been able to understand, on the plane Ginny and Silas were seated in a row with a conservative, Republican, *nuc-u-lar* Midwestern family: two irritating, video-game-playing kids, a father with a face as white and blank as his polo shirt, and a taut-skinned, aerobicized mother who, for all fifteen hours (including the plane change in Chicago), never once removed her *W*-emblazoned baseball cap. It stayed on even as she slept, whistling reedy snores through an obviously surgically altered nose. Ginny didn't sleep the entire flight. She sat in that infernal row, with those infernal people, and seethed, preparing in her mind a righteous speech she lusted to deliver straight into the woman's pinched, ignorant face. *Fifteen hours.* When they finally disembarked in Cedar Rapids, Ginny waited at the bottom of the boarding ramp for the family to emerge, Silas hovering behind her like he was the muscle of the operation. Trembling with rage, buzzing with adrenaline, Ginny caught the woman by surprise, stepped right in front of her—the bewildered children and clueless husband bumping to a stop behind her like serfs—and Ginny said she just wanted to thank the woman for wearing that hat and reminding everyone of the astonishing ignorance in this country, and spurring Ginny to work that much harder to make sure that the self-serving, war-mongering, lying, draft-evading, overgrown frat-boy son-of-the-rich didn't steal himself four more years to grind down and snuff out anything that had ever redeemed this godforsaken country. Then she took Silas's arm and stalked away, leaving the family there to try to figure out what in hell had just happened.

Ginny and Silas waited in the car while Michael retrieved their baggage, Ginny sobbing from the endorphin release, the frenetic energy. On the drive to Prairie, relating it all to Michael, Ginny'd said you couldn't change the minds of people who didn't use their minds, just followed blindly their idiot prophet—and all she could hope was that something might register with the kids, something they couldn't understand now, but might rise, years later, if they ever stopped playing video games and became sentient humans. Something might tug at them, some nagging idea that their parents' way might not be the only way, and maybe something wasn't right with the pre-paved path before them. When that crazy woman at the airport long ago said those damning things to their mother . . . what had that all been about, anyway?

When Michael seemed finished, I drew a breath. "What did you *say?*"

He shook his head, minutely, like he was trying to remember something from the far-distant past. "I don't think I said anything." His voice quavered. "I kept checking her in the rearview, to see what's going on in her head. I don't think I *said* anything. Silas either. By the time we were off 380, she just stared out the window. This is angrier than I've seen her in years, Phil." And then Michael was looking to me for help. "Not since 2000—" He broke off there so as not to cry, and maybe Eula sensed that, for she stood abruptly, joggled Oren to her shoulder, and looked out over the fields, whether in real or improvised contemplation I don't know. And Michael and I sat there staring at each other with that dumb helplessness we knew so miserably well.

When Ginny descended that evening, I'd already poured myself a glass of wine and was out on the porch, where Eula was spooning mashed carrots into Oren's gummy mouth. Ginny pushed through the screen door wearing the top of a scissored-off full slip and a pair of boxer shorts so enormous and rolled over so many times at the waist they looked like a toddler's bathing suit with a built-in flotation device. She'd knotted her hair up off her neck, but it was sweaty at her face. Still bleary with sleep, her cheek pillow-dented, eyelids swollen, she went straight for the porch swing, curled her body into a cannonball—arms tight around her legs, chin propped on her knees

—and wrapped her skinny toes over the edge of the seat. My daughter, the roosting canary. She said, "I'm sorry," and Eula and I were both poised to protest any need for apology, but didn't get the words out before Ginny asked, "Where's Daddy?"

"He went home," I said.

"Oh." Disappointed, she looked off toward the fields. When she turned back she said, "Daddy went home, but you're still here. What's going on, Ma? I saw your stuff upstairs. This isn't just about Grandma Ma being at the house, is it? Are you and Daddy separating?"

It seems moronic to say I was caught off guard, but I'd been so ready to question *her*, I'd all but forgotten the need to explain myself.

"Mom." Her eyes were clearer now, focusing. "Tell me."

Michael always said I'd make the worst spy. Torture wasn't an issue; if someone asked a question, I was powerless to refrain from answering. I said, "We're spending some time apart."

Ginny narrowed her eyes. She did not have to say, *You just spent six months apart.*

"Some more time apart," I added.

She shook her head. "He looks too wounded to be having an affair."

How in hell, I wanted to ask, *are you in a place to assess your father's emotional status?*

"Did you meet someone in Ohio?" Ginny asked point-blank. Down the porch, Eula spooned orange mush into Oren's mouth as if it might be the only thing to save us.

"Ginny . . ." My face contracted; my eyes went pleading like a dog's. "Gin, are *you okay?*"

"I'm fine. What happened in Ohio?" And suddenly, perched on the Yoders' porch swing before me was a Ginny from the past, a Ginny who would not be distracted from her compulsion, whose brain couldn't leave a question alone until it had been answered satisfactorily. Or until her mind knotted in on itself and nothing would help but another round of shock. I stared. Fear of telling her about Lucius was replaced with fear for Ginny's sanity, although the young woman before me looked sharp, poised, and way too savvy to be lied to.

I spoke like an automaton: "I got involved with someone. We didn't mean for it to happen—we tried not to—but I love him—" A ragged gasp from my throat alarmed even me.

Ginny perched, chin on knee. Diplomatically, she said, "Okay, Ma." That was it.

I wiped my eyes. I needed to blow my nose, but took a sip from my sweating glass instead, and choked as cold wine hit my throat. I coughed until it was ridiculous, then got up for some water. I blew my nose. When I came back, I sat beside Ginny on the swing.

"He's very sad," she told me.

"Daddy? I know, Ginny. So am I." Maybe my tone was colder than necessary, but I didn't need her to tell me Michael was sad.

"I don't think you're quite as sad as he is." She gave me that piteous look of hers that says how pathetic it is that I cannot grasp the tiny fact that the world doesn't revolve around me.

"Well," I shot back, "good to know he's winning in morals, righteousness, *and* sadness."

Levelly, she said, "I can't live like this." She stood, went inside, and pounded upstairs.

Eula was trying to wipe Oren clean, but succeeded only in smearing the carrot around. "Phillipa?"

I shook my head, pursing my lips to keep from crying again. "I'm sorry," I said, and though Eula shook her head to say I needn't apologize, it only felt like further admonishment.

I GOT A room that night at Prairie's only hotel. The Gas Stop Inn stands on a treeless, grassless lot at the intersection of Highway 1 and Main, with a view of Prairie's only four-way stop. The adjacent gas station is the original Gas Stop from whence the other corner establishments derive their names. The Gas Stop gas station's convenience store is also Prairie's community gathering place: one booth beneath a wall-mounted TV, a bulletin board of ads for FREE KITTENS: ASK AT REGISTER, and AMISH-MADE DOG AND BIRD-HOUSES — I MI., LEFT AT HOFER, 2 MI., ON RIGHT. Almost no one around here's got a telephone, let alone email. Triangled between the Gas Stop Inn and the Gas Stop Gas-Mart sits the Gas Stop Bar and Grill, which is Prairie's only bar, and would be Prairie's only grill if in fact there were a grill on the premises, but the Gas Stop Bar and Deep Fryer doesn't have the same ring. This is the evening and weekend hangout of most every quasi-Mennonite day laborer in the county — boys raised in the tradition, lapsed when they came of age, opting not to farm their father's land but to be roofers and drywallers, masons and plasterers. The lapsing is not such a big deal among the Mennonites as among the Amish, but still, these young men drink like they've got a lot to forget, or prove.

That night at the Gas Stop I ordered fried clams with cottage fries, each with its own mayonnaise dip. I drank a Bass. The instant I'd drained it, another appeared before me.

"Compliments," said the bartender, pointing down the bar, "of the gentleman."

Bearded and grizzly, the "gentleman" wore a workman's jumpsuit over a hooded sweatshirt — way too much clothing for the weather. Even in the Gas Stop's AC, he must have been boiling. His plastic-framed glasses were so thick they looked like safety goggles. I lifted my beer glass in thanks, but he didn't turn my way. The bartender, though, nodded at my left hand. "You might want to show Creamer your wedding ring," he said in a voice that this *Creamer* could surely hear. He seemed to be telling me Creamer was insane, because who in his right mind, the bartender implied, would look twice at a middle-aged woman eating dinner alone at a bar? The barkeep turned to wash his tools. On the back of his T-shirt was one of those little peeing-boy images you see as truck window decals or silhouetted on mud flaps. The boy appeared to be pissing over the bartender's shoulder and down his arm.

Two pints of beer and a bellyful of grease later, I walked across the trash-strewn lot to the Gas Stop Inn. Stenciled above the front desk was the Iowa state motto, OUR LIBERTIES WE PRIZE AND OUR RIGHTS WE WILL MAINTAIN, but something about the font made it look militaristic, threatening, as if what it really meant was: OUR LIBERTIES WE PRIZE AND OUR RIGHTS WE WILL MAINTAIN *with guns.* The lobby fluorescents flickered, and the wall art—John Deere prints and framed watercolor renderings of "Klassic Kountry Kwilt" samplers—quivered with static life. Fucking white Americans, taking any opportunity to tuck a "KKK" in wherever they can. My room featured further examples of the oeuvre, plus a knockoff La-Z-Boy and an overturned ashtray with the international No Smoking symbol emblazoned in red on its bottom. I switched on the air conditioner. What the Gas Stop Inn also had going for it was a nearby cell tower. I sank into the recliner and called Lucius in Ohio.

"It's me," I told his voicemail. "Quite a day. Ginny and Silas are back and she kicked me out. I'm at Prairie's own Gas Stop Inn. I'm a little drunk. I think I just got hit on. Call me?"

I ran a cool bath, waiting for the AC to chill the room, and lay in the tub, in the dark. When the water and my body temperature equalized, I lost my boundaries and became a bathtubful of Phillipa, a Wicked Witch of the West puddle without so much as a pointy black hat to show I'd ever lived. *What a world, what a fucking world.* I pulled the plug and sat while the tub drained, my own contours returning. When the water slurped away, I heard revelers drunkenly pinballing toward the Gas Stop Bar. I'd gotten in and out before their night even started.

The AC so effectively cooled the room that I climbed into bed under the sheet and the red, stretchy, faux-velour blanket—a material that would, I suspect, melt instantaneously in contact with fire, encasing the sleeper in a red plastic shell like those mini Gouda cheeses I used to pack in Ginny's school lunch, before I learned she'd stopped going to school and that she gave her lunch to the guy who hung out by the Tobacco Shack collecting change to buy cigarettes. I dialed voicemail in case Lucius had called and it somehow hadn't registered. *There are no new messages. Main menu . . .* I lay there a minute, longing for the comfort I wanted his voice to bring me. Then I dialed my home phone number.

Michael's hello wasn't morose or petulant or spiteful; it was just Michael saying hello.

"It's me." There were now two men in the world to whom I was just *me.*

"Hi, Phil." That sounded normal too, not spiked with restrained venom or fraught with checked hope. "How's it going there?"

"I'm not there. We fought. I'm at the Gas Stop Inn. She said she couldn't live with me."

"Oh, Phil." The earnest tone of his sympathy made me grateful.

"She wants to get *pregnant?*" It was nearly impossible to imagine Ginny bearing a child.

"I know," Michael said, "but what are the chances? With all she's done to her body . . . Maybe that'll be the saving grace, and she'll give up and go back on the meds."

I wished for it too. I didn't want Ginny near the unknowns of pregnancy; I wanted her medicated and stabilized, happily cocooned with Silas in a straw-bale house built for two.

By the time Lucius called back, I'd fallen asleep and apparently wanted to stay that way, or so he told me the next morning when we actually spoke. I relayed the story of Ginny and the woman in the *W* hat. Lucius said it sounded like something I might well do myself.

"Might well," I said, "yes. But *had not.*" That was, I maintained, an important distinction.

"Okay," he said. "I don't know her. But she sounds an awful lot like her mother."

Well aware that if it had been Michael presenting this argument, I'd've initiated divorce proceedings immediately, I had to remind myself that if I dismissed Lucius when he said things I didn't like to hear, there'd be few people in my life whose opinion I remained willing to consider. Eula I trusted, but she kept her opinions close, and even I could recognize that if the only person's opinion I valued was a fallen-Amish teenage single mother, I might be in trouble.

Lucius and I talked a long time that morning, hanging up only after he promised he'd visit the next weekend, before he left for France, to stay with me at the Gas Stop Inn, the notion of which seemed to charm him. I resolved to go talk calmly with Gin, apologize, and say that there came a certain point when parents and children should no longer live under the same roof. I'd stay at the Gas Stop for the time being—the weekly rate was more than reasonable—and in three weeks my stupid class would be finished and I'd join Lucius in France. In the meantime, I'd look for a rental for the fall. Part of me wanted to stay in Prairie, find a place there. Despite River City's convenience, I dreaded its familiarity. A town like ours is wonderful, the way you can walk everywhere and run into seven friends en route to the co-op, where the coffee guy knows how you take yours, and the cashier wants to hear how your basil plant is doing. The ped mall's full of your students—working the crêpe cart, reading Foucault on a bench, chasing toddlers in the public fountain—and the leafy side streets are lined with your colleagues' homes. Everyone's in Iowa-summer mode, drinking coffee on front porches, picking aphids off cucumber plants, mowing dandelion lawns. It's lovely. Unless you've just moved out of your husband's house, and rumors of your infidelity have probably whipped through the college like a regular Iowa twister, and the prospect of running into anyone makes you want to toss yourself in front of a convenient cam-bus. In that case, it might be nicer to live in Prairie, among the Amish and the Mennonites who either don't know you, or recognize you and politely look away, or ID you as the Yoders' *Modern* mother-in-law and warn their children not to get within sniffing distance of your corrupting influence. If I stayed close by, I might be of help to Eula. And I could keep an eye on my daughter.

I caught Ginny at the Yoders' the next morning before they went to Jazz Fest, and I apologized, and she apologized, and we agreed space was important. I told her about Lucius's upcoming visit so that it wouldn't be a surprise, and she said "Okay" but nothing more. My car loaded with everything I had at Eula's, I drove back to the Gas Stop.

The inn was owned by a couple, Donna and Henk Presidio. Donna had the desk that day. The Presidios weren't natives; they'd moved down from Mason City to make a go of the inn. The monthly Prairie horse auction assured them regular business, now further bolstered by the new, annual Trek Fest in nearby Riverside — "The Future Birthplace of Captain James T. Kirk." The Presidios had two kids, one who drove trucks in Iraq, the other itching to finish high school and enlist. It was my inquiry about staying on at the inn that occasioned the conveyance of all this information.

"We got room for you till Trek Fest," Donna said. "That's the last weekend in June, and we don't got a bed, recliner, or scratch of carpet not spoken for by April. But once we get past that, and Fourth of July, we got the rooms to spare. Even got July Fourth openings. I think maybe folks is staying at that new Comfort Inn by Liberty, closer to the fireworks. Now" — she opened the ledger — "we *could* get you in the movie room, and you'd only have to vacate one night, June 20. Gentleman comes from Missouri to the auction every month, standing reservation on the movie room. Otherwise it's yours." Her hand was poised to pen me into the vacancy.

"The movie room?" I asked.

Donna riffled for something under the counter, pulled out a laminated sheet, looked at it, scowled, and ducked to continue the search. Eventually she resurfaced with the correct tattered laminate, and turned it proudly toward me. It was a homemade promotional flyer advertising the Gas Stop Inn's claim to fame: *With advanced reservations, guests can stay in the room where FBI agent Sally Russell (Lolita Davidovich) stayed during the arson investigation into a rash of Amish barn burnings in the 1996 film "Harvest of Fire."* It had been a Hallmark Hall of Fame/Patty Duke vehicle, and I wanted to ask if Patty Duke had played Amish, but Donna was already speaking: "We got an official poster framed on the wall, with all the stars signed it."

"Wow," I said, "that must have been quite a time around here."

"Sure it was," Donna confirmed.

"You know," I said, "I'm really fine where I am. Keep this for drawing people in."

"You sure?" Donna seemed concerned. "Makes a good story . . ." And though Ginny has accused me of doing most everything I do in the world because I think it will make a good story, I told Donna I was too lazy to move down the hall. She laughed, said "I hear you," and penned me in for another two and a half weeks in 116.

I did not venture into River City for Jazz Fest that day. I stayed at the Gas Stop instead, reading *This But Begins the Woe: From Cooperation to Collaboration.*

Ginny can't read. Okay, that's not true. It's not that she can't read —she was an English major for a time, once upon a time, and she can get through sales tags and purchase orders at work at the Sheibels' nursery. It's hard to know just what she's capable of, post-shock, but it definitely curtailed her ability to read extended narratives. No one can tell us why. Shock's like that: they don't know exactly how it works, but it's effective in some cases, so they persist. And, to be honest, Ginny's trouble reading began long before. After high school —or when she should have finished high school—she spent a year, inpatient, at the eating disorders clinic at U of I Hospital. She stabilized long enough to get a GED and apply to an alternative college, a place for kids not suited to standard curricula, the sort of place she belonged, in theory. Her first semester there she took a lit class, but had trouble finishing reading assignments. She talked to the professor, got extensions. The semester ended and she took an incomplete, promised to get the work in by a certain deadline—they were used to students like Ginny; it was, in theory, a school *for* people like Ginny —but ultimately she could not get the work done.

Ginny has attempted, mostly unsuccessfully, to explain what happens when her mind derails, but the one illuminating metaphor she's ever been able to provide me was when she likened her brain to Tetris. I didn't know Tetris then, but soon familiarized myself. Compelling, dizzying, Tetris's constantly accelerating, geometric shape-fitting could threaten the soundest of minds. It's the crack cocaine of video games, and I wouldn't wish it on my worst enemy. When Ginny tried to read, she said, a page of text turned into something like a Tetris screen, words descending like emergent Tetris worms, falling continuously in an eternal rain. To understand what she read, Ginny had to seamlessly fit her comprehension of each word up against her comprehension of the preceding word. The words kept coming ceaselessly and she'd scramble to keep up. Unrelenting words streamed from the page into her brain, and Ginny struggled to fit each snugly against the one before. In real Tetris, if you mess up and leave a hole in the matrix, it's okay, you get a chance to correct it, but if Ginny left a gap in her understanding of a text, she'd failed. All sense and meaning collapsed, got "vacuumed up." If she left a hole in the Tetris wall of a text, the entire narrative got sucked out the hole, meaning lost —and not just the meaning of the text at hand, but all meaning. The vacuum consumed everything. Her mind ate itself like a black hole, left Ginny free-falling in infinite nothingness. Reading   or failing to understand what she read—lost Ginny her grasp on the world. But college students, even at progressive schools for troubled kids, can't *not* read. So Ginny developed strategies to slow the words. If she kept herself empty and hazy, refrained from food and resisted sleep, she had a better chance of not "fucking up and leaving a hole." She spoke with revulsion, like she was confessing to bludgeoning a baby or taking a cleaver to the family cat. It was nightmare logic: she'd be doing something, not realizing it was wrong until she'd already hammered the child's skull or hacked the cat into chunks of bone and meat and fur. Only afterward could she see the irredeemable horror of what she'd done, faced with the evidence: dead baby, butchered cat, block of uncomprehended text.

Ginny's trouble with reading went as far back as high school, but by college she'd developed ways to talk about it, to make Tetris metaphors and try to let us in. When she was a teenager, Michael and I and the doctors were the enemy threatening to take away the only things—starvation, mind-altering chemicals—that kept her going. But by the time she got to college—and she was twenty or twenty-one by then, with all the detours and lost years—she didn't want to be sick anymore. She knew something was wrong with having to deprive herself of sleep and food in order to read her schoolbooks without fucking up and bludgeoning the baby. We'd also erected enough of an emergency system around her—a safety net of therapists at school to check in with, people attuned to the warning signs—so someone would know if she didn't, say, move from a chair for entire days, needlepointing to calm herself until her fingers blistered. But Ginny was also a master of deceit. Though she wasn't eating or sleeping, she could still pull herself together, wash her hair, put on lipstick, go out, and be with people. It was when she couldn't maintain *that* anymore, and started self-medicating with Valium to slow her brain, that it all fell apart. We drove to get her, brought her back to the clinic at the U, and I can say with certainty that had Michael and I not worked for a university with a teaching hospital and clinical network, a university that provided insurance that availed us and our offspring of those services, Ginny would be dead.

The evening of the day I didn't go to Jazz Fest, I called Michael from the Gas Stop. I knew Ginny and Silas would have gone by to visit him and Bernadette after the festival, and I wanted to know how Ginny had seemed to him. I could just see Michael shaking his head, choosing his words. He walked a few paces on the wood floor, sank onto the couch; I knew those sounds. He said, "Okay, I guess."

"Did they stay long?"

"Visited a bit with my mother, then came up and had some coffee with me. Not a long visit, but . . . Have *you* talked to her?" Our lines were so stupidly familiar.

I had not, I told him, since the morning.

"She picked up campaign papers downtown, said she was 'going politico.'"

I said, "That's worrisome," and Michael snorted — as if my giving voice to my worry was to suggest he didn't share it. To make things worse, I began enumerating my fears, riling my own anxiety. "Does she not recall what that did to her in 2000?" and Michael was saying "I know," but my tirade continued: "*She* used to know. For two years she's had sense enough to know what she can and can't take on. Now she ditches the meds and forgets it all? Silas doesn't know her like this, he's never dealt with this before. What's it going to do to him? To them?"

"You're getting ahead of yourself, Phil." Michael and I were good for each other at these times. One of us launched on a flight of panic, and that seemed to anchor the other to ground. We flew each other like kites in blustery, shifting winds. "Let's try to sit tight a little while," he said. "Maybe things *are* different. Maybe we're being alarmist. Maybe Silas *will* keep her steady."

When lucius visited me at the Gas Stop the next weekend, it was the first time someone besides the housekeeper — Donna Presidio's fifteen-year-old niece from Decorah — had knocked on my door, and I tripped getting up from the La-Z-Boy, nearly impaling myself on a floor lamp.

At the door, Lucius was just as flustered. He said, "That's a long drive."

I panicked, god-awful clichés running through my head, all in the voice of Bernadette Maakestad: *When the honeymoon was over with this paramour of hers, she crawled home. Why Michael took her back I can't understand. Good riddance to bad rubbish, I say.*

"Phil?" Lucius looked concerned. I was standing before him envisioning our demise and my simpering return to the old life that still seemed to exist alongside this new one. I could take it up again at any moment, which made me feel that I had to keep choosing not to, keep choosing Lucius, and myself. Which is the sort of thing that can make a person feel really self-centered. *Selfish:* Bernadette's go-to descriptor for me. Her voice in my head was nightmarish; I couldn't remember who I was. If Lucius stopped loving me—if our love proved to be anything less than everything—I feared I'd be free-floating alone through infinity.

"Phil? What's going on?" Lucius bent himself into my field of vision, found my eyes, and hovered there, pupils twitching back and forth searchingly. Later, he told me his first thought was that something had happened to Ginny, and it made me love him all over again. What I did not admit to Lucius is that my greatest fear was not that I'd lose Ginny, but him. Granted, I had a lot more experience imagining the loss of Ginny; she'd kept me in good practice. Most of her suicide attempts—slow-acting, time-release methods like starvation, promiscuity, recklessness—get classified as "cries for help," not fast tracks to death, but even Ginny's one true attempt—the one I'm aware of, anyway—was not dive-from-the-Golden-Gate decisive, though I do believe she was serious about wanting out when she swallowed those pills. Many pills, of many kinds, all at once. We were lucky Linda found her and got her to the hospital. By that time, it seemed that Ginny had been trying to die for so long, in so many different ways, that something in me was hardened to it, steeled against the possibility of her success. I hate her a little bit for that, and part of me—a shameful, unspeakable part—thinks that if she'd succeeded, my hate might be justified. Maybe then, later, I could get past the hate and move on to pity, sympathy, maybe even healing. My own mother nursed my father through a decade of hideous Alzheimer's decline, during which she loathed and cursed him, hated him for not being the man she married, hated him—and herself—because she hated life as his nursemaid, hated what they were reduced to. But then he died, and it was over, and she could stop being angry and remember who he'd been before the decay. Then she had room to love him again, assemble the photographic mantel-shrine to her lost love, speak of him as he was in his heyday, mourn. She spent a year in adoring widowhood—a tiny window of redemption—before a stroke got her, too. Sometimes I fear that Lucius is my reward, the porthole of respite and joy in my life as Ginny's mother. Murphy could so easily whisk Lucius away, fell him tomorrow—heart attack, brain clot, interstate pileup, house fire, falling piano. But then there's this: what kind of mother imagines more easily bearing the loss of her daughter of twenty-five years than her lover of two months?

"Phil," Lucius said again. "Phillipa, where are you?"

"I'm here," I said. "You're here," and I melted into him. He held me in the doorway, whispering to my hair, kissing my temples, my eyes, and I felt such relief, hushed by his caress, safe at his insistence of safety. It's the kind of relief I never gave Ginny. I may have dragged her kicking and screaming to a modicum of health, but I've never given my daughter comfort.

Lucius and I moved to the bed and held each other there until he said, "I need food," and we ventured out, hand in hand, into rural America's Friday night. The Gas Stop Bar was packed—families with too many children too close in age; mothers in stretch pants hammocking great fallen bellies; big, crew-cut, goateed dads in acid-wash jeans. The pool table was ringed with swaggering young former Mennonites gone soft with beer and hard with menial labor. Girls'-night-outers—hair teased kinky, bangs blown straight—played drinking games at a corner booth, slinging back Windex-blue shots, vamping like everyone else was there to watch them party.

Lucius and I entered and hovered a minute by PLEASE WAIT TO BE SEATED until a waitress swooped in. "Two for dinner?" Before Lucius had the "yes" to his lips, she'd launched a gossipy spiel about how they'd been hammered all day and the only seats were at the bar, and I thought at first she was telling us that the staff had been drinking so hard they needed all the tables for themselves. Lucius's "That's fine?" came out as a question, as he looked to me for affirmation, but our hostess was already waving us toward the end of the bar, to the only two seats together in the place, directly beside Creamer, the man who'd silently paid for my beer the week before. He'd taken down the top of his coveralls, but his sweatshirt hood was still up, and between hood, beard, and safety glasses, he exposed almost no skin. I was unsure whether his disability was physical or mental, but felt certain that something about him was not right.

Lucius pulled out a stool for me. He was raised not to seat his woman beside another man, and the situation thwarted him: he could seat me beside one man, or a long bar of men on the other side, and he understandably chose to put himself between me and the rest of the bar. "It's ninety degrees out," he whispered, with a perplexed glance toward Creamer.

I nodded, mouthing words only Lucius could see: *He's the one. Who bought me the beer.*

Lucius stiffened and gestured to suggest we switch seats, but I waved away his concern. I didn't fear Creamer, not with Lucius there.

The bartender was a furry-lipped woman with long gray pigtails and a T-shirt that read: *Delicious Fried Eggs at Skyway Jack's.* Up where her breasts may once have been were drawings of two sunny-side-up eggs, side by side. "What can I get you kids?" she asked us, her voice so gravelly it was like she had rock tumblers for lungs.

"Hi." Lucius smiled broadly, a flirt without exception.

"Watch out, gorgeous," she told him. At me, she winked conspiratorially and asked what we were having. This, I thought, was a dame who didn't negotiate with men she wasn't bedding.

"Bass for me." I stuck a thumb toward Lucius. "He speaks for himself."

She said, "Right on, sister," and turned to him obligingly.

"Make it two," said Lucius.

"Two Basses." She slung a couple of pint glasses on the bar, and I watched the muscles twitch under the tanned, crepe-thin skin of her upper arms. She probably could have lifted a truck.

We ordered and ate our deep-fried starches, drank our beers, and listened to the sassy, country-girl rock that the girls'-night-outers kept loading on the jukebox. Lucius ate with his left hand and kept his right on my thigh beneath the bar. On my other side, Creamer mashed himself against the wall, maybe afraid I'd accidentally touch him, hunching over his beer as though I might steal it. I focused on Lucius, attempting to ignore Creamer's strange, lurking presence beside me. Lucius was trying both to get a better look at Creamer and not to look at all, the impulses battling in his eyes, fascinated and knowing better than to stare. He whispered, "I think he's drinking beer through a straw."

I nodded, mouthed *yes*.

A few minutes later Lucius's eyes got wide: the fried-egg bartendress had engaged Creamer in some kind of wordless dialogue, and I watched Lucius, trying to gauge from his expression what was going on. He looked like a kid seeing television for the first time.

There was shuffling and bluster from my neighbor's barstool. Lucius looked momentarily stricken, and the bartendress said, "Okay, Creamer, you're done for the night." Movement behind me ceased. "*Now.* Creamer, go on home." She could have been talking to a dog. Creamer dropped from his stool, heavy boots thudding to the floor, and hauled himself off. He bent into the exit door with his shoulder like he was running a football or heading into a blizzard.

"Did he pay?" Lucius asked our bartender.

"Creamer? Oh, Norma pays up front. We deduct through the month. Tip, too. Twenty percent."

"Norma?" I said.

"His mom." Her face puckered up sourly, then she gestured like she might cross herself.

"Why does he . . ." I began. "Why the hood, the clothing . . . ?"

Lucius sat mute, as though we were speaking a language he didn't know.

"Oh, he works at the dairy," she said, and I must have looked perplexed, for she continued: "In the 'frigeration. With how cold it is in there and how hot it is out, he'd get himself sick to death going back and forth. Takes a while to reclimatate, after, you know?"

Lucius nodded, then asked, "Why'd you kick him out?"

The bartender lifted her chin in a gesture I couldn't decipher. She smiled slyly and leaned an elbow on the bar. One fried egg stared up at us. "You remember that Unabomber guy?"

Lucius and I nodded like schoolchildren.

"When Norma dies, God friggin' knows what they're going to find in that house!" Then something got her attention down the bar, she made a quick "'Scuse me," and ducked away.

"*He's* like Kaczynski?" Lucius asked. "Or his mother is? Should I fear for your safety? Am I going to be forced into early retirement to move to Iowa to protect you?"

"Your retirement, old man," I said, "would not be early in the least."

Half an hour later, as Lucius and I left the bar, a huge vehicle rumbled into the lot, a military-looking monster truck with an enormous rusting snowplow in front. It pulled across three parking spots and *humph*ed to a halt. And then Randall jumped down from the driver's seat. The passenger door opened and Linda lowered herself to the ground.

"Hey hey," Randall called, coming toward us. With discretionary instinct, Lucius dropped his arm from my waist, then replaced it protectively an instant later.

"Randall!" I tried to sound bright, but I fear I was unconvincing. "Linda!" They wore T-shirts pinned with campaign buttons that read: MENARDS WORKERS FOR KERRY. Menards, the Midwestern home-improvement box store on the outskirts of River City where Randall and Linda worked, could not have allowed its name to be used in a political campaign, especially since I'm pretty sure they're Republican owned. Randall probably made the buttons himself, saw all those other "for Kerry" slogans—ARMENIANS FOR KERRY, GA-

RAGE SALE MOMS FOR KERRY, CHIROPODISTS FOR KERRY — and figured why not?

Linda lifted an arm hello, and Lucius again removed his hand from my waist to raise it in greeting. He let it drop to his side. I introduced him simply as "Lucius," then said, "This is Ginny's best friend, Linda. And our own Reverend Randall, who married Ginny and Silas."

"We just left all them all at Eula's," Randall said, and we then learned what I already suspected: the past weekend at Jazz Fest, amid the macramé jewelry and deep-fried-Oreo vendors, Ginny'd found the Iowa Democrats at their red-white-and-blue booth and, true to her threats to the W-hat woman, volunteered herself to the campaign. ELECTROSHOCK PATIENTS FOR KERRY!

"See my new wheels?" Randall gestured to the tank parked before us. "Insurance gave me seventeen hundred for the van. Picked this puppy up at Surplus for five hundred."

Linda said, "He donated the rest to Kerry." She looked proud.

"Least I could do," Randall said. "We just was at the Yoders' now, campaign planning." He paused as if ready to define his lingo, but seeing we were on board, continued. "Figuring how to get to folks. The party don't have much by way of records in the area." He said "the party" the way my parents' old Berkeley commie friends had. "Amish *can* vote, but don't, and"— here his voice took on an affectation like he was quoting someone — "they don't register a . . . what's it called?"

"Affiliation," Linda said.

"Most folks do that at the DMV," he went on, "when you get a license, which Amish don't, so mostly we'll be doing this thing farm to farm. Find ones who're less strict, Mennonites, *Moderns* in the family, you know? Just got to figure the best way to get to people."

Lucius said, "This bar would be a good place. You'd get them in a good mood, too."

Randall's face opened. "That'd work — where they drink is where the *change* happens."

The change. I thought of my own encroaching menopause, of Je-kyll and Hyde. I pictured Randall, that bull in a china shop, swaggering into the Gas Stop to effect change. Randall wore his hair as though he were Charlie's fourth Angel. On one meaty shoulder blade —so that he could only see it in a mirror, but it was visible to all in the muscle shirts he sported—he bore the life-size tattooed face of a baby son he hadn't seen in years. The kid was a teenager now, un-aware that somewhere in Iowa, on the back of a gigantic former meth head, rode his creepy tattooed baby face. The boy'd been named for a grandmother, but backward, and this was inked below the face in fussy, scrolling calligraphy: *Tenaj.* Tenaj, wherever you are, your fa-ther is off to effect change.

Randall was still musing. "Campaigning at the Gas Stop." He looked to Linda. "I say we start A-SAP. 'Magine if we could just stick a ballot in front of 'em—*sign here, buddy!*"

I was about to say goodbye, but then Randall asked, "How long you here for, Lucius?"

"Just the weekend," Lucius said.

"Great, great. So what'll you-all be up to, then?"

I should have made excuses and gotten out, but it seemed sud-denly, stupidly necessary to demonstrate that Lucius was not here to spend the weekend in my bed, but to see the sights of southeast Iowa, and I started chattering like a demented magpie: "We'll see the university. Drive out to the covered bridge, maybe. Or the fossil gorge?" I looked to Lucius; he leaned on a pickup in a pose of ef-fortful leisure and lifted his eyebrows gamely. "Or the raptor center: blind owls, one-legged hawks . . ." As I rambled, Lucius tried to look as though these were, of course, all the reasons he'd come to town. "I thought maybe we'd have lunch out at the Liberty Grill . . ."

Randall's face assumed a sagacious authority. "They got a new wine bar there down the street. If you-all like wine. The Liberty's got real good food, if you like good food."

"After eating dinner here tonight, we deserve it," I said, then felt embarrassed, like I'd just insulted Randall's own cooking. My throat constricted with anxiety, but sensing it, Lucius leapt to my aid. He put a hand to his belly. "Speaking of which, I could use to walk off some of those fries." It was absurd, but Randall and Linda smiled, and soon we said our goodbyes, and Lucius and I headed for a post-prandial stroll around the Gas Stop triumvirate of Prairie, Iowa.

"Would you believe," I told Lucius out of earshot, "he's her NA sponsor?"

"They let couples sponsor each other?"

"Oh, they're not—not a couple, not in that sense. That'd be nice, huh?" I held the thought: Randall and Linda in love. "That'd be lovely, but no, just sponsor and . . . sponsee?"

"Hm." Lucius wagged his head, surprised, trying to clear away the idea of Linda and Randall as a couple, which he'd thought so obvious he hadn't imagined otherwise. I watched him doing what I seem to do so often: rearrange my assumptions when I'm made aware I've misread a situation. "Hm," he repeated, as if to say *Go figure*, which is something I should say to myself a lot more often: *Go figure, Phillipa. Go figure it out before you make an ass of yourself, would you?*

Lucius and I saw no sights that weekend—no university land-marks or regional points of interest. We refused to share each other with waitresses, birds, or sommeliers. Save a few dashes out for sustenance, we stayed in room 116, in bed, until he had to drive back to Ohio. Letting him leave was like trying to stop breathing. The body fights for what it needs. The body—fragile as it may sometimes seem—fights for life. We gasp, we clot, we vomit. We keep on.

AS MY STUDENTS SAY —and probably *did* say on the course evalua-tions for that summer session I can't bring myself to read—I phoned it in. Do they still say that? Texted it in? Neither is accurate: I was present, but in body only. Lucius left for France and our correspon-dence was limited. As forewarned, I had to check out of my room at the Gas Stop when the Trekkies arrived en masse the last weekend in

June. By then, Ginny and I had come to a familiar truce-like peace, and she invited me back to the farmhouse for the week and a half until I left for France. Trepidatious but desperate—Trek Fest had the area hotels filled beyond capacity—I packed up and returned to the Yoders' on Friday morning, June 25. Ginny and Silas were at work, and Eula was out in the garden, with the baby in a bouncy chair under an umbrella. I waved and went in to put down my things, only to discover that Orah and Obadiah's family room had been transformed into Kerry HQ. John Kerry yard signs were stacked six-deep against the walls, every horizontal surface piled with papers, handouts, flyers. A glance at the far wall could make a person think she was in the wrong house: floor to ceiling, it was patchworked in 8½ x 11 color printouts—white print on a royal-blue background—of BUSH-CHENEY '04 posters, aligned and Scotch-taped with the precision of an Amish quilter. And how I wished Eula had hung those flyers—wished anyone but Ginny was responsible. Each sheet bore a different slogan above the BUSH-CHENEY logo, and at the bottom of each, in blue letters in a tiny white box, was: *Paid for by Bush-Cheney '04, Inc.* But the slogans were all twisted, like: *The Solution to Poverty. The Final Solution Bush-Cheney '04* and *America for Rich White Christians Bush-Cheney '04* and *Jews, you're successful . . . vote like it! Bush-Cheney '04.*

I asked Eula about the signs, and she admitted—with an embarrassment that made me angry at Ginny—to not really understanding them. "I think they're meant to be funny?" she said.

That night, Ginny and Silas stayed out late with Linda and Randall at Trek Fest's opening. I went to bed before they got in. Saturday, I got up with Eula and Oren, and was standing in the family room looking queasily at the Bush-Cheney wallpaper when Ginny came downstairs. She sidled up, like a museumgoer hitting on a fellow art gazer, and said, "Aren't they fabulous?"

"What *are* they?"

"You didn't hear about these? For like a day, they had this thing up on their campaign website." She dipped her chin into her neck and did an Arnold Schwarzenegger voice: *"The Sloganator."* This is how it went with me and Ginny: we'd act like things were fine, and then they'd *be* fine, to all appearances, until the whole thing inevitably exploded, again, repeat, ad infinitum. I didn't know how to respond. Ginny had plenty to say about *The Sloganator:* "They made a program on the site so people, *supporters"*—she let out an airy little snort to highlight the restraint she was showing—"so Republicans could write slogans and create official flyers or yard signs or whatever. But, of course, other people, nonsupporters, started using it for our own nefarious purposes." She looked positively gleeful, eyes twinkling. "The Bush people shut the whole thing down pretty soon, but a bunch had already made it through the censor. This"—she waved a hand to the wall—"is only a sampling of the really prize ones. *Leave Every Child Behind!* Every time I think I've found my favorite, another one pops out. *Axis of Idiocy . . . 'I believe what I believe is right.' Don't change horses mid-Apocalypse!* That one kills me."

Permit me a self-indulgent moment here to say that I don't think people who've tried to commit suicide should be allowed to idly enumerate things that "kill" them. Maybe especially in the company of those who gave birth to them, and had to go back to the same hospital—where once upon a time things had looked so promising—in order to visit a red-eyed wraith who'd been revived by health care professionals and forced to remain in the life you foisted on her. She'd vomited so violently she popped blood vessels in her eyeballs.

"So," I said, "you printed them and arranged them like this?"

"It took eons." She grinned conspiratorially. "Lots of repeats—*Leave no billionaire behind, No billionaire left behind.* I'm surprised there aren't more Nazi slogans—*Tolerance is a sign of weakness,* et cetera—they're so fitting . . . There're tons—we could do the whole room."

"I'm sure Orah and Obadiah would have loved it," I said, snide and biting.

Ginny stopped. She turned from me, shoulders rising, then falling as she let out a choppy breath. She faced me again. "I will not contend with your sarcasm right now."

"I'll be earnest, then, Gin. Does Silas know you when you're like this? Does he know this side of you? Did he know it *before* you got married?"

She drew another breath and let it out, her body clenched, lower jaw thrust forward in defiance, face washed in rage. "Silas knows every side of me." She breathed again. "He actually cares for—loves—those sides of me, not just the pretty ones, not just the nice, easy ones. Silas actually loves the whole person I am, not just the palatable parts my mother's willing to engage."

"*Pardon* me." I had the sense that we'd said this all before, already had this very fight. "Pardon me for not loving your sickness. *Pardon me* for not loving what *attacks* the person I love. For not embracing your disease with adoration! *Excuse* me for not loving . . . If you had cancer, would you want me to love the cancer? They'd be your own cells—technically part of your *whole* person. You'd want me to love that cancer? Just root for those cancer cells. *Goooo cancer! Woo-woo!*—because they're part of you and I'd be a terrible, unaccepting mother if I didn't love the cancer that was eating your body from the inside. Oh, I'm so sorry, Ginny. So sorry for not loving *all* of you. For not being as good a person as Silas. For not being *Amish*. I'm so sorry I don't love and forgive and accept and think everything is just the way *God* wants it—"

She was screaming by then, spitting venomous words. Terribly unimaginative words she'd spat at me many times before. Still effective, caustic despite their ubiquity. "Fuck you," she said. "Fuck you. I won't do this. I will not do this anymore." She was almost speaking to herself, like I'd already disappeared from the frame. She'd walled me out, didn't see me, was contending only with the mother in her mind. She closed her eyes: "Fuck you." Resolute in her conviction: "Fuck you." She said it like a mantra, a religious chant that took over when real thought failed, a mantra to protect her from the enemy

—me, the meds, the doctors. "Fuck you." She turned back upstairs and left me alone in the Bush-Cheney–papered family room. A door slammed on the second floor—Ginny loves to slam a door—and a long beat of silence followed. Then the wailing began. It was Oren, startled by the wall-shaking slam, but it was like a return to Ginny's infancy, when the wailing never stopped, the tornado siren of that horrible wail. I covered my ears. I could not bear it; in a moment I'd start wailing myself. If I didn't get out of that house I'd be standing there with my eyes pinched shut, hands over my ears, mouth gaped in a gruesome, Munchian, Howard Dean scream.

I grabbed my handbag and left. At the Gas Stop I bought the *Prairie Community News,* sat at the booth with a lousy cup of coffee, and opened the classifieds. There were plenty of available rentals—no shortage of vacant farmhouses on a half acre of what used to be the family farm, now with genetically modified corn in rigid rows. I made an appointment for that very afternoon to see a place over past the cheese factory.

Aldous Bontrager, landlord of 1867553 John C. Wolffson Road, got to the house before me to weed-whack a path to the front door. His trousers were spattered with grass, and when he lifted his cap to resettle it on his head before extending an arm toward me, his hair stuck to his brow in a wet band. The house was surrounded not by lawn but by a bizarrely ordered and organized junkyard: a pile of bicycle parts sat beside a reserve of household appliances; a nearby depression held vacuums, shop vacs, and electric brooms. Broomsticks, yardsticks, trim molding, and other long, skinny things were bundled in twine and stacked against the house like firewood.

"I own it all." Bontrager swept his hand, indicating either the farmland or the junk.

Past the junk piles, the house itself had a dilapidated, Hobbit quality. I thought the front window was boarded up until we approached and I realized it was just filth-caked. Bontrager pushed open the door to reveal a moldering electric wheelchair, and I imagined the home's resident sitting there, shotgun in lap. Bontrager said, "Needs some airing out is all."

I said, "Thanks for your time, Mr. Bontrager," and turned to leave.

"You're the Yoder mother-in-law, aren't you?" I heard him say, and I spun back around. Bontrager paused, and I steeled myself as the man looked me up and down, then said, "Nice to meet you." Sarcasm? Utter sincerity? I have no idea. I drove straight to the Gas Stop and asked Donna Presidio to put me in the first thing she had available once the Trekkies left. I reserved a room for my return from France, too. "Welcome back!" Donna said.

"I still have to survive until tomorrow — don't welcome me back just yet."

Donna looked confused, but said, good-naturedly, "Well, we're glad to have you."

"Getting to be the closest I've got to a home." I meant that the inn gave me comfort, but Donna looked hurt, as if I'd disparaged her business, and I couldn't think of a way to remedy it.

I stayed away from the farmhouse until they'd all left to go campaigning at Trek Fest that evening. KLINGONS FOR KERRY! Though Trek Fest's better attended than, say, the Marion Bar-B-Que Rendezvous or even Solon Beef Days — especially by out-of-staters with prosthetic Vulcan ears — it's really just a town fair: fried dough, lemonade shake-ups, live local music at the bandstand. And while Ginny, Silas, Eula, Oren, Linda, and Randall were out riding bumper cars and persuading Starfleet to vote Kerry, I crept back to the house, went to sleep, and was gone Sunday morning before I had to see anyone but Eula. "Back to the Gas Stop," I told her. She'd obviously heard some version of events from Ginny, and nodded, her forehead creased in sympathy. I kissed Oren's peach-fuzzed crown and fled. One more week at the Gas Stop and I'd be gone to another land. My last class was Thursday, July 1 — Final essay topic: How One Professor Managed to Make Musical Theater More Boring Than Statistics — and I was scheduled to fly out of Cedar Rapids on the Fourth, Independence Day. That was the best available flight, and it was a relief to escape the festivities: when the president's a diabolical moron, British colonization doesn't sound so bad. I've never been a huge fireworks fan. We always went because Michael loves them, and I suspect his enthusiasm for zooming, flaring explosives has a lot to do with Bernadette's abhorrence of them; she loathed fireworks like someone who'd lived through the Blitz. Ginny never liked them much either, and when she was small she'd stay with Bernadette on the Fourth while I went with Michael to City Park. The thought of being in an airplane, literally above it all, was comforting, which is saying a lot, as *I get no kick in a plane.* I don't refuse to fly, but I don't like it. I concede to the ways of this warp-speed world.

MY TRIP TO FRANCE took place in a dream bubble. Mornings, I'd wake beside this beautiful man on hotel-crisp sheets, my arm across his warm back, a breeze lapping through floor-to-ceiling windows. We'd shower together at the pension, then amble down cobbled streets to the *pâtisserie* for butter croissants and café au lait so creamy and strong it made me hum with energy. Then we'd set off on our own: Lucius to his collaborationists at their family home on rue des Brebis—the Street of Sheep—and I to wander the town. Down a tiny side street I found a used bookshop; a plaque on the door read LIBRAIRIE BRUNO BLUM, and there was a big, old-fashioned knocker that I lifted on instinct and tapped. A click sounded within, the door unlocked, and I pushed inside, where the sweet dust of old pages and powdery leather enveloped me. A large old man with a bald pate and wiry gray hair tendriling down to his collar hunched behind a great battered wood desk, books piled around him like fortifications. He peered up at me over tiny reading glasses. The same wiry gray hair sprouted from his ears and sprang from his nose, and he'd've been terrifying—a child's vision of a human monster—if he hadn't just then flashed me a tremendous smile and, removing his glasses and sweeping them about him in a gesture of expansive welcome, said in heavily German-accented English, "Welcome to my kingdom!" I thought of a story my grandparents told about a friend of theirs in Dresden, a storekeeper, maybe a bookshop or a music shop? A quiet man who kept to himself, no family anyone knew of. And then one day, my grandparents said—and they heard it from other friends and relatives, for it was the early '40s when this happened, and Bubbie and Zadie had been in California for years already—one day the shopkeeper was gone. His store, empty. No one saw anything go, just suddenly empty, proprietor gone. That's how it went: the Nazis arrived and people disappeared, never to be heard from again. I had a pang of missing them—my grandparents—both gone since I was a teenager, and my parents, then, too—a pang like a hole in my heart. And probably to soothe myself, to fill that unfillable gap, I bought from Bruno Blum, to bring home for Oren, an ungodly expensive 1979 translation of Maurice Sendak's *One Was Johnny*—"*Mon premier s'appelle Jeannot; tout tranquille il lit sur un escabeau . . .*" Because that's what my parents would have done.

In another shop, I splurged on a pair of gorgeous red leather shoes —though God knows when I'd wear them in Iowa—but that was the extent of my extravagance. Most days, I found myself a lunch spot and ate while reading *Blood Will Have Blood: The Occupiers and the Occupied, France 1940–1944,* by Lucius Bocelli, PhD. Or I'd be walking and the taste buds at the back of my tongue would flare and swell, drawing me down a side street to a *charcuterie, saucissons* strung from hooks like bunting. I'd buy a baguette, some cheese, and sliced *jambon,* and plunk down in a plaza by a fountain, or at the edge of a pasture, to eat my picnic and watch the cows flick their tails at flies. Lucius and I met up in the late afternoon for a glass of wine at a sidewalk café, then we'd go back to nap and make love, the early-evening breeze lapping at the window curtains. We'd shower again, dress, and stroll out to find dinner, over which Lucius would tell me about his day with the collaborationists. They were good people, Lucius felt, who'd grown up in a time and place that turned their lives into mind-boggling survival stories. Lucius sat with them and talked, hour after hour. Then he came to me and unfurled the stories they'd spooled upon him, and we drank wine, filled ourselves with gorgeous, rich food, and then walked the streets, hands entwined, practically skipping, like lovers in a movie musical about to burst into song, bellies full, heads lofty with wine, hearts beating with joy. I have never been so happy in my life.

It lasted five days. My sixth morning at the Pension Hébert, Lucius and I went downstairs and there was a message at the front desk. It was from Michael, asking me to call home. I'd left the number just in case, not expecting anyone would use it, and my first response was, of course, panic. Ginny. It would be past one in the morning in Iowa, but I had the concierge place the call, dial all the international codes. Lucius stood by as I waited, my mind tripping through horror scenarios.

Michael's "hello" was withered and dry. He didn't sound as though he'd been asleep.

"Michael, it's me. What's going on?"

"Phil." The relief in his voice surprised me; I didn't know I could provide that for him anymore. A small pause, a breath, and then he said, "My mother died."

I gasped. That may sound like the sort of melodrama of which my daughter accuses me, but when one is taken by surprise, one may very naturally gasp. I'd probably already been holding my breath in fear of what Michael might say, and what came was shocking, but not what I'd anticipated. I gasped, and Lucius stiffened beside me. "Michael — what . . . what happened?" I felt Lucius relax: he could hear that the calamity was Michael's, not mine. Not Ginny's.

"The day before yesterday . . ." He was remembering, placing things in time. "She didn't come up for breakfast. She was in bed." He choked, then regained himself. "They don't know exactly . . . I thought stroke, or heart attack, but they don't . . . all those meds. At the home she got help . . . They say it happens: old people *get con-*

fused." He was bitterly parroting some doctor or paramedic. "*They get confused* and simply OD—*simply* . . ." He choked up, and didn't continue.

"Oh, Michael, you should have called sooner. Is there . . . What can I . . . ?"

"I wouldn't bother you—it's all arranged—but I wanted you to know." The bitterness in his tone now seemed leveled at me. "There's no funeral. She didn't want one. Just cremation, no service. I don't expect you'd come home because a woman you couldn't stand—"

"That's not fair," I cut in. "I'd—"

Michael kept on: "—but Ginny's having a hard time." He paused. I felt his exhaustion. "A really hard time. I always knew this would be rough on her, when my mother . . . but now, off meds, she's not coping, she can't. She's way off. I don't—" He recalibrated again. "I don't expect you to come home. Neither does she, I don't think. But I wanted you to know—"

I didn't let him continue. "I'll call when I have a ticket. Should I call her? Or just come?"

"She's just fetal, crying. Silas can't . . . She won't come to the phone. Not even for Linda. I drove out . . . yesterday . . . ?"

I interrupted again. I said: "I'm coming."

MY JOURNEY HOME was beset by so many delays and trials I might as well have crossed the Atlantic by steamer ship. Technical troubles grounded the flight in Paris, but not before we'd sat five hours on the runway, eating peanut packs and breathing each other's stale breath. After hour two, the drinks were free, but plastic-bottled Chardonnay did not, wonder of wonders, radically improve my mood. Perhaps I should have been drinking rum and Cokes like the three American dudes in the row behind me, who, by the time the crew finally started to unherd us from that plane, were so wasted that one of them flicked the clasp on the overhead luggage compartment and let it slam open into the back of my head. Arms laden with carry-ons, my knees buckled—it was a hell of a hard thwack—and I'd've fallen if there'd been anywhere to fall. Instead I partially collapsed into the seats and the crush of bodies around me, my stagger causing others to waver and catch themselves. If they'd opened the aircraft door just then and created another foot of clear space, we'd've all gone over like dominos. I was fine, if a little mortified, though I developed quite an egg on my head as I sat another six hours in the airport while our plane got fixed. Or maybe they procured us another one. I don't even know. I wanted desperately to sleep, but had the idea that I might have a concussion and shouldn't doze off. With no one to watch my carry-ons, I couldn't get up and move around, and I wasn't about to hump it all with me, so I felt bound to my seat. My head ached and I had no Advil, nor any more euros. It didn't matter: the airport shops had closed for the night. To stay awake, I tried to read. The book I had with me was Lucius's *Give Me Your Watch and I'll Tell You the Time: The French Under Nazi Occupation,* but I don't think anything could have engaged me enough to keep my eyes open. I'd read a passage, drift off, head lolling, wake with a jerk, try to refocus my streaming eyes on the page, and read another few incomprehensible lines before dropping off again. At some point I must have become incapable of rousing, for I fell asleep and didn't startle myself awake. I came to, groggily, some time later, neck cricked, hot drool down my cheek and chin. An announcement was coming over the PA, people around me moving and gathering things. The middle of the night, and apparently we were boarding for Chicago. I was alive, which I thought probably meant I didn't have a concussion.

On board, I fell asleep before we left the ground, then woke to a putrid stench—a young Frenchman diagonally across the aisle vomited during takeoff, and no one could do much of anything about it until we reached cruising altitude and it was safe to move about the cabin. I found a ChapStick in my bag and held it under my nose with the airline blanket tented over my head and tried not to retch. An announcement came, "possible tornadic systems near O'Hare," and I lifted the blanket to hear the flight attendant say we'd see how things were looking once we'd crossed "the pond." If we had to make a landing elsewhere before our final destination, we'd do so, because their first concern was, of course, our safety.

I slept fitfully, in snatches, barely knowing when I was asleep and when awake. A movie played on the drop-down screens overhead— something moronic, with Adam Sandler, that kept repeating itself, like *Groundhog Day,* because every time I looked, the same scene was playing out, over and over. When it was finished, finally, they put on that dreadful Donald Trump reality show, and I'd open my eyes and see his bulging red face screaming so violently I could hear it without hearing it. There was turbulence in the black of the night, nothing outside the windows, our teeny tiny plane jouncing through infinite space. A blessing, Bernadette would have said, to be so tired I barely cared if we tumbled out of the sky or hit a twister and swirled into oblivion. Or maybe we had and I was dead already. Dead and drifting through the churning static limbo that is sleep on an airplane. And then I wasn't on an airplane, but in our River City basement, waiting out a tornado, clutching my dear old dead cat, Maude, who morphed before me into a beast called Chou-Chou, a dog, first, and then a cat. And then I realize I'm in the basement with Bernadette, lying dead on a pull-out couch. But then she's up, rocking in a chair on the Yoders' porch, stitching at something in her lap, and then she's Eula, rocking and stitching, a great quilt spread over her knees and legs, and it's growing—the quilt—blooming like time-lapse photo flowers, unfurling and spreading down the porch, the steps, out into the fields, a furry quilt of animal skins, and it's all moving and undulating, and I can see they're not skins but live animals, cats and rabbits, howling in pain as Eula—no, Bernadette, now, again—weaves her needle in and out of their flesh, the whole quilt—which is the land now, quilted like the land in a Grant Wood painting—the land writhing and rolling and becoming an ocean on which two gray-haired men row by in a dinghy. They see me and wave. I wave back, then realize who they are and stop waving. It's George W. Bush and Dick Cheney, and then I understand they aren't waving but saluting, arms outstretched, their boat turning so I can see the swastikas on their armbands. *Zieg Heil!*, they cry, *Zieg Heil!*, rowing off into the black-black sky as a bicycle comes speeding by, Donald Trump pedaling madly through the night, wicker basket shimmying, dogs barking, his hair swirling tornadic around his head as he morphs into Adolf Hitler, not pedaling an old-lady bicycle but standing in the back seat of a convertible, in a motorcade, greeting the crowds as he's driven through the streets of the little French town where Lucius is interviewing his old Nazi brother and sister in their house on rue des Brebis. This motorcade isn't the customary slow processional; Hitler's car is reckless, speeding and screeching through the town. Driverless now, and unbound by gravity, it's climbing the building walls like an insect, fast as a video game, Hitler cackling Wicked Witch cackles as he zooms through the streets looking for Lucius. Because Lucius is a Jew, and Hitler's after him. And there he is—Lucius—with his Nazis, at their table, the three of them eating furry, bloody raw rabbit, ripping flesh from bone with their teeth, blood dripping down their chins. Lucius has to eat a live rabbit sacrifice or else they'll know he's a Jew. They're watching to see if he flinches like a Jew, watching him with their bloody faces, rabbit fur in their teeth and smudged on their cheeks. And then I see they're not Lucius's brother-sister Nazis, but Bernadette and *her* brother, but her brother is Michael, my husband. The Nazi brother and sister are Michael and his mother, and they're goading Lucius on, sneering with their bloody teeth. *Esst, Juden. Esst gesund, Juden.* And I dream, and I dream, and I dream, the black sky swirling around me, horrors reeling interminably by, as if the projector's caught and will spin forever, images upon images fusing, overlapping. I know we should land, but a voice is saying we'll be circling until the tornado clears. We've got plenty of fuel to circle around, around and around. But I want the circling to stop. I want out of this nightmare, its circle and spin. I want to hit the ground with a great *thunk,* to land, *thud,* and know the witch is dead, the wicked old witch. But we only circle, never land, the ground keeps not coming and not coming, like it will never come, and all we'll do is forever turn. And then, *thud,* there it is, the stillness. And a quiet so quiet it can only be death. Except I'm alive, here in the flaming wreck of the plane, the flaming Technicolor fuselage. I'm alive and everyone else is dead. I know this somehow: that I'm the only survivor. A bright yellow cup is batting me in the face—my oxygen mask!—and there's a yellow flotation vest at my feet. I know I can pull the red tabs if I need to, or blow in the tubes to inflate it. And, if it's night, yellow lights on the shoulders will illuminate me, floating in blue water, clutching my purple seat cushion which can be used as a flotation device, but it's not night and there's no water. I'm tugging at my blue nylon seat belt to unclasp the silver buckle, and when I stand it's like I'm spilling from a burst piñata amid rainbows of detritus and debris, like the piles of scraps on Eula's quilting room floor, shreds of every color and pattern and texture in the world. Here, though, they're scraps of clothing but with people still attached, in bits, bits of people attached to scraps, and there's blood everywhere, red, red blood. Could there have been a bomb? In someone's shoes? In my shoes—my new red shoes? I stagger, barefoot, from the glinting, splintered steel and see the ghoulish red-white-and-blue of the plane's painted tail, cracked and dangling, flames all around—orange and red and deadly blue —and clouds of gasses, too, blue and vaporous, and I'm pushing through an emergency exit, past its red and white signs, a bright yellow life raft unfurling before me. I've left my bag behind like I'm supposed to, but where is my cat? My dog? My Chou-Chou, my Maude? Chou-Chou! But it's too late. I must jump, jump onto the glowing yellow slide and follow it down. Down. Down into the monochrome world.

4

TO THINK THIS COULD HAPPEN
ON RUE DES BREBIS

> But it wasn't a dream. It was a place. And you and you and
> you . . . and you were there. But you couldn't have been,
> could you?
>
> — *The Wizard of Oz*

IT DOESN'T LOOK all that different from Prairie, but I know it's
not Iowa in that way you just know things in dreams. It's a French
town—unnameable, the location too tactically critical to reveal—
known cryptically only as V——bourg, as if this were a Victorian
novel, though what it looks like is a black-and-white film. Is it true
that we dream only in black and white? Not for Dorothy . . . But this
is like Leni Riefenstahl's propaganda films, or something by Truffaut:
beautiful grayscale, crisp as a gelatin silver print, the cobbled road
glinting with flecks of mica. A sign mounted on a corner building
—white letters, dark background—says *rue des Brebis*. This is Sheep
Street. And here come the Germans.

On foot, apparently. No tanks or armored vehicles like in the
newsreels—the streets are too narrow for marching formations—so
the Nazis saunter casually into V——bourg like soldiers on furlough.
A few officers ride horseback, but most come as pedestrians. And

above, on balconies and terraces, children peer over rickety wooden railings to watch the Nazi arrival. It's less like an invasion than a parade—smiling Germans tossing sweets to the crowds, boys and girls jumping from their mothers' laps to catch the prizes. It's like New Orleans at Mardi Gras! It's the German invasion of France! In black and white! With candy!

As the march dwindles, soldiers break off in twos or threes to assess the town's billeting options. Where will the officers sleep? The enlisted men? Where to set up a communications center? At the library, perhaps. Or the dance hall. Or here, in this tailor's shop, on rue des Brebis.

Three Germans wait on the stoop for the proprietor to answer their knock. *"Bonjour, Monsieur,"* says the lead soldier. *"Je vous demand pardon . . ."* And Jean Armond, *tailleur* of V——bourg, steps aside to welcome the enemy with a sweeping gesture: *Come in!* Polite, mannerly, they wipe their feet, careful not to track mud. The officer in charge is handsome, like a young Ed Harris—pre–*Right Stuff,* the Ed Harris of *Borderline,* or even *Coma*—already losing his hair, but he's so handsome it seems only right to clear away anything that might distract from that beauty. He begs pardon of the tailor, regrets bothering him and his family on such a fine spring day. Would Monsieur care for a cigarette? Some sweets for the children?

All smiles and generosity, the Germans offer chocolates and marzipan fruits to Armond's children as their spokesman introduces himself: he is Karl Perlmutter. Just then, the shop cat slips down from its perch in the window, and Jean Armond introduces him, too. "This little fellow," he tells the soldiers, "is Chou-Chou." The cat, in turn, stretches, plants his front paws on one man's tall black boot, and tries to use it as a scratching post. At this there's a chirp of laughter from the back of the shop, and Karl Perlmutter looks up to see, in the arch dividing the tailor shop from the Armonds' kitchen, the only woman besides his mutti he will ever love.

Flustered, Karl stiffens, shuts his eyes, tries to remember his place, what he's there for. He tugs at his tunic, straightens himself in that high-cinched belt. His decorations shiver like spangles. When he speaks, it's loudly, as if to make up in volume what he's just lost of his heart. "We must inspect the barn," he declares. And then, by a miracle, Armond offers up this lovely girl, his eldest daughter: "Mignon, *ici!* Show these gentlemen the barn."

Whatever Mignon's reaction, Karl can't see it, for the girl's mother has stepped in and placed her own body (short, but imposingly bosomed) in the kitchen arch directly between her daughter and the Germans to block passage. But Perlmutter is undeterred. In brusque German the Armonds cannot understand, he takes charge, orders one soldier to stay and keep watch, and tells the other, "Follow, but not too close." And Madame Armond, cowed by this foreign exchange, simply recedes as the Nazis step forward to claim her lovely daughter.

Mignon ushers the men through the dark, oniony kitchen and out into the streaming sunshine of the yard. It's long and narrow, both sides fenced, and lined with rhododendron, peonies, forsythia — you can almost see the yellow in the black-and-white buds, as if they've been hand-painted by Georges Méliès, tiny dots against the plush dogwoods. The young couple strolls this flowering walk; the other soldier — Diederick Auslander, a buddy of Karl's from back home — keeps his distance behind. And behind them all, from the back door of the house, Idette Armond watches her daughter take that blooming lane as if she's walking a flower-strewn wedding aisle. Mignon, a bride. But the bride of a Nazi. A Nazi who's just invaded France.

"Mignon," Karl says, "this is your name? Mignon?"

"Oh!" she replies. "Yes, it's what I'm called."

"Then I shall call you Mignon. And you must . . . you must talk to me as Karl."

Mignon smiles shyly. Karl thinks she seems eager, though for all he knows, at the end of the path, in the old sheep barn at the far end of the property, her eager-to-please father may have fugitive Jews hiding in his unused stalls, munitions cached in the hay. But what Karl fervently hopes is that there are no Jews or armed French defenders secreted in the barn. Since his knock at the tailor's door, Karl's vision of the war has changed. Leave the Jews to the generals! Karl wants only to billet himself here with Mignon. Never mind the invasion, the Führer, the war. It's spring, and the ground is plush with young grass, and Karl is ready to give up his country, trade Germany for France, anything for the chance to lie down with this girl upon the achingly soft lawn. Maybe, thinks Karl — this newborn, reborn Karl — maybe France will surrender, and the rest of Europe, too, and there won't be a war so much as a redistribution, a semantic business, really.

The German troops won't stay long in V——bourg anyway; they'll have to push farther into France. Not much to accomplish here, just over the border, so close to Germany there's little to differentiate one country from the other, one people from its enemy. Karl is nineteen. He's never been away from Bavaria before, or from his mutti. When he left, she cried at the gate, *"Mein kind, mein kind,"* until he was down the road. He didn't look back, but knows that before he was out of sight she'd have taken a breath, arranged her face, and fetched her broom to sweep the road in front of their house, to sweep away the footprints of her only child.

INSIDE THE SHOP, Idette Armond whispers angrily to the obsequious toady who is her husband. "Tell me," she hisses, "what do you gain, welcoming them?"

Jean Armond is a sycophant, yes, and also a veteran of the Great War. He fought Germans in the trenches, and this current reversal in France's fortunes evokes in him not so much anger but embarrassment. For his hereditary enemy Jean also harbors a kind of fraternal solidarity. It feels sometimes as if they were all in those wretched trenches together, not combatants, but brothers-in-arms. He can't help but admire Hitler's well-trained army and accord them due respect — it's his way of contending with shame. And now, supercilious in response to his ignorant wife's accusations, he replies, "There is everything to gain through the favor of those in power."

Idette gawks. "So they've won already? You give up on France just like that? *Pffft.*" She flicks her hands to show his callousness: brushing off his country like crumbs from the table.

BACK OUT IN THE YARD, with the sort of bravado that so often accompanies falsity, Karl Perlmutter decrees the ramshackle Armond barn unsuitable, inadequate for the Germans' use, the disrepair too great. It's a lie; the barn is ideal: sheltered stalls for the officers' mounts, proximity to town, a bit of grass on which to graze the horses. But Karl is no longer serving the German army. Karl has turned traitor, allied on the side of love. "But," he tells Mignon, "the house will serve nicely." He's acting a part — it's not war, it's theater! "There are guest rooms, yes?"

"Guest rooms?" Then she understands. "Oh, no. You'll have ours — you must!" But Karl is shaking his head, refusing to displace anyone in the gracious Armond household, so Mignon must lift her jaw and defiantly insist: "You will have my brothers' room. Not another word about it. The weather's warm — they'll take the hayloft, where they slept as children. It's settled."

So Karl and Diederick move into the boys' room. The third German billets elsewhere, and the Armonds will never see him again. He's the first of many nameless Nazis. The two Armond brothers are exiled to the creaky, cantilevered sheep barn, which is fine with Fiji, who's nearly eighteen and more than ready to get out of his parents' house. On his birthday he plans to join the French army. But sixteen-year-old Michel is annoyed. He doesn't mind sleeping in the barn, but he's angry that France's defeat should also dictate his family's humiliation. Michel would prefer to stand tall before the invaders and show himself worthy of respect. Karl and his buddy Diederick are just a few years older than he is, and so impeccably trained. They're not admirable, these Nazis, nor enviable, but they *are* impressive.

ON THE FIRST MORNING after the invasion, at the large farm table in the Armond kitchen, Michel laces his school shoes while his twin, Virginie, sips absently at a café. Virginie does everything absently. She is always elsewhere, but Michel serves as her earthly tether, grabbing on to her skirts or a hair ribbon, keeping his sister with him. The twins look young for sixteen, but especially Virgie. Known as delicate, touched, *troublée,* ethereally beautiful Virgie is not quite of this world. Think Gene Tierney in *Tobacco Road* — that kind of beauty.

Bernadette, on the other hand — thirteen, the baby of the family, her chair at present pushed back from the table while Idette roughly plaits her hair — Bena looks like Idette: solid, short-waisted, scowling. No one could blame her just now — Idette would have done better dehorning goats or castrating cattle than braiding girls' hair — but Bena's scowl is perpetual, and an accurate representation of her general disposition. Gnawing bread as Idette braids, Bena looks like she has to restrain herself from taking a bite of her mother's yanking hand.

Idette inventories the kitchen. *"Où est Fiji?"* she asks. Fiji, her eldest, she named Jean, like his father — Père Jean and Fils Jean, Johns father and son — and over time "Fils Jean" has become "Fiji." And it's Fiji who's conspicuously absent from the breakfast table this morning. Idette jerks Bena's braid, repeats her question, *"Où est ton frère?"* And when Bena mumbles, "With the guests," Idette slaps the girl's head, snaps, "Don't be smart," as the shop door jangles open, although it's not Fiji coming in but Père Jean Armond, up and out early, just returning now. Idette eyes him: he's pleased, self-satisfied, waving a sheaf of papers.

"Advertising!" is his answer to the question she's not asked. His eyes are a-twinkle. He's as jolly as Père Noël, casting about, saying, "Now, who's got a café for old Papa?"

Mignon obliges, tying on an apron over her frock, a smart, starched dress with a Peter Pan collar. It belongs to her mother. So do the shoes—a size 37, though Mignon takes a 39.

"*Si jolie,*" Jean says, noticing her pumps and stockings. "What's the occasion?"

"We'll be expecting new customers, won't we?" Mignon sets to making coffee. The invasion's brought out the adult in her: she feels like the woman of the house today.

"Indeed!" Jean cries, snatching up his daughter's hand to twirl her around. The invasion's turned him into bloody Dick Van Dyke, the twinkle-toed tailor of rue des Brebis!

So Mignon and Jean are dancing in the kitchen when Fiji and the Germans appear at the back door. Fiji pushes to the table to saw hefty slices off the bread loaf and Frisbee them to his buddies, and Karl and Diederick catch their breakfasts with the easy grace of natural sportsmen.

"*Du café?*" Fiji calls, and his pals nod greedily.

"Don't forget your father!" calls Père Jean, and there's the clang of the door again as he lets himself out, tub of paste in one hand, flyers in the other, a brush clenched in his teeth.

For Idette, that's it, she's had quite enough of this mayhem. She wants everyone out of her kitchen, now. She wants silence. With one hand she hoists Bena up by the braid and shoos the twins with the other. "Off to school!" she cries, then turns on Fiji: "Look at you!" He's in old work clothes, his hair flecked with straw. "Get dressed," she orders him. "You'll be late."

"I'm not going," Fiji says, scrounging in a cupboard so he doesn't have to face her.

Idette's voice pitches up: "Jean-Paul Armond!"

"Maman," he says, impertinent, "there are things more important than school right now."

At first Idette doesn't understand. "Mignon's here with us— you'll help at the shop after school, as always." She nearly apologizes; he was only being thoughtful.

Except he wasn't. "Maman, not the shop, the situation. In V——bourg."

She softens—such patriotism! "I think the *gendarmes* have this in hand, Fiji," she chides, uncharacteristically playful for Idette, especially with Nazis in her kitchen.

But to Fiji this is no playful matter. He's furious with his mother, mortified to be treated like a schoolchild in front of the soldiers. Livid, feeling infantilized, Fiji storms from the house.

When he's gone, Idette turns to the Germans, palms up as if in surrender. "Children!" she cries, as if these two weren't children themselves. All of them, children!

Fiji doesn't go to school that day, or any other, ever again. Truth be told, in the midst of an invasion, school's a bit of a farce. Teachers duck out to whisper portentously in the hall. Students huddle in groups, sniffling like mourners at a wake. Some stand by the windows, just out of sight, to watch, for the school sits on a rise at the edge of town, and from the classroom window Michel can see the Nazis' horses in V——bourg's yards. He watches a soldier behind the Thibauts' currying a chestnut mare, rubbing vigorously at the beast's velvet flanks with a kind of maternal affection—not that Michel knows much of it. Idette's smacks don't count.

Lycée pupils are sent home for lunch, and the three youngest Armond siblings make their usual way along the cobbled streets, past Chez Sylvie where the outdoor tables spill over with Nazis enjoying the midday sun and the swishing legs of young French girls. Of course it's Virginie's beauty that first excites the men's desire, but when they find themselves invisible in her faraway gaze they turn to Bena, who's not unattractive; she has Virgie's golden-lit hair and peachy smooth skin. But Bena's squat, barrel-bodied, a spark plug of a girl, though she's becoming a busty little thing, an early bearer of breasts she's still not wholly sure what to do with. Suffice it to say the German soldiers do not share her ambivalence. Her scowl isn't pretty, but there's a challenge in it these Nazis may enjoy. It's what they expected from the French: resistance. The army didn't put up any, but now here's Bena, atoning for France's supplication with that pouty glare of hers. However she intends it, whatever she may be feeling inside, it's a look that reads one way to the German army. To them she's saying, *I bet you think you can fuck me,* and they're saying, *You bet right.* They're saying, "Mademoiselles!" Calling out from their café tables, tripping over themselves to stand, to make room. *"Bitte,"* they shout, pulling out chairs, *"nehmen Sie Platz!" "Ah-say-eh-vouz!" "Jolie, belle. Du bist sehr hübsch."*

When the Armonds reach home and everyone's seated at the table for lunch, Virginie, unusually talkative, thinks aloud about the soldiers in town. "I felt like a ball on a billiard table," she says, but if it's amusement she's feeling, she's misunderstood, as usual. Jean Armond reprimands Michel for not taking proper care of his sister. Idette scolds Bena, for why should Michel take the flak when there's another competent child to blame? Mignon soothes Virgie, although Virgie's not distraught, while Michel fumes at everyone's unfailing inability to understand Virgie. He's most upset with Idette, though, for her unconscionable, relentless cruelty to Bena. And this—Michel's anger on her behalf—might be the greatest kindness Bena knows.

WHEN KARL PERLMUTTER finishes his lunch at Chez Sylvie—*jambon, fromage, tarte Tatin*—he lays some marks on the table, bids his friends *"Guten Tag,"* and walks to rue des Brebis. Not the most central location, but if you're the only tailor in town . . . The German army has indeed found the Tailleur Armond. Peering in from the street, Karl sees soldiers pressing their bundled, soiled clothes—the shop must smell rank as a bathhouse—over the counter to Jean, who's gladhanding away, obsequious and inefficient. But Karl doesn't see Mignon. The sun on his back is unpleasantly hot, and he quits rue des Brebis for a smaller, perpendicular lane, which he follows, alert for a chance to cut over, maybe approach the Armonds' from the back. Sticking close to the buildings, he catches sight of a depression in the wall, a shallow arched alcove that contains a door, narrow as a broom closet's. He shouldn't be surprised when the handle turns; the Germans have yet to discover a door locked to them in all of France. Slipping through, he finds himself in a tight, shaded alley, but it soon opens into a grassy lane, and there, up ahead, is the Armond barn. He strides on with casual assurance, as if he walks this path every day.

The barn isn't so decrepit from this angle, causing Karl a pang of fear, imagining the trouble he'll face should the wrong person discover he's billeted himself and Diederick in a house with a perfectly good horse barn while several higher-ups are sleeping half a mile from their own mounts. The property is fenced and further fortified by overgrown shrubs; there's no way into the yard but through the house in front or the barn in back. But to get into the barn, Karl sees only one hayloft window, twenty feet up. Above that, the roof's ridgepole extends out a good meter, but there's no hay pulley, just a single rope looped far from Karl's reach. He notices a low corner of the barn where the land has eroded from the foundation posts and left an opening where he might squeeze through. He stretches out on the ground and works his head up to the barn floor, crab-scuffling himself in. His eyes adjust: Fiji and Michel's makeshift bed of quilts thrown over old hay bales.

There are any number of tactical, militarily defensible reasons for Karl Perlmutter to inspect the Armonds' hayloft. None apply here. He goes partly out of curiosity: Mignon said the boys would sleep up in the loft, but they've made their bed on the lower level, and Karl wonders why. Mostly, though, he wonders if there might be a private spot up there, on a pile of soft, sweet-musty straw, where he might lie with Mignon Armond and draw her body to his own.

Karl mounts the hayloft ladder, the temperature rising with every rung. At the top, the air's almost too pulpy to breathe. It's not for laziness that the boys are sleeping downstairs; the hayloft is unbearably hot. On the far wall is a painting—a trompe l'oeil of a window, Karl thinks, until he realizes it *is* a window, the one he saw from below, its frame curtained in dusty spider webs. Back at home in Bavaria, the attic has windows at either end, for cross-ventilation, so Karl crosses the loft and finds the hidden window, but it's stuck shut. He'll need a crowbar.

Recalling a spigot he'd seen by the house, Karl descends and goes to it, splashing his face with an abandon probably unbecoming a Nazi soldier. Then he enters the house through the back door. Mignon is there, busily attending to customers, arguing in a jumble of French and German, but she sees Karl and says, *"Excusez-moi,"* turns her back on the crowd, and leaves the shop to Jean and Fiji.

Karl needs a crowbar, but does not have the words. *"J'ai besoin d'un . . . Brecheisen?"* He mimes its use, though he could well be shoveling coal or spearfishing. "To lift? A tool, for lift?"

"Ah!" Mignon cries. *"Une pince à levier!"* Delighted, she pivots Karl around and takes his arm. "And it is for . . . ?" she asks, as if he might have sly and sexy plans for this crowbar.

Embarrassed by his undeniably sexy plans, he admits, "To open the hayloft window."

"Oh, you're sweet," she exclaims, "thinking of the boys."

Karl doesn't understand, and then he does. "Well, we have displaced them, so . . ." But lying to her is awful, and he vows: never again.

No crowbar, but they do unearth a screwdriver, a hammer, and a file. "I'll go try it, then," Karl says, expecting Mignon will return to the shop. But she makes no move to leave, and when he starts for the ladder, she follows. He takes a few rungs, then glances back: she's slipping off her shoes, steadying herself with one hand to unclip and unroll her stockings. She mounts the ladder. The sight of her nakedly vulnerable feet on the rough floor of the loft dizzies Karl. *"Attention,"* he warns, but doesn't know "splinter" in French, and she only smiles, saying, "We walked all over here as children. I'm tough," though her feet look anything but tough. They look terribly tender, little plumps of his mutti's doughy spaetzle, yet she walks about, clearing cobwebs while Karl wrestles the window. With much prying and levering, it opens, letting in a paltry breeze.

Mignon says, "I should get back," but her reluctance to leave him is plain.

"May I see you again?" Karl asks. "Soon?"

"Tonight," she offers eagerly. "We could go to the movies tonight."

He clenches in regret. "We have a . . . there's . . . I don't know what time I'll be free."

But she's got it figured. "I'll wait here, in the hayloft, just before eight. Come, if you can."

He agrees, then remembers what it took to get into the barn. "But how will I . . . ?" He doesn't need to finish; she's already got this answer, too, is treading those sweet bare feet toward the open window. "There used to be . . ." She braces against the frame, cranes up. "Aha!" Fetching a stick of wood, Mignon pokes at something, then snags it—the rope he saw from below! She corrals it in, checks its integrity. "We used it to sneak out as kids." It's knotted with loops —footholds. It is, he can see now, a ladder.

"Where did you sneak?" Karl asks hesitantly.

Mignon laughs. "Nowhere! Just plotting escapes, how we'd run away. You must have . . ."

Karl shakes his head. "It was just me and my mutti. I couldn't run away."

"Just you and your mother?"

"My father died before I was born. We own an inn, in Bavaria. We run it. I help her."

Mignon's forehead creases in sad sympathy. "She must miss you so."

Karl thinks his mutti's sanity may well depend on pretending she never had a son in the first place, but for now he keeps this to himself.

When the children return to school after lunch, Monsieur le Proviseur turns them away. The Germans have discovered the building's strategic perch: the high school is going to be Nazi HQ! Of course, it wouldn't be proper to toss schoolkids into the street, so the Feldkommandant dispatches men to find a new lycée, and this is how the children of V——bourg come to be educated in the cinema. Relocation begins that day, Nazis scurrying like worker ants with books, papers, chalkboards, and it's not until everything's moved, spilling from the concession stand onto the street, that anyone thinks to ask where the school offices will go. The students themselves need about every inch of the *ciné,* so where will they put the principal, the records? Chez Sylvie is out of the question—the Germans need a place to eat and drink, don't they? And the *boucherie,* the *crèmerie,* they can't be moved just like that—you can't just string up a ham anywhere. Scouts take off around a corner and find a bookshop. The proprietor's name is spelled in peeling letters beneath an old iron knocker; eyebrows are raised, glances exchanged. A young soldier from Munich takes hold of the knocker and raps with authority, and a warbling elderly voice calls out as if from deep in a cave, *"Oui? Qui est là?"*

The Münchner tries the door—locked—and another soldier tries the window. It, too, is fastened from inside. "Either of you have any French?" They shake their heads no: *Why the hell would we want to speak French?* The Münchner bangs again, angry now: Jewish name on the plaque, locked doors and windows. Why must they make things difficult? In German he says, "This is the authorities. You must open the door."

Perhaps the bookseller *does* understand and simply does not do as he's ordered. *"Je ne peux pas bouger!"* he calls feebly—but is it true frailty or affectation? *"Je suis un inferme!"* And he may be an invalid for all they know, but the language gap only makes them shout louder: *"Aufmachen!"* They hammer the door. *"Aufmachen, alter Jude!"* Is he an "old Jew"? He sells books, *reads* books, keeps to himself . . . Perhaps the Germans eject him simply because he's old and sick and they need a place to put the school secretary and the spare chalk. Who'll miss him? Who buys books during an invasion? This is how war goes: one day there's a bookstore, the next a principal's office. *Wasn't there once a bookshop here? What happened to that old man? You don't think he was . . . ? A Jew? You think he fled? Did the Germans send him packing? To the next town, or the next life? Maybe he had family nearby. I don't think he had family. Everyone has family. Maybe he'll come back . . . They can't stay forever, can they?*

JUST BEFORE EIGHT that evening, Mignon hurries up the hayloft ladder to find Karl below the window, testing the rope. They speak at the same time—"The cinema's closed"—and then laugh. Karl assures her it will reopen soon; Mignon will believe *that* when she sees it. "It will," Karl says. "Our Feldkommandant likes his flickers." Maybe it's the way they're positioned—Mignon at the hay window like Juliet on her balcony—but she feels like a character in a play when she says, "I will see you whenever I am able," her words flowing involuntarily, as if she's powerless against this truth. "Since we met, it's all I want." She draws back, arms crossed protectively at her chest, but all fear evaporates when Karl says, "You've changed everything." He reaches for her, and she for him, but their fingers are nowhere near touching.

AS HE'S LEAVING rue des Brebis, Karl runs into Fiji, who invites him to the bar. Steamy with anger, Fiji wants to talk: the problem is his mother. "She thinks this will all blow over, that we'll look back and say, Remember we thought there'd be a war?" He snorts at her ignorance.

At the pub, the two meet Diederick, and when they return to

chez Armond that night, all three are blotto. But there's no scene, no drunken fracas or slapstick tripping over chairs, none of that. The billeted Germans collapse in their beds, and Fiji drags himself to the barn, where he falls to the hay beside Michel to sleep it off.

THE FOLLOWING EVENING at eight, the movie house not yet re-opened, Karl climbs the knotted rope to the hayloft and, like a mir-acle, not a minute later, Mignon rushes up the ladder, and they fall together: a *pince à levier* couldn't pry them apart. He's trembling, she is too, and also crying. His hands rise to her face, tilt it up to his own. *"Oh, mein Liebling,"* he whispers. *"Meine Süße, meine Liebe."* He kisses her tears—*"Oh, meine Liebe"*—then his mouth is at her mouth, lips to her wet lips, trembling, quivering there together.

A sob catches in Mignon's throat. "My mother is furious . . . all day . . . so very angry!"

"What, what, *meine Liebe?* What—why? Why is she angry?"

"Fiji. That Fiji . . . that he went . . . with you, drinking."

But Karl can only think: *If she's furious with her son for drinking with Germans, what of her daughter, here, in a German's arms?*

"It's the drinking," Mignon says. "I think"—oh, it's too preposter-ous!—"she likes you. But Fiji's quit school." And while Idette thinks well of Karl, and a week ago might even have thrilled at his attentions to Mignon, now things have changed. Karl is the enemy.

The Germans occupy V——bourg for another week, then move on—Diederick's so eager to take Paris, he can barely keep his pants up. Karl, though, would rather turn in his uniform, forget the army, stay in V——bourg the rest of his life with Mignon. There's a gruel-ing goodbye; the men get little warning, just an order to move out. Minutes before departure, he finds Mignon, promises to write, to re-turn, and then he's gone, a heartsick Nazi off to seize Paris.

They take the city streets without a fight; the citizens simply evac-uate. Another prime minister has already resigned; France is running through leaders like undershirts, the government decamping and relocating like a band of wayward gypsies when Philippe Pétain assumes the helm. Eighty-four years old and a hero of the Great War, Pétain's a trusty anti-Semite with a fascistic bent that endears him to the Nazis. He's also a comfort to the French: in V——bourg, they're relieved to be in the hands of an honored father figure. So what if he's ancient and senile. As the Americans will one day love Reagan, the French love Pétain like a grandfather, love him for the swaggering bigot he is. Oh, will humans ever tire of paternal, self-righteous leadership by dilettante pricks?

Out of the gate, Pétain surrenders to Hitler, veritably leaping to autograph an armistice that lops France in half: the north and the western Atlantic coast will be German-occupied; the south, unoccupied, will be governed by Pétain and his crony cabinet from a new seat in the resort town of Vichy. In the south, the Germans will mostly leave the French alone, but up north, by German-annexed Alsace-Lorraine, Nazi resistance and collaboration will walk hand in hand.

In V——bourg, on rue des Brebis, thanks to Jean's enthusiastic cooperation, the Armonds will run a tailor shop/laundry/canteen/boardinghouse/information center/café, and the Nazi occupation will treat his family very nicely indeed. For a time. It seems that Jean is modeling his gracious hospitality on Pétain's back-bending acquiescence to the Germans, but complicity can't go on without consequences, whether immediate or eventual. Great Britain, for one, severs diplomatic ties with Pétain and refuses to recognize him as the leader of France, but the Armonds' comeuppance won't come until later. These early months of occupation are in fact ones the Armonds will look back on somewhat fondly. There's a war on, yes, and they're running a Nazi hostel, but nothing's *that* bad. Supply and commerce routes are interrupted, and local farmers can't export their goods, but there's plenty to eat in V——bourg: cream, butter, meat. Even when Pétain enacts his anti-Semitic laws there's no real alarm, since there aren't any Jews in V——bourg, are there? *Whatever* did *happen to that old bookseller? Was he a Jew? Really?* When the radio trumpets Vichy's

slogans—*France is strong! Vive la France!*—in the announcer's confident baritone it sounds like good news.

Good news? Great Britain begs to differ. Like those less obliging
to the Germans, Britain clings to one great hope for Nazi resistance
in France: General Charles de Gaulle, de facto leader of the Free
French. De Gaulle sees through Pétain's congenial façade, recognizes
Pétain's government for the Nazi pawn it is. The Armonds must
know of de Gaulle, right? The man's in charge of a government in
exile, commander of the resistance. He's got fugitive cells scattered
throughout the country in both the unoccupied, French-governed
south and the Nazi-occupied north. There may well be Gaullists in
V——bourg for all the Armonds know. If they're listening to the radio or watching newsreels at the cinema, they're getting all propaganda, all the time. But there are dissenters, French men and women
who are mortified on their country's behalf. In 1940, France has two
governments, each convinced of the other's illegitimacy. Even if the
people of V——bourg know of de Gaulle, should they pledge him
their allegiance? For ordinary French citizens just trying to survive
the war, the right choice—that's to say the left choice, to oppose the
Nazis and their puppet, Pétain; the "right" choice as seen from the
bird's eye of retrospect—is not an easy choice. The right choice will
not keep their children fed, their families alive. The right choice is
dangerous. France's seemingly irrepressible national pride is already
crippled by national humiliation. Shame and terror: that's France,
circa 1940.

Now, like in an old movie, it's the old flying-calendar-pages trope.
Watch the calendar nailed to the wall of the Tailleur Armond. A
fierce wind blows through the shop, tearing off pages, day by day
until the wind dies and we understand that it's now the summer of
1941. More than a year after Karl Perlmutter left to take Paris, he's
welcomed back at the Armonds'. Just him this time, and he refuses
to take the boys' room; *he* will stay in the barn. Idette prepares linens

for a hay pallet, as good as making the bed for her Mignon's deflowering. In the stifling heat of the hayloft, Karl and Mignon make love, and once they're past the first-time fear and pain and awkwardness, nothing can stop them. They've been apart a year, and God knows when they'll meet again. Propriety's irrelevant. Pétain's decrees be damned. They have just a few days.

Lying on the quilt, entwined despite the heat, they talk not of war, but of Mignon's family, the deepening discord between Jean and Idette. Michel is yet angrier, Virginie more muddled, more dependent on her twin. Bena's ever petulant, taking everything personally: *I don't like how that soldier looked at me. The butcher skimped on our ration.*

Karl laughs softly, face shiny with sweat in the moonlight. "And Fiji? He's been cold . . ."

"He *has* been different since you're here," Mignon admits. "I think it's jealousy. He's a kid, living with his parents. You're the soldier he wants to be."

"Well, I'm jealous of him, too," Karl says. "To have spent a whole life with you . . ."

They gaze up in the dark, old barn, moonlight shining in the roof cracks like stars. Then Mignon begins to speak. "Some years ago, we had a hole in the roof. In the house, in the girls' room. It was just mice, but Virgie was terrified. Of the hole, not the mice. She was scared to sleep. Papa said *ridiculous,* but Virgie couldn't sleep until he fixed it. The hole wasn't big, but Virgie stayed awake guarding it. She thought it would suck her away. *The earth is so tiny, floating in nothing,* she said, *eternal nothing."* Mignon's quiet, and Karl waits for her to go on. "When Maman saw Virgie, gaunt, dark under her eyes, she told Papa, *Fix it,* so he patched the hole. *I know I only fool myself,* Virgie said, *but the roof —it's all there is keeping us here.* And Michel, I think. Michel binds her to this life, holds her here."

Karl takes Mignon in his arms and, sweat-slick, they cling to each other, Karl whispering, "I will hold you here," and there they stay until Mignon must go back to the shop to work.

EARLIER THAT SUMMER, and with great enthusiasm, Jean Armond joined La Légion Française des Combattants, Pétain's coalition of veterans. Pétain says France's 1940 defeat was the result of bourgeois egotism; the French have grown soft, vulnerable to Bolshevism. His answer? National revolution! Jean pledges fealty to the Victor of Verdun, takes Pétain's oaths — self-sacrifice before pleasure, country over self — and swears to follow blindly and unconditionally wherever the Marshal shall lead. Such is apparently a Frenchman's duty. A new European order is coming — led by Germany, yes, but Jean Armond won't see France left behind. Idette accuses him of Nazism. Jean parrots Vichy's slogans in reply: "Neither right nor left, straight ahead with the Marshal." This evening he's brought home a framed photo of Pétain for the mantel, and as Mignon's reentering the house from her assignation in the barn, she hears her parents arguing. It seems Idette has caught Jean talking to the photo — "With the Légion, for France" — and saluting his leader, and Mignon hears Idette scoff, "Why not add a *Heil Hitler* for good measure?" so she slips upstairs, out of her parents' fray. There's something she wants to find up there. It's not like she can't hear the whole fight anyway.

If Jean Armond ever had a sense of humor, he's surrendered it. "I'm not German and do not hail their Führer. My wife should watch her tongue. What if Karl heard you speak like this?"

Idette says nothing. Bena's listening silently from the kitchen sink. But Fiji, at the table drinking coffee, can keep quiet no longer. He should've been off fighting six months ago, but under the armistice France can no longer keep a standing army of any size. There's no place for him. "Hitler will be everyone's leader soon enough," he says now, and what emerges in response from Idette is a hiss so feral it sounds like it's come from Chou-Chou. Fiji looks at her with pity and loathing, his tone as patronizing as his father's but with the force of a young man's grievous self-righteousness. He spits words like automatic gunfire: "You stupid, blind, ignorant cow."

For this, apparently, Jean will not stand. "Never speak to your mother that way."

Fiji, a machine gun on trigger lock, turns on his father. "You," he growls. "You think your Marshal's going to save the day with his revolution? He's no better than the ones who handed France over. Go on with your 'We must all think and act French,' just like the Marshal says. You will die in the hole our pitiful leaders have dug. Pledging allegiance to fools—you're worse than she is!" Fiji can't look at Idette. "Even *she* knows the Marshal's a joke. Hitler's played Vichy. He *will* be Europe's leader. You think he cares for your Victor of Verdun?" Fiji pauses to breathe, but then gives up. What's left to argue? They won't be moved, and he's got more important battles to fight—on the side of the real victor. He turns and storms out of the shop.

As it happens, Karl's just come down from the hayloft when Fiji charges out the back door. "My parents are fools, clinging to shreds of a dying France!" He pushes Karl back to the barn, slumps to the wall, and sinks, forehead to palm, beleaguered-Hollywood-cowboy style. "I have to get away from this place—and don't tell me to go work in Germany. I'm not a slave!"

"It's not so bad." But Karl has no idea how it is in the labor camps, though he can guess.

"I want to fight," Fiji says. "I want to be a soldier."

"It's not impossible, you know. There's the Légion des Volontaires Français . . ."

Fiji scowls. "My father's in it. You've got to be a veteran."

"You're mistaken," Karl tells him. "The LVF is for young men. Very selective. Elite." The boy perks up at this, like Chou-Chou leaping at a dangled string. "Boys can sign up in Paris."

And Fiji's on his feet, headed fifteen directions at once. "But I have to get to Paris!"

He could let Fiji stew—make him scamper to find a ride or set out on foot—but he sees Mignon coming down the moonlit path from the house, and Karl wants him gone. "We're headed there," he says, as if offhandedly. "When we leave here, in a few days. You might tag along." Fiji's visible lust is discomfiting, but Karl goes on. "Talk to our Feldkommandant at the old school. Tell him I sent you." Gaining a recruit will speak well of Karl. "And I'd go quickly." Karl knows any young man left in V——bourg's going to want to leave with the Germans. At this point, who wouldn't want to join the LVF? Better than a work camp, which is where everyone else is going. Except Mignon: Karl's determined to see her spared. And her sisters, too, if he can.

Fiji takes off as Mignon approaches bearing the thing she was searching for upstairs, a photograph she's handing now to Karl. "So you can know the little girl . . ." She points: "Me, and Virgie there, and little scowling Bena." Karl shakes his head, smiling: of course he knows who's who! Three girls in ruffles and ribbons, but he can already see the adults they'll become, peering up at the photographer, Mignon invitingly, Virginie lost, Bena with absolute disdain.

"There's a photo studio in V——bourg?" Karl asks, full of sudden hope.

"No," Mignon says, "a photographer came through once. But you take this. You keep it."

"But surely your mother—?"

"Couldn't care less. She'd say, You're right here, what do I need with a photograph?"

Karl squints, seeming not to understand. But he does, terribly well: not one photo exists of his own father. His mutti burned them all, but Karl's always thought this a unique perversity.

Mignon's still speaking: "And if she were to lose one of us, she'd act as if we'd never been born at all. When I was a little girl," she tells Karl, "a woman came to see us, someone Maman grew up with here—she'd moved away, returned to visit. We were introduced, and the woman said, *Of course, named for Idette's poor, dear sister.* And I thought, *Maman had a sister?* I never knew this! Maman became churlish, as good as sent the woman away. I was four, maybe. My parents called me Mignon as a pet name, but after that day I was only Mignon. Papa told me Maman's sister had died as a child. I was named Hazelle, for her, but we would never use that name again. I think now she's forgotten I wasn't always Mignon. *Zzzzp.* Gone."

If Mignon expects Karl to show surprise, it's she who's made curious by his broad, brimming smile and the wonder in his eyes as he asks, "How have I found you? How am I so lucky to have found you?" He will tell her, then, about his dead, willfully unremembered father, his emotionally spectral mutti, his lonely childhood in the ever-clean inn among revolving guests and strangers. When visitors came with their children, his mutti had him wait on them, and this alone seemed to make her proud: to see her Karl as butler to these young masters, charming as a display of precious miniatures. Otherwise, her son felt he was only a burden, a reminder of her dead husband she could not simply burn. She loved Karl with more reproach than affection.

Now, in the barn, Karl throws his arms around Mignon, kissing her face, her hair, whispering, "I am so lucky, so very lucky, how am I so lucky to have found you?" And as she's kissing him back, she takes his face in her hands, making him focus on her eyes as she says, "We," her mouth forming the word, "we." She says, "*We* are so lucky to have found *each other.*"

THE NEXT DAY, Karl sends a boy with a note for Mignon. Virgie and Bena are ironing, their faces swollen, gray as boiled turnips. Michel and Idette fold sheets; Fiji's fixing a sewing machine, sweat dripping in its guts. Mignon is darning socks when the boy enters. "From Perlmutter," he says, and she sets down her work to fetch him a few sous for his trouble. Such an adult gesture, dropping coins in the lad's palm, and Mignon feels acutely aware of herself as an adult, a relish for which she'll berate herself later: if she'd been humbler, perhaps the note might have contained some frivolity, but she thought, *How lovely to be a woman, to receive a note this way,* and it said: "We leave tomorrow. Tell Fiji, please. Come to the barn tonight."

The day the Germans leave V——bourg is obscenely sunny. Idette does not see the troops off; she learns they are gone from Mignon, who runs in, her hair frizzed to a corona and littered with straw. "You were *out* like this? Before the whole town?" She slaps Mignon's head.

"They're gone," she says, teary-eyed. "They're gone." Mignon's eyes beg Idette to do something motherly, something to spare her child pain. But there's too much pain; no one will be spared.

Idette returns to her kneading—bread from good flour, from Karl—muttering, "About time our lives returned to normal." But as Mignon weeps, Idette begins to rave: "What? Did you imagine he'd stay? Here, with you, in a sheep barn?" The dough's a useful prop; she slams it down. "You think he loves you more than his motherland?" She sneers this—*mother*—a word forever corrupted. "You think a war just disappears? *Poof?*" But wasn't it Idette who thought the war might just *poof* away? When Idette retreats to prayer, that old standby, who can judge her? Who can blame her for seeking comfort wherever she might find it?

Karl takes two things of the Armonds' with him when he leaves. In his breast pocket, near his heart, he keeps the photo from Mignon. He gets some lewd comments when he's caught gazing at little girls in christening gowns, but he doesn't care. He has one goal: return to Mignon.

The second thing he takes isn't a thing, it's Fiji. In a borrowed uniform that'll serve until he joins a battalion and gets his own, which'll be a German uniform with an armband in the colors of the French flag. Really, he might as well be in the German army. Basically, Fiji's a Nazi.

And the war goes on. Jean's "business" thrives. His new project is rabbits—a food *and* a commodity! Of course, it's the children who tend them. Michel and Virgie take to it naturally, and Bena, naturally, sulks, adding "rabbit husbandry" to the list of things the twins share without her. The three of them go to some semblance of school at the *ciné,* but most of their classmates are off fighting—for the Germans, the resistance, who knows? Mignon and Idette run the shop, and Jean scampers about town, bringing home wine one day, wallpaper the next. For as long as there is thread to be gotten, Virginie stitches, maniacally, until her fingers blister and bleed, a Fate sewing as if the future depends on it. They hear nothing from Fiji. Maybe he's a lousy letter writer or maybe he's dead. Hard to know, since the mail is not what it was. Karl writes on occasion, hastily scribbled missives if he meets someone who will be passing V——bourg, but whenever the shop bell rings, Mignon's sure it's someone come to tell her Karl is dead. She cannot imagine what she will do if he dies. She plugs the hole of that possibility with mending, washing, cooking—she even joins her mother in prayer. At this point, why not?

News flash: PEARL HARBOR ATTACKED! Its meaning for France is unclear. Will they be saved? Bombed? No one's sure. French resistance grows, but so does the Gestapo. The Germans stiffen laws; so it goes. Then, in April 1942, the Franco-German ceasefire is repealed. All France is now occupied France. Frightening rumors circulate, about prisoners, about camps. June brings announcement of the *Relève:* French POWs will be released in exchange for French volunteers to work in Germany. But here's the thing: no sane person will volunteer to board a German-bound train in the summer of '42. They've heard about the Jews, rounded up, herded aboard like cattle, never seen again. A little *chug-chug toot-toot* off to Germany? Thank you, no.

Then the terms of the *Relève* tighten further: all men aged eighteen to fifty and unmarried women from twenty-one to thirty-five will be shuttled off to Germany whether they "volunteer" or not, with the French police under orders to enforce the new laws. So, like everything else in this corrupt world, the *Relève* functions on exemptions and allowances. Those with money can fight or flee the edicts, but the poor, say, or the politically unconnected? Too bad. Off to Germany—that's the law! Jean Armond appeals to the Feldkommandant, with whom he's done much business and played plenty of cards these past two years. He requests exemption for himself, Mignon, and Michel. He comes home apoplectic with rage, spinning in circles, slamming the table. "I've welcomed them in my home! My son is in their army! And this is my thanks? These are their manners?"

"Manners?" shrieks Idette. "A war, occupation, and you want *manners?*"

Jean's face vibrates like a cartoon character who's swallowed TNT. "There is a right way and a wrong—" And just then, Chou-Chou, with keen comic timing, hacks a hairball at his feet.

Idette rails: "And you expect the enemy to conduct their affairs in the *right* way?"

"How dare you?" He's speaking to Idette but looking to Pétain on the mantel. What can a woman know? She's never seen combat, death. "You know as much of war as this cat!" he cries, then kicks Chou-Chou and stomps in the puddle of vomit. It sends him sprawling across the kitchen like a vaudevillian on a banana peel. Virginie soars to the cat's rescue.

"Papa," Mignon pleads, "what happened? What did they say?"

"'Your cooperation will be rewarded. Your daughter may work for the cause in France.'"

Trembling, clutching the cat like a live grenade, Virginie cries, "And Michel?"

"They'll send back a prisoner of war," Jean offers lamely. At this, Virgie crumples, nearly smothering Chou-Chou, who struggles to free himself, claws tearing at Virgie's arms and chest. She doesn't even notice; Mignon will point out the raised welts later. But there's more comeuppance yet to come: as payback for Jean's impertinence to request *Relève* exemption at all, the Germans take over the business. Jean and Michel are deported to German work camps, and in

V——bourg, Idette and the girls become unpaid employees in their own shop, servants in their own home, the kitchen occupied day and night by Nazis, eating, drinking, carousing, and flirting—shamelessly, viciously—with the Armond girls. One of whom wears an engagement ring she claims is a German officer's, and another who's young and sour, but comely, too, in a nasty-ish way. The third's a beauty, indeed, but also crazy: woo-woo-batso as a syphilitic whore.

SEATED ON CRATES they haven't yet used for fuel, Mignon begs Virgie to eat something, but she pushes away the bread, instead reaches to stroke her sister's face, as though it's Mignon to whom the current situation must be explained. Virgie learned of the short rations allotted *Relève* workers in Germany and will not eat a crumb more herself until every worker is returned. She's in slow-motion decay. No thread left for stitching, her bony fingers go now to her hair, feeling for a patch she's clawed to stubble. She doesn't know she's doing it, but cannot stop from finding a strand to twist and wrap around a purpling fingertip until the hair breaks and she can roll it off and tuck it in her apron. It's like she's trying to collect enough to weave hair socks for a POW.

Wearily, Mignon rises to refill the Germans' cups. Steeped toasted acorns, chicory, and twigs are what passes now for coffee. For a time the Nazis stocked the tailor shop, but no one can ensure supplies anymore. Trade is interminably slow; mail, too. Mignon still writes letters, but Michel has been relocated several times—separated from Jean early on, probably for the best, his chances better on his own—and who knows if the letters arrive. She also writes to Karl in hopes he might help return her father and brother to France. And to the German authorities, as "the fiancée of Officer Karl Perlmutter." She's even bartered herself an "engagement ring" to serve her story.

If only to escape the stifling shop, Bena continues at school. Mornings, she escapes without a word, just the door's *clang-clang*. The chime alerts Virginie, who trails Bena out, though she doesn't go to school, just wanders, truant, twisting off her hair, while Bena is escorted to the lyceé by a rotating throng of Nazis. She doesn't thrill at their attentions, but it's bitter cold and the soldiers do make something of a wind block. She's hardly out the door when a pasty one approaches to say, "I accompany you." It's a statement, not a question. Then another joins him, asking, by way of conversation, "Mademoiselle, what do you go to study in the school?"

Though she'd rather hunch against the cold, Bena walks tall. "Oh," she says, "navigation, riflery, bomb-making." The boys laugh unconvincingly. Bena wishes she weren't kidding. They round a corner, whipped by a staggering wind. Bena knows this route in any weather and turns to walk backward, calling, "If you can't stand the wind, how will you fare against the Allies?"

"By killing them!" They laugh, the wind pulling ghoulishly at their open mouths.

"Mademoiselle," calls a new boy, "may I get you a coffee? Something to warm you up?"

"I know what'll warm her up!" shouts another.

"There is no coffee," Bena retorts, "only chicory tea, and I'd rather suck a twig."

"Suck *my* twig, Mademoiselle!"

"That's all you've got, a twig. Come to my forest, Miss Armond. I'll show you a tree!"

Beneath the movie theater marquee, Bena faces the boys with cutting rectitude. "If one of you got me a real coffee, you never know what might happen." She pushes into the schoolhouse.

When she leaves again, hours later, to go home for lunch, she makes sure to pass the window at Chez Sylvie slowly enough that some German will have time to jump from his table, run to the door, and shout out into the cold: "Hey, cutie! *Schnuckiputzi,* come share a bite with a soldier." He's speaking German, but what's not to understand? "There, that's not so bad, eh? I'm a good guy. What's your name? Bernadette? Pretty. Sylvie, something for Miss Bernadette!"

Sylvie's got teenage daughters herself and, in French the Kraut can't understand, asks Bena, "He bothering you, sweetie?" But Bena's been picked on by Idette far too long to fathom kindness from a woman that age and only shakes her head, says, "I'll have soup."

Sipping Sylvie's watery potato broth—the German marveling so, you'd think he's never seen a girl eat soup—Bena senses something outside the window, someone else watching, and lifts her head from the soup bowl to see a woman wrapped in shawls, a tattered blanket around her shoulders, face nearly hidden in scarves. Then the woman lifts her chin, and she is Idette, and when she commences shouting, Bena lifts the bowl with two hands, drains it, and—cheeks ballooned with broth—grabs her coat. Swallowing, pulling on mittens, she joins Idette on the sidewalk. Embarrassing, but better than sitting with a chatty Kraut. Bena thanks her maman.

"Don't be smart, you. Don't even talk to me!"

"I wasn't . . . He made me sit with him, Maman. What should I have done? I was hungry."

"*Made* you! There's lunch at home. Don't make excuses." Idette drags Bena by the sleeve, saying, "I won't lose another child to the Germans." But when they're halfway down the block Bena asks, "Maman, *quelle heure?* I'm due back at school. The others can eat a bit more today." Idette drops Bena's arm and walks on. Bena ducks back into the theater, where she'll sit in a creaking seat, shut her eyes, and hope that if the bombers come they won't aim for the *ciné.*

ALLIES LAND AT NORMANDY; INVASION BEGINS ON FRENCH COAST. When word reaches V——bourg, celebrations don't quite break out in the streets, and there's no dancing down rue de la Ville, but there are private gatherings, toasts—*To the Allies! Vive la France!* Though Sylvie's still waiting on Nazis at the café, and they continue to occupy the Armonds' shop, at a farmhouse on the outskirts of town, in a near-empty root cellar, young people go and rejoice, drinking and dancing deep into the June night. Bena sneaks out—a boy she knows has a bicycle, and lets her ride the handlebars out to the party in the countryside, where they drink to freedom, and Bena and the boy—or another boy, any boy—climb from the cellar, wander off to a barn, where they'll kiss and tease, Bena and this boy she hardly knows. But Bena swears she won't be like Mignon, copulating in a barn like an animal. She'll do it proper, in a bed. And she won't give it away for free. Her maidenhood is currency she plans to use to escape.

After D Day, liberation takes three long months to reach V—— bourg. June and July are a stalemate in Normandy, Germans holding off the Allies' advance. Finally, in August, defense lines break and rapid progress through France begins, field by bridge by village, road by town by farm. It's all very confusing, too: the French aren't sure if they're still enemy occupied or if they're a nation liberated, and they're not sure who's in charge. Supply channels thwarted, these post-liberation months are the war's hardest yet in V——bourg. The only thing getting through dependably is bad news, nothing stanching its flow at all. News of purges, *"épuration sauvage."* The French government will at some point institute official means of adjudication to hear cases of alleged French-Nazi collaboration, but until tribunals are established it's all happening village by village. A witch-hunt is on. Disenfranchised so long, the French take up the mantle of their pride again, letting loose the anger that's been fermenting four long years. Looking around, they lay eyes on those neighbors who don't seem to have suffered quite so much: shopkeepers who turned profits, women—adolescent and middle-aged, married and widowed, the lovely and the homely, all—who've consorted with the enemy. "Horizontal collaboration," it's called. And depending on how "collaborative" they've been, and with whom, and how often, the women are beaten, flogged, or stoned in the town square. There's talk of public head-shavings. Also executions. Something's needed to lift public morale! The French haven't *won* anything. Sure they're relieved to be rescued, but there's no national victory in which to take pride. Hardly a wonder that they create an enemy within. *These women,* someone cries, *these harlots, turning their tricks against France, traitors to the country, trading on their beauty. Let's see how they feel when we shave off their hair. See how they fare when they aren't so fair . . .*

Still, the bombs keep falling. Then there's this news: Fiji is dead. He's been as good as dead since '41, for all they've known, but now it's official. Word comes via the Nazis, in whose uniform he died. Return of a body's unlikely: with the German army in retreat, fighting is fierce, and no one's going back to claim the dead. The Armonds are lucky they've been notified at all.

By late summer of 1944, V——bourg is teeming with Germans. Haven't been this many in town since '40, only now they're headed east, not staying long enough to so much as launder a shirt. The Nazis are sprinting home to defend their last line at the Western Wall. Months upon months of virtual standstill, and now everything's accelerated, everyone flying backward, like a movie of the past four years on high-speed rewind, V——bourg in a frenzy, all zip and zing, and a bizarre, surreal, collective sense that the war's being taken back, retracting itself, every lost yard regained, each seized bridgehead liberated, every dead soldier resurrected. In a newsreel in reverse, the dead who stand again aren't zombies. They reanimate, reassemble, lost heads recapitating, severed limbs zooming at bodies to reattach. A foot flies from a tree, sails through the air, sweeping up a trail of debris—bone fragments, spattered tissue—and vacuums up its own insides, aims straight for its rightful spot on the end of that leg, pieces slapping together like wet clay, skin smoothed seamless. The man leaps to his feet to test the leg in a backward stride. Good as new! It's the ultimate dream: the do-over, second chance. What's hard to grasp is why they think they'll get it right this time. If you rewind past the mistakes, how do you learn from them? How do you not make the same ones over and over, in repertory, for eternity?

ONE DAY IN AUGUST, Bena's standing by the shop window when she spots a man she recognizes on the street, and something about the familiar face makes her yelp with uncharacteristic glee. It's Karl Perlmutter's Bavarian buddy, Diederick Auslander. The war has not been unkind to him—nothing a hot bath and a good meal won't fix, though the chance of either is slim. Bena cries, "Diederick!" and it's only Mignon's gasp that awakens her to what his arrival might mean.

It's been more than four years since Diederick and Karl billeted here, and he's perhaps worried, as he approaches, that the Armonds' allegiance has shifted over the course of the war. Plenty of French have changed their minds about Germany. Outside, Diederick removes his hat, and Mignon lets out a cry, sinks her head in her hands. She already knows.

He steps inside. At a table, a soldier trimming his nails lets the clippings fall to the floor. In the shop, it's just the two girls. He nods to the young one, identifies himself: "Diederick."

She returns his nod. "Bernadette," she says.

"Bernadette," he repeats. Her countenance unsettles him—a defiance in the eyes, both inviting and dismissive—and he feels an urge to command her, like a Jew. But that can wait. He approaches Mignon, sitting limp in her chair, and she lifts her head in a vain rush of hope: he's here for something else! Needs a shirt ironed, a knee patched, was passing and remembered they were tailors. But Diederick flinches under Mignon's gaze and averts his own. He pats absently at his lapel as if to recall where he put what he's brought for her, as if it's not burning there like an open wound. He sets before Mignon a letter wrapped around the photo of three little girls.

> *My Mignon, If you read this letter, I have not kept alive to return to you. I am sorry. You are the world to me. I wish a swift end to war—whoever the winner—so you and your family may return to your peaceful lives from before we came. I am sorry the strife I brought, and most sorry I cannot make amends. I wish I could had made you my wife and we might could grown old together. I wish my mutti could know the girl I love. I wish so much things. If my*

wish had came true, you would not read this, but you are a wish
that came true. I am your forever — your Karl.

Mignon cannot speak. She cannot look at Diederick Auslander, nor can she breathe. She runs from the shop, through the kitchen, past the table of Germans, and out the back door, down the path, where she walked with Karl that glorious day of the invasion four years ago when the world was so very alive. In the barn, she climbs to the loft and throws herself on the hay, into the crumpled quilt that was theirs together, presses her face in it, grabs up fistfuls and shoves them in her mouth as if to choke herself to death right there. Gagging on cotton and straw, dust filling her eyes and lungs, she retches into that quilt, retches and heaves and screams.

Back at the shop, Bena thinks to offer something to Diederick, but what's left to offer? Herself? "Some tea?" He declines, and removes a flask from a pocket. He sips, then offers it to Bena, who drinks so fast she can't tell what it is. They stand awkwardly: he's tall, Bena squat beside him. He offers again, and she accepts, and drinks in a way she hopes might be suggestive.

He says, "It's been difficult," and she doesn't know if it's a question or a statement, so nods noncommittally, then lifts her eyes to ask, "How —" But his voice is rageful: *"How?"* He'll give her a bloody earful on the difficulty he's endured! Then he understands: she's asking how Karl died, so he drops his head low, but in the time it takes him to lift it to reply, Bena's decided she doesn't want to know. If she doesn't know, she won't have to decide whether to tell Mignon or not. In this moment, Bena's vision narrows drastically: all that matters is that which furthers her escape. This singularity of purpose will be her salvation. And doom her to live out her life.

Diederick takes Bena to lunch. Sylvie does what she can with paltry garden vegetables, a rabbit, an occasional tough rooster. There's wine, if you can afford it, and Diederick orders a bottle as though there's something to celebrate. Bena doesn't refuse. She'll refuse nothing; she'll take what's offered and use it somehow to her advantage. And so they are drinking when suddenly Bernadette leaps up, jostling the table—Diederick steadies the wine—and dashes at someone she's seen: the third sister, Diederick realizes, looking like a beggar-urchin, destitute and pathetic. Observing their gestures, Diederick assumes Bernadette is furious, scolding and ordering her sister away. But before she goes, the wraith lifts her wasted arms and wraps them around Bernadette, who tolerates the embrace, though doesn't hug her sister in return. The girl takes off, tearing past Diederick, her skin pulled taut over her bones as if she were straining through a fierce headwind. With a measure of revulsion Diederick notes how much she looks like a Jew running from a firing squad. He's saddened to imagine any of those Jew women having once been as beautiful as Virginie used to be. Beauty is, he decides, a shameful thing to waste, and the thought makes him feel cultured, more refined. It's this Diederick, urbane and sophisticated, who greets Bena when she returns to the table apologizing for herself: she'd neglected to see to Mignon before they left, to make sure she was all right. It's also this mature, genteel Diederick who says, "Of course, of course," as if in understanding, and this Diederick who assures her that Virginie will tend to Mignon, for he'd like very much if Miss Bernadette will accept his invitation to join him in the room he's let at the Fourniers', around the corner. He's not afraid to stay the night; the Allies are nearing, but they're not so close that he'll show fear. This V——bourg stop is good for his men's morale. They'll be at the Western Wall in another day, and for now it's important to show that Nazis do not run scared. They calculate, lure the enemy to the lair, and then eat them alive. At the Siegfried Line, the Allies will fall.

Just inside the door to Diederick's garret room are three small steps up, and he holds the door for Bernadette to mount before him. When she's perched above him, he pulls and latches the door with one hand and slides the other between Bernadette's buttocks. Her skirt pulls taut as he cups the mound of her pubis in his hand. It's the way he'd hold a chicken back on the farm in Bavaria: cradle the belly and breast, then cover the eyes so she'll stop her struggle and let you hold her close to breathe in the warm, dusty sweetness of her feathers just before you snap her neck.

Bena, her pubic bone against Diederick's firm hand, can't go ahead and can't turn back, can only wait for whatever comes next. He withdraws ever so slightly, then presses a finger into her. She fears she'll lose her bladder — piss herself, and him. But she holds it, and the urge changes. It becomes a desire, the desire to push herself into his finger and then come away. Press toward, and release, rock to, draw back, movements so small they seem to happen inside, press and release, like a foot, softly, on the sewing machine treadle, press and release, press, release. And then Diederick lifts her up by the crotch and deposits her in his room, on the bed, facedown on a cover of mothballed brocade. He hikes up her dress from behind and drags down her underthings. Then he's rubbing her haunch, sliding his palm over her flank, circling and kneading the flesh. When he lifts it away, she feels loss, wishes fleetingly for it to return — and then it does, but not as before. It comes as a slap, stinging and sharp, so surprising she can't cry out. The blow reverberates in her body. When he strikes her again the skin is already charged and buzzing with current that flares anew with each crash of his hand. Again and again, and she's shocked by the relentlessness; each blow, she thinks, must be the last, until the next, and another. And again. She only winces, doesn't cry. Surely she can say no, can't she? Surely she can say stop? But she holds off — how long can it possibly last? Once more, she thinks, and I'll cry out. The next time, I'll shout. The next . . .

She thinks she's gone numb, for what surprises her next is not a blow, but its lack, no impact, only an intake of breath. And then, in what seems like all one sweep, he's yanked down his pants and lowered himself onto Bena from behind, pushing himself between her thighs to find where he can part her, like curtains stuck closed at the cinema, and wedge himself inside, like he's pushing his fist into a full balloon, and she fears that she, the balloon, will explode. And then she does — bursts — with a pop like a silenced gun. She yelps in horror; Diederick pushes her face into the sharp-stinking bedcover. Deep inside there's pain, and pressure diffusing into a low, spreading warmth, a sensation impossible to describe, for she's never felt or imagined it before. Facedown on the bed in the Fournier guest house on rue de la Réformation, Bena feels herself pulse and spread, expand and blur. And then there's a jolt, and another stretch follows, a slow horror before Diederick sinks onto her, and shrinks out of her, and all she can think is how full she was just then, hadn't felt so full in years.

WHEN BENA RETURNS home that day she's met by a sewage stench that turns her stomach, and her first thought is that she's pregnant. Can you feel a baby so soon? She doesn't know, and whom can she ask? Maybe it's only the wine. When Idette turns, Bena's sure she knows: Bena's been with a Nazi; she's pregnant with his Nazi child.

"Karl." Idette spits his name like a curse. "Karl's dead. And Mignon's gone mad!" She throws up her hands, shuddering, dishtowel flailing like a limp pompom. She looks mad herself. One fool daughter after another losing her goddamn mind! Idette storms across the kitchen, rag raised like a whip. Flinging it down, she grabs Bena, who cries out, the foul soup-stench coming off her mother like the rot of disease. Idette's nose flinches, like she's awakening to the reek herself, but then Bena seizes in fear that what Idette smells is the sex on her, smells Diederick, and the wine, and the mothballed bed onto which Bena's virtue has been discarded like a dirty sock.

But Idette is too far out of her mind to be so aware. She wrenches Bena's arm, her eyes flaming, voice a terrible whisper. "You're all that's left." It's a curse as much as it's truth. "I can't run this shop alone." Then her tone's shifts from manic to businesslike, as if she's discussing employees, not her own children. "*Two* crazies now, and the commanders need—"

"The Germans won't be here long, Maman. The Allies are coming."

"And *if* they get here" — Idette is dubious — "they'll have dirty shirts to be washed as well." Idette thrusts her stirring spoon at Bena. "Tend the soup. I'll see to the madwomen."

Mignon stays in the barn for two days, Virgie by her side, stroking her hair, except when she must get up to fetch a rabbit from the hutch, lift it by its scruff, and hold it to her bony breast to stroke its soft, soft fur, nuzzle it a moment before she turns it over to Idette to stew for dinner. It's weeks before Mignon's back to work, assuming a kind of half-functional catatonia. She seems soothed by the regimen of laundry, so that's what she does: wash, rinse, dry, iron, fold, repeat.

WHEN THE FIRST bombs fall on V——bourg, no one's sure who's dropping them. Allies pushing the Nazis east toward Germany? Germans shelling as they retreat? It's terrifying, but the bombs mostly target the rail station, the grain store, bridges, though sometimes they miss. One bomb lands out beyond the Armonds' barn, but close enough to the shop that Bena and Idette, both inside, find their ears ringing for days after, until the clang gives way to a hum they'll know all their days. The bombs are terrifying, yes, but they're nothing compared to the purges.

The day Bena comes running home from town, she looks like such a madwoman that Idette thinks, *That's it, all three gone!* Virgie's out wandering, and the shop is empty but for Idette and Mignon. The Germans have fled east, Americans not yet arrived from the west, and it's the first sunny day after weeks upon weeks of rain. Bena charges in, bell ringing like an alarm. "A mob," she cries, "at the café —" Panting, wild-eyed, face twitching in fear, Bena tries to convey what they must understand: "There's a mob coming — for people who . . . Monsieur from the granary . . . Madame Bijoux from the school . . . men from that dairy . . . and the Maquis — the police took Sylvie, blocked the exits, the windows were open, I heard —"

Idette wants to smack her, but only shrieks, "Speak!" Uncompre-hending, Bena stops. Isn't she speaking? She draws a breath. "A crowd —in town. Coming for girls, women—who've had relations with Germans. Pulled into the street . . . Bijoux had a scissor—chopped Sylvie's hair, shaved . . . what they're doing. To the ones who've been with Nazis. They're coming here now."

Idette whirls on Mignon with a whisper so shrill it's a hiss. "Go to the barn. Hide in the loft, under the hay, so they won't find you. Be silent. You hear me? Go!" And Mignon, eyes splayed in terror, gasps and runs for the barn. Idette turns to Bena. "You, go! Hold them off!"

But Bena doesn't understand. "Hold them . . . ? What do I—? How—?"

"I don't care!" Idette cries. "Fall down like you're dead. Give your sister time to hide."

Thus is Bena ordered out the door onto rue des Brebis. She can't see the mob yet, but Bena knows what Idette doesn't, but what some-one else might: Mignon's not the only Armond who's been with a German. There may be Fourniers in the mob who know exactly what happened on the awful bedspread in that awful room. They might be after her, not Mignon at all, and Bena's not standing around wait-ing. She runs and turns sharply down the side street. There's been so much rain that the ground is mud, and her shoes sink, slowing her flight. Midway down the street, she ducks into an archway, tugs the little door there, and slips through, shutting it behind her. She thinks to bar it somehow, but with what? She runs on. When the alley gives way to an open path she keeps her head down, heart hammering, feet tripping. Were it not ghastly it might be funny: slapping in sludge, her shoes and socks enormous with mud. But if she can get to the barn, Mignon will take Bena in her arms, wipe the mud from her face, and Bena won't make a sound; she'll stay perfectly quiet until the mob's gone. Mignon will know what to do, and Bena runs toward her, plot-ting as she goes: if the rope's not down, she'll go under the barn.

The brush out here is overgrown with blackberry brambles, thistles, and stinkweed. Burrs stick to Bena's skirt, thorns grab her hair. There's a muddy ditch behind the barn, a bomb crater that's filled with slop in all this rain, and Bena scrambles on hands and knees up the side, trying to think what she'll do if the barn corner's too eroded to climb through, the rope too rain-slick to climb.

But it won't be the rope or the corner crevice in the end. In the end Bena will climb from the ditch and see her sister, but the angles will all be wrong, and because of the erosion, and the bombings, and all the rain, the ground's slope will seem different—Bena's climbed from a ditch that didn't exist a month before. The angles are wrong and Bena's confused, because what is Mignon doing outside? She's supposed to be hidden in the hayloft. And Bena knows then she's deluded herself: Mignon won't know what to do; she can't even get herself out of sight.

And then Bena understands. It's just a change in perception, an optical illusion. Bena sees her sister outside the barn and she can't see the rope with the footholds. Then the picture shifts, and her sister's outside, but she's not on the ground. And oh, there's the rope! It is hanging down after all! But it's hanging down taut. It's hanging down looped. It's around Mignon's neck—Mignon, who's swaying.

Later Idette will say that Bena's screams led them to the barn, but from inside the fence, from the yard, they can't see Mignon, so they don't know until they climb to the hayloft and see her framed in the window, a gruesome portrait: *Girl, Hanged*. With one hayloft ladder and many people trying to climb, several minutes pass after Idette understands what's happened but before she sees Mignon. The mob is disappointed: chase a girl down to humiliate her and she goes and hangs herself and spoils everything. They disperse, but this remains: Bena on the ground under Mignon's dangling feet, Idette in the hayloft knocking her head against a beam. They're like this for some time—Idette, Bena, and Mignon. The mob's not alerting the authorities; no neighbors rush to see what the ruckus is about. So Bena and Idette stay as they are—Idette sweating in the stultifying hayloft, Bena curled in the wet dead grass—until Virginie wanders home. Finding the shop and house empty, she strolls toward the barn calling, "Maman? Mignon? Bena? *Allo!*"

Idette is shocked into motion. "Virginie!" she cries. "Virgie, *reste là!* I come!" Maniacal now, she hurtles toward the hay window as if to fling herself out, but instead hisses down to Bena: "You, stay! Stay with your sister. *Reste là.* I get the police. You stay!" Idette takes one last look at Mignon, a survey, then says, "And get that ring off her finger—it's worth something."

The next thing Bena hears is Idette walking the path with Virgie, saying, "You come with me, we're going to town," and Bena understands that Idette means for her to stay with Mignon. *Stay with your sister,* your dead sister, and pry that fake engagement ring off her dead hand so we can sell it to buy food. Bena stares, frozen, into the crabgrass. She watches ants scale blades like great monuments, up one side and down the other, as she tries to figure out—it's too horrible, too horrible to imagine, and yet she must figure out how to get the ring off Mignon's finger before the authorities come cut her down and carry her away. This task, in the end, will involve entering the barn through the corner hole, climbing the ladder to the hayloft, and hauling the ladder up behind her to lower it out the window beside Mignon's body. Bena must then climb down the ladder to retrieve the ring. The horror of it is inconceivable, though there's one tiny blessing: Mignon's grown so thin since Karl's death that the ring is loose and comes off easily. This is the universe's one small stroke of kindness toward Bena Armond.

Virgie is with Idette at the police station, and though Idette hasn't told her what happened, neither can she shield Virgie from events as they unfold. In the station, Idette has Virgie wait on a bench by the door while she approaches a desk and speaks to a clerk. A call is then made and a flurry of movement ensues. In its midst, Idette grabs Virgie up and they're shuttled to a car and rushed back to rue des Brebis, siren shrieking, gratuitous ambulance on their tail. Virgie never sees Mignon's body, so never has to know what Bena so definitively knows, and this is what enables her story: Virgie decides that Mignon has staged her death. Last month's letter from Karl was written in code, detailing his plans for their escape from France, and Mignon's pain was not due to the death of her true love, but the realization that joining Karl would mean leaving her family forever, and leaving them thinking she had died by her own hand. In the weeks after Mignon's death, Virginie is almost happy, wafting about with some of her old buoyancy, like a friendly and benevolent ghost.

IN EARLY SEPTEMBER 1944, the tanks roll up and stop outside town, its streets too narrow to pass, and like the Germans in 1940, the Americans enter on foot. Liberation is oddly less festive than invasion—they weren't all so tired back then. Now the town is liberated, yes, but the war's still on, soldiers in the streets, foreign tongues at the café calling to Bena: *Hey gorgeous, sit a spell with your savior. Have a drink on the U.S. of A. Set that gorgeous rear right down here and tell Uncle Sam where it hurts.* And Bena could barter her company for a meal or a drink, whatever they've got, but she's too sick to want food and too queasy to care. Especially in the mornings.

It's all too clear where this is going, no? Another month passes, the Americans are still in V——bourg, and Bena still hasn't bled. Like the Allied troops, halted by the Nazis just west of the Moselle, so too is this cluster of cells stuck in Bena's uterus, and neither squadron is going anywhere soon. American GIs dig in their heels—in Lorraine, on the Meuse and Moselle Rivers, in the Argonne—just as those cells are hunkering down. The troops can't move because they've run out of fuel. The Americans' August sprint across France has raised logistical problems: their men have made it to the Moselle, but the Allies have yet to command the necessary northern ports to get supplies to said men, so everything's coming via Normandy, mostly by plane, and that's no short haul. The troops are fine on rations—they seized some German storehouses in Reims and will be eating sauerkraut and tinned fish until victory and beyond—but it's gas they need, and gas they await in every village west of the Lorraine front lines.

Meanwhile, the French police are getting reestablished, regaining control, and their main initiative is action against those French citizens who've disgraced their nation. Like the mob that came for Mignon, the country needs to place blame, and with the Germans gone, they turn on their own: anyone who's aided, abetted, or made things easy for the Nazis during occupation. They can't go arresting everyone who's consorted or fraternized with Germans, or all France would be in the slammer, but they can pursue those who've clearly, outwardly benefited. Like the tailors of rue des Brebis. It's not punishment enough that Jean and Michel have been gone for years, that Fiji and Mignon are dead, and that Virginie is mad. Never mind that the Armonds have seen nothing of their own profits. They have, have they not, received ongoing aid from one Karl Perlmutter? Is Madame Idette not the Nazis' favorite French seamstress?

"Madame is needed for questioning," says the constable when they come for her. He's nervous and young, with a silly mustache he's acquired for its insinuation of authority.

Idette, not cowed by this teenage figurehead of martial law, or his mustache, says she's sorry, but she has a business to run. She gestures to Virgie. "And I can't leave her on her own."

The constable looks smugly pleased. "If she's ill, should she not be in the hospital?"

"We can care for her here at home," says Idette. "Thank you for your obvious concern."

"But you'll not *be* at home, Madame, as you're coming to the station with me. Now."

Idette flinches like he's spat at her. "And who will look after my daughter, Constable?"

He flips open a notepad, shuffles pages. "By my count, you've one child yet unaffiliated with the Nazis. Perhaps Bernadette will look after her sister while you're occupied?"

Idette sneers. "If you can find the little whore." Is this just habitual nastiness? Or a notion that whorishness might rule out Bena as Virginie's caretaker? What *does* Idette know?

The constable's smile is repulsive. "We've picked up your little whore at the café. Perhaps some greater domestic responsibility is just what young Bernadette needs."

Idette is led to the V——bourg jail, where she spends two nights "under investigation," until she and forty-odd others board a train for a "detention center," location unknown. Bena will never see her again. When they come for Virgie, they don't even need a straitjacket. She goes willingly, thinking she'll be taken to Michel. Hope is mad, and only the mad can hold on to it.

So Bena's left alone on rue des Brebis with the rabbits and Chou-Chou, trying not to lose her mind. She can't tell one bunny from another—can barely distinguish one day from the next—but somehow there are always enough that she can kill one each morning—skin it, cook it, and have something to eat, however unappetizing, every day—and the dams keep having more kits. She lets them grow as big as she can so they're worth the considerable effort it takes to get their meat, and if they're getting fat eating their own babies, so be it. These rabbits are her salvation, and though she despises tromping out to cull one for her daily meal, they feed her, and come winter they'll keep her warm, too. She salts the hides and lets them dry and cure a bit before she adds them to the blanket she's making—a blanket no one can force her to send to any prisoners of war. They're her rabbits, and it's her damn blanket!

Huddled by the stove, wrapped in the stinking rabbit throw, Bena has a vague idea that this baby in her might be her ticket out of France. *If only it were an American's baby . . .* Pregnancy turns many women into blithering idiots, let alone one carrying a Nazi's baby in post-liberation France, but it's a while before Bena has this fairly obvious revelation: her baby's not going to emerge saluting Hitler. Any number of these soldiers could be its father.

At first she looks for tall—that's her memory of Diederick: tall. He had—*has?* Is he still alive? Will she ever know?—fairish skin, brownish hair. Unable to conjure his face, she just looks for tall, until that seems arbitrary. Thinking too much makes her lose focus and hope. She only needs a man who might plausibly have fathered this baby—that is, one of the men she takes upstairs to bed on rue des Brebis. The more men she gets upstairs, the greater her chance of escape.

Here's one now, stepping into the shop, sitting to pry off his mud-caked boots, remove his threadbare socks. They reek of rot. He lifts this evidence of his desperation, asking, "Is there something you can do?" Of course, yes, she can soak his putrid things on the stove—she's been pulling the barn down board by board and burning it for fuel. Bena takes the soldier's boots and tells him: "Go upstairs to the bed with the rabbit fur blanket. Get in and take everything off." She'll wash it all and darn the holes, the least she can do for a man who might come to believe he's the father of her unborn child. It's no trouble getting men into bed. Bena's got quite a belly on her these days, but it's been a long war, and these men are just boys, and there's not one of them thinking, *This dame looks a little pregnant, if you ask me.* Most are so young they've hardly seen a naked woman before, and certainly not a naked pregnant one. All women's bodies are foreign—the swell of this one's abdomen no odder than the rolls of another's chin, a bony back, a bulbous bum. The soldier of the gruesome socks buries his face in Bena's hair as if it's lovely and clean. He'd've made a nice husband, but she'll never again lay eyes on Sherman T. Singleton. There's always the next, though, and they do keep coming. Robert G. Cass. Theodore H. Barkey. Burt Mothersbaugh. Harold R. Fine. David I. Daley—names stamped on their dog tags. They arrive with their buttonless coats and their toeless socks, and she sends them upstairs to sleep, grateful and naked, under the rabbit fur quilt while she works on their clothes. Some bring soap, otherwise she simmers their things on the stove, a witch's cauldron of bloody, muddy undershirts and piss-stinking, shit-reeking long johns. She hangs them to dry by the smoky kitchen fire, and when the man wakes up she's beside him in bed, and he reaches to take her into his arms and make love to this plush and generous woman.

Fall turns to winter, U.S. troops moving up into the Ardennes forest to fight off the last Nazi offenses: the Battle of the Bulge, that most miserable military action. V——bourg is far enough from the front to be mostly safe, and near enough to be useful, so it becomes a staging ground for troops preparing to enter the fray, as well as a stop on their way back out. Many leave as corpses, but for the survivors V——bourg becomes a sanatorium town, GIs convalescing in the schoolhouse cum Nazi headquarters cum American hospital, and this evolution is useful to Bena. Men she's known on their way to battle are turning up again. She checks the hospital every day, and the incoming trucks, her belly concealed under wraps, her desperation harder to hide. Townspeople talk: What's under there? Who is she looking for? But can anyone possibly suspect how many different men she'd be most relieved to find?

The first to show up is Pfc. Dave Daley. Sweet, fair-haired, from Hartford, Connecticut, he gazes up dreamily from a bed in the old school gym, his face lighting in apparent recognition of Bena, though he seems very ill. If not for his name at the foot of the bed Bena would not have recognized him. She has diligently recorded all her men's names on a page from an accounting ledger she keeps folded around the photo she found in the hayloft after Mignon died. Karl's letter Bena burned, but the photograph she keeps, along with Mignon's ring that Idette never got a chance to sell, both wrapped in her list, safe among the names of the men who might be her salvation. When a man makes love to her on rue des Brebis, after he's asleep she writes down his name, adding him to the list she'll know by heart as long as she lives. She recites their names in her mind as a mantra, a *k'an-hua,* a sad and desperate meditation koan. But when Bena sees *Daley, D.,* printed on a bed chart, you'd think he was the love of her life—her Dave! Alive! She leans close to his drawn face, nose and cheeks white and scaly with frostbite, and whispers in what little English she has, "David? I Bernadette, *le tailleur* . . . ? I make wash the clothes . . . ?" She rubs together the ends of her scarf. "Bernadette?"

And Dave Daley's face lifts in what might be a smile. He whispers, "Bernadette."

"*Oui!*" she says. "Yes, Bernadette," and Dave Daley breathes in, as if to savor a perfume. "David, I tell you something," she says, and he nods. "Dave, I . . . you." Gently, she touches his face, then takes his cold arm and, glancing around cautiously, puts his hand to her belly. She says, "Baby." She says, "*C'est toi le père, David.* Yours. Baby," watching his face for some sign of comprehension. "Open the eyes, David," she pleads. "Open the eyes. *Tu es le père.* You baby."

His irises are so blue it's like they froze solid up in the Ardennes, but the whites are yellowed and bloodshot. He looks so unwell, yet gazes up at Bena with seeming tenderness. "My baby?" His eyes lose focus, as if he's spotted this baby in Bena's hair or on the wall, but he smiles, and in that smile Bena sees what she needs to see: amazement, readiness, joy. When he drifts off to sleep, Bena walks home, head held high for the first time in weeks. She doesn't know how badly Dave is wounded—she hopes bad enough to be sent home—but a porthole is opening out, and by the time she's at rue des Brebis she's envisioning herself as Mrs. David Daley, with baby Mignon, if it's a girl. And, of course, for a boy, Michel.

Later, she'll curse her own uncharacteristic optimism, an indulgence for which she's punished. Next day at the hospital, Dave's not where she left him. Annoyed to have to find him again in this chaos, anxiety edging in like wind at her coat seams, she scans the gym in an orderly fashion, up one row and down the next, until she's passed every man and not set eyes on Dave. "*Excusez-moi?*" she asks a nurse. "David Daley?" The nurse narrows her eyes, trying to make sense of these words—*Da vie d'allie? D'a vida lit?*—until finally Bena says, *"Un homme. Prénom, David. Nom de famille, Daley."* The nurse's face widens in comprehension, but then she waves Bena off: "If he's here, he's here," so Bena surveys the enormous room again, going from bed to bed: *"David Daley? Excusez-moi? Connaissez-vous Dave Daley?"*

Near the spot where Dave lay yesterday, a man whose face looks mauled by animals calls out, "She say Daley?" He glances to his buddies. "She looking for Daley?"

Bena whirls around, excited. *"Dave Daley? Oui, je cherche Dave Daley!"*

The man's lacerated face draws in, lips pursed as far as his scabs allow. "Aw, honey . . . it was some infection or something. Jeez, I'm sorry. He died last night. Mort. He's *mort*. Dead."

Bena gasps. And maybe it's the way she moves that tips him off, for the scratch-faced man glances at her belly, then back up to her face. "Aw, sweetheart, you his girl? *Amour?* Oh, hell." He looks about to cry, and for a moment Bena thinks she will too, until she makes herself remember it's not the truth. She'll forget this story, and begin another.

In January, a Brit called Pete G'schwind comes through. Usually, when their clothes were dry, the men went back to their barracks, but last fall Pete G'schwind stayed all night upstairs with Bena. In bed, the men mostly just knew how to please themselves, but Pete G'schwind also tended to Bena's pleasure—not to be taken lightly in wartime, maybe anytime. Entering her throughout the night—twice, three times, again, like he couldn't stop, saying, "Oh, God," and "I love you," and "My God, I love you." When Pete again shows up in town, he's in the hospital with a badly frostbitten left foot and no right foot at all, but neither seems to bother him; he's headed home. Grizzled as a woodsman, he won't let anyone near him with a razor: "You got my foot, now you want my beard, too?" Bena catches him when he's wheeling himself to the lavatory, but he cuts her off mid-tale, lifting the dog tags from his chest, a wedding ring waggling on the chain.

"But my darling, I've already got children. I'm married, my love." His eyes, for a second, seem to focus right on her. "Oh, but you *are* lovely, aren't you? So sorry, darling, really, truly, I am."

IN THE END, it's Cliff Johnston who finds Bena. February 1945: Dresden is firebombed, and that's the mission Lieutenant Clifford O. Johnston of Deacon, Iowa, has just accomplished, ending his tour of duty. He's got his orders, is nearly the fuck out of Frenchie-land, but makes one last stop in V——bourg, where he knows a girl he'd sure like to throw another fuck into before he sets off stateside, goes home, marries his high school girl, and spends his life farming Daddy's fields, like his daddy's daddy before him. For the rest of his life, Cliff will love to watch crop dusters fly over Iowa, raining down their poison chemicals, for it'll stir a nostalgic pride, take him back to the war, seeing the pests of Iowa kablooeyed, just like Dresden, to oblivion. But right now all Cliff Johnston's thinking about is throwing one last fuck into a big-titted Frenchie and finish this war up right. So he stops in V——bourg, delivers some supplies. He's got a whole afternoon to kill and a bottle of French cognac to kill it with, so he goes to find the girl with the great big *parley-voo* tits to throw himself a send-off. Imagine Bena's surprise when, after months of stalking the makeshift hospital, searching transport convoys for any man she's ever bedded, Cliff Johnston walks up rue des Brebis and knocks on the tailor shop's door. He's from the middle of the list, between Sid Grogin and James Cork, and he's *here,* looks healthy, is holding himself tall, with a swagger, 'cause he just bombed the living shit out of them Krauts. He's pleased as fucking peach punch to see Bernadette, whose tits, he'd swear, are even bigger than—when was that? Christmastime? Oh, if she isn't just what the army doctor ordered!

Cliff's spirits are high, in bed beside this fulsome mademoiselle, the thrill of the firebombs still coursing in his veins, Europe nearly behind him. He's twenty years old and this may be the best fucking mood of his life. The room's light is soft, dappled, and it's blissfully warm under the rabbit spread, a hell of a lot nicer than he's used to. Spent, Cliff spoons around Bena, drapes an arm over and palms her belly, cups it like a pumpkin in his big hand. He's a farm boy, Cliff Johnston, knows cows and pigs, husbandry and breeding. "How come everyone's starving and you're plumped up like a Christmas goose?" This is a compliment; it was another time.

It takes much effort, but Bena turns to face him with a combination of trepidation and joy, and they speak at the same time, him saying, "You're not . . . ?" and her saying, "Baby."

Blame it on the moment. Blame it on the war. Blame it on some MGM-concocted notion of what a real American man does when a pretty naked lady tells him she's knocked up and it doesn't cross his mind that he's maybe not the only guy who's been knocking. Blame it on Cliff's never having been all that thrilled with his Becky back home and her wilted-parsnip tits, but when he gets the notion his seed's taken root in this luscious French hottie, he lets out a whoop that Bena wouldn't know from pain if not for the irrepressible grin lighting his face like a firebomb. She doesn't have to convince him. It's more of a fairy tale than she's let herself dream.

With a grandiose flourish Cliff leaps from the covers and swoops to one knee beside the bed, wrapping himself in the rabbit blanket. Teeth chattering, he takes Bena's hand. "Well, then, Mademoiselle Bernadette. I guess that means we'll be getting married!" And though Bena doesn't know all the words he's used, she grasps the sentiment just fine. And then she's laughing, for the first time in ages she's laughing, and saying *"Oui!"* saying "Yes!" as if he's asked a question.

They leave the next day, but beforehand she'll run to the barn and free the rabbits. Chou-Chou will feast on fresh rabbit till he's ancient and portly. He'll still be there on rue des Brebis in the 1950s when Michel finally makes it home. It'll be years more before Michel is able to find Virginie and get her out of the institution where she's been stashed since '44. Chou-Chou's a scrappy survivor, living on rabbit all that time. Chou-Chou Chat, bunny-tending cat, long dead by now, of course, but the bunnies in the hutch out back on rue des Brebis are surely the infinite-great-grandbunnies of Jean Armond's wartime rabbits. And inside the house that was once the tailor's, there just might be a rabbit stew simmering on the stove right now, a home-made meal for the lunch guest of the elderly Armond twins. They're hosting the handsome American professor of history who's come all this way to hear about their lives.

BENA AND CLIFF are married by a chaplain en route to the port at Le Havre. Now, Cliff's not all that bright, and it probably seems only fair to him that with all he's done for his country, his country'll grant his wife a berth on the ship home, but when they reach Le Havre he's met with a very different reality. The reality of Request for Permission to Marry, section 2, subsection (b): "The United States Government is obligated in no way to transport the wife or dependents to the United States during the present emergency." The reality of: "You gotta be kidding me, soldier."

"Look," Cliff tells the clerk, "I'm decorated military, going home, and *she's* coming."

"Look," says the clerk, who volleys like this daily, "you want that? What's in it for me?" For there's a way around every regulation, and it so happens the clerk's got something he needs flown somewhere, ASAP. "Boost me up my ladder," he says, "maybe I'll boost you up yours."

Before leaving on the clerk's errand, Cliff makes a phone call, Le Havre to Iowa. "Hey, Ma—no, everything's fine. Hey, hang on, wait, I got news. First is that I'm coming home. Yeah, and the other is—hey, don't go yelling or anything, okay? Becky's not over there, is she? Okay, so, I'm a married man! Hey! Hey, hang on—wait. Ma . . . look. Look, Ma . . . Hey, just *wait* a sec. *Hang on.* Look: I'm gonna be a father. Uh-huh . . . yup, a great girl . . . Bernadette . . . No, *Ber-na-dette*. Yeah, French . . . I know it is, Ma. No, yes—a chaplain. No, well, no,

I don't guess she's real religious. Just a, you know, a Christian. I don't know, Ma. She doesn't got family. They're gone—I don't—just gone, okay? Um, around December. Sure, three months, sure. So, yeah, I guess September, yeah. Hey, so, I kinda wondered—about Becky . . . You're better at that stuff than me. She'll . . . no, Ma, wait . . . it'd be better from you, okay? *Bernadette.* I don't . . . just Bernadette *Johnston,* okay? *French,* Ma, okay, for chrissake . . . Dunno—end of the month? Not by Easter, but—okay . . . *Ma!* Tell everyone hi, 'kay? And you'll tell Becky? You're the best, Ma."

Cliff takes off on the port clerk's bidding, but it seems the clerk's got a bid for Bernadette, too, and she doesn't need any English to grasp what he wants: he wants *thanks* for getting her on that ship. She knows what to do. After all the men in V——bourg, he's just one more.

There's no cure like travel? Tell that to Bena, seasick across the Atlantic as they move in a military convoy aboard a repurposed cruise liner. She spends the frigid March voyage on deck, barfing over the rail, wrapped in her rabbit fur shawl. When they dock at New York harbor, port authorities refuse the putrid pelt entry into the United States. It's an ugly fight, like taking a blanket from a screaming child. *Filthy immigrant,* one cop says to another. *She's probably a Jew,* says the other, with some pity. *Should we let her keep it? I don't care if she's the Queen of Sheba—no!* And that's the end of the rabbit fur quilt, rest its moldy bunny souls.

An overnight train to Chicago, then another four hours into Iowa. No one would take this traveling couple for married, Bena's near-term pregnancy notwithstanding. They don't even talk, let alone touch. Cliff mostly sleeps, and everything about Bena says *Don't come near.* Cliff probably thinks that's just how pregnant broads are. What does he care? He's alive! A hero on his way home from war, a good-looking girl beside him, proof of his manliness on display. She and this baby will be a good buffer between him and his family, a cushion against his childhood and the childhood sweetheart he never was all that sweet on. Cliff'll work the farm like always, and his dad will help with a down payment on a house. Hell, he might even get a home-town parade.

Cliff's father, a man of vague, limp goodwill, greets the newly-weds at the train. Shy as a novice porter, Harlan Johnston takes Bernadette's small bag, all she has in the world. *Nothing like packing a suitcase and sailing away . . .* He barely nods when Cliff introduces her, keeps his head down as if it would constitute a certain obscenity to regard straight-on a woman so fecund. "She don't have much English," Cliff tells him, and Harlan says, "No, I don't guess she would."

Vida Johnston, waiting in the truck, is not altogether unlike Bernadette: capable, wary, stubborn. By way of hello, she rolls down her window: "Car's in the shop, or we'd of come in it 'stead of this. You going to introduce this—" A stream of disorderly consonants emerges from her mouth as she eyes Bena's belly. Whether in ignorance or in a cunning takedown, Vida decides Bernadette's name is Brenda, with an extra *da* on the end, and won't hear different. She deems it dangerous for "a girl in Brendada's condition" to ride in back of a pickup, so while Cliff sits in the truck bed and watches the fields, Bernadette is wedged between the Johnstons inside on the bench seat. She and Vida are both squat and wide, Harlan's a big-and-tall, and it's three hours to the farm. And Vida, for one, won't waste breath on a knocked-up girl what can't even speak English. She suspects the tart's got tricks up her ratty sleeves. Just that morning she said, "Harlan, I bet we come to find she's one of them Jews, using Clifford to get herself out of Europe over there." Harlan, who picks up a newspaper from time to time, said, "War's near over. They're letting the Jews go free. Cliff wouldn't have relations with a Jew girl anyhow, that's silliness." Now the girl's here, though, Harlan can see, Jew or what-not, she's fine-looking, a sure improvement on Becky Boyer. Hell, you get some bourbon into him, he might admit wanting to throw a fuck into Frenchie himself. But Harlan doesn't drink, and honesty, he knows, can be dicey at best.

BERNADETTE'S FIRST SPRING WEEKS in Iowa are remarkably peaceful. The Johnston farm is nothing fancy, but the house is clean, the kitchen porch a nice place to sit. She takes her chores to the table out there, to chop carrots or knead bread dough or roll a pie crust without Vida over her shoulder. Cliff and Harlan work long days on the farm. Vida tends house, one eye on Bernadette. Vida birthed plenty of children herself; she knows from pregnancy. Bena may be the Armond baby, but she knows nothing of birthing them and tries to think of it as little as possible. When her chores are done, she occupies herself making clothes for the baby she's not thinking about from scraps in Vida's sewing room. Bena's dressed in hand-me-downs from Vida and her sisters and cousins and aunts, all of whom have borne their share of babies, all asking, "How far along she say she is?"

"Due in September's what she *claims*," Vida says, pious as a TV preacher.

Taking another gander, Vida's guest whispers like a bad stage actor, "*September?*"

Vida raises her eyebrows, leans in closer, says, "You think she looks like a Jew?"

Another glance, the woman shrugs. "Don't know I ever saw one but in the movies."

"Hm." Vida's not an entirely ignorant woman. She seriously doubts Cliff's so-called marriage is legal in America. This whole *France* place feels made-up, part of Brendada's ruse. Cliff can't see things for how they are, but Vida thinks it won't be long before certain truths reveal themselves. The girl's up five, six times a night to make water — don't think Vida isn't counting. It was like that in her own pregnancies, near the end. Vida prays for Brendada's baby: that it's born soon, and it's the biggest, least-premature baby Deacon, Iowa, has ever seen.

Spring of '45 is busy: Roosevelt's death, Hitler's suicide, VE Day, and finally there *is* a parade in Deacon, and Cliff's practically the star, waving from Becky Boyer's father's convertible, because even the Boyers are being nice. Becky, too. Cliff doesn't totally understand, thinks it's because he's basically a hero and everything. He's got no idea what-all his mother's said to the Boyers, Cliff's just feeling good, riding this thing out. Bernadette's a sourpuss, sure, but not much trouble. That is, until suppertime on the May afternoon when she goes into labor.

"Early, isn't it?" says Harlan.

"Yep," says Vida.

"You sure?" Cliff asks Bernadette, who grunts confirmation through gritted teeth.

Vida says Cliff should drive Brendada in the car, since the hospital's a ways and the truck's shocks're bad, but all the sudden Cliff's a nervous wreck, and it takes Vida a minute to figure it out: he thinks the baby's coming way too early. "What if something *happens?*" he keeps saying, until Vida agrees to ride along. Probably for the best —Cliff might need things explained to him. Vida would like to think he's a trusting soul, but sometimes she's afraid he's simply a fool.

So Cliff and Vida and Brendada set off in the car, Vida sitting prim and tall in the front seat, Brendada heaving like a tipped cow in back, Vida fighting to contain her giddiness and keep from gloating. To distract herself from Brendada's bovine moans, Vida rolls down the window and sings hymns into the rushing air. Maybe their message will reach Brendada; the Lord never faulted anyone for trying. *"I dreamed that the great judgment morning had dawned and the trumpet had blown. I dreamed that the nations had gathered to judgment before the white throne."* By the chorus, Vida's having a fine time, tapping hand to thigh. *"And O, what a weeping and wailing, as the lost were told of their fate. They cried for the rocks and the mountains, they prayed but their prayer was too late."* She's just starting in on *"Too many, Lord, abuse Thy grace"* when Cliff says maybe Bernadette could use some quiet, and Bernadette nods through her pain. Vida sucks her lips and stays mum; she's got to keep on Cliff's good side.

Nothing moves fast enough on the drive, but once they get there it all goes double time, contractions included. Bena's hoisted into a wheelchair and swept inside so fast Cliff's left calling feebly, "See ya later." Vida collects the girl's things; they hardly fill a cardboard valise.

Cliff parks the car, then joins Vida in the waiting room. A moment alone to think, and he's worked himself up. "Ma," he asks, "can a baby, y'know, make it, so early?" but when Vida pats the chair beside her, saying, "It's in the Lord's hands," Cliff howls in terror: *"The Lord's?"*

"Oh, stop," she scolds. "I don't mean *dead!* Just that it's God's will," but Cliff's dashing for the nurses' station. "I'm looking for my wife. She's having a baby . . . Bernadette Johnston?"

The nurse, wide face placid as a soup bowl, coos a low "Honey, hon — they're fine."

"But it's early!" Cliff says. There must be some other word, but he can't find it.

With regard to expectant fathers, the nurse has, of course, seen it all. "It always feels too soon, honey, but a baby's ready when it's ready. Why don't you try sitting down awhile? Rest."

"But she's not . . ." Cliff gets hold of himself. "It's not supposed to come for months."

The nurse's chin lifts and her moon face ripples in a smile. "Maybe time to double-check that math." She winks. "Your baby's getting born," she says, but this daddy-to-be is not letting up. Nurse looks to her clipboard. "Mr. Johnston, tell you what." Now she's flirting — sometimes it helps these guys. "Soon as he can, I'll have Dr. Maakestad out here to talk to you, 'kay? You might just've been a little bit off. Nothing to worry." She's smiling; he's not. She musters her professionalism. "Mr. Johnston, it's fine. You have a seat. Doc'll be out just as soon as he can."

Cliff's head spins as he returns to Vida, singing hymns to herself now: *"For the day is approaching, it must come to one and all, when the sinners' condemnation will be written on the wall . . ."* Cliff sinks to the chair beside her, pinching his eyes shut, counting on his fingers, nodding his head along. "December, January, February, March, April, May . . ." Eyes open, he turns to Vida. "Nine, right? Don't laugh at me—just tell me it's nine months you count, right?"

Vida wouldn't dream to make fun now. "Yes, son," she tells him soberly, "nine," and as he shuts his eyes again to resume counting, Vida makes her voice newly grave. "Clifford, I need to say something, son." She's losing faith he'll make the connections on his own. "I don't mean nothing against Brendada, but I need to ask: could she of had another boyfriend, from before you and her—?" Cliff cuts her off: "No! What're you . . . ?" And oh, it's painful for Vida to watch this revelation enter her son's head, apparently for the first time. "Cliff," she says, softer now. "You never did meet her people, did you, son?"

"How'm I supposed to meet dead people?" he asks, but he's riffling through layers in his brain. "She had a big family before the war . . . one sister dead . . . a brother, too . . . and someone in a hospital, I think. Her father got sent to some work camp. She's the only one was left." Cliff's breaking up now—and in front of Vida, who'll probably smack him for it—at his own story, how he found Bernadette, alone in that pitiful place, and saved her, and the baby, too. He's a savior!

"Clifford, now, nothing against it, but . . . they was in *camps?* German camps?" and Cliff's nodding, eyes straight ahead. "Son, you heard the news, haven't you? Those camps is where they put the Jews, son. Where they sent the Jews." Cliff's nod, Vida sees, is winding down, like a toy. "Do you think maybe she's not what she says, son?" This, Vida realizes, is all beginning to sound like the best story anybody in Deacon, Iowa, ever had to tell. "Son, you're a war hero and a good, trusting boy. But trusting too much can get you in trouble. Ever since you and her first got off of that train, I been scared she's lying, saying another man's baby was yours. She's one of them Jews,

Cliff, a Jew girl, telling lies because you got a giving way about you, and she took advantage." Vida's voice is growing angry, a raspy whisper. "She got you to marry her—if you're all even married for real —and risk everything you fought that war for." Is she going too far? She's already got him: slunk down, head in hands between his spread knees. Vida's story is nearly done, crystallizing from *could of been* into *was,* past tense, no conditional. "Son, she lied."

This, of course, is when the swinging doors slam open and a doctor emerges, smiling, bulbous-nosed, bespectacled. Cliff's and Vida's faces are expectant, like so many Dr. Maakestad's greeted in his career. A half-century in obstetrics, and still such a pleasure to say, "It's a boy!"

Cliff can't speak. Vida either. This is usual. Dr. Maakestad says, "Come see your son."

Cliff's voice is a squeak: "It's alive?"

"Alive?!" cries the doctor. "Well, of course he's alive, Mr. Johnston. Quite so. And that's one brave little lady. Eight pounds, fourteen ounces. Haven't seen many bigger in all my years."

Cliff can't move. Shock is nothing new to Maakestad, but here's where the story diverges from anything the doctor's yet seen. Cliff Johnston, in a tremulous death rattle, asks, "It a *Jew?*"

Clearly Dr. Maakestad misheard. He begs pardon. "Come again?" But Cliff's shaking his head, seeing the wrongness of his question, its unanswerableness; he won't repeat himself.

But Vida can control herself no longer. She stands and, for the benefit of the doctor and anyone else in range, declares: "It's not his baby. That girl, she tricked him. He never even met her before December. Met her in December and a few months later she's saying it's his baby, but my son never even had known her when she got herself in trouble. My son's a *hero.*" She feels righteous, but her speech is backfiring: Cliff's standing, disregarding her, striding purposefully toward the doctor. Maakestad fears the man's coming for him, but then sees in the distant aim of Johnston's eyes that he wants to be led to the woman and the child, whoever they may be, so Maakestad takes him down the hall. The doctor knocks, peers in, a bit fearful. "Hello there," he calls to the tired new mother, infant swaddled in her arms. Then Johnston pushes in, and Maakestad's got a sudden vision of him raising a Luger stolen off a German corpse—he's going to kill them all! But then Johnston goes shy, drops his head, neck cords taut and pulsing.

Bernadette knows it's gone bad. Could she really have expected otherwise? Cliff's yelling now: "You lied! You—I don't know what—liar! Jew whore! You—" And then that's it, that's all Cliff Johnston's got in him. He turns and leaves, and Bernadette will never lay eyes on him again. She'll never know how he and Vida explain things back in Deacon. Maybe they'll say the baby died. Bernadette, too, and they had them cremated, sent the ashes back to France. But it's hard to imagine Vida keeping mum about a story that makes her come off as smart as this one does, how she figured it all out long before Cliff could see it for himself. Once Cliff's married to Becky, with kids of their own, and the whole thing's over and done, people might tell how Cliff Johnston was so nice of a guy he brung a pregnant Jew back after the war, told them at immigration it was his wife and baby. He was practically Oskar Schindler, Clifford Johnston was, practically.

It's Dr. Maakestad—and his wife, also Dr. Maakestad—who give Bernadette bottles, diapers, and a small wad of bills, and put her and the baby on a bus to River City. She carries the cardboard suitcase of baby clothes and her sewing bag, in it the photograph of three little girls, and one of a young, handsome man. Also the list, and the ring. They're all she has: these things and Michel, named for the young man in the photo. "How about *Michael?*" Dr. Maakestad suggests. "He's an American baby, after all, you know? How about an American name?"

The good Drs. Maakestad arrange for the nun who greets them at the River City station, takes Bernadette and Michael to the County Home for Unwed Mothers, run by the sisters of Our Lady of the

Prairie. Registered as *Bernadette Maakestad,* that's who she'll remain. And grateful as she is to those good sisters, even they cannot draw Bernadette to God. She pities them their naive faith, even as she envies the comfort and consolation it brings them. But Bernadette has a child to care for, and God does not change diapers or strain peas. It's skilled work, not faith, that earns money, and she needs money, and she has skills. The sisters find her a job at the university, sewing parachutes for the troops. After V-J Day, when the war is finally over and normal life resumes at U of I, Bernadette is relocated to the Theater Department, where she'll stay forty years, moving up from seamstress to costume mistress, all the while keeping quiet, learning English, raising her boy, honing her story, making it his, and ours.

5

NO PLACE LIKE HOME

"Lead a simple life," the neurologist advised. "Not that it
makes any difference we know about."

—Joan Didion, *The White Album*

Our chicago landing's going to be a bumpy one, folks," the
flight attendant announced. We were dipping and swaying. Nausea
roiled through me, and I was Bena, pregnant, on that crossing with
Cliff. Or maybe it was later, and she—I?—was somehow going back,
returning to France. But where was the child? Where was Michel—
Michael? "The captain has turned on the fasten seat belt sign. As you
can . . . *feel*, we're experiencing some turbulence." Static cracked.
"We should be on the ground shortly." I hate when they say that:
should. A crashing airplane's clearly not behaving as it should. "Please
make sure your personal items are stowed under the seat in front
of you." The plane bucked. We jounced blindly through the cloud
cover, dark and gray as ash, the plane jumping and falling. The noise
was tremendous—thundering, groaning, the aircraft creaking as if
it were about to break apart at the seams, the wind or the engines
or my ears howling ferociously. I couldn't hear people retching, but

I smelled it. I have little doubt but that bowels were voided on that descent. The plane careened through the storm.

And then we slipped from the clouds, just plopped right out, like a scratched cue ball, returned. The noise changed, as if someone had flipped the station, sounds more abstract, farther away, somehow once-removed. We got spit from the clouds, and the plane banked so sharply I thought we were nosediving. I closed my eyes and prayed, and thought of Erica Jong: "There are no atheists on turbulent airplanes." And then, *plunk,* we hit land, and went screaming across a tarmac that was presumably beneath us, rain sheeting at one side of the plane, falling horizontally, the pilot pulling hard against it. Wind screamed, brakes skidded, wheels fishtailed. I braced for the slide from asphalt to grass, to pebble and rubble, waiting for a wing to hit something solid—tree, truck, terminal—and send us flipping toward explosion. My ears popped so violently I thought I was having an aneurysm. The plane, miraculously, slowed. I opened my eyes. The plane slowed some more. A smattering of applause, a small hoot, a laugh. People sobbed.

We deplaned in a haze—shock, probably—like we'd just been born, or given birth. We'd come through a traumatic rite of passage, but now the cabin lights glowed warm, and everyone was extraordinarily respectful, helping others, making way. A flight attendant gripped my hand with both of hers and wished me well, sent me up the jetbridge, cut loose, free.

Inside the terminal, the world seemed on fast-forward. Someone clasped my arm; I flinched. Then a warm female voice said, "Connecting?" I thought she was asking if my body and brain had synced themselves again. I didn't know the answer. She said, "Are you connecting from O'Hare today, ma'am?" I must have told her yes, and where to, because suddenly I was on one of those elongated golf carts *beep, beep, beep*ing to a gate where a plane to Cedar Rapids was boarding, and then we were up, and then we were in Iowa. Home.

The airport shuttle van dropped me at the Yoders', where someone stood leaning on the porch rail, back to the road, someone I couldn't place. Someone with cropped hair shorn uneven as a horizontal collaborator's. I called "Hello," and the person turned, and it was Eula, her hair cut short as a man's. She was stunning. "Eula!" I cried. "You're beautiful!"

Oren in one arm, Eula lifted a hand to her head for one instant of vanity, then waved to dismiss the compliment. "Phillipa—" She sounded anxious, unlike herself, speaking as if tending to a task she'd sworn to remember. "I'm so sorry for your loss," she said. It took me a second to understand she meant Bernadette, who seemed, just then, not lost at all. Far from it! Bernadette had cheated death, a Jew who'd conned her way out of certain extermination. Or a French collaborationist's daughter, escaped to Iowa to raise her bastard Nazi son.

"Phillipa," Eula was saying, "I'm sure everything is going to be okay." And then, of course, I was present, instantly apoplectic, saying "What? What's wrong? What's happened?"

"Ginny and Silas have gone to the hospital, to the—"

"Hospital? Why the hospital?"

"Not the hosp—the infuse . . . infusion—infusion center."

"The infusion center? What is that? What's—?"

Eula grabbed the reins at last: "It's all right. Ginny's become . . . de-hydrated?" She said it like a foreign word, stressed in the wrong place. "The doctor wants to give her fluid?"

"Why does she need fluids? Why is she dehydrated?" I felt I was falling, grabbing.

"The vomiting," Eula said. "She's been vomiting."

"On purpose?"

Eula looked at me uncomprehendingly. "She's been ill," she tried. "Sick to her stomach?"

Disoriented, jet-lagged, probably truly in shock, I put down my bags, found my car keys, and drove to River City, to Ginny. Silas hadn't yet navigated her through the health care labyrinth. The Sheibels' nursery job had no benefits; Michael and I paid for Ginny's very rudimentary coverage. Silas had nothing. The Amish care for their own—though not their own lapsed.

THE INFUSION CENTER is apparently where cancer patients go for chemo drips. Ginny had gotten fluids in the ER and the psych ward, but hadn't been here before. The place had a lazy feel to it; everyone appeared to be dying, but slowly. It smelled like a cafeteria steam tray: bleach and boiled plastic. On vinyl loungers amid hulking beige bunkers, bald and turbaned people strung with tubes lay hooked to medi-bagged concoctions and watched TV or slept as their potions dripped and exhausted caregivers worked crosswords under ticking fluorescent lights.

I stood at reception, scanning the patients until the desk nurse pointed me to a semiprivate enclosure with frosted-glass half-walls. As I approached, Silas emerged. He doesn't dress traditionally anymore, but his clothes are still plain: work pants, a T-shirt or long underwear top, a work shirt, maybe an old Shetland sweater in winter—always shrunken-looking, boiled, the sleeves too short, hem stretched wide. His tawny hair is wispy—he'll be as bald as Lucius by thirty—and he wears a few days' worth of blond beard. His face is deeply creased for such a young person, with crow's-feet and smile lines, and he's small, wiry with muscle, his eyes warm and lively. I could be describing Lucius, I realize, though I'm not struck in person by their resemblance.

Before he could greet me, I said, "Silas, what's happening? Is she okay?"

"Eula didn't tell . . . ? Oh, no—you'd left already when I called." A shy grin was breaking over his face. "We're . . ." He laid a hand on his stomach. "We'll be expecting a baby."

"She's not—it's just . . . it's just morning sickness?" Did the Amish say that? "Sick from the baby?" Silas looked uncomfortable. "Congratulations?" I offered. I was thinking that unless female fertility had been deemed a preexisting condition, this care would be covered.

Silas thanked me. He looked tired. "She has an IV now, with medication for the nausea."

Just then, from behind the partition, Ginny cried out, a horror movie scream, and Silas and I flew to her. Contorted in a lounger reclined as far as it could go, Ginny writhed and kicked, her face red and wet. A blanket and pillows had been flung to the floor. She wore a sweatshirt, hood up and tied, but she was clawing at the strings like she was choking, moaning as if she were in labor. "I can't move my limbs," she cried. "It's like I can't stretch . . . I can't . . . they're—" She thrashed in the chair, then shook violently, smacking the armrests.

Silas pushed the call button, then steadied Ginny, undid her hood, and helped her out of the sweatshirt. When he raised her arms, she began to gag. I grabbed a bin—there were already clots of spit and bile at the bottom—and tried to get it under her mouth, but she was thrashing, gulping for air, pushing everything out of her way, yanking her shirt collar away from her throat. "I'm scared," she kept saying. "My limbs. I can't—" She heaved, but there was nothing in her. "They're trapped. In my skin. I can't push out. I'm so scared—"

A nurse strode in, elbowed me and Silas aside with unflappable nursely efficiency, checked Ginny's tubes and connectors, and took her vitals. Though she did it all quickly, nothing felt urgent enough. I wanted her to call in reinforcements, to bark *Stat!*, rip things off, jab things in. But she just went through her maneuvers like she was completing the Stations of the Cross—or whatever you do at the Stations of the Cross. I clutched the plastic bile bin. Ginny gripped Silas's hand as he stroked the damp hair from her forehead. The nurse said, "You're fine."

We waited for more. It didn't come. "She's got pain in her limbs," I said.

"Not *pain*," Ginny moaned.

Silas intervened. "Her arms and legs are . . . cramped?" He looked to Ginny.

Her voice quavered: "I can't stretch them. They're too big for my skin—" Midsentence, she began to heave. My own gag reflex kicked in and I had to look away.

The nurse nodded but didn't seem to be listening. "Side effect of the Reglan, probably—paranoia, panic, anxiety . . . I'll check. Be back with more water." She turned and left.

"Probably a side effect?" I looked to Silas. "Paranoia and panic? What's the drug she said? Regulan? Do they know anything about Ginny? About her history?"

Ginny sobbed, then heaved, which set off more of the same. "Oh, God, I can't do this—" She convulsed. I couldn't watch; I wanted to cover her body with my own. Silas tried to hold her, but she bucked in the lounger, then began to shudder. "The blanket," she begged. I tucked it around her as best I could. Her teeth chattered. "I'm so cold. I was so hot—now I'm—"

"This is insane," I said. "They have to do something." I ran to reception. Two nurses stood chatting, one absently flexing a stethoscope's pincers like a stress-relieving device; the other dangled Ginny's water pitcher in her hand. "My daughter"—I gestured, frantic —"is having a bad reaction to meds. Is there a doctor around? Who's prescribing the—what is it? Rogaine?"

Laughter burst from the nurses. I wanted to slap them. They sobered; one said, "Reglan."

"Reglan. Fine." God, I've dealt with so many nurses. It was a god-awful flashback, the recurring nightmare of Ginny. Will some concoction render her functional? A few milligrams of this, a tablet of that. Pinch of mugwort, sprig of chirping cherrybark. It's sorcery! I said, "My daughter has a long history at this hospital." *Mental illness* was all over her charts, but I couldn't bring myself to say it; they had the files. "She tapered off her psych meds"—I didn't even know what she took anymore—"to try to get pregnant, which she managed, apparently. Then her grandmother died." I sounded like my undergrads with their countless grandparents all dying every semester. "She can't handle paranoiac side effects." The nurses' eyes glazed over, a look I knew all too well, reserved for ranting mothers, always so sure they know what's best for their babies.

Unsurprisingly, I got nowhere. Someone refilled Ginny's water. Then came a shift change: the scrubs remained, the bodies — the heads atop the V-necks, the badges — changed. We got new Kims, different Melissas and Debbies, Lawanda became Renée. Silas got Ginny quieted. She was off the Reglan drip, just on fluids, and the panic had dulled. She'd stopped gagging, managed to sleep. I stood staring at the blank television screen in the corner. TVs everywhere in these places — as if television ever made anyone feel better about anything.

I called Michael with the news, then dozed in a lounger for the hours it took Ginny's IVs to drain. When she was discharged that afternoon, I drove behind Silas's Festiva to Walgreens for an antinausea prescription and waited, listening to "Anything Goes" on my car stereo — *The world has gone mad today, and good's bad today* — parked between two defunct storefronts, both now churches, and proud rivals in the Great American Church Signboard Bad-Pun-Off. River City Church of God: COME ON IN FOR A FAITH LIFT! Iowa Calvary: JOIN OUR PROPHET-SHARING PROGRAM! Pray tell, who exactly do such signs hope to draw?

On the strip out of town, Silas signaled and I followed them to a McDonald's drive-thru where he bought Ginny a shake she apparently imagined being able to keep down. Milkshakes were a fixture of teenage Ginny's diet when we needed to ply her with calories. If we got one into her, and kept her in sight while she digested it, we'd made a modicum of progress — although milkshakes are also easy to coax back up, appealing to the bulimic, who takes such matters into account. These are things in which I am, so help me, an unintentional expert. Five minutes past Mickey D's, Silas pulled to the shoulder, hazards blinking, for Ginny to vomit milkshake out the passenger door. We idled, Ginny vomited—sometimes that felt like the story of our lives.

That night was a long one. Ginny couldn't lie beside Silas—food smells trapped in his beard, hospital smells on his skin. He bathed and shaved at two a.m., but the soap scent made her heave; he lay on the floor by the bed so he'd be able to help her to the bathroom, which she finally refused to leave. She curled up on the floor, her cheek against the tub's cool claw foot. I got up to pee and found Silas asleep in the hall. In the bathroom, I got a wet washcloth and squatted beside Ginny, offering the compress. She only moaned. I brushed back her bangs and laid the cool cloth on her forehead. Softly, I stroked her skin. She groaned, "Don't—" and I jerked away. That's us: she rebukes, I retreat. "No," she choked, straining against the nausea, "the cool. Is nice. Just don't move." I left the cloth on her forehead and didn't touch her again. I sat perfectly still; air movement sickened her. The moon shone in through a tiny window above the toilet, and a patch of white enamel bathtub glowed in its light like polished bone. Ginny's face was shaded by the tub's overhang, but the light would find her as the moon crossed the sky. I thought: *I'll sit here all night and shield my daughter from the moon.* Then Eula got up to pee, and when she was done I went to resume my vigil but found the room dark: ever resourceful, and far more sensible than I, Eula'd fashioned a curtain from a hand towel and some straight pins.

Silas returned to work early the following day. He'd already taken a month off, and the tornado had plowed a steady stream of jobs for construction-carpenter types like him. Silas had to grab work when it came and hope it kept coming. I was the one to call the Sheibel nursery to explain why Ginny couldn't work. The Sheibels would be fine. Like every River City business, they had college kids lined up, desperate for summer jobs, but Ginny felt she'd let everyone down: the Sheibels and their staff, and then on out to the DNC, John Kerry, and America at large. "Ginny," I said, "the U.S. presidency is not riding on your ninety-two-pound frame."

From her bed she looked up and it seemed she was going to hurl until I realized she was giving me a look I knew all too well: the if-you're-not-joking-you're-an-even-bigger-idiot-than-I-thought look. When I didn't respond, she summoned strength and said—excruciatingly slowly, her eyes closed, as if looking at me was more than she could bear: "I haven't weighed ninety-two pounds." Pause. "Since high school." She wasn't done. "Not less. Than a hundred. Since the shock." Her eyes opened. "Why. Must everything. Be *the* most. Dramatic story. Possible? I'd be so grateful. For a boring. Story that was. True." Her voice hung in the air. I felt like she'd kicked me in the stomach. And like I'd been completely had. You can't argue with someone in Ginny's condition, but I couldn't trust her: she'd lied to us so often about her weight, about everything. The opposite of The Boy Who Cried Wolf, Ginny was The Girl Who Cried I'm Fine. A fairy tale for a new age: The Girl Who Yelled Leave Me the Fuck Alone. We hadn't discussed her weight in years, but I could see how I'd seized on ninety-two as a number that captured Ginny's tininess without raising instant alarm. You say your adult child weighs sixty-eight pounds—which has been true, believe me—and you're saying: *My daughter is Karen Carpenter. My baby is dying.* But *ninety-two* captured Ginny's tininess without signaling clear, immediate danger. *Ninety-two* had served me well. That day at the Yoders', though, I choked everything down and said simply, "I'm sorry, Gin. I only said it as a figure of speech. I didn't mean anything. I'm sorry."

Ginny absorbed this, inhaled deeply, and said, "Me too," and we stayed there together, in our sorrow and our sorriness, until Ginny rallied to speak again. "Ma, I need. To ask something." Her eyes were closed, and I shut mine—easier for us both somehow. Haltingly, she said, "You think. Grandma Ma. Killed herself?" It was the first she'd spoken of Bernadette.

I chose my words carefully, opening my eyes to see how I was affecting her. "Bernadette wasn't senile." I felt so kindly toward the woman then, proud of her for her strength, or fortitude, or some-

thing. "She didn't suffer spells of confusion. It's hard to imagine anything befalling her that she didn't orchestrate." Tears seeped from
Ginny's eyes and into her matted hair. "Maybe she was ready?" I
started to choke up, too. "Maybe she felt it was time?"

Ginny let out a cry, turned her head to vomit, but only dry-heaved,
then lay there panting. When the nausea passed, her tears flowed
again and she spoke in a voice both plaintive and terrified. "How can
I. Have a baby? How can I. Inflict life. On someone?" Then she wept.
I had things to say, but they would've been no comfort. I couldn't
even hold her while she cried. I could do nothing, and that impotence
is the most miserably familiar feeling I know.

That evening when Silas came home, I went out, just to drive
around. A shredded truck tire on the shoulder of Highway 1 reminded me of the apple skins Bernadette used to peel with a par-
ing knife in one long spiral and bounce up and down like a Slinky to
charm Ginny. Passing a farm where big white plastic rolls of silage
lay fermenting at the edge of the field, I remembered little Ginny saying they looked like giant tubes of refrigerator cookie dough. Beside
a Century Farm plaque was one of those black-and-white scripture
signs framed in white PVC that are everywhere out here, probably
all from the same evangelical mail-order catalog. This one said something that ended in GOD IS NO RESPECTER OF PERSONS. ACTS 10:34.
People are supposed to read that and go rush to worship? I do not for
a minute understand humanity.

I wound up in River City, so I went to the co-op, then sat in the
parking lot trying to call Lucius, to hell with international charges.
But I was thwarted, of course, by my damn cell phone. Fifty, and I'm
already *that* old person, flapping anxiously in the face of technology
as my students roll their eyes. Before I went back to Prairie, I stopped
by the house — *our* house? — to pick up a book, but really to see Michael, who'd calmed me through years of Ginny-conflict. To go to
him was instinctual, yes, but also, his mother had just died, and I'd
discovered for her a compassion I wanted to share with him.

Michael was out back watering his perennials. In our division of garden labor, he did flowers, I did food. Thus, no vegetable garden that year, only a fenced patch of thriving weeds. Like a neighborly Iowan, I sidled up and said, "Hollyhocks look good."

Michael scowled. My alarm surged until he spoke and I realized his anger wasn't at me. "Something's at them. Tiny green caterpillar. I smash every damn one—next day they're back."

"And the slugs?" Married twenty-six years and chatting like garden club acquaintances.

"They're okay." He sounded defeated, by the garden pests or me, I didn't know. He made as if to set down the hose, but didn't, just stood holding the nozzle limply. "How's Gin?"

I lifted my eyebrows, my shoulders, and shrugged to say, *Who the hell knows?*

Michael nodded, his mouth a grim line. A moment later he said, "You need something?"

I lifted my book, my paltry excuse. "Michael, if there's anything I can . . . help you deal with her things . . . ?" We'd done this together twice already; both my parents were dead.

Michael inhaled—I feared he might blow—but he said, "There's surprisingly little. We did most of it getting her out of Carpathia. It's all in the attic boxes there. I'll get some students to help. There's still her East Prairie boxes here . . ." On impulse, and unchecked, I laid my hand on Michael's forearm, and he did not flinch. He lifted his own free hand, placing it over mine as if in appreciation, and we stood there in the garden, our arms crisscrossed like we might begin a promenade. We stayed longer than was comfortable, but his hand was on top and I didn't want to be the one to pull away. Finally, Michael spoke. "Bring something to Gin, would you? My mother's sewing basket. It's inside." And he lifted his moist hand from mine to sweep it toward the house, as if I might not know this "inside" of which he spoke. "Hall table. Needlework stuff. Maybe Gin'd like it, something to do while she's laid up."

"Aren't you taking her to tomorrow's OB appointment? Give it to her then . . . ?"

Michael shook his head, and I had the impression he'd thought this all through. I'd removed my hand from his arm, but didn't quite know what to do with it, so I fiddled, passing my book from hand to hand, then wrapped my arms around it at my chest like a *Bye Bye Birdie* schoolgirl.

"Maybe it's time to sell Carpathia?" Michael shrugged, talking mostly to himself, a conversation he'd been having for days. "It was for Ginny. She won't need it now. They're set. Or will be, in the straw bale." He paused then, turning to address me. "That's you, Phil. That's all you." He was nodding to acknowledge the truth of something, or to concede a point to me.

"Wait, what is?" My heart raced. I needed to formulate a defense, fast, and didn't yet know the crime of which I'd been accused.

"Gin. Living a life. Married . . ." he marveled. "You were a pain in the fucking ass," he said, "but it's what got her here, to this. You got her to this."

"*We* did, Michael. We *all* did. I'm hardly—"

Uncharacteristically, Michael cut me off. "*You* did, Phil. I'm too nice a Midwesterner to have gotten results like that, to push her, and the doctors, the way you did."

"Bring in the pushy Jew when you want results, they always say."

But again Michael was shaking his head, not willing to let me deflect this praise. "Don't do it, Phil," he said. "She's really good, and she's got you to thank for a whole lot of that."

I couldn't reply or I'd've sobbed, so I only stood there, trying to thank him with my eyes. Michael returned to the debate he'd been having with himself about the house on Carpathia, now taking up his own rebuttal: "The tenants have it through the new year, so I guess we've got till 2005 to figure it out." He gestured, then, as if into the future, and the hose nozzle, leaky for years, sent out a spray. I yelped, jumping back, but a splash caught me. Michael dropped the hose—

"Shit, I'm sorry" — and took the book from my hands to inspect for water damage. It was Joan Didion's *The White Album,* which I had no reason to suddenly need; I thought he'd surely see I'd fabricated the excuse to come by. But the book didn't seem to register except as a thing he'd accidentally wetted, and he laid it over the vegetable garden fence as if to save the place, saying, "Sun'll dry it in a minute." A minute — a minute to look over my sad vegetable garden, its towering green fuzz of asparagus gone to flower. I wondered if Michael'd eaten any that spring or let it run riot. Probably zillions of dill and cilantro volunteers in there, tomatoes reseeding themselves, peppers, melon sprouts, squash, cucumbers. No telling what thrived under cover of all those lamb's-quarters. I found the latch and stepped in, and Michael said, "I just haven't . . ." He shook his head at the mess, as if he were to blame for its disarray.

"Michael, please, no." I waved off his apology. "Hell, there's probably a salvageable garden in here yet." Grabbing a stalk of garlic mustard — an invasive as big as a damn sapling — I yanked, and it came free easily. I lobbed it onto the weed pile, got a grip on a massive dandelion, and pulled it up by the root. It's very satisfying when a weed comes up with the full root intact like that; it made me want to pull another. The hose went back on. Michael continued watering while I weeded. It was like stepping back in time, so vertiginously simple, like pressing Undo. I would rise from the vegetable patch, overgrown zucchini in hand, and say, "Dinner?" and we'd discuss what was in the fridge, then head inside to shower, pour a glass of wine, and slice up the mammoth squash and turn it into a meal. It felt as if we could simply resume, set the needle back on the record, and suffer nothing but a slight strangeness, a déjà vu. Early evening, in the weeds, the *whoosh* of the hose spray, and beyond that the sounds of our neighborhood — calls, cars, phones, static, the far-off tinkle of the ice cream truck. I pulled lamb's-quarters from a cluster of dill sprouts and thought how effortlessly I could step back into this life just as I'd left it.

. . .

I BROUGHT BERNADETTE'S sewing basket back to Prairie and gave it to Ginny the next day. Half sitting in bed, she took a breath, picked out a piece of embroidery, and tried to remove a threaded needle from the cloth. It required more strength than she had. Another breath and she was gagging. I rushed over, swapped the basket for the barf bin, and held it while she retched. I thought of Michael the previous evening when he'd said, "You got her here," and I thought, *Great, here*, as she gagged and spat. *Great.* If I'm due any credit at all for her stability, it's because I've taken responsibility for her collapses, too, stood for her when she couldn't on her own. But I was tired, goddammit, really tired. And I'd thought she was finally making it on her own.

A few hours later, Michael arrived to take her to the ob-gyn. Eula left for market with Oren. She'd arranged things with a van-driving Mennonite family who worked the same venues, and now the Wingers gave Eula a ride whenever she needed—they even had a spare car seat.

When Michael and Ginny returned that afternoon, she went right to bed. Michael updated me: her due date was February 25. The morning sickness would improve past the first trimester; she'd made it through eight weeks, the doctor said, what was four more? I hated him already. He prescribed a prenatal vitamin and said to try saltines and ginger ale for the nausea. For that you need a medical degree? He'd also prescribed a new antinausea drug, but Michael hadn't filled it on the way home, so I said I'd go if he stayed with Ginny. He agreed, and I got my keys while he settled on the porch with a beer. As I passed, I reached out to put a hand to his hair, and we rested there a moment until I let go and moved on.

When I got back with the drugs, Michael was gone. Silas sat on the porch, looking tired, drinking beer from a can. I poured a glass of wine and sat with him. We didn't talk, just sipped our drinks, watching a turkey buzzard circle and dive for roadkill. Fireflies were twinkling over the cornfields when Ginny cried out from upstairs. Silas jumped to his feet. I tried to beat him to it, saying, "Stay, enjoy the evening," but he shook his head. Evening meant little to him without Ginny. She doesn't exhaust him the way she does me. He was twenty-two years old that summer.

Silas bid me good night and went to his wife, and I — a fifty-year-old woman with the emotional maturity of an eighth-grader — took my laptop, drove halfway to River City to a strip by a condo complex, got an iced tea at Subway, and sat in my car listening to Andrew Lloyd Webber, writing an email to Lucius. We'd planned to be together; we hadn't made provisions for overseas phone calls. I didn't get cell service at the Yoders' anyway. In the car with my laptop, I wrote quickly, then found a Linksys that wasn't password protected, and managed to jump on the Wi-Fi. I waited after sending, sucking waxy ice, hoping maybe I'd caught Lucius online and get a response. My car sat in the shadow of the All Souls signboard: GOD ANSWERS KNEEMAIL. At ten, anxious and lonely, I gave up and shut down the computer, but the idea of going back to listen to Ginny heave the night away felt untenable. I thought maybe I'd go sit in a River City bar, stay out all night — or what passes for all night in a town like ours, which is two a.m., when everything closes. I didn't want to go to a café full of students eating cheesecake, soft jazz piped in like carbon monoxide; I wanted to sit on a barstool, scowling, drinking whiskey, talking to no one. But I don't actually like whiskey, and my scowl just looks like patrician disdain.

Across the lot from Subway a sign announced *Hoagie Heaven Coming Soon* — only in America does a half-rural mini-mall need two sub shops — but I saw *Heaven* and thought of The Haven, near our house in town, where the pizza's good, there's nice beer on tap, and the lighting is blessedly dim. I imagined tucking into a corner booth, drinking Pilsner Urquell, running my fingers over illegible names carved in the butcherblock. I'd risk seeing colleagues, students, but the prospect of that booth was so comforting, I got on the road toward River City. And no, I didn't *have* to drive past our house to get to The Haven, but it was one possible route, and I took it. The lights were on, Michael in the living room watching TV. I pulled over with the notion that he might not've had dinner either. We'd spent countless evenings at The Haven; it might comfort him, too. I got out of the car and went to knock on my own front door.

Michael was barefoot, in gym shorts, his eyes squinty. "What's going on?" he asked.

"I had to get out of the house." I felt absurd. "The heat . . . Ginny . . ." It didn't explain what I was doing on his doorstep. What *was* I doing on his doorstep? "I thought of The Haven. Have you eaten? I was passing by —" But Michael cut in: "And thought you'd drop in to see if I wanted pizza?" I just stood there, and he seemed to deflate. Stepping back to allow my entry, he said, "I'll go put on some clothes," and left me marooned in the hall, afraid to step off the doormat. Part of me was ready to bolt, but I held my ground, studying the decor like I was a stranger. The Lasansky print: a dour woman, hair pulled in a tight bun. Framed silkscreen from a 1970s production of *Hair*. Wooden pegs hung with Michael's lawn-mowing ball caps. A quilt sampler hung on a dowel, its cord over a nail I'd likely hammered in. Michael used a stud finder and drywall anchors so things lasted. I'm not as foresightful or painstaking.

Michael came down in light pants and a shirt — he's a handsome man. I forget that. Our walk to The Haven was so familiar; it's often too hot in summer to think of eating until the sun goes down. We went silently amid the college town cacophony, droning crickets and chittering night birds, porch chatter, bursts of laughter, the clink of glasses, bottlecap *fittz*, shouts — *whoa-ho!* — of frat boys tossing beanbags into cornholes. We went through the night streets of River City the way we always had. My old life seemed to lie just on the other side of a flimsy screen door.

The Haven's AC was blessedly cool; everything else — the amber lighting, wood benches and tables, small stage hung with a worn oriental rug — exuded warmth. The place wasn't crowded but buoyantly full: the booths were all taken. Michael leaned into the bar to order us a pitcher while I looked for a table. Then I heard a voice I knew, calling, "Maakestads! Hello!"

A half-empty pitcher sat on the table before Randall and Linda, and I had my usual pang of confusion at the nature of their addiction and recovery. When Michael approached with our own frothy pitcher, he motioned to me with a jerk of his chin toward the bar, but I didn't know what he meant. Finally he mimed holding a cup and drinking. I apologized and went to fetch glasses, but then I realized Ginny might not've told Linda yet about being pregnant, and dashed back to make sure Michael didn't spill news that Ginny didn't want spilled. Conversation had stalled, and Michael looked ready to find a distant table, so I started to say goodbye, but then Randall was saying, "Hey, I was real sorry to hear about your mother. Real sorry." Michael thanked him, sincerely but obligatorily, not encouraging further dialogue, but Randall's not much for social cues. He asked about a memorial, a place to send flowers, and would there be a service? Did Michael have a lot to deal with, wills, testaments, whatnot? Michael shook his head, muttering half mutely. Linda sat hunched over her pizza, also shaking her head as if to say *Such a shame,* but I felt that she, too, was embarrassed by Randall, dreading a moment when he might climb on his chair and clink knife to beer stein to recite a eulogy for Bernadette Maakestad.

Like Linda, Michael retreated into himself, hunching over the pitcher, swaying a bit, then jumping back as a little wave of beer washed over the lip and splashed to the floor at his feet. "Oh!" Michael said, but his surprise didn't quite sound right. "God, better get this to a table before I drench us. Really good seeing you both." He turned to go and I raised our two empty beer glasses to Linda and Randall, then followed my husband to a table out of sight.

I sank down, sighing. "Phew! That was close."

"What was close?" Michael set down the pitcher. I could see, then, that he was near tears.

"Oh—I just—I don't think . . . I don't know if Ginny's told them yet—about the baby."

Already over it, Michael said, "Oh." I laid my hand on his arm, and he lowered his head, breathed deeply, then sat back up straight, eyes wide. A waitress approached, stopped short at the sight of our "moment," but bopped on over anyhow. She was Chelsea, and she'd be taking care of us. "I see you've got drinks. C'I bring you a nibble while you decide? Jalapeño poppers? Fifty-cent wings?" So eager, this Chelsea, plucked brows raised in exaggerated friendliness. I do pine at times for a surly urban waitress, pen poised in profound annoyance.

Michael pushed his menu away, ordered a large pesto-chicken, add artichokes, and Chelsea popped off to the kitchen. Michael poured our beer. He was close to the very frayed edge of his own respectability. Knocking on his door had been a stupid, selfish idea.

Linda passed our table on her way to the restroom, and we all waved awkwardly. A minute later, I said, "I should pee too," just to get away. As I entered the ladies', Linda was exiting the one flimsy, shuttered stall, and another woman was going in. Uneasy, we laughed. I stood to wait in the cramped sink area while Linda washed her hands, hunched like an adult in the preschool bathroom. When she turned off the water, our eyes met in the mirror. "I *know,*" she said, smiling into our reflection.

"Know what?" I said.

"Silas called. Gin got on the phone, and she couldn't hardly talk, but she told me." Linda dried her hands on a brown paper towel as if the drying itself were a pleasure.

"Told you *what?*" I wasn't taking chances.

For all her burly toughness, Linda can be charmingly prudish. "About the baby."

I exhaled audibly. "She's not telling other people, not this early. Just you."

"I know." Linda shifted. "I didn't even tell Randall yet. I was going to tonight."

"Oh?" The intricacies of what Linda and Randall did and didn't tell each other was unknown to me then, and if I thought anything of her hesitation to disclose Ginny's pregnancy to him, I probably chalked it up to some kind of squeamishness.

"I'll try and visit soon," Linda said, moving aside as the other woman exited the stall.

"Ginny would love that," I said, no idea if it was true, and Linda nodded, holding her towel like she couldn't decide whether to toss it out or not. "Well, see you out there, then," I added.

"Yeah, see you." Linda balled the towel in her fist and left the bathroom with it.

On my return to the table, Michael nodded at me the way he would to a colleague arriving at a department meeting. "Sorry," I said, sliding in. "I ran into Linda in the bathroom."

"Hope she's all right." It took me a second to understand it was just that old punch line: *You ran into her? Ouch!* It was something we did; it was silly, not even funny. I pantomimed a laugh and reached out to him, but the gesture felt rote, the only comfort of which I was capable: a hand on his arm. He let it stay.

We sat silent until the pizza came. Michael reached to serve, but then didn't. He stood, said, "I need to go," and pushed in his chair, then paused as if to say more, but didn't, just left.

I flushed with shame, like I'd been dumped in public. Sipping my beer, I lifted my eyes slowly. No one gave a shit. Still, my heart beat fast. Staring at my coaster, I tried to rein in my thoughts. I looked at my watch as if I had someplace to be. Michael could've darted out to save theater seats, teach a class, catch a train. I'd been left to get the to-go box, pay the bill, meet him there. I flagged Chelsea and gobbled a slice as she fetched our check and a box. Some grad students sat nearby and I walked over, pitcher in one hand, pizza in the other.

"We've got a—" I gestured toward a mythical *thing* I had to get to, *out there.* "The pizza'll travel, but not beer."

A guy in a Goodwill Hawaiian shirt cleared a spot beside him, saying, "By all means!"

Driving through town, I ate two more slices, then went by the bus station where River City's young, modest, and seasonal homeless population congregates after dark. I pulled over, rolled down the passenger window, and lifted the box. A group of Mohawked, tattooed kids sat against a brick wall, their dog rope-tied to a water meter nearby. I said, "You guys want some pizza?" and a combat-booted boy stood and loped across the sidewalk. He leaned in, took the box, said "Peace," and turned back to his cohort. As he walked, he inched the box open. "Pesto-chicken!" He sounded pleased. A whiff of that pizza would've made Ginny hurl.

On the way home, I paused in the Subway lot: no email from Lucius. Back in Prairie, I lay awake a long time in my hot little room, trying to think of him; we'd been apart mere days and already I could barely see his face. I fell asleep. At four a.m. I heard Ginny vomiting. I must have fallen back to sleep, for I next woke in the late morning, Silas long gone to work, and Eula tending Ginny. She lay propped on pillows in bed, in tears, watching a pair of mourning doves in a hickory. I took a straight-backed chair—just sensing the motion of a rocker made her sick—and we became an eighteenth-century cliché: I, the relationless spinster, caring for the infirm in exchange for room, board, and a meager inheritance. If I pulled my hair into a taut bun and put on a dress of Orah's—if Eula hadn't quilted them all yet—I could've passed for Whistler's mother.

"How did I think I could make it through a pregnancy?" Ginny said.

"You didn't know, Gin," I said. "Everyone doesn't go through *this* having a baby—"

She cut me off: "It's not a *baby.* It's a nonviable cell cluster."

"Gin, it'll get better—"

"What if it doesn't? I can't do this for nine months. I can't. Right now I want to die." Those are words she'd never before spoken to me, aloud and explicit. "I won't," she sobbed. "I wouldn't. Not to Silas. Not ever." Relief, but a twist of pain, too: she had someone to stay alive for, someone she wouldn't punish as she'd punished us. "I keep thinking about Grandma Ma," she said. "I saw her last at Jazz Fest. I tried to register her to vote, but you know how she was . . ."

"Gin, don't. Don't do it to yourself."

"How can I not? She was so depressed, her arthritis, not able to do what kept her sane. And I badgered her." The sewing box sat on the nightstand. "She was so depressed for so long."

"Bernadette?" I was confused, but Ginny wasn't really talking about her grandmother.

"I don't know how I could have wanted this, but now I can't undo it—or I *could*, but—"

"Is *that* what you—? Are you thinking of abort—"

"*No!* I don't *know!*" She was breathing hard, quick, heavy breaths. "Sometimes it's the only thing that makes sense, but we'd definitely never have kids, then. No adoption agency in the world . . . Me? Raise a child? With Silas I thought I could, but . . . if Bush's reelected? Bring a kid into *this*? How's it fair to inflict . . . How could *I* have anything *but* a miserable, suicidal child?"

"Ginny, please . . ."

"Ma, if you'd had a clue how I'd turn out, you'd've raced for Planned Parenthood."

"Ginny!" It wasn't true. I'd never thought of aborting. I could have—*Roe v. Wade* was decided while I was in college—plenty of my friends did. It had honestly never dawned on me.

"I want to miscarry," she was saying. "I keep hoping it'll expel itself. Then it wouldn't be my fault." She dissolved; the nausea descended. Soon she was retching red Popsicle spit, and I was thinking how if Bush got a second term and stocked the Supreme Court with Jesus-touting imperialists, they'd overturn *Roe* first chance they got, and choice would be history.

It was into this warren of joy that Randall and Linda descended that afternoon, like Santa, except through the front door. But, like Santa indeed, they came bearing bundles. Christmas in July! And came in trumpeting, literally. Randall blew a toy horn, bellowing, "Halloo, Mama!" and swooping triumphantly inside, teeming Menards bags slung over his shoulder, feathered hair pulled off his face with a terry sweatband. He waved greetings to me and took the stairs. Behind him, Linda toted more bags, and gave a small head-bow I read as apology. I followed, anxious, but when Randall threw open the bedroom door, my violently sick daughter seemed to have been replaced by their shy, sleepy friend, so serene you'd think she'd just stuck a needle in her vein.

"Little Mama!" Randall looked ready to pounce on the bed and bounce Ginny off. Linda reined him back. Ginny held still, fragile but persevering, as Randall and Linda unloaded their offerings, bestowing gifts until the quilt was piled with packaging detritus. Minutes later, the two were collecting themselves to go. Linda said, "We're just on break." Randall bellowed farewell, and as suddenly as they'd come — roar of engine, cloud of driveway dust — they were gone.

When the truck pulled away, I went back to Ginny. She'd shrunk amid the wrappings and looked small and overwhelmed. "Ma, can you put it all somewhere? I can't look at it." She closed her eyes. "I just can't." So I gathered it all: child-sized Adirondack chair, set of gardening tools for tiny hands, blow-up kiddie pool, orange onesie stamped CARPENTERS DO IT WITH TOOLS. I'm sure they'd swiped it all from Menards, or took an "employee discount" that made it nearly free. *Kinehora* on all of it. Jews don't buy gifts for unborn babies: too much can go wrong.

I put everything away and returned to Ginny, pulled my spinster-aunt chair over to the bed, and we sat watching the sun descend to the summer fields. In a few minutes she closed her eyes, and when her breathing deepened I crept downstairs to pour a glass of wine. When I got back, golden light streamed in on the wedding quilt. Eula had finished it while I was in France, and this was my first look at the whole thing spread out. It's all white, shades and gradations and textures, and in that bright sun I couldn't tell what I was seeing. A bit of oat-colored burlap gave way to something filmy and sheer as a negligee. A band of thick white, like a boat's sail, and an overlapping crescent of geometric-print cotton—maybe a hospital gown? Some shapes looked like flattened bonnets, until I glanced away and couldn't see them when I looked back, saw only a white whale spouting a spray of chenille fringe. Upside down in one corner was a word, faded blue print on worn sackcloth. It took me a while to read H-A-T-C-H-A-B-I . . . An electronics company? A Japanese steakhouse? Then I worked it out: HATCHABI-l-i-t-y. A poultry feed sack. I sipped my wine, watched my daughter sleep, and for a little while nothing felt so bad.

When Ginny woke again the sun had mostly set, though the sky still glowed. Fireflies popped out and we watched them against a dark that seemed to rise from the ground. I felt full of what I can only describe as a great goodwill. Maybe it was the wine. "They're such good people, Linda and Randall," I said, "such good friends to you." Ginny didn't respond, but I knew she agreed. I was thinking aloud on a warm, lovely evening. I felt good—so help me! Good and relaxed and gabby. "I wish I didn't see them as siblings," I said, "like Linda's his tomboy kid sister he looks out for. Don't you sometimes wish they'd fall in love and live happily ever after?"

Such an earnest sense of hope, envisioning these two ungainly, awkward people finding joy—passion!—together, but Ginny's expression made it clear I'd gotten something very wrong. *You,* said my daughter's gaze, *are a moron.* What? Linda was gay? Or Randall? They *were* brother and sister? With great rebuke, Ginny said, "They've *been* together since they met."

"They have? They—what?" I could not hide my confusion.

"Since they met, at NA. You're not kidding? Jesus." Her revulsion made me think it wasn't the pregnancy making her sick, only me. "They don't display it, parade it around, but . . . Jesus, you're really that oblivious? Are you aware of anything outside yourself at all?"

It was just the question I so often wanted to level at her. I said, "That's not fair, Ginny."

"Life isn't fair, Mom." She spat it out, every word sarcastic, like she couldn't talk *to* me, could only relay what she *might* have said if she'd deigned to converse with such an idiot.

SILAS'S CREW REGULARLY worked past sunset, using all the daylight they had. When he got home, I left, drove until I got cell service, then pulled over. On the shoulder, between pavement and corn, hundreds of tiny birds were giving a synchronized air show, swooping up and diving down, all of them at once, lighting for a split second, then taking off again, looping the loop like they were caught in a vortex. It whipped them up and deposited them back, over and over again.

I called Michael. We hadn't parted on easy terms at The Haven, but I was trying not to dwell, not take things so personally. "Michael," I began, "how would you characterize . . . how would you classify Linda and Randall's relationship?"

There was a pause before Michael said, *"What?"* He drew it out, as though I'd just spoken in pig Latin and expected he'd answer without inquiring: *Pig Latin, Phillipa, really?*

It was nothing but wishful thinking that let me respond as I did, some notion that Michael was struck as dumb as I'd been by the news of Linda and Randall's coupledom. "You *knew?*"

"Knew *what*, Phillipa? What the—? I'm a little taken aback here, okay? I'd been expecting, I don't know—I wasn't surprised you called, but I thought you might say something before . . . what? Gossiping? What are you asking? Without any mention at all of last night?"

"Last night? I don't know what happened last night, Michael. You stormed out—no, you didn't—you got up and left, but you didn't explain. How am I supposed to—?"

"*How? How* could you . . . ? Well, Phil, you could ask. You know, you could ask."

"Ask what? Ask what's wrong? I'm sorry—I'm sorry I didn't ask. I thought I knew what was wrong. Your mother died. Our marriage is falling apart. Our daughter's off her meds, vomiting and acting like a lunatic! I'm sorry I didn't ask—did I really *not ask* what was wrong? Last night? Or now? When I called just now? I was supposed to start by asking what was wrong? I'm sorry, I'm sorry. I forgot! I forget where we are in time sometimes, I forget for a second—"

"How nice for you," Michael cut in, "to be able to forget."

"Michael, I'm sorry, I'm sorry! I don't know how to do this! I was trying to stop thinking everything was about me. I was trying to let you do what you needed to do."

"Don't treat me like a tantruming child, Phillipa. Don't." He was still angry, but calmer. These were familiar lines, familiar ground. How many times over the years had Michael told me to stop treating him like a tantruming child? I should've stopped already.

"I'm sorry." Sometimes it seems like the only thing I say. Is it irony that there was a time, when Ginny was two or three, when "sorry" was *the* thing she could not say? If she did anything—even totally accidentally—that called for apology, she'd freak out. She'd curl up, bury her head and limbs into her stomach, and wail in horror or shame at having made a mistake she couldn't undo. To apologize was to admit wrongdoing, and consent to living with that imperfect and unretractable wrongness, and that was intolerable to her. She'd tantrum, but she could not apologize. Then something clicked and she figured out that if she *always* apologized, for everything, constantly, and atoned for wrongdoing before she could do wrong, then she could maybe live with herself. So suddenly everything was "sorry." You'd say, "Good morning," and Ginny'd say, "Sorry, hi." "How'd you sleep, Gin?" "Good, sorry." "Hungry?" "Sorry, yes, sorry." Like a tic, it came as if involuntarily, yet sounded blithe and utterly insincere. We tried to explain that "sorry" lost its meaning when repeated so often, that words grew dysfunctional with overuse, that crying "Sorry!" was like crying "Wolf!" and one day — when there really was a wolf, or she really was sorry — no one would believe her. Now, twenty years later, *I'd* become the perpetually sorry one, overusing my apology words.

Michael sighed deeply.

I took a breath and said, "Do you want to talk about last night?"

He let out a short, bitter laugh. "Not really," he admitted, then laughed again, but more kindly. "I just couldn't be there, with you, in that place — the same —" He broke off. When he spoke again, a false jollity masked the hurt: "A little too far down memory lane. Not the trip for me just now, thanks. Anyway, so, what were you asking? About Randall and Linda?"

I told him. "Did *you* know they were a couple?" They had their own places: Randall lived in a trailer park, in a mobile home he owned outright via some complicated provenance of drug dealers and jail stints, debts owed and claimed. Linda had lived in a halfway house for a while, but for the past few years she'd shared a crappy apartment in town with some other former addicts.

Michael said, "I guess I assumed if they were that close they were probably sleeping together." Then he asked after Gin, and I suppose I might've said something simple like, *She's okay.* Or, *I'm not sure.* Or, *You know, up and down.* But I was all too eager to switch topics, and for twenty-five years Ginny was the subject we shared, so I launched in: "She said today she wants to miscarry. Or abort. That any child she had would be depressive and suicidal, and that she wanted to die, but wouldn't kill herself. She talked about your mother, too, about *her* depression. She's worried that with her own suicidal impulse, and now Bernadette's, too . . ." I'd like to think that had we been face-to-face, I'd've seen Michael's reaction and shut up sooner, but as it was, I didn't know until too late that I should have already stopped talking.

"Jesus Christ, Phillipa," he said, "you never fucking stop! Ginny's grandmother's dead—she's trying to deal with that—and all you can do is harp on this idea that she died just to piss you off!" I tried to break in, but Michael wouldn't let me. "It's that hard to get past your own egotistical notion that my mother OD'd to interrupt your European tryst? That she took her own life just to inconvenience *you*? Your self-absorption is downright pathological sometimes."

"*My* self-absorption?" The opportunity for defense had passed. So, too, apparently, had my empathy for Bernadette. "Your mother didn't spend five minutes of her life thinking of anyone but herself. *Pathological self-absorption*? Pathological self-absorption is what it takes to kill yourself. Did she think about Ginny? Did she even think what it would do to—"

Now Michael was shouting over me. "My mother didn't *do* anything to Ginny. She *died*. *You've* decided she killed herself. You *decided* it. That doesn't make it reality. She just died."

"She *did* kill herself. That's not even a question—you told me yourself. She swallowed the pills. Accidentally? In confusion? Did she seem confused to you? Really?"

"What do you think?" he demanded. "You think showing you the 'family album' was her last worldly act? She came clean, to *you*, and then offed herself? Is that—"

"That album's bullshit, Michael. Not a picture in it has anything to do with—"

"The woman is *dead*, Phillipa. My *mother* is *dead*. I am not having . . . I cannot . . ." His tone was changing, his words slower, deliberate, his anger palpable. "You don't get to decide what's true. You don't get to ferret out some truth-at-any-cost just to satisfy your own need for it. My mother's life was harder than yours will ever be, than we can even conceive."

"She never allowed us to conceive—never told us one true—"

"Stop," Michael commanded. "Stop it. Now. She is dead. She's dead. She is dead." Then he broke completely: a gasp, a wrenched sob, and everything got muffled. He must have been holding the phone against his chest or a sofa cushion to mute his breakdown.

I felt broken, too. I spoke softly into the phone. "I'm sorry, Michael. I'm sorry. I'm sorry." I repeated it, hoping he'd hear, hoping there was still something left in the word.

I hung up and drove to the nearest Wi-Fi, stopping at a Burger King drive-thru for a chocolate shake. I hadn't had one in years. It tasted like liquefied marshmallows and I drank it greedily, slurping the dregs as I pulled into a spot. The Calvary Church signboard read: BE CAREFUL WHO YOU HATE IT COULD BE SOMEONE YOU LOVE. In my in-box was a brief, unsatisfying email from Lucius, but what did I want? Epic, elegiac declarations of ardent longing? I was tired of longing. When I was young, before Michael, longing was exactly what I wanted: the ecstasy of yearning, that insatiable, orgiastic reaching. Now I didn't want to *want,* I just wanted Lucius, and I couldn't have him. I was mad with longing. I know sometimes only madness preserves us, but I'm not Virginie, steeled inside madness to survive a war, or Ginny, whose existence has been ruled by it. I've led a good and easy life. My madness—if I can call it that—was first-world, American-made, white bourgeois madness. It was roller coaster, carnival madness, and I'd bought my own ticket. I'd asked for it all.

I STAYED ON at the farmhouse, taking care of Ginny while Silas was at work. Late at night I'd hear them argue: Ginny crying, "I shouldn't be pregnant," and Silas saying, "Intense illness can be a sign of a strong pregnancy, Gin. Your body's fighting to keep the fetus safe." She'd snap at him, then, in a tone I thought she reserved for me: "It's not a fetus, it's a parasite." If it *were* me, a screaming match would have ensued, the two of us shrieking back and forth: "Fetus!" "Parasite!" "Fetus!" "Parasite!" With Silas, Ginny just wept. "I don't feel anything I should, no instinct to protect it. It's poisonous. I want it out. It's like it's Bush, and I'm America, and this *thing* took over. I want it out like I want him out. I hate what I am—what our life's reduced to." And then the wailing gave way to vomiting, which was almost a relief. To me, at least.

Late July, the Democratic convention: a tiny yet bold ray of hope arrived in the form of a young Illinois state senator named Barack Obama. A candidate for the U.S. Senate, he gave the keynote speech, and people were talking *rising star of the Democratic Party,* etc. At Ginny's request, I brought a radio to the bedroom. We turned up the volume to compete with the fans required to blow Silas's and my human odors away from her, but in her farmhouse sickroom—wind machines howling, crickets sending out their high-pitched drone, dim kerosene lamp on the bureau, the crackling radio blaring a solitary voice interrupted every few seconds by thunderous crashes of applause—we listened. "Do we participate," Senator Obama asked, "in a politics of cynicism, or do we participate in a politics of hope?" We listened as this black son of a single mother took the national stage and raised goosebumps on our bodies despite the thick prairie heat. He spoke and I wanted to denounce every cynical thing to ever come from my wiseass mouth. Why wasn't *this* man running for president? Kerry was middle-of-the-road; Obama was audacious. Audacity was what we needed.

One evening in early August, I took an email outing to the strip, and returned—sucking down a Subway pop, flipping off BUSH-CHENEY signs (with a particularly stiff bird for a lawn sign on 490th: WHOREMONGERS AND ADULTERERS GOD WILL JUDGE. HEB. 13:4)— to encounter a situation at the Yoders'. When I'd left, Eula and Oren were still at market, and Linda was looking after Ginny until Silas got home. I came up the drive and saw something was wrong: Silas's car was there, and, beside it, a big humanish shape was rocking back and forth like a davening rabbi. It almost looked like two people having sex against the car, but I got closer and saw it was Eula with Oren clutched to her chest. They rocked, halting and jerking, Oren's limbs flailing. Something had happened to him—he was choking, or having a seizure, or anaphylaxing. I leapt from my car. I heard him screaming, which eased my fear a bit, but still I rushed to them, now imagining spurting blood, mangled limbs, skin sliced unstanchably deep. There's a certain hysteria specific to parents of mortally sick or injured children, and Eula was in that kind of distress. Market crates at her feet, she sobbed, wrenching against Oren's thrashing.

When she saw me, Eula froze, then let out a cry that twisted her face, and from some primal resource I didn't know I possessed, I tapped skills unexercised in a quarter-century. I scooped Oren from her arms, assessed him for damage, and, finding none, swung him onto my hip and began thumping my hand to his back—good, solid, resounding whacks, like when a ball hits a tennis racket just right. I may have appeared, just then, like someone "good with babies," and though I am not, Oren calmed some, laid his head on my chest, jerked, switched cheeks, rested, switched again. He was flailing from exhaustion, overdue for a nap that was being prevented for a reason I now understood: Ginny and Silas were inside, quarreling.

"I can't go in." Eula batted a hand at her face. "I'm so ashamed." Beautiful even then: those wide cheekbones, skin unblemished as a cherub's, her strong jaw even more striking without the long hair to soften it. I'd pieced together the story of her haircut: she'd fallen asleep in the bathtub, homemade candles burning on a shelf over her head. Unpeeling her wax-bound mane from the porcelain tub was easy enough, and so was finding her sewing scissors and styling an emergency, impromptu pixie cut. She looked like someone's Amish lesbian dream girl.

I bounced Oren, who wasn't yet asleep but was nearly out of fight. "You're ashamed to go inside, Eula? I don't understand." Bobbing, I felt the muscle memory of it, the isometrics of baby-mothering.

Eula tried to collect herself. "I know it's for Ginny to choose . . ." Instantly I understood: Ginny was going to abort the baby. "She's so sick. I cannot blame her for wanting it to end." Eula struggled to render her feelings in language. "In my head I know, but in my heart—" She sobbed. "In my heart, it's pain. Pain I can't—" She scowled, raised her hand as if to slap her own face, but let it fall limp against her thigh. "Oh, I'm stupid—*I can't bear*—so stupid!" She drew a choppy breath and placed a palm against the back of her own neck as though she had to be two people in one, the comforter and the comforted. "Ginny says it's nothing—fluff, cells, not viable. She says it's not a baby. But it *could* be. I think of my parents, unable to have more children after my birth—the joy they'd take in a baby of Ginny and Silas, and my heart—" The anguish in Eula's face—I didn't know how Ginny could see it and not crack. Then I realized Ginny *hadn't* seen it; Eula'd hidden it from her. Of course she had.

Standing by the car, Eula seemed determined to make sense of something. "My parents' death was an accident. No one meant them harm. That is—it's one thing." She drew air. "I am trying to understand how Ginny—Ginny, that I love—how Ginny can bear—and I—" She tried to pull it together again. "I am ashamed of myself, too stupid to understand. And making like *my* feelings matter. Making a . . . a . . ." She searched. "A *fuss!*" She swatted the air dismissively. "I'm a stupid girl. I know nothing. But all that will be lost—it is the loss of my parents over again."

I couldn't hug her with the baby on me, so just wrapped an arm awkwardly around her shoulders. Eula dropped her head toward me but lifted it again, uncomfortable, and we stood as if we'd happened to come outside to lean on the car and enjoy the sunset. The words thrumming through my head would only have confused Eula more, and I had no right, so I just stood there, my arm around her, crying and thinking, *Jesus Christ, I've gone pro-life.*

What I could glean from Eula was that when the Wingers dropped her off after market, Silas was already home, and Eula'd started inside with Oren but heard the arguing, understood its subject, and retreated. She'd been standing at the car ever since, unwilling to go in and let them know she'd witnessed the fight, or let them see her reaction. Her own tears, she felt, were inappropriate, and she refused to inflict them on Ginny and Silas. The logic didn't totally track, but she was adamant, and in her conviction she reminded me of no one so much as my daughter.

Oren was asleep for now, but we had no idea how long Ginny and Silas would fight. It was unprecedented. I did the only thing I could think of and had Eula load Oren in my car. We drove until I got cell service, and called Michael. "I know you're upset with me," I said when he answered the phone—he *had* answered it, even with my name on the caller ID. "And I'm sorry, but . . ." I described the gist of the situation. "I need to bring Eula and Oren to River City. I'll put them in the basement, so they have space. I'll take Ginny's room. It's only for the night."

Michael sounded resigned. "I'll make sure there're sheets on the bed down there." I wondered if he'd been in the basement since he found his mother dead in it.

I called Silas's cell next, blessedly got his voicemail, and left a message as to where we were. Eula didn't speak on the ride. When we pulled up and began to gather ourselves, I realized she might be hungry and wondered aloud if Michael might have anything or if I should go pick something up, but Eula shook her head. "No, Phillipa, please. We'll go right to bed. Please."

I knocked, Michael called that the door was open, and we went in. He waved a somber hello from the living room. Eula waved back and I made a sleep gesture and led mother and child to the basement. When I came up, Michael was still in the living room, having a drink. He lifted it at me as I entered, as if in greeting, but there was something in the gesture that made it clear he was commenting on the absurdity of lifting a glass in cheer to the woman who was making his life miserable. He couldn't get rid of me, and I was the one who'd left him! It was ludicrous. I stood in the door gauging the situation, watching him resign himself: *Well, she's here, might as well talk to her . . .*

"So," he said, "no grandkids after all." He was a little drunk. At another time I might have flared at him for his flippancy, but I only shrugged. "Did something do it," he asked, "or just . . . everything?" He's not an eloquent drinker, Michael.

"You know, she talks about Bush, the state of the world," I said, "but maybe it just lends her legitimacy." I didn't know if he was listening. "Is a 'politically imperative' abortion easier to justify? *Surrender George or I'll abort!*" I was talking like I'd had a few too many. I couldn't seem to stop. "Maybe she thinks she's like a Jew in the ghetto—Nazis breaking down the door, smothering her baby to save it from Treblinka."

Michael stared at me in astonishment. "There are times," he said levelly, "when it makes no sense that she is your child." He stood—not very steadily—set down his drink, pushed past me, and climbed the stairs. My mind spun. I couldn't process his comment, so instead I drained his drink—ice-watery whiskey—and went upstairs to sleep in Ginny's old room, under the ticking gaze of the shifty-eyed cat clock.

When I woke, I knew it was early by the hazy light, and I was still the last one up. Slipping on shorts and shrugging back into my bra, I caught a whiff of myself, T-shirt sour with sleep and yesterday's dried sweat. I pulled my fingers through my hair on the way downstairs, splashed water on my face in the kitchen, and poured coffee. All my mugs sat in the cabinet—Michael chose cups by their handle grips, I liked whatever held the most coffee. How awful it would be to go through that cabinet, sorting them: *mine, yours.* When couples split they should take turns smashing every piece of crockery and glassware until there's nothing to divide but a pile of shards, and they should walk across those barefoot so they have physical wounds to nurse along with the psychic ones. I'd rather tweeze ceramic splinters from my feet than go through the kitchen cabinets telling Michael which pieces of CorningWare I considered to be rightfully mine.

I heard Eula and Oren in the basement. Michael was outside watering, and I went to him. *Good morning* struck me as thoughtless—*What's good about it?*—though Michael would never say something like that. When the back door slammed and he turned, I said only, "Hi."

He didn't turn the hose off, only looked at me over the spray. "Hi." He sounded worn, not mad. We both turned to the flower bed and watched the spray catch sunlight.

"I'm sorry," I said, "again. Always. I'm sorry." I fought against any tone of steeliness; I didn't want to sound obligingly contrite when I was really just sorry.

My husband turned to me, letting go the trigger. He was tired— of my apologies, of his need for them. Maybe we needed a blowout to end the stalemate of our separation. If we fought and I *didn't* apologize, would we get somewhere? Maybe my sorries stalled us. Always creeping back, tail between my legs. Michael gestured vaguely at the house. The leaky nozzle dribbled down the front of his khakis, like he'd zipped up too soon after a pee, and I looked away. "Or maybe don't sell Carpathia," he said, as if we were in the middle of another conversation. "Sell this place instead?" He waved the hose, flinging a splash in my direction. I jerked back; he thought I was balking at selling the house, and responded accordingly: "What? You're coming back?" Then he softened. "Neither of us could afford this place alone. Who needs all this room?"

I squinted at him. "You want to move back to the house where you grew up?"

"It's a perfectly fine house."

"Sure, yes, I just . . ."

"This one'll be easier to sell."

"Okay." It was true, and I had no leg to stand on. I missed my home—missed having a home—but couldn't see returning to live there by myself. I certainly didn't want Bernadette's house. Largely unchanged since she bought it in the '50s, the place had now been a student rental for four years; it was probably a wreck. But Michael and I had different issues, different ghosts. Ripping up linoleum and tearing down wallpaper might be good for him. Maybe it was easier to imagine living in the house he'd shared with his miserable, nasty mother than the one he'd shared with his lousy, cheating wife. "Okay," I said again. I readied myself to go. "Please, Michael, call when you're ready to deal with her things. The boxes. Or if you don't want to deal at all. I'm glad to . . . before the semester starts . . ." Did I have ulterior motives? A desire to root through her possessions? I don't know. I think, by then, I really didn't. I think I felt done.

Michael nodded absently, then seemed to remember the hose in his hand, and pressed the trigger, returning to his coneflowers, his black-eyed Susans. You don't have to be a real gardener to garden in Iowa; all you have to do is toss down a few seeds, throw them some water occasionally, and the earth makes plants, and the plants bloom and flower and fruit like magic beanstalks. But Michael's never lived anywhere else, and he thinks he's a gardener, and that gardening is easy: you pick off a few aphids, squash some leaf eaters, fence out the rabbits. Rich soil and humid, hot summers are all he's ever known. God forbid the man encounter a blight, or clayey, sandy, lousy dirt. He'd do what he's done all his life: plant seeds, water, and wait for them to grow. And if they didn't, he'd simply stand there watering, shaking his head, bewildered.

WHEN EULA, OREN, and I got back to Prairie, Silas's car wasn't in the driveway. A note in his hand said they'd gone "to the doctor." I didn't know if that was a euphemism or just Silas's Amish-ish-ness. "The doctor" was Planned Parenthood, I assumed—how could I not? I left home and drove to my strip-mall Linksys to look up Planned Parenthood protocol. Drinking a drive-thru insta-latte, I learned that Iowa doesn't do same-day abortions: she'd have a diagnostic visit first, then the clinic would have a specially designated weekday for fetal extractions. For obvious reasons, that day wasn't listed online. I had no email from Lucius, but wrote him anyway. *Ginny's aborting, and I've apparently joined the right. What's wrong with me? Politics hit home and suddenly it's not a choice, it's a child?*

I was back in Prairie in under an hour. The Festiva was still gone, but Randall's monster truck now sat in the drive. I parked, already uneasy. Eula was rocking on the porch swing, clearly distraught, with Oren crawling nearby in a wooden baby-jail that's surely illegal by modern safety standards. I castigated myself for leaving them at all. "Why's Randall's truck here? What happened? Are you okay? Gin and Silas aren't home yet?"

She shook her head. "Randall's inside, waiting for them."

I found him in the Bush-Cheney den, bowed over, his fists clenched. Alone with him, I felt strangely vulnerable: Randall's a very large man, and though he'd never intentionally hurt me, he was in a highly emotional state and I didn't know how much self-control he had. When his head lifted I feared he was about to howl, but as he raised his face, his arms fell limp to his sides. Tears coursed down his pocked cheeks. He dropped to his knees, and I must've moved toward him, because his head was at my rib cage, so I held him, stroking his hair as he wept into my shirt. "Please don't let her do it," he begged, and I started to say, "I wish I had the power—" but he cut me off: "She can't. She just can't." Then he was weeping again, and I remember becoming aware for the first time of the crushing enormity of Randall's love for Linda, so huge it was inconceivable I'd been unaware of it so long. No one knew their whole story—what came out that afternoon and what I've patched together, piecemeal, are no longer distinguishable in my mind—but there were things not even Ginny knew about Linda, and I'd be lying not to admit to a hint of vindication at seeing Ginny proven a little clueless herself.

Linda, I learned, could not have children. Something genetic I don't fully understand, and she won't, or can't, talk about. What I've gleaned is that she once had a pregnancy that ended gruesomely, a preterm birth that happened in a public place, Linda stoically bearing the pain until it felled her. I'm no longer sure which lines here are ones I've drawn myself to connect the stars in that vast dark sky to try to make a picture, but I think the lost pregnancy may have been followed by a hysterectomy. My limited understanding is that Linda and Randall wanted a child, couldn't have one, and knew no adoption or foster agency on the planet would place a kid with a pair of heavy-drinking recovered drug addicts with a handful of suicide attempts and incarcerations between them, even if they were two of the best-hearted people on this planet. Silas and Ginny's child would be the closest Linda and Randall got to parenthood, and the idea of Ginny aborting it sent them into desperation as helpless as when Linda lay hemorrhaging in a Babies "R" Us break room, her dead fetus wrapped in paper towels and nestled among packing peanuts in an old diaper box.

I told Randall the incontrovertible truth—if I asked Ginny not to abort, I might as well offer her a ride to the clinic—and miraculously managed to do so without breaking into "Never Say No," from *The Fantasticks*. Randall had a much better shot himself. Best, also, to remove myself from the premises so as not to remind Ginny that what he wanted was also what I wanted. I got Eula and Oren back into my car and drove to the nearest air-conditioned place I could think of. Which is how we wound up, in the middle of that blazingly sunshiny summer day, carrying a sleeping Oren in his car seat into the dark and nearly empty Gas Stop Bar. Only the pigtailed bartender was on duty —we learned her name: Regina—so we set Oren on the bar and sat there to save her from traipsing across the room to serve us at a booth. She peeked in at Oren. "Few too many already, I see."

I was starving, and Eula hadn't had lunch, so we ordered full meals and Cokes and sat in that strange, quiet place, sleeping baby on the bar between us. Eula's hair was starting to grow out, and she'd taken to tying it off her face with a scrap of fabric. Dressed in Obadiah's old, plain clothes—dark pants, a blue-gray button-down—and her own scuffed boots, she might have been lunching in a SoHo dive with Jackson Pollock and Lee Krasner. A cheese factory worker came in, sat at the end of the bar, and started chatting quietly with Regina. Inside the Gas Stop it's easy to forget there's a world out there at all; not one window in the place. Not a one.

Patrons trickled in, and by the time Oren woke, the happy hour swell had begun. Eula leaned toward me, a hand to her breastbone, and said, "Phillipa, I must feed Oren," so I paid, tipped too much, and we left. Randall still hadn't called. "We could drive someplace where no one's around," I suggested, and Eula directed me down a dirt road just out of town. We parked and got out at a riverside clearing beside a trashy fire pit surrounded by stumps: a townie drinking spot. I could picture Ginny there, back in her partying-with-the-druggies days. She probably *had* been there, partying with the derelict Amish youth of Prairie. I thought to wonder, then, if Ginny knew who Oren's father was; it wasn't hard to imagine this hangout as the site of his fathering.

I followed Eula past the fire pit, down a herd path to a rock outcropping over the creek, where she sat, undid a button, and offered Oren her breast. Instinctively I looked away, then back again so as not to be one of those women who avert their gaze at the sight of another woman's breast. You'd think once you've been a mother and nursed a child, you'd have joined the ranks of people who know what to do with their eyes, but not me. Straight out of my nursing bra and back among the awkward, worried that looking away will appear disapproving, and watching will seem untoward. I attempted, pathetically, to affect the carriage of someone so at ease it would never cross her mind to worry where she was looking. Late-afternoon sun dappled through the tree canopy. Eula switched Oren to the other breast. My phone rang. I stood to answer it. "Randall."

"Hey," he said, and I held my breath. "Hey, so, I'm here with Ginny"—he couldn't talk freely—"um, and things're good, so it looks . . . well, like I'll head home now."

So we drove back, lightheaded with relief. Ginny was already asleep upstairs; Silas sat at the kitchen table. The doctors at Planned

Parenthood had been alarmed at Ginny's state, he told us, and prescribed a host of medications, all of which started with Z and sounded
like superheroes or planets from *Land of the Lost*. Antidepressants,
antiemetics. Ginny scheduled an abortion, but Silas persuaded her
to give the drugs a chance first. With two weeks left in Iowa's legal-
abortion window, Ginny was slated just under the first-trimester wire
for Friday, August 20. They could "cancel at any time," Silas told us,
and I didn't bother saying it was like one of those old record club ads
on TV, which Silas wouldn't have understood on so many levels it
wasn't worth explaining. I also did not share that on Wednesday, August 18, two days before the appointment, Lucius was due to return
to the States.

After everyone went to bed, I drove back to Subway. Lucius had
written, and his note was lovingly, if patronizingly, chiding. I'm not
sure if it made me feel validated or just dumb.

*Phillipa, stop it. Just stop. No one's gone pro-life! Your happily married,
grown-up daughter who* wanted to have a child—*and got pregnant* on
purpose, *with planning and forethought, pregnant with your first and probably only grandchild*—*now wants to have an abortion, and you're upset
about it. That doesn't make you pro-life, it makes you human.*

THE NEXT MORNING, I ate breakfast, went to the porch, and then
must have dozed on the swing. I heard the creak of the screen and
opened my eyes to Ginny, standing in the doorway. I hadn't seen her
upright, unaided, in weeks. "Hey, Ma." Her eyes were squinty, but
there was a softness to her affect, her body not bracing against the
next wave of sickness.

"Gin, how are you?" It was the wrong question, I knew instantly,
and I feared she'd snap from her sleepy calm to rip my head off: *How
am I? Jesus fucking Christ, is that the only thing you can say?* I steeled
for it, but Ginny stood there in a pair of cutoff sweatpants and a
stretched-out T-shirt, took a deep, steadying breath, and said, "I think
I'm not so bad."

"Aw, Gin . . ." I wanted to hug her, but tried to conceal my relief lest that set her off. I only slid over, patting the spot beside me. She shook her head no, but shook it too fast—her balance faltered. Closing her eyes, she refocused, then said, "Maybe don't swing?" I dropped my feet and ceased all movement. "Thanks." She smiled, with effort, leaned against the house, and slid down to sit, knees into her chest. "I got some heinously expensive pill they give chemo patients. It's like ten bucks a dose." She was gauging me; Ginny didn't have prescription coverage.

"We can help," I said.

"But you can't, really," she asked, "can you?"

"We *can*," I said emphatically. "We're *glad* to." With Bernadette gone, and no more nursing home care, money would go a lot further. But I didn't know what was left in her savings. I bit my bottom lip to keep from speaking, then stopped because that gets Ginny's ire, too: *You think I don't see you biting your lip to let me know you're not saying whatever it is you want to say?* I closed my eyes and tried to stop from doing anything, realized I was unconsciously rocking the swing, and stopped abruptly. I attempted to sit and breathe in a way that wouldn't upset her, and when I opened my eyes she was looking down the porch with a contentment I hadn't seen in far too long —since the wedding. I closed my eyes to the warmth of morning sunshine.

"I love that," Ginny said. I feared it was sarcasm, but when I opened my eyes she wasn't sneering, or even looking at me at all, just gazing down the porch. "It makes me remember how I could've thought bringing a child into the world might be an okay thing to do."

"The farm?" I tried to follow her gaze. "The farm makes you feel like that?"

"The light," she said.

"The sun does feel good . . ."

"Yeah, but not that. The shadow." She pointed at the house's white clapboard siding. Somehow a silhouetted window frame was being projected onto the porch wall. Shadows from a willow, too, its branchlets swinging and fluttering inside the four-paneled shadow-frame.

"It doesn't make you sick?" I asked. "The fluttering?"

Ginny shook her head minutely, shrugged a shoulder to say, *Who knows?*

I said, "It's kind of like a Japanese scroll, but elongated." She nodded. This—a pretty silhouette I'd never have seen if she hadn't pointed it out—this was what made Ginny not need to abort her gestating fetus. A shadow on the wall—that's where she found salvation.

A short-lived peace. By noon she was vomiting again, but we were all grateful for the reprieves, however brief. She was still asleep that afternoon when Randall and Linda drove up, pulling Randall's trailer behind the truck. He rolled down the window: "Figured, I live in a damn mobile home, why not mobile it over here till this all's done?" He waved a hand in the region of his belly. They parked, hooked the trailer to the well and to a generator, which made the yard sound like a helicopter landing pad, and took up residence on the Yoders' lawn.

Silas roofed from dawn to dusk on those long, hot Iowa days. Michael came out to Prairie a few times a week. I made dashes to Subway to email Lucius. And then it was mid-August, with pre-semester faculty meetings on campus and appointments with my student assistant director, choreographer, musical director. We had *Drood* auditions to plan, rehearsal rooms to reserve, pianos to be tuned. I'd done no class prep, and I'm no Lucius, who could waltz in to lecture brilliantly and charm everyone without any planning. He was due back that Wednesday, and I was to spend the weekend with him in Ohio before classes began the following Monday. Abortion Friday, nestled right in the middle, was hard to plan around, since no one knew whether it was happening or not. Wednesday evening, when Lucius was due home, Linda and Randall had an NA function in Ames, Eula worked Bluntmore's Auction, and Michael had a meeting and couldn't look after Ginny. So, as Lucius was returning Stateside, I was home with my daughter, without cell or Internet service. I left once on the pretense of an errand and stole down the road until I got a cell signal, hoping to have a message, but the only voicemail was my assistant director rescheduling our Monday meeting for Friday. Pissed, I called back to say I couldn't do Friday; maybe I should have explained, but I didn't. He was confused, then overly apologetic, and I had no patience for any of it. As his anxiety mounted, I met it with defiant indifference. The poor kid. Sure, he'd heard talk that Phillipa Maakestad was moody and erratic and could be difficult to work with, but he hadn't seen it himself before. Once upon a time, I cared more what the students thought of me. Used to be I cared about the shows, at least. But when your daughter's about to abort your grandchild, and the love of your fucking life is finally in telephone range after weeks and weeks away but doesn't care enough to call, it's really hard to give a shit about a musical revue. An entire career, such as it is, in the theater, and what I have to show for it is a head full of peppy harmonic rhymes I'll never shake from my consciousness. There's undoubtedly an echelon of hell reserved for those of us who can't hear the phrase "try to remember" without needing to chime in, "*and if you remember, then follow . . . follow follow follow follow follow . . .*"

Lucius did not call me from the Chicago runway the instant the plane's wheels touched down, and he didn't call before or after the attendant okayed the use of personal electronics. He didn't call while awaiting his connecting flight, nor from the baggage carousel, nor as he waited for the U of O colleague who was fetching him. And he didn't get home, flop on the bed, kick off his shoes, and dial my number. No, Lucius called me that night after he'd showered, poured a drink, gone through the mail, skimmed his accreted *New Yorkers*, and took a gander at the coupon packets—*1000 address labels for 1¢ with an order of 200 personalized checks! Large pizza* = FREE BREAD-STICKS!—never once thinking I might be anxiously awaiting his call.

I left the Yoders' as soon as Eula got home, and when Lucius's call finally came, I'd been sitting in my car on the side of the road for an hour, desperate and fuming. Travel-weary, Lucius was distracted, preoccupied, just checking in to let me know he was home. I was exhausted and distracted too, and also envious: I wanted to be in *my* own living room, having a drink, nothing more to do than sort junk mail. Would that I had a living room! I had a Bush-Cheney–papered Amish den. I ached to be with Lucius, and it killed me that he was probably very happy, just then, to be alone. We had our first real fight that night on the phone. I told him what I'd gone through, waiting for him to call, driving back and forth to be in cell phone range, and he suggested—quite innocently, I know—that I *could* go to the mall and buy a new phone, get whatever plan Silas had, and be able to talk from the comfort of my own bed. However innocuous his intention, I blew. I didn't know what cell plan I had! Michael took care of it; he still paid the goddamn bill. "I don't have my *own bed*," I told Lucius. "I sleep in the discarded single bed of an Amish child. And I don't have time to go to the mall because I'm babysitting my vomiting daughter, and I have to teach in four days, and direct a fucking show and—" I drew a breath. Lucius was saying, "Whoa," trying to talk me down, "whoa, whoa," but his comfort was no comfort to me now. "I'm not a horse!" I yelled—yelled into my phone on the side of a rural highway. "I can't *whoa*. There's no *whoa*. Nothing stops. I can't just gallop to the mall for a new phone!"

"Jesus Christ, Phillipa." He started to say *whoa* again, but stopped for a long moment to reassess, recalibrate. I saw myself becoming someone he'd look back on, one more ex among the wives and lovers. The thought came at me like a knife, so well hidden I never saw it flash, so sharp I didn't know I was stabbed until I was dying. "It's okay, Phil," he was saying, "it's okay."

Apparently I'd apologized. If you don't remember your apology, does it still count? Was I indeed sorry? I was certainly filled with sorrow. I could have wailed and keened with sorrow! But is that sorry? *Yeah,* I imagined my undergrads saying, *that's seriously sorry.* I tried again: "I'm sorry." I meant it all: *I am sorrowful, I'm a sorry excuse for a person,* and *I apologize.*

"It's okay, Phil." He didn't sound like himself; he sounded like the Lucius other people knew, and I didn't want their Lucius. I wanted mine. I felt like Michael: *Undo it. Make it like it was before.* "I'm sorry," Lucius said, placating and diplomatic. "I don't mean to minimize what you're going through." Then he said all the things I should've wanted to hear—that he missed me, felt far away, selfishly wanted me to himself—but it buzzed like filler in my ears. I felt eviscerated. In a juvenile stroke of retaliation I wish were beneath me, I told him I'd be unable to visit that weekend—a meeting I just couldn't miss. Far from stricken, he sounded relieved.

That night was such a low—a low of lows. Back at Eula's everyone was asleep, Linda and Randall not yet home from Ames. I crawled into bed—Eula's childhood bed, and Silas's before her, and probably that of half the children of Prairie. The Yoders weren't the only ones making use of the Highway 1 Mennonite thrift shop. All I wanted in the world was to call Lucius back, say "I'm sorry" again, and try to get it right this time. I wanted to hear his *"I'm sorry,"* and his "It's okay," and believe them. I went so far as to go downstairs and look for Silas's cell phone—God help me, I went through his pockets. Back in bed, crying indulgent, self-pitying tears, I heard the creak of a door, footsteps, and Ginny's heave, and pulled the pillow over my ears.

ON THURSDAY, August 19, Linda and Randall both had to work. I said I had a meeting at school, so Michael stayed with Ginny, but I actually went to the Prairie View Mall, which is neither near Prairie nor in view of a prairie, except in the sense that the interstate and condo development, industrial park, municipal airport, and county landfill were all once prairie, *long ago, when the strip mall was grassland.* At the cell phone kiosk, I was humiliatingly lectured on incomprehensible details regarding texting surcharges and cancellation penalties. What I grasped was that parole from my current contract would incur mind-boggling costs. Such things must be covered in divorce settlements these days: *parties agree to remain on existing cell plan until expiration or death.* I left with a "prepaid disposable phone," which did not mean I could throw it out. What it *did* mean, I had no idea.

Ginny sat propped on the family room couch, looking better. She always did after I'd been away. "I let Daddy go home," she said by way of greeting, her affect visibly shifting as I approached: posture sinking, color fading, jaw slackening. "Silas'll be home soon. Eula's here. I thought you didn't need another encounter." On the subject of her impending abortion: nada.

"Your dad and I are dealing with things, Gin. No need to police us. Really, we're fine."

She looked out the window, at Eula's sunflowers bowing their enormous heads. "Right," Ginny murmured. "Of course." Then she said something else I couldn't hear.

"Excuse me?"

She turned on me. "Do you really think the first person plural is appropriate? I'm sorry, I just—maybe he'd like to speak for himself. You can't just decide someone's fine to make it true."

"Why is it, Ginny, that you're so compelled to state the obvious to me?"

She gave a puff of futile laughter. "Maybe because you never seem to get it."

"Great to see you feeling better, Gin." I left before she could say anything more.

Upstairs in my tiny room, I tried my new phone and got a screen message that said service was unavailable: *Press any button to accept roaming charges.* I hurled it at the wall. It didn't make much noise, just a hard, plastic clatter, but one beat later came the cry of the baby and Eula's quick tread along the hall. "I'm sorry," I said to the air. I lay on my bed and cried.

That evening, Silas gave Ginny a bath while I helped Eula with dinner. All the windows were open, fans blowing to keep the smells from reaching Ginny. Eula gave me beans to trim, and I took the bowl to the back steps, tossing ends into the grass. At the stove on the other side of the screen door, Eula stirred a cast-iron pan of onions and tended pots of beets and potatoes. The screen had torn in several places, but Eula'd sewn and patched them: meticulous, artful repairs in this ridiculous, disposable world. "Your Frankenstein screens are so beautiful," I told her.

"Frank and Stein screens?" she asked.

"Oh—" I apologized. *"Frank-en-stein?* It's a book. People mostly know the movies, though. There's a sort of mad doctor who's builds a man in his laboratory and brings it to life."

Eula listened intently, but was understandably confused. "And the screens . . . ?"

"The monster's stitched together, like your screens, but he's hideous, patched from dead bodies, I think, dead people sewn together—" Eula looked horrified. I backpedaled. "But your screens are beautiful! They're stitched, and so was the monster. And he's actually very sweet, but huge, and doesn't know his own strength. He hurts people without meaning to—he doesn't understand they're fragile. And people are afraid since he's so ugly. It's a scary story—like for Halloween? In fall, when kids dress up and knock on doors . . . ? Trick-or-treating, for candy? Ghosts, witches . . . and a big, green, blockheaded guy with bolts on either side of his neck. His skin's like a clumsy crazy quilt, crude stitching—which is not *at all* what your screens look like! But if something's stitched together, people say it's like Frankenstein." I was ludicrous, a blithering, blockheaded oaf.

Eula nodded uncertainly. Oren, who was crawling now, clambered at her calves, whining to come up until he exhausted himself, curled around her feet, and fell asleep on the floor. One by one, Eula shut off the flames under her pots, and stood there, embarrassed of her idle hands, but not wanting to wake him. Through the screen, she said, "Is everything all right, Phillipa?"

Is *anything* all right?, I wanted to say. I arched my neck, closed my eyes.

Eula revised her question: "Are things all right between you and your—your friend?" It's the way my grandparents spoke of my boy-friends as a teenager: *your friend.*

"I don't know." My voice broke. "It's hard to know."

"I am coming to understand," Eula said, "that if your child isn't well, everything becomes very difficult." She peered at me. "May I . . . ? Would it offend if I told something to you that I have noticed? About you and Ginny?" Of course I felt nervous, but stronger than fear was a nearly carnal desire to hear her observation, and I urged her on. "In the time I have known your family, Ginny has often been ill, but sick as she's been, it always seems when someone comes around—someone from outside the family, but from inside as well —Michael, Bernadette, Linda and Randall, even Silas. When they're present, Ginny acts as if she's better, though there's a cost to this, and, after, she is worse. But with you she doesn't pretend. She's just as she is."

I laughed ruefully. "Well, I can tell you that from *my* end, it feels like everyone else brightens Ginny's mood and all I ever do is make her more miserable."

"Oh, no!" Eula cried. "No, that's not it at all! I've watched. You give a gift to Ginny—" I was shaking my head at how absolutely un-true it all felt. "For you, Ginny does not pretend. That is a gift. I never had that gift from my mother, though this perhaps is more than I ought say."

My eyes welled. I looked at Oren on the kitchen floor, curled at Eula's bare feet around the cuffs of Obadiah's droopy overalls, and I prayed right then—to Murphy, or whoever it is I address when I beg things of the universe: *Let Oren be well. Let Oren be well, and let Eula know love. Let her know great love. Let Eula have a love like Lucius. A love like Michael.* For I have known two great loves in my life, and that's more than most people get. I prayed for Eula to do better than

Bernadette, with her lifetime of secrecy, devotion to a son born of a union void of love—but then realized I was thinking of Bernadette Armond, the Bernadette of my imagination. I had no idea if Bernadette Maakestad knew love. Maybe her story was true and there had in fact lived, and died, one David Maakestad, whose death closed Bernadette to all other loves except her son—and, later, that son's lone daughter—for the rest of her life, until—old and bitter, ousted from her umpteenth nursing home, a festering annoyance to all but those two blood relations—she gave up and swallowed a handful of pills, as if to say: *For this I survived the Nazis?* Of course, that's not Bernadette's voice in my head. It's my own grandmother's German-accented English with which I've turned Bernadette Maakestad into Bena Armond, the conniving Jewess of rue des Brebis.

ON FRIDAY, August 20, less than an hour before her appointment, Ginny canceled the abortion. Always the last minute, these stays: final supper eaten, appeals exhausted, relatives flown in, lethal injection poised . . . But wait! Randall dashed to the trailer, returned with a bottle of Asti Spumante, and popped the cork with celebratory gusto. Cheap champagne frothed onto Eula's kitchen floor, everyone cheered, and we sipped bubbly from jelly jars, toasting to Ginny's health and the health of the Yoder-Maakestad-to-be. Gin was upstairs, exhausted, and it felt strange to rejoice in her absence. Silas looked beat but relieved, and Eula looked like she'd been granted her own stay of execution. Linda appeared to be reeling as Randall lifted his jar, clearing his throat dramatically. We hushed. He looked to Linda, and she must have wordlessly agreed. "Me and Linda" he said, "we wanted you-all to know—" He grinned wildly, eyes brimming, laughing and weeping, both. "We wanted to let you-all know that I'm maybe the happiest man in the world, since a couple weeks ago we snuck off to city hall while no one was looking and we got married. So I just want to say—" Randall sucked in a breath, held back his tears, and thrust up his glass, nearly hitting the ceiling. "To my beautiful wife!" We all whooped, jars raised to Linda. She'd set hers down to hide her face, but behind her hands, she too was smiling.

In the flush of the morning's news, I felt decisive myself. I wasn't going to Ohio, but instead would do the responsible thing, attend my *Drood* meeting that afternoon and spend the weekend finding my-self a place to live. Meanwhile, I took a room at the Gas Stop again. I called Lucius, who was relieved for the continued gestational life of my fetal grandchild and seemed genuinely disappointed that I wasn't coming to Ohio. We plotted some logistics and, in the end, Lucius promised to drive to Iowa to see me the third weekend in September. "Maybe I'll have a home by then," I said, "though I know you're fond of the Gas Stop."

"I am fond of wherever you are," he said, then added, "I'm glad you'll be phonable."

I perused the Gas Stop bulletin board, circled every mildly prom-ising rental in the *Prairie Community News,* and set off on Prairie's back roads. I could take money from home equity if need be and pay it off once we sold River City. We'd make money on the house, no question. I was not destitute, begging for a job at the Gas Stop. When the house sold, we'd be fine. And no longer a *we*. Financially, Michael and I would be okay. I just had to tell him that I wasn't coming home.

A few miles out of town I passed John C. Wolffson Road and was remembering the crumbling stone house and Aldous Bontrager when I came around a bend on White Rabbit and nearly missed the hand-lettered FOR SALE BY OWNER sign in front of a tiny, abandoned-looking cottage. White paint peeled off in scrolls, and the porch was so canted I mistook it for a wheelchair ramp. It sat closer to the road than I'd've wanted, but was perched on a little bluff-like rise, so if cars took the turn too fast they'd crash into the hill, not the living room. The sign also said: OWNER FINANCING AVAILABLE. The area code was Des Moines. I drove toward Prairie until I got a signal and reached Brent Furman at his Ankeny law office. His father, the former occu-pant of 16524 White Rabbit Road, had moved to East Prairie Elder

Living—did I know it? he asked. White Rabbit had been vacant for some months. He drove out that afternoon to show it to me.

An apologetic and accommodating country lawyer, Brent Furman was so pleased by my interest in the house it was clear no one had ever inquired about it before. The place was filthy, a ramshackle one-bedroom with only a woodstove for heat, but it had electricity and running water and telephone wires came out that far; I could get a landline. He wanted nineteen thousand for the house and the half acre it sat on. I explained my situation and asked if he'd consider a rent-to-own thing. He looked ready to weep with gratitude. He said, "We might-could work that out."

"When would I be able to move in?" I asked, using great effort to refrain from asking when I *might-could* move in. What a glorious phrase! Like things are changing as you speak: *I might—no, I could!* I wanted right then to become a might-could kind of a gal: *America, We Still Might-Could!* I wanted a bumper sticker: *Kerry-Edwards Might-Could!*

"Still got a few things of Dad's to clear out the basement. Might-could bring the trailer tomorrow, do some cleaning." I pictured him with his wife and kids, mops, brooms, Swiffers, sprayers. "How's September first? Make it easy—what's that? Wednesday?" And I'll admit this, with embarrassment, but it's true: before I let Brent Furman get back in his car, I hugged him.

I ditched *Sweeney Todd,* which had been in the tape deck too morbidly long, and put on Jones and Schmidt's *Celebration* (critical flop, fabulous show) to drive to the Yoders' to get my things. Belting "Somebody," I passed Bontrager's junk house: the piles had been pushed away from the house, which sat like an island in a mown-grass moat. The front-door window looked as if it had been squirted with Windex, a small porthole rubbed clean, and as I passed I saw, framed in that circle, the face of a pale, white-haired woman. I could almost swear she lifted one skeletal hand to wave as I went by. I remembered peering in at the wheelchair, and suddenly I didn't know if I'd just seen a woman or conjured her. I could see my life on White Rabbit Road: one more old lady rotting alive, farmhouse decaying around her. The canvassers and evangelists, the Mormons and door-to-door Oreck salesmen would wonder how I'd come to be a toothless, lonely specter. At the bar, people would say: *You know she was once a professor? Then there was the buggy wreck, and some other business —affair, tornado, suicide, pregnancy. Now she lives on Jell-O. Only one ever visits is that shunned Amish girl, kooky quilter with the bastard son. Queer bunch, that family.* Even so, in my mind my new home took on a glow. Brent Furman would descend like a fairy godmother with sprites and industrious woodland helpers, and they'd scour and scrub until the little house shone with the promise of a new life.

At the Yoders', Ginny was propped on pillows like a consumptive Victorian heroine, her skin the color of skim milk. I could barely stand to look at her. She probably did weigh ninety-two pounds after those weeks of vomiting. We hadn't spoken since our nasty exchange the night before, but I felt suffused with new energy, that I could be magnanimous for once. I apologized, said I was proud of the hard decision she'd made. She took it in, her equilibrium so bad she couldn't even nod. I told her about White Rabbit, how I'd be nearby, but without crowding them.

Ginny was gearing up to speak. "It's going—" She broke off, drew a breath, then continued, "To be. So close. In Iowa." She was weak with fatigue, purple under her eyes, lips cracked white. I didn't know what she was talking about: *what* was going to be close? My mind was on rural real estate. "Please. Help," Ginny pleaded, and I moved closer to do whatever she asked, get her water, a bucket, ice chips . . . She took a breath and spoke again. "The campaign," she said. "They need. Everyone. Whatever you can. Especially. If you're going . . . to live . . . in Prairie. Don't just . . . sit here with me. It's not like"—she tried to smile—"I'm going anywhere."

I'd be lying if I claimed I wasn't holding my tongue, but all I actually said was "Okay, Gin." I felt manipulated. She was asking this of me on the very day when she'd complied and done what we'd all asked of her. I said, "I'll do what I can," because I would, in the end —and the middle, and the beginning—do anything in the world for her. Any godforsaken thing in this godforsaken world, including going door to door to convince the good people of Prairie, Iowa, that nothing had ever been so important as getting to the polls on November 2 to vote John Kerry for president.

6

THE SCREEN DOORS OF DISCRETION

In an age of madness, to expect to be untouched by madness
is a form of madness.

—Saul Bellow, *Henderson the Rain King*

I HAD NEVER BEEN so ill prepared to teach as I was that autumn.
Fall semester often catches me by surprise, despite the fact that I can
see it coming like a storm over the cornfields. I suppose I have what
they call poor planning skills. The first few weeks were madness:
add/drop, *Drood* auditions, callbacks, casting, commuting from Prairie. Sweet man though Brent Furman is, he's no Mary Poppins. Magically industrious bluebirds hadn't descended on White Rabbit Road
to sweep the cobwebs with tiny brooms clasped in their wings, and
the house did not sparkle with Disney shine. I made a few attempts
to render it habitable, but the place needed an industrial cleaning and
I finally shelled out for professionals. It also needed a paint job, and
though I wasn't about to tackle the exterior unless I bought it, the
interior was imperative. I bought a few gallons of white paint, but
then Randall said something about primer, and I didn't know—was
it necessary? I couldn't deal; the cans sat in my kitchen, patient as

toadstools. I spent hours on hold with the phone company trying to get a land line installed: the earliest appointment was late September. What possibly had them so busy at Prairie Country Telephone? I wondered if the ghost lady had phone service. I called Lucius on my cell when I could, but there was little time. Probably for the best. I was resigned to being a lousy professor and virtually turned *Drood* over to the AD, a perfectly competent senior. I did not possess the necessary exuberance for musical theater. My life had fallen apart, and everyone knew it.

Lucius came to visit in September as planned. My directions took him past the stone cottage, but he arrived late and road-weary and forgot to look for the ghost lady's window. We'd been apart more than two months. Shy, we held each other on my futon mattress. I offered him a drink, but Lucius said what he really wanted after that drive was a shower. One look at my rust-streaked stall, though, and he said, "Why don't we go get a room at the Gas Stop?" It felt like a painful step backward to admit my new home was uninhabitably depressing, but I agreed. Donna Presidio found us a room, and I allowed myself to be led down the familiar hallway. Lucius took a shower, and then I let him make love to me on the red velour blanket I knew so well.

The next morning we woke late, anxious and ill at ease. I suggested brunch at the Liberty Grill, so we drove Lucius's car out into the stunning day — *the kind of September when grass was green and grain was yellow* — and started to feel better. Even the W barn on 26 didn't look so menacing as the sun streamed in our rolled-down windows and we zipped toward fresh orange juice, eggs Florentine, house-smoked bacon. We parked at the hardware store just as the owner was locking up — *Saturday 8–12, Always Closed Sunday* — and walked to the Grill. A small crowd waited out front for tables; I should have known it'd be packed. The sun grew too hot. We hadn't had coffee, and by the time we were seated, Lucius and I were both peevish. In a corner of the café sat a few U of I administrators; I didn't say hello. A colleague with out-of-town guests was seated a few tables away; I pretended not to notice. I felt incapable of exchanging pleasantries.

We frittered the afternoon away at what passes for tourism in southeast Iowa: walking the fossil gorge trail, visiting the raptor center and the octagonal barn. We drank a beer at the covered bridge and browsed the antiques mall on 24 where Lucius, impressed by the vintage postcards, spent the better part of an hour flipping through the contents of two oak file cabinets. He found a few that were relevant to his work, and I bought one of Le Havre, a steamship pulling out to sea. I imagined Bena on deck, wrapped in her rabbit fur quilt, watching France recede.

We spent another night at the Gas Stop, and on Sunday morning, before he left to drive home, I called the Yoders to see if we might stop by. I got Silas on his cell, down at the straw bale site, and caught him off guard. He sounded hesitant, but he agreed. I couldn't bear for Lucius to just get in his car and leave, everything between us feeling false and wispy and unsaid. Childishly, I'm sure I was pushing until something gave. I knew the stop at Eula's was wrong.

We went to the Prairie Bakery for cinnamon rolls and carried them to the house like an offering. People were congregated in the kitchen. At the door I called, "Hi, all—this is Lucius."

"Hi, Phillipa. Hi, Lucius," their voices in unison, like a twelve-step meeting or a kindergarten class. I handed Eula the cinnamon rolls; icing had seeped through the box. Linda was at the table beside Randall, who had one foot on sleeping Oren's bouncy seat, pumping it with vigor.

"Hi, everyone," Lucius said with a little wave. I was awful to put them through this.

"Lucius," I said, "you remember Linda and Randall." They looked suspicious and wary. "And here's Silas!" I cried, too exuberantly. "Silas, Lucius. Lucius, Silas." My tongue twisted idiotically. Silas gave a little bow, and Lucius bowed back, and I thought how much these two would like each other if given the chance. "That's Oren," I pointed, "and Eula. Where's Gin?"

Movement stalled. Everyone looked to Silas, who said, "She's lying down," and I saw what was happening: she'd told him to say she was sleeping, but he didn't want to lie, could only say "lying down," which was technically true, though it choked him nonetheless. An awkward moment ensued, then Randall's foot slipped from the bouncy chair and Oren woke screaming. Eula swooped, whisked him up, and fled to the porch to nurse. I tried to speak: "Oh, okay. Well, tell her . . . that I'll see her this week . . ." I looked to Linda and said, "I'll call you about Ginny-sitting?" and she nodded quickly. I stammered that Lucius needed to hit the road, then said, "I'm sorry. We'll go. We should never have come." I turned to Lucius in tears, and his look was so piteous I spun from the kitchen and flew past Eula and Oren on the porch—"I'm sorry!" I tripped down the steps, a bumbling moron, my every support cast wantonly aside. Free-falling, I stumbled to the car. If the Honda had had automatic locks, I was sure Lucius would have aimed the remote and kept me out. I'd thrown away everything; if Lucius left me, I'd have to hitch back to White Rabbit. I was a foolish woman who'd trashed her life for some whim she'd been calling love.

I skidded past the car; the humidity gagged me like a wet sock. I heaved, hands to knees, and hung there, gasping. I'd catch my breath, I thought, and then keep running until I dropped dead in a cornfield or got hit by an SUV. But Lucius came from behind and took hold of me, arms around my waist. I coughed, Heimliched; coffee lurched in my throat. "Whoa." His voice was low, modulated. "Whoa." I let him bear my weight as I panted like a horse. "Whoa."

"I'm so sorry." I couldn't look at him, couldn't bear my own reflection in his eyes. "I don't know what I was thinking, how I even thought for a minute that would be okay—"

"Phil, stop." He turned me around, let me burrow into him. "It's okay," he said, and it wasn't okay, but God, I wanted his comfort. I wanted so much to feel comforted.

Lucius dropped me at White Rabbit. I had pushed, and something had given, but as I lay on my futon, hours passed, and though I didn't feel whole, I didn't feel quite so broken. I lay there thinking how we humans are all like a big field of reeds, all propped together and sway-ing — the weak, the broken, the strong, and the hale. *Swaying reeds for Kerry-Edwards.* I slept, woke in my own drool in the midday sun, got up, and went into the bathroom to pee. From the floor I grabbed a bottle of rust remover stuff I'd bought and, still on the toilet, sprayed it at the shower wall. In the kitchen, I drank water from a jug, got a scrub brush, and returned to the shower, where I went at the livid rust stains with toxic chemicals, then with baking soda and vinegar, until it no longer looked like Janet Leigh was murdered there. Then I pried open a can of paint. I was totally unprepared for my classes that week, but I whitewashed my goddamn house.

IT WAS LINDA and Randall who called me to action, to hit the streets, door to door, for our Johns, Kerry and Edwards. Randall changed out of his *Dedicated to Service & Quality* work shirt and into *A Stronger America.* He collected buttons   *It Ain't Over 'Til Your Brother Counts the Votes, One Nation Under Surveillance, Show George the Door in 2004, Reelect Gore* — and Eula gave him a pair of Obadiah's suspenders to pin them to. I like to think Orah and Obadiah would have supported us, to imagine them at the farmers' market with Eula, *NOV. 2* flyers wedged between dill loaves. Quilts and propaganda: *Plain People for Kerry.*

Randall's truck was impractical for campaigning — even with the snowplow removed, it got the gas mileage of a double-decker bus — so we took my car, but that meant I had to drive, since neither of them could work a stick. Randall had to push the passenger seat all the way back and wedge his legs under the glove compartment. Linda navigated from the back seat. There were rules: we had lists of registered Democrats but we weren't supposed to tell anyone to "Vote Kerry-Edwards," only to stress the importance of voting in such a close election, encourage those inclined to cast a Democratic vote to get out and cast it. At our first stop, Randall was so eager to extract himself from the discomfort of the car that he was up the walk and knocking exuberantly before Linda and I unfastened our seat belts. A curtain moved, someone peered out, then ducked away fast and ran through the house shutting off lights as if no one was home. Our second stop was a modular "Victorian" in a cornfield where we interrupted a dinner party. The hostess looked me in the eye and said, "I sure as hell *will* be at the polls, and sure as hell *not* for Kerry." She spat his name like a foul taste, then turned with gutsy pleasure to her guests—not the Democratic crowd we'd expected—inviting them with an exaggerated eye-roll to join her in mocking us. I stared for a moment at their twisted faces, then turned away. Randall and Linda followed me down the poly-pebble walkway. My anger rose like a hot flash. Driving away, I fought the urge to ram the cement tigers that flanked the asphalt driveway. Sentries of the stupid.

We quickly realized that the registered-Democrat lists were useless, so we drove up and down country roads, stopping at farmhouses, trailers, sagging prefabs, scrub-yard ranches strewn with broken lawn chairs, rotting insulation, Walmart play sets, plastic blocks and animals and vehicles coated in the same black-green mold. Linda kept track of where we went. Some people invited us in, some said *Go to hell.* Our uselessness hung from us like Day-Glo crossing-guard ponchos. If Eula'd been there, things might've gone better. Eula makes bitter humans go soft with kindness; when Linda, Randall, and I arrived on doorsteps we angered everyone—even the university hippies. Did we not see, they demanded, that wasting gasoline to hand out dead-tree leaflets in our leather shoes and Made in China clothing solved precisely shit?

We retreated to the Gas Stop to lick our wounds, ordered a pitcher, and raised our glasses. "To Iowa's seven electoral votes—for

Kerry!" At the end of the bar sat weird, mysterious Creamer, hooded, hunched over his soda-straw beer, an empty stool beside him like an enforced buffer zone between him and the general populace. The top of his coveralls was unzipped, but his hood stayed up. He put away a good many pints, then rose unsteadily to leave.

I turned to Regina. "Please tell me he lives within walking distance."

"Creamer? Nah, they're out by Scooter's." Regina looked amused, a little coy.

I shook my head: not a landmark I knew. Nor did I know to whom "they" referred.

She gestured off behind her. "Five miles, about."

"After that much beer?"

"Keeps him in shape," she said. "You can't see" — Regina gestured as though she were clad in Creamer's voluminous clothing — "but that's a *fine* body." She winked, as if she knew this personally.

I was confused. "Drinking keeps him in shape?"

"Wish it did!" Regina hooted. "Ha! Not drinking — running."

"Running?"

Regina's patience was expiring. "Running. Home. From here. Five miles at least."

AS THE SEMESTER charged on, *Drood* rehearsals amped up (I attended just enough of them to keep my guilt at bay), and it became impossible to coordinate campaigning schedules with Randall and Linda. If I had a snatch of time, I'd go on my own, door to door, farm to farm, and I know there are meth dens and shotgun-wielding lunatics, but mostly there are Yoders and Bondorfs and Bontragers. Yes, there are decrepit cottages where junk mysteriously migrates in the yard, but mostly you've got old ladies tending lawn statues or watching from wheelchairs, waving at passersby. Mostly it's *Bless This Country Home,* cozy homilies stenciled on faux-distressed wood, everything quilted in barn-red gingham and pine-green plaid and stamped with Holly Hobbie ducks and dusty-rose hearts. All that kountry kupboard kitsch, and most of them don't have a clue that's the old-fashioned way of saying *No Negroes*. They just think it's kute.

I stopped at 1215 710th Avenue, ostensibly the home of registered Democrats Norma and Burton Kramer. Prairie's western edge is largely suburban ranches on two-acre lots with spindly trees, truck-tire planters in the yard, and cement deer with crumbling ears posed pastorally atop septic drain fields. But 1215 was a tiny farmhouse on a dead-grass rise above a swampy pond, its sloped shore ringed in cyclone fencing with coiled barbed wire on top. In the pond were two enormous, filthy swans. A cantilevered breezeway extended from a shed at the edge of the swan pen and stopped just shy of the house, its end propped on stacked cinderblocks. A side door seemed to lead to a room whose windows were covered in plywood. The house was worn free of paint but for traces between planks of an ancient aqua the color of public pool bathrooms, and though the yard had been mowed, it had no walk. A rutted trail like a herd path led up from the road. I pulled the screen door and its frame torqued in my hand. The front door behind it was so spongy with rot it barely sounded when I knocked, yet was answered by a hunched woman who stood before me in a wig like a swatch of matted camel's hair coat. Her face was barnacled with warts and moles. She said nothing. A wheelchair sat behind her as if she'd just stood from it.

"Hi, I'm looking for Norma Kramer?" I sounded like a demented Girl Scout.

"You found her." Ill-fitting dentures clacked in her mouth. Norma Kramer looked as if the life she'd lived afforded her the right to tell me to take my Thin Mints and Do-si-dos, my Johns Kerry and Edwards, shove them up my skinny white ass, and get the hell off her property. This was a white woman who could've called my ass white and made it the insult she intended.

"I'm sorry to bother you. I'm Phillipa Maakestad, a volunteer for the Iowa Democrats?"

Norma Kramer's wig stayed put as she shook her head beneath it. "My son's not here."

I studied my sheet, as though oblivious to her annoyance. "Burton? He's on my list too."

Norma Kramer's head went back and forth. "I don't talk to people. My son talks to the people. He's at work, else at the bar. He talks to the people. Not me."

I stalled. "Your son's at work? Is there a better time to come back? Later this evening?"

"Nights he's at the bar. He don't live in here anyway. The cottage's his." She jerked her head toward the swan pen. "Now, you ready to leave me alone?" She slammed the door.

I headed back to the car, swans hissing behind their chain link as if trained. The shack wasn't *their* home, I realized, it was Norma's son's. And I'm a little dense, as Ginny would be eager to corroborate, so it was only as I started down the path that I put it together—the son, the bar, the name—and: *lightbulb!* Burton *Kramer* was *Creamer*. He lived here with his mother. Here, à la Sweeney Todd, where the demon fowl-keepers of 710th Avenue probably butchered unsuspecting visitors and meat-pied them into swan feed. *These* were the registered Democrats of Prairie County. Kerry should have just conceded and spared us the pain of our own hope.

At home on White Rabbit the next day, I was readying to head into town for an evening rehearsal, making some coffee in a one-cup drip for the road. I set the kettle on and ground the beans, and then a strange thing happened: the grinder's whir ceased, but the house kept rattling. A knocking, it sounded like steam heat cranking on, but I didn't have steam heat. A long moment passed before I understood that it was coming from outside: someone was at the door. I'd lived there a month and this was my first knock. Stepping back to get an angled sight line out the front window, I tried to see who was on my stoop—what I wouldn't have given for a couple of pubescent, neck-tied Mormons, or prim African-American matrons inviting me to witness prophecies at Kingdom Hall. But no. In the October dusk, a lone figure stood silhouetted there, large and hooded, and I thought: *It's Creamer. Burton Kramer's at my door.* In one hand he held a spherical object; too big for a softball, too small for soccer, it was about the size of a human head. In the other hand he held a knife, and I understood. Creamer had decapitated his mother, then run here, carrying her head, to kill me, too. Add me to the meat pies.

In the shadows, I flinched, and he saw, and raised his knife and began rapping its blade against the window. He leaned to peer in, and I saw it wasn't Creamer. He smiled, gesticulated. Fear and confusion unbalanced me. When the kettle began to whistle on the stove, I lurched toward it, a Pavlovian response. Lifting it from the burner, I felt its heft and saw my hot pot as the weapon it could be. The man on the porch could get into my house whether I opened the door for him or not, but if I answered it with a boiling iron teapot and things got weird, I could heave it at him and run. I palmed my car keys off the counter and went, kettle raised, to the door.

The stranger was already speaking as I opened it, smiling as he lifted his knife-wielding hand. I jerked involuntarily, muscles clenched, ready to fling my scalding pot at him. But then he seemed to be lifting the knife toward himself. I had the crazy thought that maybe this was a *thing*: knocking on a stranger's door to slit your own throat for an audience. He lifted his arm, pushed back his hood, and then—incongruously, disorientingly—seemed to be talking about fruit. "Evening, ma'am. Drove by on my way, Prairie to Hills, saw your light on, figured I'd stop. Florida grapefruits today, drove all night right out the citrus groves—nothing like Florida citrus with winter coming on." He shifted his stance and, in a move that looked choreographed—a swirling sweep of his arm—he produced the grapefruit, as if he'd conjured it from the autumn air. A sudden kamikaze Benihana swishing of hands and blade, and a punch of citrus hit the air. My salivary glands flared. Another flourish and I was presented with a wedge, still attached to an impossibly twisted segment of rind he held between his fingers. I was clearly meant to sample this grapefruit, but I didn't have a hand to take it, although hands might not've been required; I had the sense I was supposed to snatch it up with my teeth. The man seemed oddly unprepared for any hesitation—did other people gobble it right up? I lifted my hands—teakettle, keys—to display my inability to accept, then heard myself say, "I just brushed my teeth." He softened, let out his breath, relieved by this apparently reasonable explanation as to how a lone Iowa matron could conceivably refuse a taste of fresh grapefruit in the October dusk. "Some for later, then? Keep well. Though . . ." He stepped too close, peering around me and inside. "Don't got much storage, do you? Ought to get you a 'frigerated chest for the basement. For items what could go bad. These'd keep good in a root cellar." He said "root" like it rhymed with "foot."

"I have to go," I said, and his expression went funny. I thought, *He is going to kill me.* Then something snapped, and I said, "I can't buy your *frut,* okay?" I was imagining what would happen if he knocked on the ghost lady's door: he'd peer through her Windexed porthole and give her a heart attack. Norma Kramer, no question, would've heaved the kettle and sent Frutman to the ER with third-degree burns. All those doors I'd knocked on in the name of John Kerry, and any one of them could've been answered by someone as insane as I was right then, a lunatic ready to hurl a kettle of boiling water, and with nothing to shield me but a clipboard of DNC flyers. My voice cracked as I opened my mouth and yelled—screamed—at this man: "You can't just walk up to someone's door with a knife drawn and ask them to buy grape*frut!*"

The man on my porch, knife-speared grapefruit and sample wedge in his hands, looked at me as if I was the craziest fucking person he'd ever encountered, and he backed up slow, like he didn't want to get hurt. Eyes narrow, he almost sounded sarcastic—which is nearly unheard of around here—as he said, "You have a nice rest of the evening, ma'am."

My hands were still shaking when I got in the car to drive to rehearsal. My face was numb, and I couldn't feel my fingertips. It was stupid to drive like that, but I did anyway. Coffee no longer necessary —I had so much adrenaline coursing through me I'd probably never sleep again—heart hammering in my chest cavity, I drove under the speed limit. Passing the monstrous *W* barn on 26, I wanted to drive up onto the grass, get out of my car, and hammer on the door, shouting "How do you *live* with yourselves? Why not put up an *I'm a Greedy Bigot* sign? What's the difference?" Then I thought: I'm a Sloganator, a living, breathing Sloganator, no different from my lunatic daughter accosting that stupid woman in her stupid *W* hat. I am her, and she is me, and there's only so much sanity to go around. I kept her alive all those years, no life of my own, my existence devoted to keeping my death-bent daughter alive, and now—wonder of wonders, miracle of miracles—she's still here and planning to stick around. So do I finally get to live my own goddamn life? No. I get to lose my fucking mind! And, of course, my goddamn brain—ever coursing with the lyrics of every musical ever written—my fucking brain kicks in with the voice of *Drood's* John Jasper. Inside my head: a raving, opium-addicted madman, bellowing ferociously—stage lights picking up every speck of spittle that flies from his mouth—bellowing, *"A man could go quite mad!"* Because in this stupid fucking world, a *man can* go quite mad. A man can lose his mind and buy his Corvette and fuck his undergrads and spit across the stage. But I am not a man! I am not a man, and I'm going stark fucking mad! If I drove up to the *W* barn and got out carrying a knife like the Frutman, those fetus-festishizing, *W*-loving, white-is-might-is-right motherfuckers inside could pull one of the guns they so adore and shoot me dead without a second's thought. And maybe *that's* the difference between us and them: we don't come with knives. We come with words, spitting and spewing our furious, self-righteous, sanctimonious words, and they come with their guns, and they kill us. And if I were black—if I were the African orderly from East Prairie out knocking on doors, canvassing for Kerry—they'd've shot me already, because that's the world we live in: where a burly white asshole can march up to my door with a blade in his hand and treat me like I'm the one who's crazy to be afraid when, if he were black and I were a Republican gun-toting lunatic, I could kill him without so much as a ripple of repercussion in this miserable, pathetic, reprehensible, justice-starved world. The world into which we'd just convinced Ginny it was okay to bring a child. The miserable world into which I brought my own miserable child, now a miserable adult, fully aware and sickened to the marrow of her bones by the injustice of this godforsaken place, and as wholly incapable as her pathetic mother to do a goddamn thing about it. About anything. How does anyone with a conscience—anyone with any moral sense at all—do anything but cry, all day every day, navigating this godforsaken world? And I *know* they think the same thing about us. I *know* they weep over our slaughtered, butchered babies, wring their hands and tear their hair over a world where we can rip children from our wombs and call it a choice. I *know*. If it were just the abortion people, I think I could manage some sympathy. Empathy, even. But why are they also the gun lovers? Why are they the conversion therapists and gay bashers? The ones lobbying to drill Alaska, pave paradise, put up a parking lot, and give a tax break to the zillionaire? If they'd put down their fucking guns and take off their white hoods, I'd be willing to talk about fetal rights until the goddamn cows come home! And I know—I *know*—they're saying the same thing: if we'd just stop murdering babies, they'd be willing to talk about letting our beloved faggots wed each other, letting our beloved darkies walk to the store without fear of being shot. How's there any hope at all for a country like ours, like this, a country stolen from its people—a people we killed as deftly as Hitler killed the Jews? We: the imperialist whites who sailed across an ocean, stomped ashore, and took what we wanted. We stole this country. Stole it and whipped our slaves into building it up to suit us. Senator Obama called for participation in a politics of hope, but where is it? Where in this miserable country can we find that hope? Where does *he* possibly find that hope? It's not a choice between hope and cynicism, Senator. This isn't cynicism; this is despair. This is unremitting, fathomless despair.

My body was shaking uncontrollably. I couldn't keep my foot on the gas pedal. I pulled over and sat in my car, crying in the dark on the side of the road, thinking: *How does Ginny do it? How does she rise from this?* Because *this* is my daughter's life, this unrelenting cognizance of that which is intolerable in our world. What does she ever grab hold of to pull herself up?

Shadows, I remembered. Shadows. Shadows cast by a flickering sun on the farmhouse wall. But it was dark out; everything was shadow. I sat in my car and wept.

By the time I thought I might be able to drive, I was so late for the rehearsal it seemed pointless, but the alternative was turning around and driving back past the *W* barn, and the idea of being home alone felt inconceivable. I drove to campus and sat another long while in the car before I could collect myself enough to rise and enter the auditorium. They'd started long before without me, and the house lights were blessedly low. I scurried to a rear seat, sank in, and burrowed down in my coat, clutched to my body as though it might protect me. I wished I had a flask of Jasper's laudanum wine, or a drag from Princess Puffer's opium pipe. I'd've liked to smoke myself into an opium coma, Puffer crooning over me a woeful tale of the man who'd been her demise. It was a man who led her down the garden path to hell. Hell, where I now resided. And where *I* hadn't been led by anyone: I'd plowed this path all on my own.

I DIDN'T SPEAK to Lucius until a few days later, when I called him from my car in the Gas Stop parking lot. The sky went dark as we talked, staying on the line as if the length of our phone call could

make up for the lingering awkwardness between us. We were too formal and cautious, both of us tired, and longing, and tired of longing.
We wanted to be together, and beyond stating that, again and again
until it felt stupid, what else was there? When we hung up I was worn
low, and weak from hunger, and well aware that whatever I got at the
Gas Stop would just perpetuate the downward drift. Fill up on fried
breadiness, wash it down with a big cup o' carbs, and head to sleep!
What I wouldn't have done for a salad, some steamed broccoli . . .
Well, apparently what I wouldn't do was drive to River City. I didn't
have it in me, probably because for days I'd had only fried crap, beer,
and coffee. It was a cycle, and it was vicious.

Slow night at the Gas Stop: pigtailed Regina tending bar, Toni
Braxton on the juke, a couple of little kids slamming pool balls
around like tabletop shuffleboard, parents pleading with them to
come eat another chicken strip. I took a seat, ordered a beer, and felt
like a regular.

"How's that cutie?" Regina asked, and my train of thought was so
herky-jerky I started saying Ginny wasn't due for quite a while, but
then wondered how Regina even knew Ginny. Then I understood she
was talking about Oren, and began to say he wasn't technically mine,
but then realized the "cutie" she meant was Lucius, and I gasped. He
didn't feel like mine at all. My eyes welled and my throat closed, and
Regina saw it all, fast, like the longtime bartender she is.

"Trouble in paradise." She nodded. "Say no more."

I nearly protested, galled to be that cliché, but I let it go. I ordered a seafood combo with a side of jalapeño poppers as my green.
Someone passed behind me, returning to the bar from the restroom,
and Regina began tapping a beer. The figure slunk into my peripheral vision, and I saw it was Creamer—Burton Kramer. He took his
seat. No words were spoken. Regina slid him his Bud. He unwrapped
a straw. And a moment later, I heard him speak for the first time,
though I didn't realize who he was talking to until he'd had to repeat
himself several times, and I looked over to see who was ignoring him.

Apparently, I was. "I'm sorry?" I asked, frazzled.

"You were looking for me." His voice was garbled, like he had rocks in his mouth.

"Oh! I . . . and your mom . . . the DNC list. I didn't . . . Kramer, Creamer. I talked to her."

The lenses of his spectacles were so thick they bugged his eyes out. "I know." He held his lips oddly pursed, as if attempting to move them as little as possible, maybe so as not to reveal bad or missing teeth. He said something then that sounded like "Do not capitulate."

I waited for sense to coalesce around the words, but it didn't. "Excuse me? I don't . . ."

"The DNC," Creamer said, leading.

"Oh! Oh, it's the Democratic National Comm—"

"I know what it stands for," he said, and I felt like a jerk. He kept nodding, though I didn't know what at, then said something like "Beinsta Bows," the sounds of which I couldn't reconfigure into something comprehensible—*Bynes Da Bows, Pines To Poes.*

"Excuse me?" I finally said. "Buy insta—?"

"Pints," he said slowly, lifting his glass. "To. Polls." I must've looked uncomprehending. "Just Randall's thing, I guess." Creamer snorted, shook his head. "Kind of genius, really. Pints to polls—guy's buying beer for anyone who'll vote for Kerry."

"Is that legal?" It was the first thing that came into my mind.

"Who cares? Hey, you get my mom to vote, I'll buy you a pitcher. Hell, a keg!"

I sipped at my beer, swallowing clumsily and gulping air. I began to say, "Does your mom—" but a burp rose up out of me. When it passed, I finished: "—need a ride to the polls? 'Scuse me." I patted my sternum. Creamer didn't exactly smile, but something shifted, like he'd taken a gratifying bong hit, and he regarded me approvingly, and I relaxed. "Do *you* need a ride to the polls?" His pleasure disappeared. He mumbled, "Under control," and hid his head under his arm. Regina was watching. Like an idiot, I pressed on. "We're giving rides on

Election Day." Creamer grunted inaudibly, sucked up his beer dregs, then slid off his stool and out the door.

Regina leaned in. "Creamer don't got a car. Gets embarrassed."

"But we've got rides!"

Regina kept shaking her head. "Norma needs the para-van, for the wheelchair and all."

"But we have all kinds of accommodations. I'm sure we could get them to the polls."

The look Regina gave me was like Ginny's when she's waiting for me to realize what a moron I am. *Go ahead and chop the man's balls off, why don't you.* Then someone ordered a drink and she turned away.

ELECTION DAY 2004: I taught in the morning, then returned to Prairie to Ginny-sit. Her nausea somewhat abated, she'd risen from her sickbed only to get bitch-slapped back down: a routine ob-gyn check-in got her diagnosed with high blood pressure and—and this is a quote, the clinical name—"an incompetent cervix." They put her on "modified bed rest," which meant she could get up only to pee. Noncompliance would land her on "full bed rest," with attendant bedpan indignities. When I arrived, she had one hand submerged in a bowl of soapy ice water on the nightstand. Swelling, she explained; her wedding ring was cutting off circulation. We wrestled the band from her chafed, throbbing finger. "It was Grandma Ma's," she sobbed.

"You'll wear it again once the baby's born, Gin." I awaited a sarcastic sneer, but the bite never came. I slung the ring over the top of my index finger. "I don't remember her in a ring . . ."

"She couldn't." Her voice broke. "The arthritis." Thin, gold, engraved with flowers and vines, like the one Bena pried from dead Mignon's hand.

I settled downstairs in the family room, in the shadow of the Sloganator wall, to make last-ditch calls on Ginny's cell. We'd gotten updated phone lists of registered Dems who might yet be nudged to the polls. Still on it: Norma Kramer and her son, Burton. Strangely excited, I dialed the number, but it just rang and rang. I made other calls, to other people who were not home, or not answering their phones. I certainly wasn't answering mine.

Late in the afternoon I called the number of a Jaycee Spendler, who was, according to my printout, an "infrequent voter," age forty. A woman answered with a faraway hello. I launched in: "Hi, I'm with the Iowa Democrats. If you're supporting Kerry, we hope you'll vote today."

She gave a hoarse, tired laugh. "You're all really into this, huh? Going all out?"

"Well, we're scared," I confessed. "Four more years of Bush? That terrifies me."

"Anybody but Bush, right? Just not Bush." She laughed again. "So, it's only today?"

"Yup, last chance. I can tell you your polling place . . ."

"Let me get a—" She held the phone aside. "Angel, where's that pen at?" Scuffling ensued. "Look, we can't find the location of that —just tell me it. I could maybe get there."

"I can drive you if you need . . ." I said.

"You know it matters if you have a record?" It took me a second. A record? Vinyl? Voting record? Then I understood: a criminal record.

"I don't know," I told Jaycee, "but I can ask." I started up the stairs, calling, "O precinct captain, my precinct captain!" Ginny gave a pained snort to say what sort of a precinct captain she was. In her doorway, I covered my phone. "Rules on voting with a record?"

Her eyes were slits. "Depends." She took a deep breath. "Misdemeanor or felony?"

I don't know how Jaycee heard her, but cell technology's a mystery to me. Jaycee's voice came through the phone: "Felony." Then louder, as if to really claim the deed: "It's a felony."

Ginny said, "If she's on the list, it can't hurt. Might have to do a provisional ballot . . ."

In my ear, Jaycee said, "I'm just trying to raise my kids, y'know? It was a *bad* summer."

"Jaycee," I said, "are you still at 499½ Sunset View Way? I could come get you now."

There was a pause. Then she said, "Sure, what the hell? Why not, right?"

I'll admit to feeling an anxious giddiness as I drove to Jaycee Spendler's. Adrenaline, the slightly insane rush of doing something I'd never done before, some crazy notion of doing something that might possibly, in a teeny tiny way, matter. Ludicrous, I know, but it's like an infection, the idea of "making a difference," and I gave in to it, to that hope.

Across the street from an abandoned farmhouse, its land long subdivided and sold off, Prairie Dairy's thirty-foot fiberglass mascot, Carrie, watches over Commerce Drive. I didn't know this part of town, Prairie's industrial sector. A scrawled sign in one duct-taped window of an auto body shop: *Will work on buggy's too.* A storage facility—part Quonset hut, part cement-block box—with a sign: *Call Joe M, no number.* Between the farmhouse at 499 Commerce Drive and a badly listing garage cut a dirt alley: Sunset View Way, the view metaphoric. Number 499½, a double-wide behind the farmhouse, must have once housed a day care center. The yard was strewn with crushed mini-trampolines and broken-wheeled exer-saucers, a toppled basketball hoop on a warped plywood backboard. Plastic pastel Easter-egg shards littered the patchy fescue. An enormous stuffed panda lay out on a cement slab like a sacrifice. I knocked and waited on the stoop, staring into a glass storm door etched with mildewed dolphins.

The girl who opened the door was very put together: new jeans, a clean sweatshirt. Only when she turned did I see a knot in her long, fine hair that would need to be worked through with baby oil and tweezers, or just cut out. "Mo-om," she hollered, "it's a lady!" When no answer came, the girl went back and left me staring in the storm door. The place was a disaster of sherbet-hued baby paraphernalia. Something was wriggling in the rubble.

When Jaycee Spendler emerged, she was talking on a cordless, and paused, receiver clamped ear to shoulder, to scoop up what I figured was a battery-powered toy, plastic legs beating furiously. It turned out to be a baby. Less than a year old—Oren's age, maybe younger—it smiled in that thrilled-baby way, flailing and slamming its head into Jaycee's shoulder. She was little and thin, her dark brown dyed hair hanging over an acne-scarred face, gaunt, puffy, and preternaturally exhausted. The baby beamed at her in unmitigated adoration. "Look, I'll call you back," Jaycee said to the receiver, and I had an odd sense that it was pantomime, no one on the other end. Jaycee looked at me like I was vaguely familiar.

"I'm your ride to the polls," I said.

Jaycee chuckled a little. "They really got you working, huh? *Not Bush. Not Bush.*"

I smiled wearily. "We're trying to get to anyone who might possibly vote for Kerry."

"Yeah," she said. "Terry, Terry, right."

I tried to stay focused. "Can I take you to the polls to vote, Jaycee?"

She glanced down at herself: acid jeans, a black T-shirt, fiery insignia, scrawl as illegible as Randall's *Tenaj*. "Don't got a car. Lost my license. You got one, I'll go."

"I even have a car seat," I told her. The adrenaline rushed again.

I don't envy parents attempting to get out of the house with a baby these days. We didn't know how easy we had it before everything was officially dangerous. Jaycee adjusted Oren's car seat for baby Travis, while Angel, age seven, readied a diaper bag. Travis: a name destined for the meth den, his face probably already inked on some guy's hairy shoulder. Travis's diaper bag knocked the back of Angel's knees, but she carried it with poise. Gripping a fresh-from-the-freezer teething toy in one hand and a milky bottle, warm from the microwave, in the other, Angel climbed in beside Travis like a tiny au pair. Jaycee got in front with me. I wished I'd cleaned up the car.

"Angel voted in school today." Jaycee stuck a thumb at her. "Didn't you, baby?"

"That's great." I smiled. "Who'd you vote for?"

Angel thought about this for some time. Finally she said, "I think it was a male."

I sighed—"If you think we're crazy today, just wait till there's a female on the ballot!"—and backed down Sunset View Way, the Prairie Dairy cow looming in my rearview. "How is it, living right here by Carrie?" I asked, expecting, I suppose, delight—from Angel, at least.

"Loud," Jaycee answered. She meant the dairy, I realized, not the cow.

"It's loud," Angel agreed.

"Trucks all friggin' night," Jaycee said. "Exhaust fans. It's worse than the train tracks."

"No, they were way worse," Angel said. "Right when you fell asleep, that bell ringed."

Jaycee nodded. "Those bells sucked rocks."

"It's better here," Angel added. "The dairy people are nice."

"Angel Dawn," Jaycee cautioned, "you don't go talking to them at the dairy, you hear?"

In the back seat, Angel murmured, "Sorry," as Jaycee turned to me: "I come home, find her talking out there to them men work at the dairy. She's got no idea. No clue." Jaycee shook her head. "Fucking cow," she muttered. She meant Carrie, not Angel, but it felt nasty anyway.

I tried to change the topic. "I know someone who works at the dairy."

"Hey, look, I don't mean offense," Jaycee said. "There's decent people there. I don't mean no offense. Angel's just too fucking friendly—excuse me—for her own good. Right?"

Behind us, Angel nodded obediently.

"He's not really a *friend,* really," I said. "I mean, I just know him."

"No offense," Jaycee repeated. And then, as if she had something to make up to me, she started shaking her head, repeating, "No Bush, no Bush," marveling over the phrase.

I spoke, as if to Angel: "*I* voted for the Democratic candidate, John Kerry."

"Kerry," Jaycee said, "Kerry."

"Right," I said, slightly relieved. "Right. Kerry's the Democrat."

"Creamer's a Democrat," Angel said.

"Creamer?" I nearly gave myself whiplash. "You know Creamer?"

"Course," Angel said. Jaycee didn't react, but I wasn't sure if she'd stopped listening or if maybe Angel was allowed to talk to Creamer. "He voted for that one you said," Angel told me.

"Creamer did?" In the rearview, Angel was nodding, and I said, "He told you that?" She nodded again and I shook my head, grinning. "Good man, Burton Kramer. Good man."

"Who's that?" Angel asked.

"Who? Burton Kramer? Creamer." I was excessively pleased to be more in the know about Creamer than this seven-year-old. "It's a nickname."

"I didn't know that," Angel admitted, and I imagined her telling Creamer about our conversation: how the lady who took them to vote for John Terry said Creamer's real name is Burton. He probably loathed "Burton," was taunted as a child—*Bur-ton, Bur-ty, creamy, dirty Birdy*—though for all I knew he could've hated "Creamer." Maybe he'd thank me.

"Where's his bottle?" Angel asked. About Travis, I realized, not Creamer.

"In the bag?" Jaycee looked around her seat. "Guess we forgot it."

Angel seemed worried; I was anxious too. Would there be Republicans monitoring the polls, challenging the votes of convicted felons? Was I leading Jaycee into something awful? But we were already there: Arnold J. Stoltzfus Middle School, no turning back. Angel asked, "Will I go here if we keep living here?" and Jaycee said, "Maybe, probably." I felt suddenly drunk, my depth perception off, like the car had stretched and I was piloting from the back seat, my arms and legs extra long and rubbery, feet working pedals somewhere far ahead. I pulled over and we tumbled out. Someone unclicked the car seat from its dock, and Travis, silent and dull-looking, watched skeptically from his padded half shell. The world careened past; my voice was too loud. We slammed car doors and marched to the entrance like we'd come to the end of the yellow brick road —*Here we are, Emerald City!* I prayed we wouldn't be turned away at the gates.

Inside, white-haired ladies and gray-scalped men behind cafeteria tables strained over huge binders of dot-matrix printouts. "This woman's here to vote!" I called, and a hunchbacked poll worker shook his head as if afraid I'd do something dangerous or obscene. Or maybe he had Parkinson's. I was shaking too, couldn't get my bearings. The geriatric poll workers greeted each voter like the first voter ever, rediscovering the check-in process anew every time. Jaycee produced an ID, lists were checked and cross-referenced, and she had to fill out a card. No big red FELON stamp. Small favors. Awkwardly, Jaycee juggled pen, paper, and baby, and I stood uselessly by until it dawned on me to take Travis. "You don't mind?" She seemed surprised.

"Oh, no, not at all." I'm not a woman grubby to get my hands on a baby. I often sense I won't be trusted, given how I did with my own. But Jaycee passed Travis right over. Freed from the car seat, hitched on my hip, he flailed once, then stilled, staring out, listless. He was so placid I wondered if something was wrong with him; then, as if to disprove me, he commenced to howl. Angel fumbled in the bag and produced a grimy, gnawed pacifier, but it placated Travis, who laid his cheek on my chest, shut and opened his eyes several times, and fell sound asleep.

At the next table, a man in a urine-yellow shirt slid a ballot into a privacy folder, his hands also shaking with Parkinson's. Jaycee opened the folder and looked for something to lean on. Divested of the baby, she was freer, confident and performative. We were a whirlwind of paper and people and baby junk, and she seemed to like the attention we attracted as our entourage moved toward the voting "booths," a row of folding podiums with bright blue privacy screens. Angel trailed behind us, collecting drool cloths and chew toys in our wake. In a rickety booth, Jaycee slapped down her ballot, circling her pencil hand above it. I balanced baby Travis against me and drew the line with my finger. "Connect those," I instructed, "arrow tail to tip," so she did. One pencil line—*Felons for Kerry!*—and then everything went warp speed again, Jaycee flailing her ballot at the Parkinson's man who—arm quivering like someone had a gun to his head—pointed her to a ballot-counting contraption. Jaycee let the machine's mouth suck in her card, the analog counter clicked to 416, and she was done. Of those 416 votes, how many were for the hell we already knew? How many of these poll workers had drawn their own shaky lines for the plain-talking rancher they just really related to? Did they, too, feel misunderestimated? As we flew toward the exit, I cursed elderly right-wingers at large: *May your quavering pencil marks be too faint to count. May your chads forever hang!*

Back at 499½, Jaycee struggled to extract Travis from the car. "Can't believe I'm forty and voted for the first time!" And I chirped back like a public-service ad, "Now that you know how good it feels, maybe you'll be back!" They went up the walk—me waving, them waving, Angel yelling, "Bye!" Me yelling, "Bye, Angel! Travis! Jaycee, thank you!" And then they were in and I was driving away, daylight dying, headed for the Gas Stop, very ready for a beer.

Halfway down the hill, cruising on the great success of the Spendler outing, I thought of Norma Kramer and imagined swinging by the swan house to spirit her off to Arnold J. Stoltzfus. It went Disney in my mind: Norma's wheelchair hitched to the pair of harnessed swans, honking triumphantly as they took flight. I drove by the house, but no lights were on. I thought briefly of driving to John C. Wolffson to see if my ghost lady wanted a ride to the polls, but in the end I drove to the bar, listening to NPR's heartening news that Kerry was ahead in the electoral count, 77 to 66, but scared to let myself hope.

Regina slid me my pint, saying, "That asshole wins, I don't even know what," her gray eyes cool behind beige plastic grandma glasses. In that moment I questioned everything, seized with sudden horror that I'd read Regina all wrong: far from being an old leftie, was she actually a back-of-a-Harley chick, skinny arms wrapped around some Libertarian's barrel belly? I stared, paralyzed, until her face broke in a grand, crooked smile. "What? I done my bit." She thrust her bony pelvis toward me to show the I VOTED sticker on her belt buckle. "Creamer'd've had my hide!"

Linda and Randall arrived soon thereafter in buoyant good humor, fresh from NA, where consensus said Bush was out — and that was mixed company: drug addiction crossed the aisle freely. "A round of shots on me for everyone," Randall proclaimed, "even Republicans!"

"Of what, honey?" Regina asked, and he cried, "Make 'em red-white-and-blue!" Regina concocted something that looked like a lava lamp in a shot glass, and I tried to wave mine away, but Randall was insistent. I went zero to sixty in about one second, boiling mad, ready to yell, *What the fuck kind of NA sponsor shoves alcohol on people?* He hovered, like he might force the shot down my throat, and I cowered as its colors blurred to a purple bruise. Then Linda came into focus beside Randall, and she was laughing, and I saw Randall was laughing too, and then, slowly, I understood: he was *acting the part* of a bullying peer-pressurer. It was parody. Parody, but I couldn't laugh. Everything was too raw-edged, my nerves frayed. When the president's straight out of *National Lampoon,* his vice from central casting, and Mennonites are drinking Bud Light and feeding Bon Jovi to the jukebox, parody and reality have become one.

Randall dropped the act. "Whaddya like, Phillipa? You name it. On me," and I felt too frazzled and drained to do anything but accept. I gestured to my glass, and Regina whisked it off to tap me a new one. A night to get drunk if ever there was one. "It's too early to celebrate," I said, "to count our chickens. My grandmother would've said we were giving it a *kinehora.*"

"Can-a-horror?" Randall said it like *Cannes-aux-horreur,* which sounded like an upscale slasher film festival, but I didn't really know how to pronounce it myself.

"It's Yiddish, or Hebrew, I think," I told him. "You say something's good, it goes bad."

"What, you going Amish out here?" Randall laughed. I tried to join in.

He and Linda went off to play pool at some point. Someone came in and sat down in Creamer's seat, and I was beer-emboldened enough to think to say, *Go find another stool—that one's reserved,* but I only half turned, gave a politely dismissive Midwestern nod without actually seeing at whom, and resumed watching TV. The guy beside me breathed heavily—it was quite off-putting—and Regina set his beer down without a word; he was clearly a regular. As the booze hit the guy's bloodstream, his panting quieted. Then he said, "Got my vote in," and I whipped around, confused. It *was* Creamer. He wore a T-shirt, his sweatshirt tied at his waist. I'd never seen him without a hood, and the effect was disconcerting. I realized I'd imagined him curly-haired. His beard was brown, black, and reddish, woodsman-bushy, but his hair was straight and thick, cowlicked and sticking out in all directions, a lot more salt than pepper. It never dawned on me that Creamer was my age; I'd thought him young enough to make a relationship with Regina unseemly. She had to be sixty-five, and I'd thought Creamer forty, thirty-five. Now I could see he was a good bit older. He was asking me something. "You okay, Mrs. Maakestad?"

"*Mrs. Maakestad?*" I was surprised he had any idea who I was.

"Just being polite." He seemed very normal. Not Ted Kaczynski–like at all.

"Phillipa," I managed to say, but Creamer nodded; he already knew that, too. "Do you prefer Burton or Creamer?" I asked, but he just shrugged. "Regina and Angel call you Creamer."

"Angel Spendler?"

"How do you know her?" I asked.

"How do *I* know her?" Creamer said. "How do *you* know her?"

"I drove her mother to vote today." I puffed my chest with childish pride.

"Nice," Creamer said.

"She was already registered," I told him.

"Yeah, well, I did *that*, but voted's a whole diff— They didn't give her trouble about . . . ?"

"Wait, you registered voters?"

He waved it off. "Just pushed a little in the right direction." He nudged out an elbow.

"So how do you know the Spendlers?" I asked.

"I work at the dairy . . . ?" His tone was odd, like he thought I was trying to trick him. "They live across the street . . . ?" Then, without warning, Creamer sucked down the rest of his beer, pushed away the glass, signaled Regina for a refill, and strode off toward the bathroom.

When Regina came to collect the empty, I said, "I got his next one."

She slanted her eyes. "Bartering himself for beer now?"

The nastiness of her tone confused me and tied my tongue. "No," I stammered, "I just . . . he—" She was halfway down the bar before I managed to say, "He registered voters!"

The look she shot back was of withering skepticism. "Yeah? What else'd he tell you?"

"What do you mean *what else*? What else what . . . ? What are we talking about?"

Regina leaned in to me. "Look, you want to talk about Creamer? Ask me what you want to know." I feared she'd reach over and wring a question out of me.

"Okay," I said, "why does he drink his beer with a straw?"

Regina straightened. Her face spread in a dopey, chinless grin, and she threw back her head, hooted one big "Ha!" then said, "Because he's a fucking freak!" and went to tap his beer.

Creamer returned. He thanked Regina for the drink.

"Thank your lady friend," she said. "Or should we all thank her? It on her account we're seeing your fine form tonight? He don't strip down for just anyone, you know."

Creamer glared. "I ran to the fucking middle school. I got hot, okay? Let it fucking lie."

"I'll say you got hot," Regina snapped, then pushed through the swinging door to the kitchen.

I didn't know if she didn't believe he'd gotten overheated, or didn't believe its cause, or if she was calling him sexy, or hot and bothered. You spend a lifetime in student musical theater, every line bolstered with gesture and action to telegraph emotion to the half-deaf, half-dead guy in the last row, and your appreciation for nuance and ambiguity shrinks appreciably.

Creamer sipped his beer, one eye squinted behind his thick glasses as if he were in pain.

"You *ran* to the middle school?" I said. "To vote? That's miles away."

Creamer shrugged.

"I could have given you a ride. You *and* your mother."

"My mother," he said flatly, "hasn't voted since my father left her in 1969."

"Your mother stopped voting when your father left her?"

"Meant too much to him," Creamer said.

"Your mother stopped voting because voting meant too much to your father?"

"She stopped *voting*," he said bitterly, "when the man abandoned her, me, his job—fucking *tenured*, too—to go 'homestead' with a nineteen-year-old in fucking Idaho."

"He was a professor?"

"Associate," Creamer grumbled, nodding at his beer.

"At U of I?" I asked. "Of what?"

Creamer gave a disingenuous laugh—"Poli-sci!"—then drank, squinting in pain.

"Are you okay?" I asked.

He shrugged and nodded, though noncommittally. "My fucking teeth."

And then, just like that, the straw made sense. "You have a toothache!"

He didn't see why I was so gleeful about it. "Something," he said. "Sensitive as hell."

"Have you seen a dentist?"

"Yeah, no—not much for the dentist," Creamer said, "even if I had the insurance."

I wanted to take him all in, to really see what Burton Kramer looked like. I'd clearly had too much to drink. I said, "So, you're going to use a straw for the rest of your life?"

He gave a soft, resigned snort. "Fucking hope not. Pain comes and goes, you know."

Creamer's teeth were just one of those things, I realized: you put it off and put it off until you're the guy who drinks beer through a straw, and then why bother? Pain comes and goes. The man was the fucking Buddha: all life is impermanence, everything is change.

Linda and Randall finished their pool game. The Gas Stop was dividing by affiliation: scant Democrats at the bar, god-and-gun lovers by the pool table and jukebox. "They got the entertainment," Creamer said, "but we hold the booze." He said it like that Billy Joel Vietnam song: *We held the liquor, they held the entertainment.* Was Creamer a vet? I wondered.

On TV, the Carolinas went red, then Virginia. C-SPAN had people phoning in their voting stories—*Voices of America*—the anchorwoman asking callers about their poll experiences. She was looking for strife, she wanted, *I walked uphill both ways through a snowstorm and got told "No niggers allowed,"* but people were only grandstanding. Another southern state went red, and a cheer rose from the pool table. Creamer slid off his stool—to punch someone, I figured—took one step left, and plunked himself down beside me, and I'd be lying if I said I didn't thrill to it: this man who kept himself so insulated from everyone had removed his armor and moved closer to me. He leaned in and said, "What are you doing here?"

Flustered, I said, "I don't have a TV. Where I'm staying."

"Not the bar. I mean Prairie," he said. "Why you're in Prairie. Get sick of the city?"

"Oh." I was the infamous Yoder Mother-in-Law, didn't everyone know that? "My daughter and her husband . . . he's a Yoder?" Like half the county. "Silas and Eula?" But Creamer was saying, "I just didn't know why *you* were here," and then I was telling him: "My husband and I split up." I hadn't yet spoken that aloud, so plainly. "I had to get out of the house." It was true, though it sounded, in summary, like a much simpler situation than the one I felt I was in.

"Bald guy?" Creamer asked.

"Bald?"

"Your husband."

"No, why?" I asked.

"The one who was here," he said. "Bald on top? Here at the bar, talking to Regina?"

"Lucius?" My surprise was unfeigned.

Creamer lifted his palms as if to say, *I don't know the guy. He's* your *damn husband.*

"No, that's . . ." What was I supposed to say? *That's my lover?*

"Hey, look, none of my business," Creamer said. "Sorry, look, never mind, forget I . . ."

"Look," I said—why do I adopt the speech patterns of whomever I'm talking to? "Look, no, that's someone else. My life—is not usually like this. It's been a very strange time."

Creamer shook his head. "None of my business. Really not my fucking business."

God, I wanted the night to be over—the election to be over, the semester. I wanted Lucius to take me to bed and fuck me until it was done. *That's* what I wanted. But then, as if in a perverse response to my desire, every TV in the Gas Stop was taking us inside a White House living room where the entire Bush clan was photo-opportunistically gathered to watch the returns. Scene designers had them all absurdly positioned, smiling their cheeky, false smiles on white sofas that wrapped the room. They'd even gotten someone to perch on a couch arm, like a contortionist, and managed to smush in a token black, way in a corner, far stage left. I saw her only when Randall began talking loudly to the TV: "How much you pay her to sit there, Dubya? What'd it cost to get her to pretend she don't know about your people out scaring black voters from the polls, you shitwad?" The camera zoomed right in, then, on the shitwad himself, who was saying, "I believe I *will* win, thank you very much," and I laid my head on my arms and watched the TV with one open eye, like a bird who's smacked into a window and stares up from the ground, unsure whether it's dead or not. I was still in that position when someone came up behind me to order drinks. Lefties weren't feeding the juke or shooting pool, but party sequestration hadn't stopped the right from boozing. The guy waited a few paces back while Regina got his drinks ready. She was passing them over the bar when some state got called for Bush and a buoyant *whoo-hoo* rang out, and just as the guy took the drinks and turned to go, he leaned in to me, beer breath hot in my ear, and said, "You're gonna lose, River City bitch."

I was up, wheeling around on my stool, cursing—"What the fuck?"—before I even laid eyes on the guy, and I must have clipped him as he tried to scuttle away. He stumbled and the drinks leapt from his hands, and then everything took on the slow-motion affect in which all accidents seem to unfurl: the drinks splashed up from their highball glasses, pausing at the apex, ice cubes glinting, limes hovering glossy and ripe, until the glasses decided to follow their contents as if to try and catch up to prevent a spill. Creamer cried out as the liquid hit him, soaking his coveralls. The highball glasses, industrially sturdy, clunked to the floor unharmed, but Creamer jumped to his feet, landing hard in his steel-toed boots, crushing one glass on impact, the other as he stumbled forward. Such a familiar sound —glass breaking underfoot, a classic moment in any Jewish wedding —though it's a sound always followed by cheers, and their absence felt strange and foreboding. I did a staging years ago of *Fiddler on the Roof* where it's the smash of Tzeitel and Motel's wedding glass that sends the cast into song and dance—into *L'Chaim!* Rest assured, the Gas Stop Bar and Grill did not burst into musical revue, but the glass-smashing did return us to real time. No cheers of *Mazel tov!*, just gasps, shouts undulating through the bar. All around me there was flapping, like a flock of frightened birds. From the beating frenzy came shattering echoes as the glass ground underfoot and shot out against metal chair legs. Creamer lunged for the guy who'd heckled me—who'd no doubt expected to drop his insult in my ear and make a getaway with his drinks, fast, like Ginny in the airport with the *W*-hat woman. Instead he found himself bereft of beverages, flat on the bar floor, and flailing under Creamer's bulk. With the top of his coveralls down and his sweatshirt tied at his waist, Creamer had four sleeves flapping at his thighs. Even stripped of his layers, he was a big, bearish man, well over six feet, and burly. The heckler was no match for him. Creamer might've held him down until he apologized if every other able-bodied man there hadn't swarmed in to wrench them apart. Each side staggered back; empty floor opened between them. The site of the scuffle was slick-wet, scattered with ice cubes and glass shards and muddled wedges of lime. A pair of eyeglasses lay a yard from my feet. Creamer, restrained by four men, looked plucked and denuded and wrong without his spectacles. I picked them up off the floor.

Regina rose over the crowd, calling "Whoa, whoa, whoa!" just like Lucius. She stood on the bar in a pair of tiny, ratty tennis sneakers far too demure for a woman so tough, and took charge, yelling, "Creamer, out. Get him out of here." The men restraining Creamer nodded the way they do at Bluntmore's to confirm a bid with the auctioneer, and Creamer was led from the Gas Stop. Regina turned on the guy who'd started it. "Bondorf, what the fuck?" she demanded, and he hung his head for the scolding. "Get the hell out of my bar. I don't want to see you for at least a week, hear me?" Bondorf nodded, was released, and made a walk of shame out the door. Regina paused to take stock. She looked down at the crowd: "Someone make sure Creamer's ass gets home safe." A few men nodded assurances, but I seemed to be saying, aloud, "I'll do it." Creamer felt like my responsibility; I had his glasses, after all. I pushed in my stool and was digging in a pocket for cash to lay on the bar when I saw Regina shaking her head at me, an eyebrow cocked in disbelief, her mouth saying "Nuh-uh," then more emphatically, "Nuh-*uh*." I understood that I was supposed to retract my offer, but I didn't see why. "It's not necessary," Regina said as I stood there stupidly, looking up, still digging in my pocket. She spoke as though I were a dog with a squirrel in its jaws. "Drop it," she ordered. "Just drop it."

The crowd began to turn away, and Regina made a surreally graceful dismount from the bar, Linda and Randall supporting either hand like backup dancers. She landed beside me. "You think you can keep from starting any more bar fights, or should I kick you out now, too?"

I was so embarrassed and cowed, I only managed to squeak out a lame little "Sorry."

Regina nodded once, as if to say *You should be,* and stalked off to the kitchen.

I stared at the TV's scrolling closed captions. C-SPAN's correspondent took a call from Bloomfield, New Mexico. "Hi," said a young woman. "This is actually my first time to vote, so, yeah, pretty proud to vote for President Bush because I believe we have a lot of the same agreement on morals like partial-birth abortion and, you know, stuff like that."

"Partial-birth abortion is a moral?" Apparently, I said this aloud. Randall sat on a nearby barstool. Now I addressed him: "I didn't start it," I said, and maybe he didn't hear, or was looking across the room at another TV, or maybe his silence meant: *But you did, Phillipa. Just by being where you don't belong, you* did *start it.* I didn't belong, and it wasn't about red or blue; I was the only person in that place who didn't work for an hourly wage.

I stuck two twenties on the bar—too much, no matter how many beers I'd had—said good night to whoever might hear, and left. No one tried to stop me. I was too drunk to drive, too drunk to bring Creamer his glasses at the shack behind Norma's, which was what I'd imagined doing. Instead I crossed the parking lot to get a room at the Gas Stop. Henk Presidio's not a talker, and he had the desk, for which I was grateful. He didn't ask what brought me back—probably didn't care. I was a guest; we came and went. He put me in a new room, not 116, though it had all the same accoutrements, just in a different arrangement. This compounded my disorientation, but I didn't really feel my drunkenness until I sank down in a La-Z-Boy that turned out not to be under me. I lurched to the opposite corner of the room and tipped myself into the actual chair. I wanted, and didn't want, to turn on the TV, so I called Lucius, who didn't answer, which was just as well, since the thought of telling him what had happened made me recoil. He'd side with Regina and make me feel worse. Or was it Michael who'd've done that?

My humiliation burned. For this night, and for all the others—a radiating, retroactive embarrassment—I'd sat at the Gas Stop bar, sipping beer and dipping fried nuggets, people around me sniggering at my every bourgeois move, sneering silently as Lucius and I held hands between the stools, rolling their eyes as I bantered with Regina —Regina, whom I'd vainly, ignorantly, arrogantly imagined to like me. I'd enjoyed the delusion that she was happy to converse with an intelligent woman her own age, that it pleased her to talk with someone other than meat-headed meatpackers or meth-headed roofers. But really, Bondorf had only expressed what everyone there had wanted to say for months: *Go back where you belong, bitch.*

In the La-Z-Boy, I stared at the ceiling. Parking lot light edged through a crack in the curtain. My eyeballs felt swollen, my brain buzzed, and my heart hammered with beer. I don't remember closing my eyes, but my phone startled me awake. "Hey." Lucius's voice was heavy.

"What's wrong?" I asked—too quickly, on instinct. Then I remembered: everything.

I heard him force a puff of air out his nostrils, the exhausted imitation of a laugh.

"I got kicked out of the Gas Stop," I told him. It felt true enough.

"Oh, Phil . . ." he said, but I couldn't tell if it was a sympathetic *Oh, Phil,* or a chiding one, or just something to say. I hadn't wanted to tell him what happened until he seemed not to want to hear it, and then I did want to tell him, and to bring Creamer into it, to threaten Lucius into claiming me, or declaring something. None of this, I know, excuses my behavior.

"I'm drunk," I said, and that seemed to make it all the more true.

"Don't," he began, "you're not . . ." and I don't know what he was going to say, because he never finished. "Where are you?" He wanted to know I was safe, but it made me feel judged, not loved. Yes, I'm aware of the juvenile nature of my reactions. I'm ashamed that I wanted to tell him I'd started a bar brawl, that a man—a rival suitor—had defended me. I wanted him jealous, wanted to see if I could provoke it, see what it did to him. Lucius is not a jealous man —I don't *want* a jealous man—but that night I was desperate for something I couldn't name, and stabbing blindly for it. Lucius said, "I can't watch anymore," and this is what I lashed at.

"You don't *know?*" I asked, galled—or sounding galled. Was *my* television on?

"There's nothing more I can *do.*" He sounded exhausted, but I was not kind.

"Maybe you should've done more when you had the chance," I spat.

"Please, Phil," he said, calmly, rationally, *soberly*. "Not now. Not about this. Please?" And like the tantruming child I am, I hung up on him. Just like Ginny slams doors on me, I hung up on Lucius. I sat a long time afterward, phone in hand. He did not try to call back.

Which is what propelled me to the Gas Stop convenience store. I think I intended to buy cigarettes. I hadn't smoked since college, but if I were ever to take it up again, that was the night. Maybe I'd buy junk food, chips to soak up the beer in my belly, though I kept thinking about more beer, too, imagined getting wrecked, by myself, in my hotel room, the election washing boozily over me. In reality, I'd probably take two sips and fall asleep in the La-Z-Boy.

I pushed in through the chiming front door, and there, seated at the single booth, nursing a Styrofoam cup of coffee through a straw and staring—near blind, I figured—at the television, was Creamer. He looked at me like I was the last person he'd've expected, but also as if things had gotten so weird that night it almost made sense. And he appeared to be seeing just fine, not at all like someone who'd lost his thick glasses. "You didn't go home," I said.

"No TV. And crap radio reception." He laughed ruefully into his coffee. "I'm sobering up," he declared, and lifted the cup in cheers.

At the beverage station I splashed scaldingly hot, pale brown coffee into a cup and added five tubs of half-and-half just to occupy my hands. To Creamer I said, "I have your glasses."

"Oh? Thanks," and he lifted a hand to accept their return.

"Oh—not here. I'm sorry, I didn't know you'd . . . I left them in my room. I got a room, at the inn." I gestured in its direction. "I couldn't keep sitting there. At the bar." Creamer was nodding. "Do you want your glasses? I could get them." But he'd gone back to the television and seemed to only dimly register my words. I asked, "Are you staying here till it's over?"

"Over?" he said, like he didn't believe it ever would be. "She loves kicking me out."

"Regina?" I gestured vaguely. "I have a TV. Your glasses . . . you could watch with me . . ."

Creamer looked at me hard. He buried his hands in his sweatshirt pockets and hunched his shoulders, eyes jittering in confusion, or pain. "You're asking me to your hotel room?"

I lost it: "Why does everyone think I'm trying to lure you into bed?"

Creamer's eyes went to his cup, and he stared into it a long time. I got nervous, set down my coffee, and searched my pockets for some imaginary lost ChapStick or hair band. I feared he might not respond at all and started to say, "Never mind—" but he put out a hand as if asking me to wait for his answer, so I waited. The door chimed, and a young guy came in. He and Creamer exchanged nods, and he squeezed past me, filled a cup, then waited at the register for the clerk. All this lent Creamer some time. I sipped my coffee—which was either repulsively flavored or I'd accidentally added something like fake Irish Cream—and studied the bulletin board business cards. *Tawney Laffler, MA, LMHC, Specializing in self-discovery and compassion-*

ate connection. Bart Yoder—Free Standing Timber. Sigourney Gahl, Intuitive Gardening Coach—call for prices. Prairie is close to Fairfield and its Maharishi University of Management and Transcendental Meditation, where things tend to float toward the New Age.

The customer paid and left, the clerk retreated, and Creamer lifted his eyes, saying, "I'm sorry if I made things—" I started to protest, but he shushed me. "This is a small town. I . . ." He paused and looked up at me, questioning. "We?" he asked, but I didn't understand the question. "*We* live in a small town. A small town where nice-looking ladies don't—"

"Creamer!" I protested, embarrassed.

"What?" He took a deep breath and lowered his voice. "You're a nice-looking woman."

My insides went watery. I felt deranged. Something was very wrong with me. I'm mortified that what I said was "Well, if you're used to Regina!"

Creamer squinted in disappointment. "Don't," he said. "Don't. That's beneath you."

"Beneath me? How do you have any idea what's beneath me?" My voice was too loud, I couldn't help it.

Behind the register, the backroom door swung open and the clerk, who could obviously hear everything we said, gave a melodramatic *ahem* to announce his entrance.

Creamer lowered his voice. "Maybe we could talk somewhere more . . . private?"

"Well, I invited you to a more private place, but apparently that was too shocking to—"

He cut me off— "Okay"— stood, tossed his cup in the trash, and gave the TV a last pitiful glance. Then he took my arm like I was his daughter caught out after curfew and led me out of one Gas Stop and into another. Three in one evening, a personal record. I keyed open my room.

Inside, I gave Creamer his glasses, which he took absently and soon set down on the bureau. I turned on the TV, offered him the La-Z-Boy, and began to make coffee. He refused the recliner and instead took the wooden desk chair, in which he looked like a grown-up at the kindergarten table. He sat very close to the TV; I reminded him of his glasses.

"Oh, I don't really need 'em," he said, a little hangdog.

"You don't?"

"Nah, I just . . ."

"But they're so thick, I assumed—"

"Yeah, it's just easier sometimes."

Sometimes? I'd never seen him without them. I walked to the bureau, removed my own glasses, slipped his on. They were dirty, scratched, and off-kilter, everything blurry and foggy, but that's how the world looks to me without glasses. I wished I *had* bought beer; I was just drunk enough to wish I were drunker.

Creamer took up the remote and chose ABC, Peter Jennings, which somehow gave me license to blurt, "Did you—growing up, did you have a relationship with your father?" I hoped he didn't think I was asking if he'd been molested. The coffeemaker burbled and spat steam. I envisioned a past in which a lovely, wartless Norma Kramer, with her own teeth and hair, was married to a dashing Peter Jennings. Creamer sighed deeply. "I'm sorry," I said. "I . . . My husband doesn't have a father. Or didn't . . . you know, beyond conception. He never knew him."

"Your husband," Creamer said. "Not the bald one."

"Right," I said. "Not."

"Might be better that way. I had something to miss, you know? Had one till I was like fifteen, and then just had a falling-apart mother, so, yeah. Your husband's done a little better than me, even with his disadvantages." I didn't say anything, which should be a lesson to me: when I didn't talk, Creamer did.

"I went to the U, you know?" he said.

"You did? When?"

"Not for long," he said. "Wasn't suited to it."

On the TV, Peter Jennings announced that ABC was relinquishing Arizona to Bush. An electoral graphic flashed: Bush 210, Kerry 188. Creamer changed the channel. When the coffee was ready, I carried him a cup. CNN's take on Bush's lead was more palatable.

"You got a straw-thing?" Creamer mimed a stir. I went to the coffee tray. "Or something to put in it?"

I thumbed through a basket. "Sugar, Sweet'N Low, nondairy — that whitener stuff."

He was shaking his head, glancing around. "There a minibar?"

"I thought you were sobering up?"

"When I was going home, I was." But now he had reason to drink again, it seemed, and I will attempt to say this without shame: I went soft inside at the thought. I'd say *wet*, but that's not entirely true — not wet, but liquidy. If it sounds unlikely, go to menopausechitchat .com or redhotmamas.org and read about perimenopausal women whose "symptoms" aren't decreased libido but exactly the opposite. Maybe I was sick — with drink or anxiety — or maybe I wanted to fuck this man. Maybe I was about to vomit. I'm not sure I knew the difference that night.

Creamer stuck a steel-toed boot at the mini-fridge beneath the TV, and the square door rattled open to reveal a full-stocked array of tiny bottles. Room 116 hadn't had a minibar. Rising, Creamer set his coffee on the desk and crouched down to inspect. I heard my father's voice in my head, lecturing on the ludicrous markup on in-room drinks. And Michael's voice, telling little Ginny why we don't drink from hotel fridges. I'm sure Creamer figured a person who sprang for spur-of-the-moment hotel rooms didn't think twice about minibar costs. Squatting, he reached in blindly and removed a dark bottle, stood, cracked off the tiny cap with two fingers, and poured a splash into his coffee. He held out the bottle. I took it — Kahlúa — and emptied it into my cup, then sat on the edge of the bed in the primmest posture I could affect. Creamer took the La-Z-Boy. It was ten p.m.

Iowa's polls had been closed for an hour, but CNN wasn't venturing guesses. They called California for Kerry, then someone was saying something about Florida.

"Fuck me!" Creamer slammed his fist to the desk and started flipping channels. On CBS, Dan Rather said he wasn't calling Florida because, after 2000, he'd rather be last than wrong.

I said, "I think I'm going to be sick."

Creamer rose, then squatted down, opened the mini-fridge, and reached in for a bottle. "Guess that means you don't want another shot?" He upturned another tiny flask into his cup.

"I don't think I'm really going to be sick. Metaphorically sick, I think."

He held out the bottle: Bailey's. On ice, I thought, I could stomach it, so I grabbed the bucket, and Creamer said, "Oh, shit, for real?"

I stopped. "For real. I'm going to get ice. Yes, for real."

"Oh, I thought . . ." he stammered, and I left him there with Tom Brokaw or Wolf Blitzer and went into the too-bright hall, geometric shapes rising and hovering a few inches above the wall-to-wall industrial carpet, quivering in the fluorescent shimmy. A whoop came from behind a closed door, sexual or electoral, I couldn't tell. I steadied myself against the wall and pitched toward the ice machine alcove. I remember thinking if I got drunk enough I might not be responsible for what I did. I'd entered the mindset of an Iowa sorority girl out on a Saturday night in the middle of the winter, shivering bare-limbed in platform heels and halter top, waiting for something to swoop in and take her away—a boy, a shot, a car, a roofie, a tornado—anything that might pluck her from her frigid reality and deposit her someplace else. I thought of Eula wandering River City in the wake of her parents' death, of Bena under her rabbit-skin quilt on rue des Brebis. Sometimes you don't care what happens so long as something does. I wondered if there existed a vantage point from which I *didn't* appear to be having a midlife crisis. I don't remember filling the ice bucket; I do remember reentering the room, finding it unchanged, and realizing I'd expected it to be — for Creamer to be gone, or to be naked in the bed. But there he was in the La-Z-Boy, hair phosphorescent in the TV glow. He said, "Florida's gone," and I pictured Florida detaching and drifting into the ocean, that little penis of a state falling off, gone. *George Bush has taken the penis of America. May it float like a boat full of Cuban refugees until some good Democrat rows out, tosses a line, and tows it home.*

I sat on the bed. Every anchor had the same thing to say: *Florida has been taken, I repeat, Florida has been taken* — like it had been seized. When, finally, Dan Rather called it, I knew Florida was truly gone, and it started to seem like the election had to have been rigged. A woman on Fox — *Fox!* — was saying, "Either the exit polls by and large are completely wrong, or George Bush loses." And there's Dubya sitting cucumber-cool in the White House because he already knows how it's going down: he's paid, and he's collecting. If Creamer'd said right then, *Let's leave. Go. Anywhere: Ecuador. Honduras* . . . I'd've said yes, left everything — Lucius, Ginny, everything — run away, a refugee, to sleep on the beach, roam and beg, toothless, among goats and street dogs. Get malaria. Typhoid. AIDS. Die. "You got to stop looking at me," Creamer said. I was watching the TV light in his hair. When I burst into tears, he cried, "Jesus!" and it sounded like an appeal.

"I'm sorry," I stammered.

"I'll go." He set down his cup, and the remote, and put his hands on his thighs to stand.

"Where . . . ?"

He stood. "Wherever. It's fine. I should go. You should . . ." But he decided against whatever he was going to say. I was ready to beg: *Please, tell me what I should!*

Peter Jennings loomed onscreen: "Let's go back to reality —" *Yes! Reality!* But then: "The electoral vote of reality here: Mr. Bush, 237; Kerry, 188." Creamer looked like he wanted to reclaim the remote and blip Jennings away, so I stood and grabbed his arm. He backed down, left the remote where it was, and we stood there together before the TV. I clung to his arm with both hands as Jennings called Oregon for Kerry; then the numbers looked a little better. Creamer lifted a hand, I thought to take mine, but he was only prying my nails from his skin. Our eyes didn't leave the screen. He uncurled my talons gently and held my two hands, protected in his one. New information got piped into Jennings's ear. Graphics flashed: Bush 246, Kerry 195. "Colorado, battleground state as late as October, goes to Mr. Bush." Off camera, a voice said, "The states continue to pile up," and I was grateful they were treating it like a tragedy: states amassing like Allied bodies on Normandy's shores. When Creamer's free hand joined our other three, we must've looked like square dancers on some bizarre promenade.

On the news, as they'd been saying all along, it would all come down to Ohio. My anger at Lucius surged: he hadn't done enough. He'd spent the fall thinking about his Nazi collaborators, his French sister and brother on rue des Brebis, putting energy into ferreting out details of their catastrophe while a new one unfolded in his backyard. He should've been registering voters, like Creamer. Confused, ferocious, I clutched Creamer's hands. Washington State went to Kerry; Bush took Alaska. Some RNC dipshit told ABC that Fox had called Ohio for Bush. "I believe others will follow suit," he said, but Jennings held strong: "We have not projected Ohio."

When I finally broke away to grab another bottle from the fridge, Creamer snapped up the remote to change channels, but the maps were all red no matter the network. He sank to the bed. I filled a cup with ice, dumped in the contents of the bottle, and sat beside him, and we slugged frigid Stoli Vanil, passing the cup between us, Creamer tossing it back in his throat to avoid his teeth. I got up and refilled with plain vodka, Absolut. My hangover loomed, jeering at me from tomorrow; it had George Bush's face, his tiny teetotaling eyes.

Dan Rather looked terrible: puffy and toady and miserable. The map was a hideous red blob with tufts of blue in the upper corners, a Bozo the Clown grotesque of a country. A few white patches still gleamed out, zones of possibility where everything would be decided. Just north of Hawaii's displaced white archipelago were a few white western states, and glowing stage left was white Iowa, below white Wisconsin. On NBC, Brokaw gave up on Ohio—"This race is all but over"—but Ohio was still Rather's last white hope on CBS. Creamer and I sat at the edge of the bed on the plasticized spread, its nylon quilt stitches unraveling beneath us. Washed in gaudy TV light, voices rushing at us, I rested my head on his shoulder, and when it slid down to his chest I didn't right myself. He held me, and I was grateful to be in his gigantic embrace, his beard pressed to my neck, face buried in my hair. I didn't want to be fucked anymore, didn't want the complication of any more feeling. I wanted this: his arms around me, breath in my hair, face in my neck. We stayed there and held each other. I fell asleep.

I remember the disorientation of coming to: Creamer disentangling, extricating himself, laying me back on the awful bedspread. He stood and watched John Edwards address a crowd: "Every vote will count and every vote will be counted!" It was 2000 all over again. I felt a desperate hope, the last stage of denial before misery. Creamer hit Power; the TV sizzled off. He said nothing, just put the remote on the dresser, paused, his gaze leveled at me, then turned and left. The door latch clicked. For some minutes I waited, thinking he'd return, then remembered he had no key. Too late, I also remembered that he lived five miles away and had no car, and it was the middle of the night. At least he'd taken his glasses.

In the shadow and buzz of that roadside hotel, I squirmed to get under the covers, but a wave of nausea caught me and I lunged for the bathroom, where I swayed over the toilet bowl, disinfectant burning my nostrils. I wanted badly to vomit. I contracted my throat, straining to belch, then thought of my daughter and stuck a finger down my throat as far as I could reach. I gagged and tried again, flinched and pulled away. And then, like I'd found a secret panel to spring a hidden door, my throat dilated. A plash of liquid—chunky and hot—soaked my hand and splattered into the bowl. My eyes streamed, throat burning. I did it again. And again, until nothing more came up and I was only gagging, empty and exhausted. I flushed the toilet, splashed my mouth and face at the sink, and fell out the bathroom door into the bed, onto that disgusting, glossy quilt, and I entered a strange and distorted haze. I was floating, ensconced in a weird capsule of remove, outside everything, the world and my body. And that is how—amid the roiling muck of America and the tangled mess of my life—I fell asleep on that terrible election night in an odd and serene bubble of peace.

7

LET HOPE AND SORROW NOW UNITE

But since reality is incomplete, art must not be too much afraid of incompleteness.

—Iris Murdoch, *Existentialists and Mystics*

I AWOKE AT the Gas Stop on November 3, 2004, disoriented and dehydrated, throat raw, head leaden. On my night table sat the bucket of melted ice. I got it to my lips; it was blessedly cold. Swaying with nausea, I managed to get to the bathroom, where I peed in the dark, head in hands. Unable to bear the vanity light, I flicked on the dim entryway bulb. My ponytail was half undone, and I pulled out the elastic and redid it as I lifted my eyes to the mirror: puffy, tired—I looked like Dan Rather. I tilted my face—a canted profile's always easier to bear than the straight-on mug shot—and caught sight of a hank of hair at my neck that had escaped the elastic. I swept at it, but grabbed nothing, so I craned toward the mirror. It looked like an ink splotch, as if I'd slept on an open pen. Annoyed, I shut my eyes to switch on the bathroom light, then opened them slowly to discover by my hairline, an inch behind my ear, a dark purple bruise. A hickey. An enormous, blackened hickey, the likes of which I hadn't seen since high school. I grabbed my crotch, concentrating, trying to discern a physical memory of sex, but I felt nothing—no lingering sensation, no bodily recall. I felt miserable, but not unfathomably miserable, not the kind of miserable I'd imagine follows passed-out-drunk sex. I felt the misery of someone who'd drunk too much, slept too little, and faced another four years of Dubya. The hickey looked like it might last that long; I'd never seen one so bad. Incredulous, I kept checking, and it kept being there. I stood under the fluorescents wondering if Creamer'd intended it, or even knew what he'd done. I pulled the rubber band from my ponytail and chucked it in the trash.

The light outside was tornado-hazy, like the throat of the sky might open wide. Wearing a scowl to deter the most banal of Midwestern pleasantries, I crossed the parking lot, bought orange juice at the Gas-Mart, and coffee, and a Saran-wrapped bagel-like bun stuffed with half an inch of butter. As I drove off, I couldn't help turning on the radio. The local NPR anchor was despondent; nine-forty-five a.m. and Kerry hadn't conceded. What did we think: he *wouldn't*? He'd refuse? Every voice delivered the news with thinly masked disbelief. Iowa's outcome—undetermined, margins too small, the race so tight—might take weeks to calculate. In the end our seven electoral votes would mean nothing. There were vain, desperate hopes: for lawsuits, national recounts, a world where Iowa mattered. If Ohio got contested and turned around, Kerry would need every blue vote there was. That day, the Day After, we awaited revelations of voter fraud, electoral conspiracy. I knew I wasn't asleep, but still waited to wake from the nightmare. Driving through Prairie, past Creamer's house, I thought to stop, but what would I do? Knock on Norma's door? *Hi, your son left my room in the middle of the night* . . . Back at White Rabbit, no strength to start the woodstove, I fell to the futon, pulled up every quilt I had, and slept.

That afternoon I drove to River City in a queasy fog and presided miserably over a directing class discussion of stage furniture. After, headed back to Prairie, I stopped at the strip mall for a burrito and took a few bites in the car before I got out my phone to call Lucius. It would be easy to explain the hickey as something else—coat-hook run-in, showerhead accident—but I didn't want to lie, and though it may well have faded by the next time I saw Lucius, that didn't change anything. Not telling him about it was still a lie. The truth didn't even sound true: I'd gotten a hickey via an essentially nonsexual encounter. Allegiance to truth had compelled me to tell Michael about Lucius the morning after we first slept together, but maybe I'd lied to myself about my motivation then—maybe it had been a means of forcing a breach in my marriage. If I were willing to lie now, I was treading on very murky moral ground.

It's a testament to Lucius's emotional maturity—and to the three marriages under his belt—that he answered my call. A lesser man might have made me leave a few pathetic messages first. Still, the way he said "Hi, Phil," he could have been Michael, and annoyance overtook my remorse: one second I was contrite and full of apology, then he said *Hi, Phil,* and I was irritated and impatient. I imagined they'd formed a club, the Men Wronged by Phillipa Maakestad Club, where they sat in a circle drinking Jim Beam from Dixie cups, commiserating and practicing their *Hi, Phils* until they could pack into those two words everything they harbored against me. In my mind, a whole throng of them cropped up cancerously: Michael and Lucius circling with the others, like a community rec center NA meeting. There were colleagues I'd snubbed, dumped boyfriends of my youth . . . Oh, look there: Creamer'd made it, too. Had Creamer been wronged? I was the bruised one, though I suppose he could've been dead in a ditch for all I knew. Randall and Linda arrived—they'd never miss a meeting—and it was no longer a men's club but equal-opportunity, come-one-come-all, join Everyone Phillipa's Ever Wronged! The cast and crew of *Drood* were there, and all my Ohio students. Bernadette and Ginny sat on a bench, whispering, Eula and Oren beside them, and the mob kept growing, filling the room and beyond: Jaycee and her kids, the polling place cronies, the Gas Stop's ex-Mennonite laborers, Johns Kerry and Edwards, their campaign staffs, flanked by Democrats, Republicans, and Naderites alike, all of them, everyone, America.

"Phillipa? Hello?" Lucius's tenor had changed; now *he* was annoyed, and in reaction I swung violently back to regret, with a fervent imperative to mend this rift. Then, just as instantly, I was asking myself what kind of self-respecting fifty-year-old woman goes clambering and groveling back to a man, needing him this desperately because she's never been without a man. Eula Yoder, age eighteen, was more of a woman than I'd ever been, probably ever would be. I hated myself. I drew a ragged breath, and the sob that emerged from my throat was so like a beast's it frightened me. I gulped for a breath, swallowed wrong, and started coughing. When I regained myself and put the phone back to my ear, I was prepared for Lucius to have hung up, prepared for the sound of my aloneness in the world. But he was still there, saying, "Phil? Phillipa?" The care was back in his voice, and I broke into sobs. "I'm sorry. I'm so sorry . . ." Lucius shushed me calm, and I was too tired to fight his comfort.

When I stopped crying enough to speak, I said, "Is this it? Is it over? Are we nothing but a brief and unreal *affair*?" I spat the word. "A *fling*? Is this unsustainable in real life?"

Lucius sighed, slow to speak. "I wish," he began, then reconsidered, started again: "If we . . ." He stopped, returned to his original opening: "I wish you didn't see it as an all-or-nothing proposition. This *is* real life. I'm not trying to be difficult, but I don't see why it's real or unreal. Enduring or over. True or false. It doesn't seem fair."

I wanted to tell him: *Life isn't fair.* Instead I said, "You don't think we're over?"

"I hope not. I'm frustrated, angry—I was really angry last night. But I'm not washing my hands. Yesterday was bad, today's not so great either, but not *I'm done* bad . . . Are you done? With me?" He was turning it around. I tried to protest, but he kept on: "Last spring was glorious—fraught, but glorious. And unsustainable. Summer—

France—was glorious. And fleeting—no test of sustainability. Now here we are: jobs in different states, students, families. You're in the midst of tremendous upheaval—you don't need me to tell you that. Do I wish your daughter weren't in crisis? Of course. Do I wish the election had gone differently? That we were independently wealthy, no responsibilities, could up and quit and move to France? Sure!" He paused. When he continued, his voice was less belligerent. "I care for you very deeply, Phillipa Maakestad. It guarantees nothing, but I hope it counts for something. I hope we last, Phil. I hardly feel done. I'm here. I've signed on. When you sign on for joy, you sign on, too—unspoken, unacknowledged, maybe—you sign on for pain, too. We will, inevitably, cause one another pain." This was the same logic I'd presented to Michael. "You sign on for love, and you've signed on for heartbreak. We signed. And you're breaking my heart with this—"

"But *you're* breaking *my* heart!" I cut in at last.

"I think—and this is based on three marriages—I think if we're breaking each other's hearts, we're okay."

I can't say I wholly understood the logic, but I wanted to believe, so I did. And I think that is what some people call faith.

"When we started," I said, "my life was relatively stable. You were an upheaval, but one I could afford; everything else was calm. This sounds idiotic, I know, but I didn't see the intricacy of the balance, how altering one part can send the whole system into chaos."

"So you can't afford me? That's the point? Now I'm an indulgence you can't afford?"

"No, I just—"

"Phillipa, are you even talking about yourself? *Your* life isn't some house of cards. What can you not handle? What is this 'fragile flower' idea? What's in chaos? You've been managing the collapse of your marriage—you moved out in May. You were gone long before. And you've been okay: you have a place, you're helping with Ginny, Eula's baby, teaching, directing—"

"In absentia!" I cried. "You don't need to pep-talk me. I wasn't looking for—"

"But you're managing. Your life is not a house of cards. What's collapsed? The country? Bush was president when we met; he's still the goddamn president. *That* horror card-house is still standing, God help us. But until Ginny got sick, Bush wasn't even your fight. She took that on; you inherited it. Ginny might be having trouble—that doesn't mean *you* are falling apart."

"But I am!" I cried, but my thoughts had gotten snagged on Ginny, some kind of alarm going off: my Ginny alarm. Whatever had been holding back my worry that day gave way, the dam breached, and it seemed suddenly, glaringly probable that right now, in the wake of the election, the Yoder house was a crime scene: the drive cordoned with yellow tape, sirens blaring, lights flashing, and upstairs, in a bathtub of blood, my daughter lay dead, finally free.

"*Are* you?" Lucius asked, but I'd forgotten what we were saying, consumed now by the image of Ginny and her unborn baby dead in the bathtub.

"I have to go," I told Lucius.

"What?"

I'd already started the car. I couldn't hold the phone, the wheel, and the gearshift all at once. "I'll call later. I have to get to Ginny." I tossed the phone to the passenger seat with my discarded burrito, peeled out of the lot with a screech of rubber, and nearly jumped the median.

THE YODER FARMHOUSE was so uncommonly lovely as it came into view that it seemed impossible for anything awful to have ever taken place there. Against a blue-black sky, the house glowed, its kitchen windows lamplit—kerosene, or one of the battery-powered ones they had. It looked so peaceful I wanted to pick up my little White Rabbit house and plunk it down in the field beyond Randall's trailer, live right there, close at hand, like the Amish elders do. I feared, though, that night, that the peacefulness was an illusion. Like those creepy paintings by Thomas Kinkade—country landscapes and fairy-tale cottages that look lit from within. That "Kinkade Glow" could as easily emanate from a flaming meth lab bathtub as from a blazing hearth. The sleepy duck pond beside the gingerbread cottage, all aglimmer, is really a scum-mucked swamp, razor wire penning in the hissing fowl. At times, the whole world feels like an optical illusion: with a slight tilt of the frame, *American Gothic* becomes *American Ghoul.* Disney's castle is really Count Dracula's, not in Mickey's Magic Kingdom but perched on a Transylvanian peak. Our blood-red apples, wicked delicious, Monsanto Delicious, like Kinkade's paintings, are too delicious to be true. On November 3, I feared the Yoder house was aglow because my daughter had set herself on fire like a Buddhist monk, a great, grand finale of pregnant self-immolation. Ginny stars in her very own staging of *Pippin:* she steps into the flame, is engulfed by the flame, *becomes* flame itself, and—at last! —for one moment, shines.

The scene at the Yoders' was actually far simpler. There was fire, yes: in the woodstove, and in the kitchen, under the kettle. Eula was making tea. I looked cold, they said. "Take off your scarf, sit." Was I outside for long? they asked. Was I all right? I couldn't take my scarf off; I had a hickey the size of a black walnut. And I couldn't get my mind around their calm, thoughtful questions. Weren't those the questions *I* had come to ask *them?* I sank to the plaid couch. The Sloganator wallpaper was gone, the pamphlets and yard signs, too. The room felt safe again, like Orah and Obadiah's family room, and I sat there with my family, drinking herbal tea on a very sad night in America. The strangest thing was the calm; we talked of commonplace things.

"How's the show?" Ginny asked.

"*Drood?*" I sighed. "It'll go on."

"It must." What crossed her face might've been a shadow of a smile. "When's it go up?"

"After Thanksgiving."

"Thanksgiving," she repeated, and I feared she might turn her head to barf just at the mention, but she went on in that weird, calm way. "We should figure out what to do . . ."

Suddenly all I wanted was sleep. Lucius and I had talked of having Thanksgiving in Ohio, just us, but that was before I had a hideous purple suck-spot on my neck I'd neglected to tell him about. Thanksgiving weekend was also tech weekend for *Drood,* which didn't leave me a lot of time for anything. "I can't talk logistics tonight, Gin."

I made my excuses and drove the nighttime roads home, my cold burrito lying uneaten on the passenger seat. I had no appetite, for it or for Thanksgiving. When your parents are dead, you're not close to your extended family, you've recently and indecorously left your husband, and you're not thankful to live in the land of George W., you might not feel inclined toward the customary national slaughter-feast. My own parents so abhorred the "family holidays" that on many a Thanksgiving of my childhood we told each set of grandparents we were with the other, then stayed home and ordered in Chinese.

My breath hung in the air as I stoked the woodstove in my frigid little house. As the room warmed, I crawled into bed. The thing about a woodstove is that you have to keep feeding it, and the thing about lies is that once you're wrapped in one, it doesn't matter how many logs you put on the fire, because you're impervious to warmth. I called Lucius. "Ginny's okay," I told him.

"I'm glad," he said. "Are you?"

"Glad or okay?" I wasn't trying to be funny, I was just exhausted. I answered myself, "Yes, both," then realized I'd wasted the chance to say, *No, I'm not okay,* and tell him about the thing he couldn't see: my purple-black hickey. Unfair as this may be, his ignorance made him seem foolish. My knowledge, and his lack of it, put me in a position of power. It was just what I'd done to Michael: dropped firebombs while he slept, then woke him to tell him his bed was in flames. I tried to confess, but only managed to ask, "Are we okay? Will we be okay?" as if Lucius were the one with something to disclose. And, ignorant, he kept saying, "We're okay, Phil. I think we're okay. Nothing we can do about Bush—that's over. But we're not, okay? Is that what you need me to say? That we're not over? We're not over—I'm not over you."

Creamer's purple bruise burned at the side of my neck. I said nothing, only wept. A cheater and a liar, I'd wind up alone like the rest of my pathetic kind.

A COMMITTEE MEETING got me up and out early. In my passenger seat lay last night's burrito, bean juice leaking into the cracked seat leather. I shoved the whole thing into its bag, drove toward River City, and threw it in the first trash barrel I passed. That afternoon I had to Ginny-sit at the Yoders', and when Silas came home to relieve me, I drove to the Gas Stop and called Lucius from the lot, one hand self-consciously at my neck. "I'm afraid to go in," I told him.

"As if that's the worst that's gone down in that place," he chided. "You're unfamiliar with bar rules, Phil: every day's a new day. No one's accountable."

"I'm just another drunk who'll be forgiven by the rest of the drunks?"

"You are but a small part of a great whole."

"Who are you quoting?"

"I think it's a step," Lucius said.

"You're preaching AA?"

He laughed. "Get in there, have Regina pour you a beer, and stop feeling so alone."

"I think that's enabling."

"Fine," he said, "I'm enabling. Get thee to the bar."

Law & Order had resumed its ubiquitous place on the TVs, closed captions scrolling by, turning reruns into breaking news. Regina wasn't working. The guy tending bar tapped my beer almost without acknowledging my existence; I am, after all, a woman of fifty, mostly invisible to men. But Burton Kramer was not most men. At his end of the bar he sat, bespectacled, hooded, hunched over his beer, soda straw sticking out. I felt as embarrassed as if we *had* spent election night fucking our brains out, but I took my beer and moved to sit beside him. I said, "Hi."

"Oh." He gave a show of surprise, as if he hadn't noticed me. "Hey."

I tried to make him meet my eyes. "Could you take off the glasses? Jig's up—I see you."

Slowly, Creamer took off and folded the plastic glasses. He placed them on the bar.

"Did you get home okay?" I asked.

Creamer nodded, pursing his lips as if trying to recall what I might be speaking about.

"Five miles home, drunk, three o'clock in the morning? Remember?"

He shook his head. "Oh! I crashed at Regina and Sally's." I must've looked confused; he backtracked. "It's fine. I stay there if it's late or I'm drunk. It's fine. I have a key."

"Regina and who?"

"Sally?" he said.

"Who's Sally?"

"Sally. Her . . . wife . . . girlfriend-person. Sally."

"Regina's . . . ?"

"You never met Sally?" Creamer said.

"Regina's *gay?*"

Creamer sat there looking at me, as though my question could not possibly be complete.

"But . . ." I cocked my head, shook it, and cocked it to the other side in an attempt to rearrange the pieces into some kind of sense. "But, didn't you . . . ? And Regina . . . ? I thought something . . ."

Creamer actually looked amused. "Regina's practically my mother," he said. "I'm sorry if you worried. They're just . . ." He gestured as if to say they lived nearby.

"You want to be sorry for something?" I said. "I have something you can be sorry about." I leaned in and lowered my voice. I felt ridiculous, like I belonged on *Law & Order.* Hand to my neck, I said softly, "You left an enormous hickey on me."

His eyes bugged. "What? I *what?*"

I made to pull down my scarf. "Like to see?"

"No," he said quickly. "I mean, I, but . . . not here. Are you sure?" he asked, as if what he called a hickey and what I called a hickey might be different things.

"I know a hickey on my own neck."

"Look, I'm really sorry," he offered. "I never . . . I . . . Do you bruise easy or something?"

"I don't know." I thought of Michael's handprints on my ass. "I don't know," I said again. We drank our beers, watched *Law & Order.* There's a reason people like network TV, with its promise of resolution: give us an hour and we'll reconcile the irreconcilable.

Later that night, when I got in the car to go home, I caught a whiff of something unpleasant, remembered the leaky burrito, and cursed myself and my forgetful slovenliness.

The next afternoon when I got back into the car—late, rushing to school—the autumn sun had been shining down for many hours, and little doubt remained that something was rotting in my car. After my class, it positively reeked—like blue cheese, Stilton. There'd been sour cream on the burrito, but I couldn't understand how it possibly smelled as bad as it did. Sitting in the theater parking lot, I bent to sniff the passenger seat. It smelled okay—or as okay as a fifteen-year-old ass cushion can. I sniffed again: the stink didn't seem to be coming from the seat, but I wasn't sure. The driver of a Caddy parked beside me strode up to get into his car just as I rose, and he looked like he'd caught me sucking off my passenger.

Over the next few days, we had freakishly warm weather; Saturday after the election, the temperature hit 70 degrees. Randall and Linda carried the Yoders' plaid sofa into the yard, and Silas carried Ginny out to it. I sat with her as she finished a snack of cottage cheese and corn chips. The sun emboldened me, as if even Ginny and I wouldn't clash in its warmth. "Gin," I began, "given things with me and Daddy, I think, for Thanksgiving, maybe I should just be absent, you know? I don't . . . are you . . . do you think *you'll* really be up for it?"

Eyes closed, face serenely tilted to the sky, Ginny said, "Silas and Eula and I've been talking. I think with drugs to gird me, I might be okay with the meal itself. We thought Eula and Linda and Randall might do the cooking in town, at Daddy's, and then all come out here to eat. We figured maybe you'd go to Ohio?"

"That sounds good, Gin," I said. "That sounds like a good plan."

The weather remained warm. Silas, Linda, and Randall got some work done on the straw bale, and I was able to drive with my car windows open until real November weather arrived midmonth. One evening the temperature went down to the twenties and I had to resort to car heat. The stench got so foul I sprayed a full bottle of Febreze on the passenger seat. It took days to dry, but once the chemical stink subsided, the fetid rot reared again. Finally, I went to one of those coin-op car-vacuum places and pulled out every insert, yanked up all the rugs and mats, and found, between the passenger seat and the door, wedged deep in the crevice, Travis Spendler's pale pink baby bottle, nipple side down, the formula curdled and leaking.

I threw the rancid sludge in a dumpster, bought more Febreze, which I poured directly on the spot, let it pool in the seat track and bubble on the carpet. Until the snow came a few weeks later, I left my car windows open at night. I bought essential oil for the dashboard and burned incense until I trailed aromatic drifts of patchouli through the university halls like a hippie undergrad. The stench was undefeatable, which felt perversely appropriate.

One evening I went to get dinner at the Gas Stop. Creamer—at his usual spot, in his usual garb—removed his glasses without prompting when I sat down. "How's it going?" he asked.

I nodded, shrugging: *It goes*. He understood, or pretended to.

"How's the . . ." He patted the side of his insulated hood, around where his neck might be.

"Turning yellow," I told him.

He winced. "Look, I really am sorry."

"That's okay," I said, and it felt true. His apology was wholly genuine, and right there, right then, it all felt okay. In that moment, Creamer might've known me most fully, hickey and all. And this, I thought, is why people take up residence on barstools: because right here everything's forgiven and it all feels okay. I could imagine us, decades from now, perched on our Gas Stop stools, an old couple with a joint bar tab. On TV, a camera lingered lasciviously over a golden-plump turkey breast, and I asked Creamer if he had holiday plans.

He seemed amused. "Why? Inviting me over with the family?"

"I'm not—I won't—I'm not going to be there. I'm—"

"Spending it with your sweetie?" he asked, a snideness in his tone. Then, before I could respond, he retracted it: "Look, not my business. I'm sorry. Really, none of my business."

"I don't know where I'll be," I told him. "I'm supposed to go to Ohio, but . . ." An idea crossed my mind. "Hey, you know, if you don't have someplace, you should go to the Yoders'. There'll be a crowd, and I'm sure they'd be happy to have you join—"

"You're inviting me to where you won't be, with people I don't know?"

Then I was confused. "I thought you did know them. The Yoders and Ginny—"

"I mean, I know *about* them—everyone does—but I don't, like, *know* them. I'm going to the Spendlers', anyway. Angel made me an invitation." He held up one hand, fingers spread, and traced it in the air. "Those pictures the kids make in school—make a turkey out of their hand?" He waggled his fingers, as if the shape he'd drawn might come to life and reveal its turkeyhood.

"Well, that's nice," I told him.

"Yeah, we'll see," he said. "Might be a microwave Thanksgiving if Jaycee's cooking."

"What about your mother? Will she come?"

Total incomprehension on Creamer's face. "She hasn't left the house since last spring."

"Oh, I didn't—"

"Agoraphobic-like, you know?"

"Oh, I didn't—"

"Yeah, well."

"What happened last spring?" I asked. "Did something happen that made her . . . ?"

"No, you know, just decided, *enough*. Hard to blame her. Probably headed there myself."

"But you're . . ." I stammered. "You like this place too much!"

"Yeah," Creamer said, resigned. "Yeah, well, maybe I do."

Thanksgiving came, and I couldn't go to Ohio. The logistics were nuts and my hickey wasn't totally gone. I told everyone in Iowa I was going to Ohio, told Lucius I couldn't leave Iowa, and after rehearsal on Wednesday I drove an hour north to a Waterloo motel, where I paid cash for a room just in case Michael looked at the credit card statement. On the drive up I stopped, God help me, at a 24-hour Walmart thrumming with last-minute shoppers collecting preselected dinner fixings. They were laid out so you could go down the aisle, remove a box or can or bag from each shelf, and assemble a meal. Stuffing mix: check. Canned cranberry sauce: check. Instant mashed potatoes: check. Mrs. Smith's frozen pumpkin pie: check, just heat and serve. An enormous crate overflowed with yams the size of fireplace logs. Beside it, an entire wall had been devoted to marsh-mallows, from mini to super-colossal, star-shaped, pumpkin-shaped, tiny marshmallow Pilgrims and tiny marshmallow Indians ready to congeal in a great American marshmallow melting pot. When I en-tered, a group of Mennonite women stood at the display, engaged in periodic consultation, removing a bag from the shelf to consider more closely before replacing it. I wandered a long while — time in Walmart is very mercurial — but when I checked out, the Mennonites were still at the marshmallows, their contemplation perhaps more re-ligious than culinary. I left with a bottle of wine, snacks, a facial mask kit, a Tae Bo exercise DVD I thought would play on my computer, a compendium of *New York Times* crossword puzzles, a mesh sack of "odor-absorbing and neutralizing" volcanic rocks, an industrial-sized box of granola bars for tech weekend, a case of super-cheap cham-pagne for opening night, and, on sale for $59.99, a probably crappy espresso maker. I was in a weakened, vulnerable state, like everyone else at Walmart on Thanksgiving Eve. Also, I bought a new bottle for Travis Spendler.

My night consisted of not drinking wine (no corkscrew, and I couldn't bring myself to ask at the desk) and sleeping poorly. A Thanksgiving sun was just rising as I walked to IHOP for breakfast. I watched TV in my room until checkout time, then sat out the after-noon in a Hobbit movie at a second-run cinema in a half-abandoned strip mall. I took slow back roads toward home, listening to *Company* for company. Every house I passed was awash in Kinkade Glow, chim-neys streaming woodsmoke, children waiting on outdoor swing sets to be called to dinner, grown men with football jerseys stretched over their beer guts tossing balls in the gathering dark.

I had no plan, only a desire not to go to White Rabbit and be alone, and as I drove into Prairie I saw Carrie the cow and thought to stop at Jaycee's to drop off the bottle for Travis. The house was dark, but I pulled up and crossed the yard anyway. Around back, I thought

I saw a TV glimmer, and though it was probably Jaycee and the kids, I couldn't shake the idea of Jaycee and Creamer, naked under ratty blankets, sharing a joint, exhaling into the stale bedroom air.

I went back to my car, stuck the bottle in the cup holder, and drove off. When I passed the Gas Stop and saw lights inside, my heart sped up, a kind of relief flooding my veins like physical warmth. I pulled into the lot, where six or seven other cars were parked. Climbing the steps, I felt like an alcoholic, craving my drink, my barstool, the dim, forgiving light. Two guys at the pool table, a few couples in booths, lone men at the bar, Creamer in his seat, Regina perched on the counter. Gray, pigtailed head tilted back against the bar mirror, she was posed like a pinup, having a beer herself. I sank onto the stool beside Creamer's. "I just went by Jaycee's," I told them.

"We ate early," Creamer said. "Jaycee had to work the nine-to-five."

"Oh?" I hear "nine-to-five" and think, *Tumble out of bed and stumble to the kitchen . . .* and it took me a second to get that he meant nine p.m. to five a.m. *It's enough to drive you crazy if you let it.* I assumed Jaycee worked at the dairy, and I don't guess the cows get Turkey Day off. I also realized that it was Angel watching TV in Jaycee's bed, Travis asleep beside her, the small room warm with electric heat. They were home alone. Jaycee couldn't afford a sitter—it's why they lived next to the dairy. Angel babysat, and Jaycee could be home in two minutes if she had to. Their vulnerability hit me hard.

"How's Ohio?" Creamer asked. I couldn't read his tone. I checked Regina's face for a clue, but she was drawing deep on a cigarette, willing her shriveled, blackened lungs to inhale.

"Fine." I ran a hand through my hair, slouched into the bar. "Long drive," I said, like I'd just pulled in. I drank my beer, then got ready to go; rehearsal was called for eight a.m. I offered Creamer a lift, but he waved me on, "I'm good," and excused himself to the men's room.

"Is he okay?" I asked Regina.

She looked at me hard. "Just 'cause he doesn't drop everything when you say boo, don't mean he's not okay. That man's closest I got to a son. He's not used to women like you."

"Women *like me?*"

"Just don't fuck with him, okay? You're from another world, honey." She ground out her cigarette and slid off the counter. "You're only slumming it here and you know it."

"Is that a threat?" I was so affronted I almost laughed. "What kind of average, ordinary woman are you looking for for Creamer? I'll be sure to keep an eye out."

Wholly unflappable, Regina practically seemed game. "You know," she leaned in conspiratorially, "I always thought Eula Yoder'd make him a nice wife."

"She's eighteen!" I felt desperate. Regina said nothing. "And probably gay," I added.

Regina stared for one beat, then threw her head back and hooted with laughter. When she fixed on me again, her eyes shone. "You really do have the worst gaydar around, don't you? This old dyke's a straight girl, and Eula Yoder's chomping pussy?" Her head shook, astonished. "Honey, you need some *help*." She spoke with a measure of kindness, but my tears came fast, and I'm pretty sure I said, "Do you think I don't know that?" before I ran from the bar.

I spent the following day in dark auditorium recesses, blocking sound and lighting cues. Midafternoon, Michael dropped off some new gels for the strip lights, then came to squat by my auditorium seat and confirm a few tech details. We didn't speak of Thanksgiving. I realized it had been the first without his mother. He stood, patted the back of my seat, *good horsie,* and stalked away.

Sunday we worked until three a.m. Act 2's a bitch of a tech—multiple alternate endings, depending on an audience vote during the performance—and it took forever. I was so tired I didn't go back to Prairie; I slept on a borrowed yoga mat in my office—*our* office. Michael and I shared a position and everything that went with it. To divvy our joint acquisitions would be absurdly complicated and involve department administrators, secretaries, maintenance guys, Buildings and Grounds. Truly, it might not be the heartbreak of divorce that wrecks a person, but the logistics, the endless sorting of amassed crap: every Bank One pen and appliance manual, every takeout pack of soy sauce, unmarked key, and green-grime-covered penny, every weightless leg of every fly that ever died inside the airless tomb of the junk drawer we call marriage.

AN UNMITIGATED DISASTER, *Drood* went up in early December. The musical, based on Dickens's final, unfinished novel, stops dead halfway through the second act, mid–song-and-dance. The performance stalls, actors stagger about, confused, and the MC announces, "It was here Mr. Dickens laid down his pen forever." We're to imagine old Charles keeling over atop the manuscript. It's supposed to be funny. And the great innovation of Rupert Holmes's script is that when we come to that point in the show after which Dickens wrote no more, the MC solicits an audience vote to determine the play's outcome. In our production, from the curtain's very rise, the show was rife with so many glitches that when things broke down in act 2, it was impossible for the audience to understand that *these* interruptions were really part of the script and not just further foibles in a pathetic production. I think our audience experienced such collective relief at the news that Dickens had written no more, that to then learn they'd be subjected to participate in an enactment of the democratic process, *and* have to sit through three more musical numbers, was to discover a theatrical innovation they'd have been happy to forgo. A better teacher would have found a way to use it all— plenty of instruction in failure—but what would such analysis have uncovered? *To ensure quality, do not employ a director whose life is falling apart.* And I am, I fear, a mediocre teacher at best. Sometimes I worry I'm actually a terrible teacher who'd never have been a teacher at all but for Michael and the position *his* position afforded me. Used to be, you could say I was a perfectly competent director, but I think *Drood* proved otherwise. Lousy director, lousy wife, mother, nursemaid, daughter-in-law, and an incontrovertible failure as a political activist. At times I am hard-pressed to justify my existence.

Though *Drood* went unfinished, I've no doubt that if he'd lived, Dickens would have tied every last dangling plot thread into the sort of neat novel package for which he is known. Once upon a time, I wasn't so bothered by neatness — gathered strings and a quote-un-quote satisfying ending — but just then, tacking false musical endings onto an incomplete work felt like a worthless sham. To leave the musical unfinished — end the show mid–cancan kick and send everyone home — might've been the most honest thing we could have done.

But a musical theater audience does not seek honesty. Someone dies — say, Edwin Drood is murdered, or Bernadette Maakestad fails to awaken one morning, an empty pill bottle beside her — and though there's no sense to be made of that death, or that life, we still attempt — perpetually, eternally, unrepentantly — to reconcile the pieces left us, to connect the most far-flung of stars into a constellation we recognize. Edwin Drood was pushed into the river by none other than . . . John Jasper! Drood was killed by — drumroll, please — Princess Puffer! We can't bear to let a mystery go unsolved, a life unexplained, stars unclustered into bulls or spoons or bow-shooting archers. We cannot stand for those stars to simply float free, infinite and random, long dead, their stories ended an eternity ago. Unfinished, *The Mystery of Edwin Drood* might've been the only honest thing Charles Dickens ever wrote.

WINTER BREAK is usually especially nice in River City: no underage drinkers stumbling home at two a.m., the town quiet and echoey and a little solemn, like an empty nest, a particular quality of sadness hovering in the wake of the students' departure. I've always found it poignant and satisfying. I missed it entirely that year, for I no longer lived in River City. I was a commuter: zip in, park my car for hours in a U lot, move through the stations of my teaching life, then zip back out, preferably under cover of darkness, show tunes blaring on the car stereo.

Some decorations went up on Highway 1, and Salvation Army Santa took up his post outside Dollar General. Bible Baptist on 26 changed its signboard—WEATHER FORECAST: GOD REIGNS—and Regina decked the Gas Stop with boughs of Hobby Lobby holly, plastic berries poking out like poisoned temptations. The Presidios strung up lights at the inn and erected an artificial tree, pre-baubled with miniature tractors and fake candy canes tied with tractor-print bows. One of the Gas Stop cocoa taps dispensed peppermint mochas.

I played my Jew card. No one cared; who could have wanted me around? December 21, I turned in grades and wrapped up paperwork. December 22, I went shopping, i.e., pushed a bum-wheeled cart through the antiques mall. I collected fabric for Eula—1940s kitchen aprons, printed sugar and flour and feed sacks, bolts of bordello-burgundy chintz and pale jadeite green—but one of the great glories of Eula's quilts is how everything comes from someone and somewhere, every scrap an anecdote in the quilt's story. I put the anonymous fabrics back where I'd found them. There was a fabulous vintage aqua Melmac full dinner service with a matching child's set that I wanted to get for Silas and Ginny, but I can't buy gifts for an unborn baby without fear of killing it with a *kinahora,* and melamine probably causes cancer anyway. I gathered old Democratic campaign paraphernalia for Randall and Linda, but the *Dukakis '88* button, *Mondale/Ferraro* bumper sticker, and *Dean '04* flag in my cart looked like testaments to failure. I'd give them the Walmart espresso maker. Everyone else would have to take a check.

My hickey was barely a pale shadow by December 23 when I left White Rabbit predawn and drove to Ohio. Lucius and I were invited to a party that evening at Anthea Lingafelter's, and I didn't want to rush in, change my clothes, and race off for what amounted to our coming-out party before we'd had any time alone. As a couple, a *we,* we seemed so far fallen.

Ten hours in the car, yet I turned onto Lucius's street still unsure what to tell him. I'd listened to all of *Celebration, Jerry's Girls, The Fantasticks,* and *Company,* but hadn't figured what to say about my hickey. Snow swirled in the air, not yet sticking, as I parked behind his Honda and mounted the front steps of his Sears Craftsman bungalow. He'd been there since his last divorce fifteen years before. The porch smelled of leaves and woodsmoke, and the warmth of the yellow window light was glorious—Kinkade Glow be damned. I'd spent no more than a week's worth of nights there, yet when Lucius opened the door, the emanating smells—fire in the fireplace, Murphy Oil on the floors, sherry on his lips, Barbasol in his beard—I felt as if I were home. Except I had no home. White Rabbit was more like a squat in an empty art studio, and I was like a desperate orphan, ready to leap into any open arms. Lucius poured my favorite wine —cold, cold Sauvignon Blanc, dry and grapefruity, with a hint of cat piss. He topped his sherry and drew me to the couch. I was bleary and tingling with nerves as we lifted our glasses to each other, then to our lips, and sat looking into the fire. He reached behind me, a hand under my sweater to touch skin. I opened a button on his shirt and reached my fingers through, and we sat and watched the logs crackle and collapse. He said, "I don't want to let you leave the house."

"But the party?" He'd been intent on going, out of some obligation I didn't quite get.

"After the party," he clarified. "Is that okay?"

I don't know what sort of confirmation he wanted, but my response, issuing forth without intent or premeditation, indicated dire okaylessness. "What is it with this party?" I cried. "Why are you so intent on this party, with these people? Who I hardly know, and you've known so long—who've known *you* so long, through God knows how many women. Anthea . . . who else? How many of them have you had relationships with? How many women there have slept in your bed? Is this what you do every few years? Do they all know I'm just the latest dupe? Am I as foolish as they must think? Am I that person? Am I even the person *you* think I am? You don't even *know* the person you'd be showing up with to that party!" Nearly two months since the election, and a day alone in the car to decide how to phrase a confession, and that's what I said.

Lucius looked perplexed. "I'm not under . . . Phil, what's wrong?"

Of all the replies he may have anticipated, he couldn't have expected this: "Remember the man at the Gas Stop? Drinking beer with a straw?" Lucius nodded slowly, comprehension dawning. Then I saw his rage rise and realized where he could take this. "No! No—not that!"

"Oh, I think it's exactly that." His voice was caustic.

"No," I tried to assure him, "you couldn't think of this. It's too bizarre," and he backed off, and I told him the story of election night and the tremendous hickey.

"He did it while you were passed out?" Lucius looked horrified, but I shook my head.

"It happened before. I had my head on his shoulder, his chest, hiding myself from the news, and his face was by my hair. I wasn't aware of it then—I'm not even sure he knew he was doing it. But in that tension? Bracing against what was on TV? It doesn't make sense, but it's what happened. It wasn't sexual—it wasn't anything. Or maybe it was, for him; I don't know. That's what happened. He had no idea he'd done it. We'd drunk way too much, clinging to each other just to hold on to something. And I came away with . . . this. I should have told you then, but it was such a horrible time. We'd fought on the phone, and everything felt so miserable. I kept trying—I couldn't make myself tell you. I thought I'd see you Thanksgiving . . ." And yes, I'd omitted and glossed over things, but essentially that was it: I'd confessed.

Lucius said nothing; he stared at the fire. Finally he spoke. "What am I supposed to do, Phillipa? Spank you? Say you've been bad? You've been human. A shitty, pathetic human. But I'd be a hypocrite to say I deserve better; I deserve worse. I really wish it hadn't happened—"

"But it did."

"I understand." He shook his head. "You're an adult, Phillipa." I snorted—my so-called adulthood!—and Lucius looked at me. He said, "Is this . . . is Creamer someone you want to be with? Is there more I'm not picking up on here? Are you trying to tell me—?" And I was chorusing a stream of noes, but he kept on: "Is this something you need to explore? Do I have to accept that? I've had this entire god-damn conversation before, close enough. I've been on both sides of it. What does that say—life repeats itself? We get a chance to make different choices if we can remember the stupid ones we made and manage not to make them again? Or is it Rock, Paper, Scissors? The same choice gets you a different result each—?"

I interrupted: "But what if I've lived the wrong life? I didn't have the foresight—I didn't wait for you. I was impatient to start my life, whatever that meant at twenty-three. I fell in love, I got married; it felt right. We had Ginny—maybe that should've been proof of how wrong —"

"That's insane," he cut in. "It's crazy and you know it. Do I wish we'd met years ago? Sure. But what if we'd met and weren't . . . We met when we met, as we met, and that's what's made any of this possible. You can't regret circumstances. You'll *what if* your life away."

"But what else is there? Is there anything but *what if*? Isn't that what the future is?"

"The future, fine," Lucius said, "but not the past." And he's right, I know that—I do—but they're so entwined, and I sometimes can't distinguish. Causality's not a line, it's an unwieldy, un-untangleable knot. "You're married, Phillipa," Lucius said. "You've been married a long time. Maybe this is your midlife crisis—sow your wild oats, then go back to Michael? Maybe I'm your midlife crisis. I probably deserve that. But I'm not going anywhere. I love you. I'm not out skirt-chasing. I wasn't out skirt-chasing when we met. I was done, in so many ways I was—I had my work, my teaching. I wasn't looking for this. But you came along—*you* came along. You're tremendous, Phil. You're it." He blushed, like a boy admitting a crush: fourteen or sixty-five, love makes adolescents of us all. "And yes," he said, "if we'd met forty years ago—okay, no, not forty, you'd've been ten. Thirty years ago? You at twenty, me at thirty-five? But I was already married by then—I married, too, remember? I had kids. I did it all, too. I also stopped waiting for you. Should I have been more patient? I didn't know patience like that then. But now, here you are. You exist! But you didn't then—not for me—and I went and had my life, my children. I'm not sorry for that, for my kids, my far-too-many wives." He shook his head. "That you and I met before I'm too decrepit to be of use to anyone—I should be thankful for that miracle alone. But I'm greedy, and human; I do want more. I want to live for-fucking-ever! With you—have babies with *you*, raise them, live a life. But we can't. We've lived those lives already. We don't get to do that again; we get *this*. We get now. I was very prepared never to have this, not to know this. I never thought . . . But now it—you—you're here, and I have to take it—you, this—on whatever terms it's offered. Do I wish some man in Iowa hadn't sucked your neck in a hotel room? Yes. But life is complicated, and if your being here with me now means Creamer had to give you a monstrous hickey, maybe I need to make peace with that."

I probably don't have to say I was sobbing by then. I'd grabbed hold of Lucius's shirt, a fistful of fabric in each hand, and bowed myself into his chest, pressing my head to his sternum as if that might keep the top of it from blowing off. Our faces were hidden from each other.

"That party!" he was saying. "I couldn't care less. I thought it might segue . . . I thought—stupidly! mistakenly!—I thought it would be good to have a destination tonight. Take pressure off *us*, just do something casual. I never thought about who'd be there. There's no one else, Phil. Anthea was a long time ago. No one else would be there—I wouldn't do that to you. Those people know so little of me. They're colleagues, not friends. They're perfectly nice, but . . ."

I'd lifted my head as he spoke. My tears had stopped but my face was wet and so was his shirt. "Ginny once accused me of not having friends. She said I alienated everyone, I only had acquaintances. She said I drive people away. How can you love me? How can you possibly?"

WE MADE LOVE that night with a startling, clawing urgency. Lucius can make me come with his fingers inside me moving so slightly— such minute movements to cause what he causes. I heave, begging him to fuck me, wanting nothing in the universe but to feel him full inside me. That night I cried; he came, his beauty excruciating to me. And then we lay together, tears seeping from our eyes. This is sex in old-middle age, replete with gratitude and awe. We come, and we cry, thankful for these bodies, still capable of pleasure.

In bed, in the Christmas Eve eve dark, Lucius said: "Tomorrow I want us to make a plan. Our spring breaks coincide—I checked. I want something on the horizon." I nodded, unable to bring myself to tell him it was impossible: Ginny was due at the end of February, and I could hear Bernadette's voice in my head, informing me what *decent people* did when their daughters gave birth, and it was not jet off with their lovers. No, *decent people* whipped up casseroles and potpies and cooed at the wrinkly little thing, held it and let its parents steal a few minutes' sleep. But I'll say this: if Bernadette did *any* of that when Ginny was born, I have no memory of it.

In the morning Lucius got up to make coffee and retrieve his laptop. Then, back under the covers, he perched the computer on his knees and said, "Let us enter the travel-expedi-orbitz-elocity vortex!" That's when I told him why I couldn't go away during spring break. He understood, of course, apologizing all over himself for forgetting in the first place. We stayed in bed until late afternoon when Lucius slipped on clothes to go pick up the turkey dinner for two he'd or-dered from a catering company in town. We'd have our holiday meal on Christmas Eve, he said, like his Scandinavian ancestors, and Chi-nese takeout on Christmas Day, like self-respecting Jews.

He set the steaming takeout cartons on the edge of the kitchen counter. "No need to dirty dishes," I said, so we sat at one corner of the dining room table, boxes and tubs open before us like a little model city, and ate with forks, rooting through the cartons. The ca-tered turkey was dry, the stuffing fussy, but we ate hungrily, and I told him, then, about my lonely Thanksgiving, thinking of the Chinese takeout Thanksgivings of my childhood. I should have gone home more, visited my parents. I should have been nicer to them, should have been nicer to Bernadette. I should be nicer to Ginny. I should just be nicer.

That evening we read in the living room, fire in the fireplace, Lu-cius on the sofa, a scotch on the table beside him. I lay with my head in his lap, a glass of wine on the floor within reach. He read Bellow, I read Didion, so filled with happiness I had to keep touching him, squeezing. He'd say, "I'm so happy to have you here," and I'd say, "I'm so happy to be here," or I'd say, "I'm so happy to be here with you," and he'd say, "I'm so happy to have you here with me," and we'd burrow closer until one of us needed to say it again. Outside, snow began to fall. Then, around eleven, my cell phone rang. I sat straight up. "Why is anyone—?"

Lucius laughed. "To say Merry Christmas." He motioned: An-swer it.

The number was ours—Michael's. I missed the call and imagined Michael imagining he'd caught us in bed, so I called back as quickly as I could to dispel that notion.

"Michael, I'm sorry, I didn't get the phone in time." He had not, I knew, called with yuletide greetings, and I was instantly back in the French pension, hearing *My mother is dead,* having to leave Lucius, be-ing called home. Only now it seemed Michael wasn't talking about death, but birth: Ginny and Silas had gone to the hospital. The baby was coming. I *was* being called home. "But I can't drive!" I cried. "I've had wine!" It was all too preposterous.

"Well, sober up and come when you can," he said. "We'll be here."

I hung up. "She's in labor," I told Lucius, "or they're trying to stop the labor, maybe?"

"I'll make coffee," he said, like it was an old movie: *Hot coffee— sober you right up.*

I followed. "It's too soon . . ." I felt like Cliff Johnston: *Nine months, right?*

"How early is it?" Lucius set the kettle on the stove. "Don't quote me, but I think maybe two months isn't such a big deal anymore. There's a week they hit—I just read a piece—it's about the lungs, that's the big thing, and once you hit thirty-four weeks, maybe, it's okay."

"Is thirty-four where she is?" I asked, as if Lucius were the one keeping track. "Thirty-four weeks? It's forty all told, right? If she's two months early, that's thirty-two . . . that's two weeks too early. How is it forty total? When did it go from nine months to ten? Did you know it's ten now? They just decided!"

Level-headed and unflappable, Lucius opened a cupboard. "I'll make you a thermos."

"Maybe I should sleep? Not leave now, sleep a little and then get up and go?"

Lucius paused his search. "*Could* you sleep now? Or maybe you get a little ways down the road and then pull—" He stopped. "Do you want me to come with you?" He waited for my reaction, peering at me, then resumed speaking before I could answer. "We could take turns sleeping and driving. Or keep each other awake, drive a few hours, get a motel. I don't want to foist myself, but I'm glad to go. What else does a Jew have to do on Christmas?"

And so we drove west, Lucius and I, that Christmas Eve. Crossing time zones felt like cheating fate, as if turning the clock back an hour would help us beat Ginny's baby into the world. I called Michael at three a.m.; he said meds had slowed the contractions—"They say the longer it stays in, the better"—and everyone there was trying to get some rest. In my state of exhaustion I took this to mean that we, too, could stop for a few hours' rest, so we found a dirty-carpeted Econo Lodge and lay on scratchy sheets, listening to the ice maker thrum as we held each other, overcaffeinated hearts throbbing in our chests. The tap water tasted like Clorox and sulfur, so we filled the ice bucket and set it on the heater, but the bucket started melting, so we chugged the repulsive tap water like shipwrecked sailors drinking our own piss. Desperate, I went to the vending machine and bought the only noncaffeinated beverage therein: Orange Crush. We poured it over ice and gagged it down, sugar jetting through our veins. Sleep was impossible. Maybe we dozed a bit. When the morning hotel sounds began—doors clicking, trunks slamming—we got up, brushed our teeth, gulped coffee, drove on.

We were three hours from River City when Michael called to say our grandson had been born at 8:52 a.m. Born, and then whisked to Neonatal Intensive Care for tests, the results of which were now awaited. Lucius drove during the excruciating hour before Michael called back to say that the baby was quite small—four pounds, eight ounces—but everything was there, in the right places, and he was breathing on his own. So far, the tests were clear of major red flags. I braced myself anyway in anticipation of some horrific reveal, which is, essentially, parenthood in a nutshell.

It was after noon on Christmas Day when Lucius dropped me at the university hospital. I gave him the key to White Rabbit, but as I started to explain the quirks of the woodstove, I saw his exhaustion and directed him to the Gas Stop instead, closer to civilization, such as it may be.

I consulted a hospital directory, then made my way down hollyberry-bannered halls and through elf-festooned doors. A large window looked into the NICU, and among the crowd of holiday well-wishers before it stood Randall, nose pressed to the glass, hand raised, fingers waggling. Inside, amid a maze of plastic incubators that looked like dog crates, I saw Linda, then Michael. They stood on either side of a crib, arms stuck in through portholes, hands hovering near a hairy thing the size of a pool ball. The head! I gasped. Randall turned, tears in his eyes; "Merry X-mas, Grandma!" He wrapped me in a sumo embrace, lifting me off the ground.

"That's him?" As if Linda and Michael would be cootchie-cooing some other baby.

"That's your boy!" Randall said.

"Does he have a name?"

"Not yet." Randall waggled fingers again toward the sleeping, incubated swaddle. Linda looked up, saw me, and made motions to say she'd come out so I could go in. "Two visitors at a time," Randall explained. "And you got to wash your hands really good. There's directions."

Linda came out and hugged me awkwardly. "Are Gin and Silas up?"

I told her I didn't know. "I came straight here. Should I . . . ?"

"No, they needed sleep. You stay. They'll come up to feed him. Go in," she urged.

I washed and dried my hands, then pushed through the swinging door behind a nurse in a Santa hat with bells on her clogs. Maneuvering around parents and nurses, I passed the incubator of MADELEINE SOPHIA, hand-stenciled in dark pink on light, her birth date and vitals marked on a taped-up index card. A woman in candy-cane-striped scrubs stood folding flannel burp cloths—white with a teal and red stripe, they almost looked Christmasy. LUCAS "LUKE" JOHN and JACOB "JAKE" ARTHUR lay toe-to-toe in separate basinets, beeping and flashing screens at their heads. Another phalanx of monitors and IVs stood beside the twin cribs of MORGYN ELYSE and MADISYN ELLA; their parents sat nearby—she in a wheelchair, he in a rolling nursing seat, each cradling a doll-sized child. Disoriented, I paused to get my bearings, and Morgyn and Madisyn's parents looked up, smiled vaguely, then averted their eyes. There are rules about not looking at other people's babies in there. I spotted Michael and edged over, passing a privacy screen behind which AIDEN RYAN's mom sat, very unprivately, with suction cones vacuuming her milk into tiny cellophane sacks that looked like holiday gift bags.

Michael didn't see me approach. His hands were through the basinet's armholes, and I thought of that kids' game, Operation: *Take out his spareribs for one hundred dollars.* On my side was another pair of armholes, so I put my hands through; Michael jerked back, startled. He looked to see who was attached to the hands, and I felt a twinge of disdain: *All these years, Michael, and you don't know my hands?* I wondered if I'd know his. I'd know Lucius's.

"You made it," he said.

I smiled. "I made it. How are things? How is *he?*" I looked in for the first time at my grandson. He had a tube stuck up his nose. He looked like an iguana in a knit hat, slightly askew.

Michael fixed it. "Ladies make these for preemies—a nurse said they arrive in bulk."

I got an image, then, of Bernadette stitching, keeping the NICU in beanies. It had never dawned on me that she might have been making something useful, for someone else. I'd only ever pictured a hidden linen chest stocked with doilies or handkerchiefs that she counted, late at night, a miser at her shekels, adding hankies to the stash the way Bena added rabbit skins to the fetid blanket.

"So, he's okay?" I asked, and Michael said, "As far as they can tell." Inside his plastic box, the poor thing was covered in adhesive pads wired to hulking monitors. Eyes closed, he drew up his brows as if in concentration, a drowsy smile fading in and out as he breathed. It was probably just gas, but he did look peaceful. I asked after Ginny.

"Honestly?" Michael began, and I felt afraid, but then he said, "Honestly, she seems good. The birth itself sounded bad. She didn't get drugs—there wasn't time, once it got going. So, bad, but relatively short. Right after, she got kind of catatonic until they assessed the baby and told her he was okay. I think she was steeling for some horrible diagnosis—" Michael broke off, glanced around. "Once she knew he was okay, she was, too."

The baby was still asleep when Silas scrubbed in. Michael gingerly pulled his arms from the incubator; mine had gone pins and needles in the armholes. I shook myself out as Silas approached to steal a look at his tiny son. "I need to let Ginny know he's sleeping," he said, and went to call her. Moments later he returned. "She's asked if you'd like to visit with her?"

Downstairs, Ginny sat up against a stack of pillows. My daughter in a hospital bed is not, unfortunately, an uncommon sight, but something was different—her affect, her bearing. Women always have those postdelivery photos with baby, the mother's face drained, drawn, as if thinned by the exertion of childbirth, skin luminous, eyes strained, barely the strength to smile. None of *those* in Ginny's family album, but as I entered her room and saw my daughter as a mother for the first time, she had that look. No child in her arms, but she had the look: spent and walloped, but radiantly alive. It's an image I will hold all my life.

"Ginny." I moved toward her. "He's beautiful."

"Ma." Her voice was deep and soft, and she smiled and reached to squeeze my arm. Then her lip crooked to one side. "I think he kind of looks like an iguana."

"But a *lovely* iguana—I thought the exact thing! Maybe all babies look like iguanas."

Ginny was still smiling—I hadn't seen her sustain a smile since the wedding—shaking her head, saying, "But he's a *live* iguana, and he's okay. They think he's okay."

"I'm so sorry I wasn't here—" I began, but she waved my excuses away, saying, frankly, "It was awful. You were spared—and you haven't been spared much when it comes to me. Murphy owed you." She paused. "I'm glad you're here now." She squeezed my arm again.

The winter sun was on its westerly descent outside the hospital window. On the sill, a gift shop flower arrangement moved minutely in the recirculated air. The window was daintily splotched and dripped with bird poop, and the sun shone in, casting a cockeyed, canted silhouette onto the opposite wall. Ginny caught me appreciating it. "It's because it's so accidental, I think," she said. "Accidental beauty. The birds come pooping by, and then the sun starts setting, and it all coincides . . ." She gestured at the dappled wall and together we watched the shadows. "I'm sorry he's got no name yet," she said. "It's my fault."

"Gin, don't apologize, he's two months early."

"We *have* one, basically. I've just been so superstitious, like the minute we give him a name, he'll die." It hurt, how much she sounded like me. "But Silas says it's a disservice *not* to name him now. A name is a vote of confidence, how we claim him." It was hard to imagine Silas saying it in that way, yet it made sense, both that he'd say it and that my daughter loved him. "I know he's right, I just get scared, but we'll do it soon, I promise." She was afraid, but not paralyzed. Afraid, but moving through it, with Silas, to the other side.

Silas drove me to the Gas Stop that evening. Only a few cars in the bar's lot, but it was open; the refuge of the desperate can't close on the day desperation runs highest. I've read that more people kill themselves on Christmas than any other day of the year. I bet it's not just Christians, either. A lonely December 25 is miserable no matter what you believe, or don't.

Miracle on 34th Street was on the inn's lobby television, Christmas dinner in progress inside the Presidios' apartment beyond the front desk: stereo carols, laughter, dish-clanking. I called in to Henk and Donna, but the clamor muffled me, and the desktop bell was inaudible amid the jingle bells. I tried Lucius's cell; he answered groggily. "What room?" I asked.

"I can't remem— Hang on." I could hear him fumbling to stand.

On a hunch I asked, "Is there a movie poster on the wall? *Harvest of Fire?*"

Surprised, he said, "Indeed."

"On my way." Must not be much holiday business if we'd snagged the movie room.

Lucius—sock-footed, rumpled—took my hand at the door and led me to bed, where I sank gratefully into that soft red blanket. "How's everything?" he whispered, drowsy, drifting.

"Good. Everything's good," and I let myself fall asleep almost instantaneously.

I woke sometime later, confused, then felt Lucius beside me, pulled him closer, and slept on. When I woke again, he sat reading in the corner La-Z-Boy. I croaked "Hi," and he shut his book and leapt up, crying, "Hello! I'm starving! The bar's open across the way. I'm dreaming of fried nuggets." He climbed into the bed and held me beneath the red blanket.

"Fried nuggets." I buried my face in his neck, trying to breathe in his warmth, but he was jumping up, pushing shoes onto my feet, saying, "Let's go!" and I struggled, laughing—"This is serious!"—and he was saying, "I don't even know when I last ate," and then we were outside, the cold glorious on my face as we crossed to the Gas Stop. Regina was tending bar, Creamer in his seat, the positions in which I'd last seen them, on Thanksgiving Day, a full month before.

"Merry Christmas!" Regina waved us over; we had no real choice. Creamer barely lifted his head, gave a half nod, a nearly silent grunt, and took up his straw. Lucius, baffled, looked concerned that he'd misunderstood the entire hickey story. But the alchemy that had produced our election-night intimacy—and that bruise—now felt inimitable and inexplicable.

Lucius and I sloughed off our jackets, settled on stools. "I'm starving," he told Regina.

In a sudden panic, I asked, "You *are* serving food tonight, aren't you?"

"Whatever you like," she said. "It all fries up the same. Or I got Christmas dinner."

"Christmas dinner?" Lucius's face lit up.

"Turkey, dressing, the works. Just got to nuke it," Regina said. "Cooked a twenty-two-pounder. Thing was in the oven half the damn night so we could eat by noon."

"Hell, if you're offering . . . ." Lucius grinned. "Christmas dinner, the fixings, please."

"Sally cooks a mean turkey," Creamer said.

"That she does," Regina said proudly. She turned to me. "You too, honey?"

I felt suddenly and terribly unmoored. Did I cook a mean turkey? When had I last cooked a turkey? Had I ever cooked a turkey? A *mean* turkey? Weren't all turkeys mean? I grabbed for Lucius beneath the bar; I thought I was going to slide off my stool and fall off the world, but he said, "Get this woman a turkey dinner, stat," patting my leg, then squeezing it, tight and private. "And say congratulations," he added. "Phil's a grandma!"

Regina hooted. "Your daughter had her baby! Round on the house! What'll it be?"

"I'd take a beer." Lucius is a merciless and unrepentant flirt.

"Bass?" She nodded, then looked at me. "You too?" I nodded back, mute.

Creamer said, "It's early, isn't it?" I balked: *Creamer* telling *us* it was too early to drink? "Is everything okay," he asked, "with the baby? Being early and all?" I nodded, unable to speak.

Regina set down a frothing pint. I took a sip and choked, and Lucius thumped me on the back. "Everything's fine," he told them. "Early, but fine."

Regina set down a beer for Lucius and lifted her own. "To birth," she said. "To life."

"*L'chaim,*" Lucius said, and I managed "To life," and Creamer said "Cheers," and we all clinked and drank, and then Regina went to microwave our Christmas dinners.

ON DECEMBER 26, Lucius and I woke at the inn, gathered our things, and moved to my place on White Rabbit. I showed him how to use the woodstove, and he set to figuring out the espresso maker, which I'd been too ashamed to give to Randall and Linda in the end. By the time I showered, he had made me a lovely latte, in a travel mug to drink on my way to the hospital. He'd stay at the house, read, take a walk. I kissed him and went to see my grandson.

Michael was already there, by the NICU window where Randall had stood the day before.

"Hi." I squinted in. There was something taped to the basinet. "Is that a name tag?"

"It is," Michael said. "He has a name."

I paused. "Should I prepare myself? Is it weird?"

Michael laughed and shook his head. His eyes were kind. "Not too weird."

Silas waved from inside, beckoning me to trade places and join Ginny. I deferred to Michael, but he said, "You. I was here early—got to hold him awhile before anyone was up."

I watched Silas through the window, readying myself to wash up whenever he started toward the door. Beside me, Michael took a breath and began to speak. "I'm driving out to Prairie now to fetch Eula. If you're sticking around, maybe you could watch Oren while she visits with the baby?" I nodded: *Of course.* Michael took another big breath. "Gin and Silas can take them back to Prairie later—they're going out there to collect some things from the house and then come back to River City, stay at the house here, to be closer to the hospital. And I'll move over to Carpathia. The tenants wound up leaving before Christmas. I thought I'll get the work done faster if I'm actually living there. Give Gin and Silas some privacy, too. Easier than schlepping from Prairie every day." My heart wrenched to hear my family's Yiddish from Michael's mouth. "When they go back to Prairie, I'll put the house on the market."

"The house?"

"Our house."

"Already?"

"*Already?* How long did you want to wait? You left a year ago, Phil."

"I didn't—"

"Yes," he said. "You did."

He was right; January's when I drove off into the blizzard. "Okay," I said.

"Okay, then," he said. "Well. Guess I'll head out." Michael turned from me and strode down the corridor, past a formation of plastic nutcracker soldiers lined up against the wall like they were facing the firing squad. He passed the bulletin boards of all the NICU babies' be-fore-and-after photos, the notes their parents sent in, year after year: *Our Greyson was 1 lb. 9 oz. and spent 23 weeks in the NICU. Now he's 15, 195, plays JV quarterback. Thank you U of I NICU!* Watching Michael walk away made me want to run after him—chase him the way Lucius had chased me down the Yoder driveway—catch his waist, and pull him back. From behind, you might think Michael a younger man than he is—not much gray hair in back, and he's still slender, his belly concealed at that angle. I watched him walk away. I did not run after him. He paused at the hall's T, peered right, left, then right again, then chose a direction and took it. He turned and was gone, and I stood in the NICU hall, watching the goings-on inside, until I heard, "Phillipa, good morning."

It was Silas, beside me, asking, "Would you like to go in?"

"Hi," I said. "Yes, sure," I choked. "I would." I scrubbed in.

The crib sign had stars and red hearts around the blue-stenciled name: OBADIAH BERN.

"Obadiah," I said.

"And Bern, for Grandma Ma," Ginny said.

"Obadiah Bern."

"Obadiah Bern Yoder. We're going to call him by his initials, though," she told me.

"O.B.?" I tried to hide my skepticism. *Like ob-gyn? Like O.B. tampons?*

"Obie," Ginny corrected. "Stress on the first syllable."

"Obie, that's nice. Obie." Like Opie, but *Andy Griffith* was my childhood, not hers.

"We'll see," she said. "He'll be Obadiah if Obie doesn't work. We're fine with that."

"It's a good name, Gin," I said. "And a tribute to two people who loved you very . . ." and then I was crying, and Ginny was wrapping her arm around me, drawing me to the basinet, and we just stood there and watched the baby — Obie. We stood and watched him sleep.

THREE DAYS AFTER Obie's birth, Ginny and Silas ensconced themselves at the River City house, and Michael moved over to Carpathia. With Obie in the NICU, his parents didn't yet need help. Ginny was calling it "practice parenting," and putting on a good face, but I think she just wanted to take her baby home to Prairie, finish the house, and get on with their life. Still, sick as she was of the hospital with its cheery, scrubbed staff, she was grateful; in another age, a baby born at thirty-two weeks would have had little chance. Casseroles and one-pot reheatable meals were already showing up at the doorstep as fast as Ginny and Silas could freeze them, and I'd be of more use to them once they were home in Prairie and really needed help. So Lucius and I packed up and drove to Ohio for a few days together before the semester began. On the drive — no show tunes: there *are* limits to Lucius's love, and he draws a line at Andrew Lloyd Webber — we talked about spring break, when I'd now be free to travel after all.

"We could go back to France," I said. "To the pension. Try again?"

Lucius nodded. "We could. The weather won't be great."

"Will Ginny and Silas be okay on their own by then?" I said. "Can I really just *leave?* What kind of grandmother does that make me?" I was quiet a moment, then said, "Spring break is when the Yoders died. It'll be two years in March." Orah and Obadiah would not, I'm quite sure, have left town while their three-day-old grandson lay hooked to monitors in Neonatal Intensive Care. I know I need to stop comparing myself to them — the Yoders weren't judgmental people, and if there was any way to honor them, it might be for me to show a little more kindness to the world at large, in which I'd probably have to include myself.

"You know," Lucius began, "or maybe you don't . . . Alsace-Lorraine, that region on the German border — Haut-Rhin, Bas-Rhin, Moselle — is where all the Amish Mennonites are. Active churches, even. It's where Ammann settled when he split from the Anabaptists. Sainte-Marie-aux-Mines is the so-called cradle of the Amish movement. Farmland's beautiful."

"You're making that up."

Lucius laughed. "Making what up? No, it really is beautiful."

"There's an Amish mecca in the middle of France that you just happen to've encountered in your research travels? How does that happen?"

"Edge," Lucius corrected, "very eastern edge of France." Then: "Because the world is a strange and miraculous place? Because everything is connected? Because Murphy likes himself a good coincidence? It's not really *that* coincidental. The Amish do get around. Slowly, but . . ."

"You know something terrible'll happen. We'll get there. It'll be paradise. Again. And we'll hike into a field with rucksacks for a picnic, a bottle of local wine, the wheat waving, cows lowing, mourning doves all a-coo, and some Amish garçon will come rushing up with a telegram to deliver heinous news, and I'll hitch a buggy ride to the airport, yelling giddyup, *vite!*"

Lucius was laughing. "*Twice* does not constitute a statistical trend. Phil, you were summoned home when a miserable eighty-year-old woman died. In her sleep! May we all be so lucky." I tried to protest, but Lucius went on: "Then, you were called home for something *not* terrible. For a baby! And everyone is fine. There was no tragedy. Here we are, mere days later, headed back together to cold, unlovely Ohio. It's all perfect—everything's okay."

"But by pure luck! It might've been so far from okay . . ."

"Yes," Lucius said, "you're right." He smiled at the road ahead. "But it *is* okay. This time it's okay. Next time might not be. But try, try and be okay with the okayness of *this* time. Don't waste it worrying about next time. Be here, in this time. With me."

"*Everything is connected. Be here now.* What are you, a Zen master?"

"In my spare time," Lucius said. "Weekends. School breaks. Alternate Wednesdays."

"I love you," I told him.

"And I you." He reached for my hand across the center console. We drove east.

ON NEW YEAR'S EVE afternoon, Lucius was out picking up some things for dinner when my cell rang. It was Michael. "What's wrong?" I said. "Why are you calling? What happened?"

"Phil, Phil, nothing's wrong. I just found something I thought— it might interest . . ."

"Okay." My pulse slowed. "Okay."

"I'm in my mother's attic and I thought you'd like to know that you were right all along."

"Right about what?" There was purloined Nazi loot stashed in the rafters?

"I found my birth certificate," Michael said, "and I don't know what it means exactly, but it lists no father. It's blank." He let out an ironic chuckle. "I am officially fatherless."

"Oh, Michael . . ." *I'm sorry* didn't feel appropriate, but I didn't know what would be.

"Don't *Oh, Michael* me." He paused, and when he spoke again his voice was gentler. "I just thought you'd be interested. A weird thing, though—maybe just a typo, I don't know, but her birthday, you know, was November 24, but here it's May 14—"

"Your birthday?"

"It could be a typo—putting that day's date accidentally for 'Mother's Birth Date,' but they didn't put the year as '45. It's written May 14, 1927. And she was born in '22, anyway."

There was, of course, so much I wanted to ask, but I'm proud to report that I said only, "She just wanted people to tell her how young she looked for her age." Michael laughed, agreeing, and I laughed, too, relieved. We hung up, and I sat in Lucius's darkening living room. Nothing had really changed: the birth certificate neither conferred nor confirmed any truth, just cleared the way for different stories. Maybe everything Bernadette told us was true: her young husband, her Dave Maakestad, was killed in the war. By the time Michael arrived, she'd been forsaken by Dave's family, and proof of their marriage probably wasn't easily obtained. Records get lost in fires, both proverbial and actual, accidental and deliberate. Was Bernadette's great secret not that Michael was illegitimate, but that his birth certificate made it look as if he were? Why she didn't burn it, too, is another question to which we'll never get an answer.

New Year's was quiet; we were asleep by midnight. Before I returned to Iowa, Lucius and I bought tickets for spring break. We'd fly into Luxembourg, rent a car. The pension had rooms available—not their busy season. The weather might be crummy, but it didn't much matter to us.

I left Ohio in early January and inched my way through the eternal Greater Chicago traffic. Is it beside the point to say I wished Lucius were beside me? That we were in a car together, not driving on a U.S. interstate, but tootling down a French country road in a rented Citroën, the fertile Franco-Amish farmland unfurling around us like a quilt over the hills? We would go through the mountains and begin switchbacking down into the Sainte-Marie-aux-Mines river valley. Lucius loves driving those roads, winding and winding. I look ahead, over red tile roofs, huddled white-stone houses, church steeples poking up from the ridgelines. The hills are full of caves, Lucius tells me, abandoned mining camps, and I half expect to hear the whistle of dwarfs, Sleepy, Dopey, and Doc tromping along the road, pickaxes slung over their shoulders. *Hi-ho, hi-ho.* It's an elfin forest, a Hobbit glen. We come around a bend to an ancient Mennonite cemetery, perched practically at the edge of a cliff, its moss-covered gravestones cockeyed and cantilevered. Following directions, at the next fork we leave pavement for dirt, rattling on, pebbles thunking the undercarriage. And then, there it is, the farmhouse we're looking for. Not as crumbling as I've feared — or maybe it is, under all the ivy and wisteria. Does wisteria bloom in March? To hell with March — let's make it spring! Spring in Alsace, fictional wisteria blossoming in profusion! Sage and lavender thriving!

A few speckled chickens scatter, spooked by the car. We park, cut the engine, and they return to peck what we've stirred up. As we climb out, the old farmhouse door swings open, and Ginny emerges — why not? — with Obie slung on her hip, grabbing at his mama's tattered purple sundress. On Gin's feet are old laceless sneakers; she's ruddy, tanned, plumped, and muscled, as if she's been here for years, working the farm. When she sees me, she smiles and lifts that baby toward me and we sandwich him in a hug. They smell of earth, sweet-rich as compost, and faintly of straw, rosemary, yeast, and a ripe smokiness. I could stay all day just inhaling them, but Silas is coming out, reaching to shake Lucius's hand. Ginny and I release Obie. I hug Silas. Gin hugs Lucius. My heart is full.

Maybe that's when a shout of greeting comes from the fields — Linda and Randall striding toward us. The farmhouse door slams, and out toddles Oren, Eula close on his pudgy heels, hands out to catch him if he falls. He's wearing overalls with baggy knees so mended and darned it's as if they've been purposefully padded to protect him from his tumbles on the craggy paths. Eula has found her real home here in France. This cradle of the Amish movement is also, it seems, the country's quilting capital, meeting place of the Carrefour Euro-péen du Patchwork, the crossroads of European fabric arts. Here Eula has found her vocation and her people.

It's lunchtime, and on a cracked-brick patio behind the farm-house a great wood table is laid with quilted placemats, red and co-balt and gold, florals Eula collects on trips south to Provence. The farmhouse's screen door opens and out comes Creamer with a tray of plates and baskets, rounds of white, creamy cheese, a misshapen rustic loaf—Eula is teaching Ginny to bake. Creamer, no longer un-der cover of insulated Carhartts, wears a T-shirt and carpenter pants. He tends the dairy cows. Eula calls him Burton, and we all learn to do the same. She's pregnant again, their first together. Norma for a girl, Norman if it's a boy, even though Creamer's mom's not dead. She's here, too, Norma, living down the lane in the old gardener's quarters, there, past that blossoming dogwood. Creamer couldn't just leave her in Prairie, alone with her swans. So he's brought her to live out her final years in France, and she's mellowed remarkably here, among family.

You know what would be so nice? To have Bernadette live with her, let her share Norma's little house. If Bernadette had held out, she could have returned to the land of her birth, returned with her dear Ginny. This place—it's her family's farm, her true homestead. Neither a French Jew nor a Nazi collaborationist, perhaps Bernadette is French Amish, fled from this battle-torn place like so many oth-ers in the 1940s, sent abroad, to brethren in Iowa—Prairie, Iowa. A teenage girl, alone in a new world, she's promptly knocked up—or maybe it happens on the ship, on the way over, and she arrives, preg-nant, in America. And if you think the Amish are rough on the fallen now, imagine how it might have gone down in '45. She'd have been shunned, ostracized, and done whatever was necessary to survive: made her way to a place where she might find work—River City—and use her skills to make a life of some kind for herself and her son. All those years . . . But now, at long last, she's back in her homeland. And she and Norma Kramer, unknown to one another in Iowa, are housemates *en France*. And these two are peas in a pod, bugs in a rug, thick as thieves, stuck together like glue—they're a cliché of companionability! No one knows, quite, if it's sort of a Boston marriage, if they're merely companions, or if they're wink-wink, nudge-nudge, quote-unquote *companions*. Who even cares? They're two old ladies who've discovered some happiness, so help them.

If it's spring break, maybe Michael will be here for a visit, too—with a girlfriend, a grad student, of course, but maybe not so young as all that. Anyway, they seem happy, and I can let them have their happiness, can't I? Pull up a seat, an old fruit crate, pass the *saucisson*, the *pâté de campagne*. Some more wine? The more the merrier! Maybe we could pull up another two chairs while we're at it. Have Orah and Obadiah leave Prairie *before* the SUV hits their buggy, or let them get hit, but survive, thanks to *Modern* medical miracles, and when Ginny and Silas flee the States with Obie in the wake of Bush's second inauguration, Orah and Obadiah follow, along with everyone else—Eula and Oren and Burton, and Randall and Linda—because there's a better life to be lived, here in the land where the Amish began, among the lapsed, among family. Here, where Lucius and I will settle eventually, as soon as we can afford to retire. Because where else on this maybe-not-so-godforsaken earth could we possibly want to be?

God, I am such an American: on a highway headed west, dreaming of the lives we all might-could lead.

ACKNOWLEDGMENTS

When you work on a book for fourteen years, you run the risk of forgetting places you've been and missing folks who helped out along the way. So, firstly and foremostly, to all the people I'm surely and egregiously forgetting to thank: I'm sorry—and THANK YOU!!! Then: tremendous thanks to Vinnie Wilhelm and Katie Hubert, who generously and enthusiastically read and talked with me about very early incarnations of this project. To Allison Amend and Erin Ergenbright, who read the 823-page incarnation and deserve to be sainted. To Eric Simonoff, who's heroically read thousands of pages of this book alone and—blessedly!—hasn't given up on me yet. I am very, very, very lucky to have him on my side. To Lauren Wein, who took a chance on *Our Lady,* and without whom this book would not be a book—in its current form or any other. I am indebted to her in more ways than I can express, for her super-smarts and her intensive, devoted, and inspired work. Lauren, you are everything a writer dreams an editor could possibly be. And to Pilar Garcia-Brown—thank you! To Larry Cooper, whose patience, care, and good humor—and great fortitude in putting up with so many em-dash clauses and ubiquitous Nazis and entirely excessive adverbiage *and* utterly unnecessary *italicization,* not to mention overzealous exclamation(!) and, apparently, undue *apparentlys,* and disproportionate use of . . . ellipses!—made the copyediting process flat-out fun. To Nelly Reifler and the good people at Pratt's Friday Forum, and to Joanna Parzakonis and Derek Molitor (and Kirsten Jennings!) of Bookbug (www.bookbugkalam azoo.com), for inviting me to read from this work in progress and making me feel like it wasn't totally crazy to keep going. To Malena Watrous and the editors and Stegner Fellow guest editors of *Story Quarterly,* for publishing "The Church of the Fellowship of Something," my first attempted entry into the world of this book. To the MacDowell Colony and the Corporation of Yaddo, for the glorious residencies where I was able to get out early drafts of Phillipa's story, and to the wonderful artists and writers I met there who listened to bits of what I was working on and offered insight, feedback, and encouragement. So much gratitude to you all. I'm profoundly thankful to Stephen King and the Haven Foundation, for their support and the miracle of a Freelance Artists Assistance Grant during a time when hyperemesis gravidarum made it impossible for me to earn my own keep. Likewise, to the PEN Writers' Emergency Fund for a generous grant, and the Authors League Fund for the emergency no-strings/ no-interest loan that helped get us through that rough stretch. To Myra Nissen, who helps through all the bad stretches, and the good ones, too, and whose support in all ways has been lifelong, constant, and sustaining—thank you, Mama, for everything. And to Tony Nissen, who made so much possible—during his life, and after. I wish you were here, Papa, to enjoy the fruits of all your years of work. We are all so grateful to you in so very many ways. To Jacqueline Massey, my invaluable resource for all things French—*merci, merci beaucoup* to Jacqueline and Annick Davies, who channeled their best French schoolgirl penmanship for me. To Michelle Forman, to whom I dedicate chapter 3, with huge love (and huge apology). To Sonne, who's been patient—no joke; it can't be easy having parents who need so much time quiet and alone with their words—and who's the bunskiest Bunski ever to bunski! And, lastly and mostly, to

Jay. I tell my students: when you meet someone who reads and understands you like you most deeply hope to be read and understood, and whose edits of your work make you make sense to yourself, you should probably marry them. To Jay, without whom: nothing. And from whom, for whom, and with whom: everything. We're doing it, together. Life.